Advance Praise for Ka

Land Sharks

"Dripping with raw bureaucratic dread amid a sunny Hawaiian day, this novel does not disappoint anyone who reads the occasional legal drama. This feels like it came from an episode of 'Law and Order,' and I like it!"
—Nathan Hopp, *Reader's Boulevard*

"Move over John Grisham and make room for first time novelist Katharine M. Nohr and her cast of muscle toned, sun tanned characters chasing triathlon medals and courtroom victories. In this page turner of a thriller, Ms. Nohr takes us on a ride through the ultra competitive world of triathletes an. trial lawyers, all the while weaving a story of mystery and romance. A thoroughly enjoyable, must read story for all audiences. Five stars."
—Teresa Tico, Film Producer

"In Katherine Nohr's Land Sharks, *young attorney Zana West takes a case involving a fellow triathlete paralyzed during an Olympic trial. With millions on the line, she's hip- deep in deceit, betrayal, and romance. A likable heroine and more than a couple of sleazy villains make* Land Sharks *a fast-paced read from the first page all the way to its surprise ending."*
—Sherry Scarpaci, Author of *The 13th Victim* and *Lullaby*

"A lively Honolulu whodunit full of island flavor!"
—Lesia Sasynuik Schafer, HR Professional

"I read the whole book in one delicious sitting. As a sport enthusiast in the legal profession, Land Sharks *was a brilliant and entertaining ride from start to finish. Zana West was a multifaceted protagonist providing a rich view into the inner circle of the tri-world and the pressures facing young legal associates. Zana didn't let Rip Mansfield out of her sights and the readers of* Land Sharks *won't want to let Zana out of theirs. I can't wait to catch Zana on her next adventures!"*
—Emily Schmit, California Attorney and Water Polo Coach

6/16/16

Dear Patty,

Thanks for being All In
for IAIP and we
are happy to join
regions together. ☺ ☺

aloha,
Katharine

LAND
SHARKS

#HonoluluLaw, #Triathletes & a #TVStar

Katharine M. Nohr

Katharine M. Nohr

WD
PUBLISHING

Editor: Brittiany Koren
Cover Art Design and Layout: Beth MacKenney and Eddie Vincent of ENC Graphic Services
Cover images © Shutterstock.com

Category: Legal Mystery
Description: *A female triathlete who is a lawyer teams up with another lawyer who is a Hawaiian T.V. star to solve a high profile case.*
ISBN: 978-0-9962521-3-3
LOC: Catalog info applied for.
First Edition published by Written Dreams Publishing in May 2016.

To my Dad, Gerry Nohr, who was the biggest fan of this novel and the Tri-Angles series, and encouraged me to follow my dreams.

Prologue

Crouching in the aero position on his Kestrel bike, Jeff Paris was flying fast down the hill. He tuned out the cheering crowd as he closed in on Vic Leavitt, the last Olympics' gold medalist. When his front wheel was perilously close to Vic's back wheel, he relaxed a bit in his friend's slipstream before the steep climb up Kilauea Avenue. Jeff glanced behind to see Brad Jordan drafting off his rear wheel and confirmed they had broken away from the others.

Only two men would qualify for the London Olympics, and Jeff was determined to be one of them. He watched Vic's body adjust to the bumps of the road as he focused his attention on his rhythmic cadence. They were perfectly in sync, having rehearsed this moment for the past year, strategizing how they would beat Brad, the reigning U.S. national champion.

The three cyclists approached the narrow hill that climbed above the neighborhood adjacent to Diamond Head. The trade winds keeping the spectators cool had no impact on Jeff, who had expended his energy on the ascent, sandwiched between his friend and rival.

Halfway up, Jeff could hear his breathing over the whirring of race wheels. Near the top of the hill, the spectators, volunteers and police thinned to just a few people. Jeff gritted his teeth and stood up in his saddle, swaying side to side in unison with Vic. They struggled to keep their speed on the steep grade, but their momentum and will pushed them forward as if they were propelled by motors rather than shaved legs. Jeff sensed Brad was close behind and could almost feel their wheels touching.

As they reached the summit, he heard a revving engine and then watched as a small white sedan hit Vic's front tire, catapulting his body so it bounced off the car's trunk as if in slow motion.

Instinctively, Jeff turned his wheel sharply to the right, colliding with Brad's front tire, launching them both into the air. Jeff's shoulder slammed into the asphalt and Brad landed in a twisted position on top of him so his legs looked as if they were attached backwards, blood seeping from his mouth and his eyes staring straight ahead. He lay on the ground, listening to strange sounds coming out of his own mouth. Jeff smelled burnt rubber and tasted blood.

Chapter 1

@Zlaw Surfergirl wiped out. #Bummed.

Zana West almost swallowed her gum when her boss stormed past her and into her friend's office, because when Frank Gravelle was about to fire an associate, he didn't consult with Human Resources. His firing technique was old school. This time, he hurled a legal brief at Leilani Tam, grazing her left breast. He stomped into her office, swinging his hips far too much for a straight man, and pointed at her Donald Trump-style, shouting, "You're fired!" He then turned on his heel and marched right past Zana, stopping briefly to sneer at her as if to say, "You're next." Zana was one of the few female associates left at the Gravelle, Parsons & Dell law firm, which should have been equipped with a revolving door for the freshly hired and fired young men she affectionately referred to as "attorney-boys." Now, her friend Leilani disappeared out the door with surfboard under arm, giving her a half wave and mouthing the F word before she even had a chance to hang her law school diploma.

Zana watched Frank march back to his office with his hips swaying side to side and lifting his feet too high as if he was performing in a marching band. It was only a matter of time before Frank directed his tirade on her and left her homeless with no way to pay $80,000 in student loan debt. Her nameplate said "Zana West, Attorney," but she was a glorified legal secretary, her fingers flying over the keyboard to create fill-in-the-blank documents at an associate billable rate, of which she earned only a small fraction.

In her office, Zana's diplomas and certificates of merit snaked along the windowsill and floor next to an empty bankers box she kept handy for the day Frank hurled an unacceptable brief in her direction. She felt her phone vibrate in her pocket.

Keep in Touch, Z! Leilani texted.

Zana sighed and texted back, So sorry, and then added her signature flexed bicep muscle emoticon.

Her friend replied, Waves are 2-4 on south shore. No worries.

That was easy for Leilani to say. Her father was Teddy Tam, the owner of half the car dealerships in Honolulu, with in-house legal counsel where his free-spirited daughter would no doubt land when she tired of hanging ten. Zana's drug addict father wasn't going to rescue her. If she couldn't satisfy Frank's impossibly high standards, she would join the hundreds of fresh-out-of-law-school graduates whipping up smoothies at Jamba Juice. No one was hiring new attorneys in this economy.

Practicing law in Hawaii wasn't exactly paradise. Before moving here last year, Zana had imagined relaxing on white sand beaches, running and cycling on sunny days cooled by trade winds and swimming with dolphins in the warm turquoise water. Instead, she spent most days shivering in her air-conditioned office and only glimpsed an ocean view when called into a partner's office to accept another mundane assignment. Rather than sip a Mai Tai and thumb through a trashy novel, Zana drank water from the hallway drinking fountain and poured through piles of legal documents. There was no sand between her toes. Only bags under her eyes.

After Leilani's text, Zana tucked her phone back into her knock-off Coach bag, not wanting to be tempted with Twitter, Facebook, or Candy Crush. From time to time her secretary, Sylvia, with weight-lifter strength carried even more documents into her office to pile on any portion of her desk where wood was showing. She didn't bother straightening any of the toppling paper stacks. Messy meant productive in this law firm. When Zana had started her job several months ago, sure she was going to "change the world" and "help people" like all other newly-minted, beauty pageant-like idealist attorneys, she hadn't imagined the firm would not even consider going paperless, much less take on pro bono work. This firm was all about Dictaphones, pink message slips, typing pools and billable hours and daggum it—to Zana's misbelief—Frank Gravelle was going to keep it that way.

But she wasn't going to let him stop her. Ever since the triathlon bug had bit her at the age of seven, Zana had been competitive. She loved the idea of edging out her competition during the last few meters of a race, but in reality, it didn't happen very often. The same was true for law school. She had worked hard trying to earn more points than her fellow students, but was never one of the few awarded A's. Zana had renewed hope now after moving to Hawaii and making a fresh new start, far away from her troubled childhood. She planned to be the best associate the firm ever had and maybe even become the first female partner someday—if she didn't get fired first. That's why she rushed to the office every morning before dawn to win the "first associate in the door race." The partners didn't notice her daily triumph, but when she used her key to open the front door and flipped on all the light switches at 5:30 a.m., the victory felt sweet.

After finishing her last fill-in-the-blank legal document of the morning, Zana paused briefly to check Facebook and the "Fighting in Paradise" page for any updates on her favorite T.V. show. Realizing she didn't have time for social media diversions, she dove back into research for a motion for summary judgment on a premises liability case. Even though Internet research wasn't the most glamorous of legal tasks, at least she was using her education reading appellate court decisions. Senior associate Brian Ching was assigned to draft the motion, but Zana would contribute. She hoped Brian would invite her to hear his oral argument in court. Any associate from the firm who got to set foot in a court room during his or her first year of practice was, according to Brian, either damn lucky or sleeping with the boss. Zana told Brian she hoped to be damn lucky, then saw him press his lips tightly together and lower his head.

Poised before her keyboard, Zana typed at a speed the partners demanded of their top legal secretaries, an almost embarrassingly fast rate for an attorney. When one of the elder partners had interviewed her, he asked how fast she could type. Zana responded without thinking, "100 words per minute." After she left the interview she realized how offensive the question was and wondered if she would have been better off lying. The attorney-boys who hunted and pecked their way through their work were at least handling small motor vehicle collision cases.

Zana's legs were beginning to cramp up from sitting so long, demanding a much-needed stretch, but when she finally stood up, her panty hose ripped.

Oh, great! she thought. As a triathlete, she wasn't shy about changing out of her bathing suit and into running or biking clothes under a beach towel in the parking lot after a swim. If she accidentally flashed a nipple, her fellow athletes paid little attention. So in her office, she hardly gave it a second thought when she lifted her skirt to pull off her ruined panty hose. After all, the door was almost closed.

When two of the better-looking young male attorneys rushed in without knocking, Zana pulled down her skirt and looked them straight in the eyes.

"I see we're interrupting something," Cole Maddox said, raising an eyebrow.

"Maybe we showed up at just the right time," said Rex Sampson, the Prince Harry lookalike.

Zana smoothed her skirt and smirked.

"Could there be a man hiding under your desk?" Rex asked. "You know that's against firm policy."

"Gravelle, Parsons & Dell Policies and Procedures strictly prohibit barging into female associates' offices without knocking," Zana said, sitting back down in front of her computer.

"Sorry," Rex blushed.

"Are you eating?" Cole asked.

"Not yet." Zana clicked a few keys, delaying her entry into the lion's den of attorneys scarfing down the lunch provided the third Friday of every month—one of the few perks of working at G, P & D.

"Don't wait too long. The food goes fast," Rex said following Cole out.

"I'll take my chances," Zana said. Every instinct told her to jump up and join her colleagues for the free food. Her days on the streets were still fresh in her mind, but now she had a regular paycheck and a roof over her head so she saw no reason to go back to stuffing her pockets with any morsel she could get her hands on. It was better to focus on work.

Zana felt more comfortable without nylons, but noticed her legs could use a shave. If she wasn't putting in 12-hour days in the office and training for triathlons, she might have some time to attend to such things. Her fingers continued to zoom across the keyboard when she heard the door creak open. Her body jerked upright when she looked up and saw Frank sitting across from her, rubbing his chin. He was wearing an orange Reyn Spooner shirt with a surfboard pattern incongruous with his pale skin and old-fashioned, slicked-back hairstyle.

"I see you're the only one working while everyone is eating," Frank said.

"I just wanted to get this finished." Zana's hands shook, wondering if his unexpected visit meant it was time to make use of her bankers box.

"I have an assignment that might be right in your wheelhouse."

"I think there's some room on my desk." Zana shifted some papers. "If it's urgent, I can type it before I leave."

"It's not typing," Frank said, rubbing his chin again.

"Did Libby leave for the day?" Zana asked. "Do you need coffee?"

"I understand you're a triathlete," Frank said, ignoring her questions.

"Yes," Zana nodded, glancing over at the racing bike and running shoes she kept in the corner.

"I'm assigning you a high-profile case involving a cycling accident that occurred during the Olympic triathlon trials in Honolulu." Frank enunciated every word clearly as if he suspected that having breasts meant Zana might not have ears and could only read lips.

"Thank you," Zana said, smiling for the first time that day.

"Libby will give you the file. I want you to review it this afternoon and prepare to discuss it with our litigation team when we next meet."

After Frank shut the door behind him, Zana jumped out of her chair and broke into a happy dance. She then texted her friend Shelby, OMG, I got assigned a big triathlon case!

***

Zana snatched the case file out of Libby's hands the instant she walked in the door. She couldn't wait to work on her first important assignment. The documents told the story of how the accident killed Vic Leavitt, rendered Brad Jordan paralyzed, and traumatized Jeff Paris so badly he quit racing and admitted himself for a brief stay at Kaneohe State Mental Hospital. Brad Jordan, the plaintiff who filed the lawsuit, laid in a Honolulu hospital for three months, undergoing multiple surgeries to his spine. He was then transferred to a rehabilitation hospital on the mainland so he could learn how to ambulate using a wheelchair and function as a paraplegic. After ten months, Jordan returned to Hawaii.

Zana scanned a CD of damage photographs, including shots taken at the accident scene. One picture showed a Kestrel's tire peeled off a bent rim, twisted around a blood spattered top tube. Another showed a saddle broken off a seatpost next to a broken chain on the asphalt. There were several pictures of a bent down tube with the name Kestrel legible. Others showed a bike computer with a cracked face, a bent derailer and a water bottle with green liquid spilling out of it. After skimming the photos, she felt her stomach rumble.

The three men eating the remainders of teriyaki chicken, sticky rice, macaroni salad, and malasadas turned their attention to Zana as she walked in, the only female in the room, as usual. She would have been more comfortable grabbing a bite downstairs, but she couldn't pass up the free food and thought it was better for her career if she didn't segregate herself.

"What are you working on?" Kim McCall asked her when Zana sat down. All the guys looked up from their phones and newspapers.

"The triathlon Olympic trials case," Zana said, trying to conceal her excitement as she slipped chopsticks from a paper holder.

"You're lucky," Kim said. "All I ever get are minor car accident cases."

"I remember seeing something on T.V. about that case," Michael Lee said. "Didn't that guy who used to be a professional cyclist, but was caught doping win the Olympic gold medal?"

"That's right—Ryan Peterson. He won Stage 4 of the Tour de France, but was banned from pro cycling for steroid use. He got into triathlons, but wasn't expected to make the U.S. team until his competition was wiped out at the Honolulu Olympic trials accident," Zana said.

"I read somewhere that Peterson caused the accident," Brian Ching said.

"Are you reading *The National Enquirer* again, Brian?" Michael chuckled.

"The tabloids blamed Ryan Peterson, but as far as I know, there wasn't any proof," Zana said. She wasn't sure why she had rescued Brian.

"Zana, do you think Peterson had anything to do with causing the accident?" Michael asked, placing his chopsticks on his paper plate.

"I don't think Ryan is another Tanya Harding, if that's what you're asking, but you never know. I guess he could have hired someone or had his girlfriend run over his competitors," Zana said. "He's a slow swimmer compared to the world's top triathletes and so winning the gold medal was suspicious."

"If Peterson caused the accident, you should be able to get our client dismissed," Michael said. "Even a girl can do that."

Brian and Kim laughed loudly and let out whooping noises.

"So, what was the score of the game last night?" Zana asked, ignoring them. She actually knew the score of the baseball game between University of Hawaii and University of Nevada Las Vegas, but she knew what would happen with the mention. The guys immediately jumped into a lively discussion about the various players.

Zana smiled, listening to them immersed in conversation. And when she got up to leave the room, they didn't seem to notice.

***

Later, at Starbucks across the street, she heard a familiar voice after picking up her latte from the barista.

"Zana. Over here," Andrew Bergen called to her. He wore a black Tommy Bahama shirt and neatly pressed black slacks, as he sat at an outdoor table shaded by an umbrella, his iPad in hand.

Zana had felt an instant camaraderie with Andrew, a senior associate at the firm. He was five years older than she and, like quite a few attorneys in Honolulu, was a transplant from New York with what he told her was a Brooklyn accent. Andrew's body was fit from playing Ultimate Frisbee on weekends. She admitted to herself she thought he was handsome and matched his pretty blonde girlfriend, Kelly, even though his hairline was receding and he lacked a chin.

When she moved to Hawaii last year and found a room for rent in Kahala, one of the poshest neighborhoods on Oahu, Zana couldn't believe her good luck. Andrew and Kelly couldn't afford the rent by themselves, so they sublet their extra bedroom to Zana. It was Andrew who had coached Zana for the Hawaii Bar exam and arranged for an interview at G, P & D after she accumulated 30 rejection letters from other firms due to the poor economy. And thanks to Andrew, she'd been offered an associate's position over hundreds of equally qualified applicants. She thought of him as her mentor and confidante at the firm, answering her daily barrage of questions with patience.

"Hey, Andrew." Zana pulled up a chair next to him.

"That asshole, Mansfield," Andrew said in a hushed voice.

"You mean Rip Mansfield?"

"Yeah, he's a shark in an attorney's suit."

"I guess that sums it up." Zana sipped her latte. "I just got assigned a case against him."

"You better watch out—he made Lori cry in court a few days ago."

"Are you kidding? What a jerk."

"I'm *not* kidding. I'll bet he's made some of the younger male attorneys wet their pants."

"Right. You probably have to wear Depends when you go up against him."

"Not exactly," Andrew smirked. "Don't trust him, Zana. He'll screw you over any chance he gets. He just reneged on a settlement agreement.

Two days before arbitration, he told me that his clients couldn't agree to the terms. Needless to say, I was caught unprepared. Asshole!"

She took this all in, and more. She appreciated Andrew's candidacy.

"So, what are you going to do?" Zana asked.

"The only thing I can—tell Frank what happened and hope I don't get canned."

Later, after Zana returned to her office, she opened the Hawaii State Bar Directory and looked up Rip Mansfield. His picture was probably out of date. She wondered if he still looked like Pierce Brosnan with his dark hair flecked with gray, blue eyes, and chiseled face. No wonder he was able to be so manipulative with his movie star looks. One thing was certain, Zana refused to let the man bring one tear to her eyes. She had had a lifetime of crying as a child and resolved to be tougher than her fiercest opponents.

The ringing of her phone interrupted her thoughts and she answered it. "Hello, this is Zana West."

"Hello Zana. Rip Mansfield."

"What can I do for you, Mr. Mansfield?" Zana straightened in her chair, stunned to hear his voice.

"I understand you're representing one of the defendants in my client, Brad Jordan's, case." *News travels fast.*

"Frank Gravelle is lead counsel. Shall I transfer you?" Zana steadied her voice, hoping Mansfield wouldn't sense the butterflies fluttering in her stomach.

"I'd like to talk with you, young lady. I'm sure you're prettier than Frank."

"I suppose it depends on your taste."

"I'll bet you have sexy legs," Mansfield's voice was sleazy, as if he was talking to a phone sex girl rather than Zana, a counselor-at-law.

"Did you want to discuss the case?" Zana asked, trying to keep her voice steady.

"Not really. I'll be sending you a demand letter soon, Sweetheart."

"I'm not your sweetheart, Rip. Good afternoon." Zana hung up and stared out the window. She focused on the Dole pineapple atop the cannery-turned-shopping center in the distance, and willed herself not to cry.

Chapter 2

@Zlaw #Shark in attorney's suit has met his match.

Lying prone amongst the rumpled, high thread count sheets on his king-sized bed, Rip smiled at Kaitlin who was asleep next to him, breathing softly with one bare breast peeking out of the sheets.

"Good morning," Rip said softly, raising his body and kissing her on the lips. He'd remembered this one's name using his newest gimmick. His handyman had posted a small white board on the bedroom wall, where he had drawn a heart with their names, "Rip + Kaitlin," which he could see from the bed. On the table under it was a vase he kept full of tropical flowers for his frequent guests to enjoy.

"Good morning, sweetie," Kaitlin said, smiling with her eyes closed, pulling Rip towards her.

Waking Kaitlin meant delaying his escape, but he couldn't resist morning sex before his orchestrated 6 a.m. emergency phone call. She'd be impressed he was so important that he was needed at the office so early, and Rip would return to his main house a few blocks away for a relaxed morning of sipping coffee and catching up on the world news—alone.

Rip's ringing phone interrupted them, but he ignored it until he was satisfied. He then jumped out of bed, feigned listening to the message a few steps away from the bed, made his excuses, pulled on his jeans and black T-shirt from the night before and left Kaitlin to fend for herself.

"Stay as long as you'd like," Rip offered, kissing her before making his getaway.

"Do you really have to leave?" Kaitlin implored.

"It's urgent. I'll make it up to you," Rip said, tucking Kaitlin in with the disheveled bedding. "Help yourself to whatever you can find in the kitchen."

Three years ago, Rip had used his share of a multi-million dollar jury verdict to buy the 2,000 square foot "Date House". He had remodeled it so that its primary room was a large master bedroom with an adjacent women's bathroom complete with a white marble Jacuzzi, a nearby bathroom for him, and a black slate double shower with a view of the ocean through its clear glass window. This playground for romance was complete with a fireplace, another Jacuzzi on a private lanai, a Bose sound system, and dimmable remote-control lighting.

He kept the stainless steel kitchen stocked with champagne, strawberries, caviar, dark chocolate, and fresh whipped crème to put his dates in the mood. The living room featured an original John Lennon painting of naked bodies entwined above a soft leather makeout sofa. The white marble arched entryway to the house was flanked by imported date palms, which inspired the house's moniker. Escaping through the house's electronic iron gate, Rip chuckled, thinking of the wicked pun.

After he returned home, Rip relaxed on his white, leather sofa facing the floor to ceiling window looking out over the rippling blue and turquoise Pacific Ocean, while he read *The Honolulu Daily*. Money had bought him the peace of dating without drama. If a woman complained about his lifestyle, she was immediately dropped from his rotation.

Kaitlin, with her large brown eyes, waist-length brown hair, and slender body was the kind of girl he imagined himself falling in love with. He had felt twinges of feelings for her and others like her, but had suppressed them. He had no interest in opening himself up to hurt, which to him was the natural progression of any relationship. After his wife of three years ran off with his law partner in the early days of his career, he vowed he would never again partner with anyone either in or out of the courtroom. And that meant marriage, too.

Rip turned on the six small, flat screen televisions set up above the desk in his home office. He enjoyed watching what the women in the Date House did when he filmed them with closed circuit cameras. The most amusing of his subjects were those left alone for the first time. They couldn't resist opening up every cupboard and closet, hoping to discover something interesting about him in his absence, having no idea he was watching them. He particularly enjoyed it when they were naked or scantily clad while they snooped.

Kaitlin had been coming to the Date House for months, and so Rip had already spied her exploring every inch of it. By the time he turned on the monitors, she was already showered and dressed and sitting at the kitchen table. Her long, dark hair was pulled into a high ponytail and she was wearing a tank top and shorts, reading her Kindle while sipping coffee and eating a croissant. Rip quickly became bored and turned off the screens. He wasn't sure if Kaitlin was one of those women whose heart he had captured, or if she would soon find another man who would give her the affection she desired.

In the mornings, Rip often worked at his home office if he wasn't scheduled to be in court or at a deposition. As soon as he pressed the digits on his phone to transfer his work calls to his home number, his phone rang.

"Mansfield here."

"Hi Rip. I have an offer on the Tashima case," Melvin Yani said.

"Okay, let's hear it."

"I have $55,000. I need your answer by next Wednesday."

"That's fucking ridiculous! Tell the adjuster she's an ignorant slut. Don't call me again until you have a real offer," Rip yelled, slamming down the phone.

Rip didn't care what other attorneys thought of him, so he gave no further thought to his conversation with Yani before reviewing the draft of the complaint in the Jordan triathlon case. Drafting a complaint filed against an unsuspecting defendant gave Rip great pleasure, so much so he joked that serving it on an unsuspecting defendant with ample insurance coverage was orgasmic. He amused himself with including multiple "counts" in the complaint and citing as many possible legal theories as he could conjure. His inclusion of excess legal jargon would surely confuse, scare and ultimately intimidate the defendant who would demand his insurance carrier pay policy limits, which could be millions of dollars. If the company didn't pay, Rip stepped in and sued them for bad faith.

This strategy had worked so well in the past, it had paid for Rip's 2012 Porsche 911 Carrera S with its 3.8 liter 6-cylinder engine with 6-speed manual transmission and his latest Rolex. Rip associated a new toy with each complaint so he could visualize his prize as he strategized how to squeeze as much money out of the insurance company and the defendant as possible. Unlike most plaintiffs' attorneys, he had no conscience about seizing a defendant's house, or garnishing his wages or life savings and retirement funds. The bulk of that money would go to the plaintiff, but Rip enjoyed the forty per cent share, which funded his flamboyant lifestyle.

He believed that whoever dies with the most toys wins. In order to ensure his victory, he threw a punitive damages claim in the complaint as well, hoping the jury would find the defendant's behavior so egregious they would order him to pay millions of dollars to the plaintiff. On the last occasion this strategy had worked so well, Rip's prize was a magnificent beach house on the north shore of Kauai.

While he was drafting the complaint, the theme song from *The Apprentice*, "Money, Money, Money" blared from his phone. He quickly picked up, knowing it was Amber Penney calling to alert him to an unrepresented, seriously injured potential plaintiff, or "cash cow", as Rip called them.

"Hey, Sexy."

"I've got another one for you," Amber said. "Bad car accident. She's in a coma."

"Are there any family members there yet?"

"I called her parents just before I ducked out of the ER to call you. If you get here quickly, you'll be able to talk with them before the other ambulance chasers arrive."

"Hey, that's not very nice, Amber. Didn't you like the diamond tennis bracelet I gave you for your referral of Brad Jordan?"

"You know I need a new car, Rip."

"Why don't you come to the Date House? I can give you your money's worth."

"You wish. I need a car. A Beamer or Mercedes. Not some American made hunk of junk. Do you want me to call Preston Farnsworth? I'm sure he'd be interested in this case."

"No need. I'll take good care of you. We'll talk about it when I get there."

***

Rip stepped into his eight-car garage, making a beeline to his gun-medal gray 2010 BMW. It was his oldest car and if this referral proved to be a significant injury with clear liability, he'd give it to Amber. The car smelled musty when he opened the rear passenger door and he wondered whether it would start after not driving it since last summer when he had lent it to that blonde who moved to Honolulu at his urging.

He had met her in the wine section of a Trader Joe's when he was in Seattle for depositions. She'd suggested a 2006 Pinot Noir and he'd suggested sharing it in his hotel room. The sex was unforgettable. She was so flexible she could do the splits in all sorts of positions and her training as an endurance athlete translated nicely to the bedroom. He had finally met his sexual energy match.

Rip returned to Honolulu after nearly a month of post-deposition sex marathons, but couldn't get her off of his mind. Apparently, she felt the same way, because she announced she was planning to move to Waikiki. He sent her a one-way first class plane ticket and a few grand for an apartment deposit. He even used his connections with the school board to get her a teaching job. Rip had introduced his new Seattle girl to the sun and the Date House, fitting her in on Tuesday and Friday nights. This worked for a few months. Then, her non-stop calling and texting, dropping by his office, stalking him on the golf course and tailing him in her car turned into screaming matches of her constant demands of his time and his excuses of why he had less and less of it for her. He stopped returning her calls. Eventually, she gave up.

Rip yanked the large blanket out of the Beamer's backseat, which they had used to protect their naked bodies from sand while having sex on the beach one night. He licked his lips remembering her tanned, smooth skin straddling his body. He then pulled beach towels, a picnic basket and some rumpled T-shirts out of the trunk, piling them into an empty plastic bin for one of his maids to sort through later. A layer of fine Hawaiian sand covered the carpet of the trunk, but there was no time for detailing the car and he doubted Amber would complain.

As he climbed into the front seat, he saw it. A white lace thong had been hung over the rearview mirror with his name written in blood—R.I.P. His only concern was that she had been the one who first introduced him to Brad Jordan before the Olympic trials.

Chapter 3

@Zlaw Married to my #work. Engagement ring was a paper clip.

After spending the morning reviewing every inch of the Jordan file, Zana arrived early to her first litigation team meeting. The conference room was already set up with a pitcher of the firm's signature pineapple water, a thermos of coffee and the usual plate of fresh donuts no one ever ate. Zana poured a cup of water and opened her laptop, clicking open to her notes. Andrew had warned her that Frank's interrogation of new associates at such meetings was sometimes more grueling than his cross-examinations of hostile witnesses at trial. Her boss had even been known to fire attorneys on the spot if he caught them unprepared. Zana's stress level was so high she'd already changed from her sweat-soaked blouse into a spare top she kept on a hanger on the back of her door. Her navy blazer would have to remain on to cover up the emerging dampness under her arms.

Tom and Lori, the other associates on the team, walked in together chatting about a case. Zana had noticed them always hanging out together. Andrew had filled Zana in that they were both married to other people, but there had been some unsubstantiated gossip they were having an affair. Zana's observations and her woman's intuition told her they were merely work buddies, relying on each other for the same type of support Zana sought from Andrew, but who knew for sure.

"Hey, Zana," Tom said. "Welcome to the team. Are you ready for Trivial Pursuit?"

"I'm not sure I know what you mean," Zana said, "but I'll try."

"Are you ready to answer Frank's completely inane questions?" Lori whispered, keeping her eye on the door.

"I think I can handle it." Zana touched her right underarm with her left hand, hoping she wasn't sweating through her jacket.

"Good morning, team," Frank said as he walked in.

"Good morning," the associates said in unison.

Frank launched into his questions before sitting down at the head of the conference table. "Zana, what type of vehicle was involved in the subject accident?"

"According to the police report, it was a white, late-model compact, American-made car with no license plate visible," Zana said, relieved she knew the answer.

Not wasting a breath, Frank tossed her another one. "How fast was the car traveling when it hit the cyclists?"

"The police estimated the speed at 30 to 40 miles per hour," Zana said.

"Did any witnesses see the driver?" Frank asked.

"A witness described the driver as a female with long, dark hair and dark glasses," she answered.

"Clearly you read the police report. Tell us something we don't already know." Frank rubbed his chin.

"Excuse me?"

"If I wanted someone to recite the police report, I would have hired a third grader," Frank spoke with such venom that several drops of spit flew out of his mouth with his words. "Didn't law school teach you how to think?"

"Yes," Zana said quietly. She wished Tom or Lori would rescue her by distracting Frank from his grilling, but they remained silent.

"As a triathlete, what do you think about the accident?" Frank prodded.

"I agree with the incident report, which stated that someone intentionally drove onto the course. With all of the orange cones, signs and barriers erected to stop traffic, it's hard to believe it was an accident."

"Good point, young lady," Frank said, nodding, as he landed his fist on the table with a loud thud. "What do you think about the rumors of Ryan Peterson enlisting someone to wipe out his competition?"

"It's possible," Zana said, trying not to jump at the sudden noise. "It would have been more likely if it was a world competition. The Germans who Peterson competed against in the Olympics were fierce opponents. Wiping out the top U.S. guys didn't do anything to address the threat of the Germans, Brits, or Australians."

"Peterson won the gold. The accident put him in the position to win handily," Frank said. "And what injuries did the Plaintiff sustain? Lori?"

"Severe spinal injuries, rendering him paralyzed," Lori said. "We need to get the medical records and have an independent medical examination completed."

"I agree. Lori and Zana—you'll need to follow up," Frank said.

Zana noticed he had omitted Tom, the only other man on the team, from this assignment. Maybe Frank considered obtaining medical records the legal equivalent to fetching coffee.

"Time to get back to work. Keep me updated on discovery," Frank said and abruptly left the room.

"That was quick," Zana commented after the door shut behind their boss. She felt beads of perspiration above her upper lip and wiped them off with a napkin.

"If you hadn't been able to answer his questions, we would have been in here a lot longer. Good job, Zana," Tom said. "You heard what Frank said. Back to work."

"Billable hours," Lori hissed.

Zana carried the stack of files and her laptop back to her office. She had expected the meeting to last several hours and had even cancelled a rare lunch date she had scheduled weeks ago so she wouldn't feel any time pressure. She slipped her jacket off and grabbed a hanger so she could rehang it on the back of her door. But after seeing sweat circles as big as dinner plates under each arm, she tossed it behind her desk. The top underneath was even worse and she'd be stuck wearing it for the rest of the day.

Before returning to her computer, Zana popped a piece of sugarless gum into her mouth and texted her friend, Shelby. *Now avail for lunch,* adding her signature emoticon.

Shelby's response was immediate. *It's about time, your Highness.* Zana laughed at the crown emoticon.

Later, when she arrived at their favorite hole-in-the-wall Thai restaurant in Chinatown, Shelby and Moana were already in the long line of people spilling out the front door and onto the sidewalk. She noticed the Mayor of Honolulu standing there with everyone else. He and Zana exchanged smiles. It was nice living in a big, small town where everywhere she went she ran into someone she knew or a public figure she recognized from T.V.

"It's about time," Shelby said to Zana when she joined her friends in line just as they were about to give their orders.

"You know my work sucks," Zana said.

"Well, at least you're here," Moana said. She was wearing a flowery skirt with a sleeveless top, showing the tattoos of Chinese calligraphy down her arm.

The women took their plates of Panang chicken, beef curry and eggplant out to the garden dining area in the back of the restaurant with its rows of picnic benches covered in plastic red and white checkered tablecloths. The mayor and his entourage sat behind them, filling the only remaining empty table.

"Looks like you barely survived the grilling from your boss," Moana said.

"What do you mean?" Zana asked.

"There's only a small patch of blouse you didn't sweat through," Moana motioned to Zana's shirt before picking up a fork to eat her lunch. "Have you ever heard of deodorant?"

Zana smirked. "Mo, do you even *know* how to use chopsticks?"

"I'm calling your tattoo artist," Shelby said.

"I don't have anything to prove, like you *haoles*," Moana said. "So, how *did* your meeting go?"

"Good. I think I made it through another week," Zana said.

"Does that mean you can go out with us on Friday night?" Shelby asked between bites of beef curry. She used chopsticks like a pro.

"We're biking at the butt crack of dawn on Saturday," Zana said. "I need sleep, not a hangover."

"We'll make it an early night. We're just going to have a few drinks at Peppers," Moana said.

"Okay, maybe. It depends on my billable hours." Zana yawned. "I could use some sleep."

"Some of the single guys from my office will be there," Moana said. "Stock brokers can be pretty cute."

"You're telling me," Shelby said. "Zana, these guys are gorgeous. You'd be crazy not to join us. How are you ever going to find a boyfriend if all you do is work and train?"

"You'll have to take a shower first." Moana plugged her nose.

Zana laughed. "It's not like either of you are dating anyone right now."

"At least we're out there checking out the goods," Moana said. "With all the single guys we train with, it's amazing we never go out with any of them."

"Do they date?" Shelby pushed her empty plate away. "All they seem to do is swim, bike and run."

"That's all *we* do," Zana said. "They probably say the same thing about us."

"And you work such insane hours," Moana said.

"I'm okay with working hard for a few years to pay my dues. Then, I can think about meeting someone special." Zana put down her chopsticks, abandoning the second scoop of rice. "For now, I'm married to my work."

"And triathlons." Shelby smiled.

After lunch, Zana returned to the piles on her desk and 50 new emails. She wished for time and energy to go out with friends on Friday night, but knew there was no way she'd be able to get up at 4:30 a.m. on Saturday after a night of drinking. Despite what the girls said, the night would be a late one of fun and laughter. The Bronzeman Triathlon was a month away. She couldn't afford any extracurricular activities right now. Between triathlon training and work, she didn't even have time to take her growing pile of soiled work clothes to the drycleaner or renew her expired car registration.

Zana popped a fresh piece of gum in her mouth. She squinted at interrogatory #30 on her computer, the last of the set she'd drafted for Plaintiff Brad Jordon, clicked on spellcheck and pressed save. Andrew would proofread the document in return for a lox and bagel bribe before she handed it over to Frank for final approval. Zana swiveled her chair towards the window and noticed it was now dusk. She could see the silhouette of the Dole Pineapple against the industrial district lights in the distance. She sighed. If her new case wasn't so interesting, she would have been swimming towards the sunset in the ocean or running around Ala Moana Beach Park rather than staring at an illuminated screen in the dusty confines of this high rise.

Just as she was straightening up her desk to get ready to leave, the door swung open without a knock.

"Zana, do you have a moment to discuss the Fujiwara case?" Brian Ching walked in and sat on the chair facing her desk without even waiting for an answer.

"Sure, Brian," Zana replied. "What's up?"

"When can I expect a draft of the motion?" Brian was not into small talk and he certainly didn't care much for fashion. *Was he wearing the same rumpled aloha shirt he had worn all week?* Zana knew he must have about three or four of the 2006 nautical patterned Reyn Spooner shirt.

"I've written most of the memorandum in support of the motion. I'm just waiting for our client's signed affidavit. Do you have any timing concerns?" Zana could see from Brian's expression that he was surprised by her promptness.

"No." Brian stared at her and rubbed both his hands on his thighs in a nervous gesture, rocking back and forth. His strange behavior led Zana to suspect he had a crush on her. "Mrs. Fujiwara is sort of an airhead. Make sure she signs her affidavit."

"Sure. Sylvia is taking care of it." Zana looked away from Brian's stare. She had wondered how he could have become a junior partner until one of the other associates explained to her that he was a billing machine. The man never went home. He was also a potential rainmaker, with the promise of using his many connections to bring business to the firm.

Zana grabbed her bag and briefcase, and walked towards her office door. Brian popped up out of his chair, following her through the door.

"Sorry, I've got an appointment," Zana said, hoping Brian wouldn't guess it was with her running shoes.

He kept pace with her to the elevator. "How's your triathlon case going?"

"Good. I'm working on discovery," she said, pushing the button marked "G" for garage.

"Watch out for Mansfield. I heard he's taken a special interest in the case," Brian said when the elevator opened. "My cousin told me she saw him having dinner with some triathlete's wife or girlfriend at Duke's a few weeks before the accident."

Zana wasn't surprised by Brian's comment. The Ching family was big, wealthy and well-connected. Brian always had some inside information.

"Do you think the woman had anything to do with Brad Jordan or Ryan Peterson?" She stepped into the elevator, Brian following behind her.

"My cousin, Celia—she's with the prosecutor's office—said she was sitting close enough to Mansfield's table to hear some of the conversation."

"And...?" Zana prodded.

"They were talking about a triathlete by the name of Brad who was competing in the Olympic trials."

"Why would Mansfield have anything to do with Brad before he was injured?"

"Good question. Celia asked me the same thing," Brian said.

"Her information is really random," Zana said. "How did the subject even come up?"

"She reads all of the lawsuit filings in the Akamai Business News and saw our firm listed as counsel-of-record for one of the defendants with Mansfield representing the plaintiff. She called me, asked if I was handling the case." They stopped on the 14th floor and a cleaning lady, cart and all, stepped onto the elevator.

"So that jogged Celia's memory about overhearing Mansfield's conversation?" Zana whispered.

Brian nodded and was silent until the woman got off, stepping onto her floor.

"Celia wonders if Rip had something to do with the accident," Brian said as the elevator reached the bottom floor.

"Hmm. I suppose anything is possible," Zana said. She walked quickly to her car, leaving Brian standing near the elevator staring after her.

Chapter 4

@Zlaw Have you ever won the car #accident lottery?

Alexia Moore yawned loudly for the fifth time that morning, not even bothering to cover her mouth.

Tammy, the claims adjuster in the adjacent cubicle to hers kicked the flimsy structure between them so hard, Alexia was sure it would collapse, burying them alive.

"Shut up!" Tammy said, laughing. "Don't you ever get any sleep?"

"Sorry," Alexia yawned again, this time quietly into her hand.

"I don't know why you bother getting up so early to exercise every morning," Tammy peered at her over the wall. "You're so skinny."

She shook her head, feeling her face flush at the compliment. *If she only knew.* Alexia kept a tiny picture of the Space Needle and a large picture of Waikiki Beach on the bulletin board next to her computer as a constant reminder of her past in that gloomy city compared to the dream she was living in paradise. She vowed never to miss an early morning workout and used makeup to cover the bags under her eyes, but she could do nothing about her incessant yawning.

Alexia turned her attention back to the letter from Rip Mansfield. *Was he really demanding the insurance company pay $5 million?* She squinted her eyes and stared at the paper again.

"Tammy," Alexia said. "Can you take a look at this?"

"What?" Tammy said, her gold Hawaiian bracelets jangling as she made her way over.

"What do you think?"

"Is this a joke?" Tammy examined the letter over Alexia's shoulder.

"No, it's from Rip Mansfield." Alexia yawned again, this time from anxiety. "I hear he's a snake."

"The supreme ruler of all snakes. If it were any other attorney, this would be laughable." Tammy brushed a strand of auburn hair away from her chubby cheek.

Tammy had just celebrated her 25th year with Friendly Isle Mutual or

F.I.M. as everyone called it, and was the Senior Adjuster for the claims unit. Most of their colleagues were afraid of their boss, Caron Rossi, so they often lined up at Tammy's cubicle to ask for claims handling advice. And thankfully, she would give it freely with a smile.

"Have you ever seen a demand this high?" Alexia asked.

"No way," Tammy said. "Most of our insureds have policy limits below $100k and the attorneys seem to value their client's injuries at precisely the top amount they can squeeze out of us."

"What should I do?" Alexia's stomach felt queasy.

"You'll have to bring this to Caron immediately," Tammy said. "Document your file on everything you do. If we get sued for bad faith, you're toast."

"That's what I thought. Thanks."

Alexia sighed. Caron, who seemed to have stepped out of another era, wore 1950s mothball scented suits and scrutinized her underlings' every move through thick cat-eye glasses. She was the manager of the entire department and was almost as scary as Mansfield. Alexia didn't mind working sixty hours per week in order to keep up with her caseload, but she preferred the safely of her cubicle, reviewing and evaluating files and negotiating with attorneys or monitoring defense counsel to make sure they were on top of her cases. Emailing and talking on the phone was easy and anonymous. Walking through the maze of cubicles, past dozens of workers to drop uninvited into Caron's office made her dizzy.

Caron had climbed the corporate ladder from the bottom rung in the mailroom to clerk, then secretary, adjuster, supervisor, and finally to claims manager. She knew the law better than the attorneys she hired and could recite every obscure detail of F.I.M's claims manual from memory. Even though Alexia had been issued an employee handbook when she started, the company's top brass changed too often for her to know where the buck stopped, besides Caron's desk.

When Alexia dared to leave her work space, she often saw Caron schmoozing with different men wearing suits and ties whose balding pates were mainland pasty white. They were too important to introduce around to personnel, but Alexia noticed their presence inspired fewer bathroom breaks and lowered the volume of office chitchat.

Before trotting over to her boss's office, Alexia took a few minutes to review the thick stack of exhibits included with Mansfield's demand letter.

Big mistake. Sandwiched in between medical records and diagnostic studies were dozens of gory photographs of Brad Jordan's bloody body lying in the road next to another athlete covered in a white sheet as ambulance attendants prepared to transport them. *Who was taking pictures?* she wondered.

Alexia suddenly felt the rumble of nausea she had tried so hard to avoid and bolted to the ladies room to puke up her breakfast. She then suppressed another yawn as she splashed water on her face. She'd have to brush her teeth before breathing on Caron.

Alexia wasn't a big fan of mangled body pictures so prevalent in her claims files, but she did appreciate her salary which was much higher than what she had made working at a bank in her previous life in Seattle, so she put up with occasionally losing her lunch. Many Hawaii residents had to hold two jobs in order to manage the steep rent. She made enough to live in a tiny house in Makiki and could afford $7.00 boxes of cereal without having to cut coupons. She made sure to hide her squeamishness though, unsure if having an iron stomach was one of the job requirements. The last thing she wanted was to be demoted.

After brushing her teeth, she reviewed the file partly in preparation for discussing it with Caron and partly to procrastinate.

F.I.M. had sold an insurance policy to Aloha Athletics Company, Inc., the company that ran the triathlon Olympic trials. In his letter, Mansfield blamed Aloha Athletics for failing to block the course from traffic, and because of their gross negligence a jury would find the company to be at fault for the accident. Mansfield detailed his client's damages: $350,000 in hospital bills; $100,000 for rehabilitation; $80,000 for wheelchairs; $55,000 for medical bills and another $250,000 for future medical bills; $20,000 for medication; $2 million for future lost earnings, and $2.5 million for pain and suffering. According to Mansfield, he was offering F.I.M. a bargain to settle for a mere $5 million, before incurring tens of thousands in attorney's fees and costs to defend the case.

She certainly wouldn't cough up the policy limits so easily. Even though blood and gore were involved, the one thing Alexia excelled at was holding onto the insurance company's money, and for this, she was a rising star at F.I.M.

Caron had already assigned the case to defense attorney, Frank Gravelle, who was a good match against the repugnant Mansfield. Frank would delegate most of the labor to ambitious young associates and junior partners who would work up the case and then, hopefully, he would kick ass at trial. The reality was that the case would settle before trial for something more sensible and much lower than policy limits. However, the ideal outcome was an early win of a motion for summary judgment, which would throw the case out of court and let F.I.M. and Aloha Athletics off the hook. If that happened, Alexia would hopefully be a hero and stood to receive a good evaluation and maybe even a modest raise at the end of the year.

She popped a peppermint Altoid into her mouth, grabbed a few files, a notepad and a pen, and headed down through the cubicle maze to Caron's office. Before entering, she set the files on a co-worker's desk and wiped her sweaty palms on her black pants.

"Hey," Alexia whispered as she tiptoed into Caron's office, trying not to disturb her phone call.

Her boss motioned her to have a seat on the opposite side of her desk, piled high with at least 50 files, giving the impression that Caron was either literally buried with work or needed treatment for a hoarding disorder.

Alexia busied herself by re-reading Mansfield's letter while Caron haggled with some plaintiff's attorney, clearly holding tight to F.I.M.'s money.

When Caron finally hung up the phone, she typed on her keyboard for a few minutes while Alexia pretended to wait patiently. Alexia knew better than to interrupt her. Caron would talk only when she was good and ready, and if she wanted her to leave, she would gesture with her trademark wave of a hand.

"Alexia, what's the status of discovery on Pelton versus Wong?" Caron asked, peering over the precarious stack of files.

"Plaintiff's deposition was taken last week. I'm still waiting for defense counsel's deposition summary and evaluation," Alexia said.

"Who's defense counsel?" Caron barked in her hoarse ex-smoker's voice.

Alexia had noticed that when the laws in Hawaii prohibited smoking within 20 feet of buildings, her boss no longer loitered amongst the smokers.

"Frank Gravelle."

"Okay. That's good. What are the reserves?" Caron turned back to her computer and typed.

"$23,000. Are you okay with that for now?" Alexia asked, inwardly holding her breath.

"Yeah," Caron said. "Let's reevaluate after Frank's report."

"I need to talk with you about something," Alexia said. Her hands shook as she handed over Mansfield's letter, but in the process she knocked over the file wall, causing it to crash down onto Caron.

"Fuck!" Caron shouted, digging herself out from under the pile. She then snatched the letter off the top and skimmed it.

"He's demanding $5 million," Alexia said.

"Jeez." Caron leaned forward so Alexia could see her eyes widening behind the tortoise shell reading glasses, her face going pale. "Plaintiff was paralyzed. Is that correct?"

"Yes. Reserves are set for $300,000 right now."

"What are policy limits?"

"$5 million."

"Hmmm. Okay. Well, I need to address some other matters." Caron waved her hand dismissively towards Alexia, the signal for her to go.

***

After Alexia had left and closed the door, Caron put her elbows on a small area of her desk no longer loaded with files and rested her face in her hands. She sat in that position for at least fifteen minutes before she knew what she had to do.

"Larry," Caron said gruffly into the phone.

"Yes. Caron, nice hearing from you," Lawrence Katz, her boss, who worked out of F.I.M's home office in New York, said. "What's up?"

"We've got $5 million in exposure on a Mansfield case," she said.

"Hmmm."

"Gravelle's on the case," Caron explained.

"You know what this means?"

"Yeah," Caron said, barely audible.

"If we get stuck paying $5 million, we're done," he said.

"That's what I understand." She put her glasses on her desk.

"Our jobs depend on shutting this one down," Larry explained.

"I know. If worse comes to worse, how much could we pay without it being a disaster for the company?"

"We're undercapitalized, Caron. I'm not supposed to tell you," Larry paused, "but the previous CEO flaunted insurance department regulations."

"Oh?"

"We already paid $2 million on the wrongful death claim by Vic Leavitt's estate. I think we can only take a hit of $1 million on this claim—maybe less."

After Caron hung up, she stared at her hot air balloon screen saver until she heard the buzzing of one of the lines on her desk phone. She watched the illuminated light flash until it stopped. She then turned back to the remaining file tower on her desk, picking up the next claims file in line. *One small task at a time*, she thought to herself.

Chapter 5

@Zlaw Delicious post #workout #drink: Tri-tini.

Brad Jordan tossed another stack of unpaid bills, coupon mailers, political flyers and magazines onto a pile of unopened mail, spilling the stack on the counter to the floor.

A triathlon magazine caught his eye.

When he leaned forward in his wheelchair to grab it, he caught sight of a large envelope with the return address of The Law Offices of Rip Mansfield, LLC. His sponsors had long since stopped sending money and products, so the only mail besides his paltry disability check with any potential for a payday came from his attorney. Brad was anxious to cash in on the promises Mansfield had made in the hospital at his bedside during a time when money was far less important than his morphine drip.

He ripped open the envelope, tearing a chunk out of the first page of the document with a red DRAFT stamp in the top right corner. He shook the papers. When he saw there was no check, he flung them back onto the pile of mail. Brad then used his well-muscled biceps to push his wheelchair back into the living room, dodging dirty towels, empty pizza boxes and clothes strewn about the floor.

"Where's the fucking remote?" Brad said out loud to the empty room, before spying it on the floor, half covered by a dirty T-shirt. He reached to grab it, throwing the T-shirt in a corner. Clicking through hundreds of channels, he finally settled on a baseball game.

By the second inning, he squirmed in his wheelchair, trying to get comfortable. His back was especially sore today. So he popped a few Vicodin, washing them down with what he called a Tri-Grapetini—a grape-flavored Gatorade and Absolut vodka cocktail—served in a plastic water bottle he had used for hydration when riding his bike before the accident. The more he drank the less pain he felt, and the less he cared about his destroyed Olympic dreams and professional triathlon career. Without the incentive of millions of dollars in compensation, even the alcohol couldn't do much to get him out of bed each morning. Mansfield had offered him all the hope that money could buy, but he had also instructed Brad to have patience and to trust him while the wheels of justice turned slowly.

He saw the mess as he looked around the room, but he wasn't in the mood to tidy his small, disheveled apartment. He expected his off-and-on-again girlfriend, Heather Alexander, to stop by after work in a few hours. If she complained about having to work all day and then take care of him at night, he'd do what he always did. Play the poor paralyzed victim card. She would cook his favorite dish, clean the kitchen and then his apartment while he moaned in pain, begging for her to massage his neck.

Brad flipped through the channels again, stopping when he saw Mansfield on T.V., flashing his cheesy Hollywood smile, promising to get even with big insurance companies for denying claims and to wrestle millions out of them to compensate severely injured victims. He had never heard of Mansfield before his accident. He showed up in his hospital room the very day of the crash, shortly after the anesthesia wore off from his first surgery. Despite his persistence, Brad said he had to consider all his options. Lawyers streamed in and out of his hospital room for the first few weeks after the accident, trying to outdo one another with looks of sympathy, lower contingency fees and lofty credentials. It was Heather's identical twin sister, Megan, who had insisted that Mansfield was the best attorney in town and just the right shark to avenge his loss. And Brad had trusted her; he had no reason not to. Megan was a fellow triathlete who had also moved to Hawaii and ran in the same circle of multi-sport athletes as he did.

Brad took another swig of his Tri-Grapetini. He hoped Mansfield would make good on his promise so he could pay his mounting medical bills and escape from this dreary place. A large settlement could bankroll the kind of life he had imagined if he had won the Olympic gold medal instead of crashing at the Olympic trials. In the meantime, his survival depended on Heather continuing to pay his rent, so he decided he better at least try to make an effort to tidy up and slap some deodorant under his arms.

He rolled his wheelchair over to the window and closed the blinds. He then wheeled over to the door and locked it, making sure the deadbolt was in place and the chain was on the door. He stood up slowly. His back was sore, but the initial paralysis had gradually disappeared after three surgeries and almost a year of intense physical therapy provided at the urging of Mansfield, who had advised maximum treatment in order to increase his medical bills so his injuries would yield the highest possible settlement or jury verdict. Even though his doctors expected Brad to walk again if he complied with prescribed therapy, Mansfield emphasized that the longer his injuries remained the more money he would get. Such talk gave Brad less incentive to suffer through repetitive exercises. Yet as an elite athlete, he couldn't help but excel at rehabilitation.

He had slowly and secretly regained his ability to walk. The only person who discovered his secret was Megan when she was taking care of him a few months ago. He had heard the door shut and leapt from his wheelchair to grab a beer from the fridge and had almost knocked her down in the kitchen. She had come back for her purse.

Megan hadn't let him off easy. After days of her threatening to rat on him to the defense attorneys, they finally struck a deal. In return for her pledge of secrecy, Brad promised her a cut in his take. Neither of them thought it would be a good idea to bring his girlfriend in on the ruse. Heather loved to spread gossip and knowing such a big secret—if she managed to keep it—would give her leverage in their relationship he didn't want her to have.

Heather made it clear she wasn't thrilled he gave up a college education to train for the Olympics. She wanted him to have an education to fall back on. But, after high school graduation, he spent every waking hour swimming, biking, running, lifting weights, and eating the perfectly balanced carbohydrate and protein diet. There was little time left to spend with his girlfriend, and certainly no time for studying and attending classes.

They had been dating for five years and living together in Kirkland, Washington, where they had both grown up when he had announced his plan to move to Hawaii to train in preparation for the Honolulu Olympic trials. Heather had just realized her dream of becoming a T.V. anchorwoman after years of paying her dues as a weather girl, and so they were at an impasse, arguing non-stop about whose career should take priority. He was up against the deadline to qualify for the 2012 London Olympic Games. After ten consecutive days of riding his bike in the rain while his competitors trained in the sun, Brad decided his yearning to be an Olympian was far greater than his feelings for his girlfriend. While Heather was at work one night, he packed up his belongings and left a small post-it note apology with no details of his plan.

Once he settled in Waikiki, he changed his cell number and email address to avoid distractions from Heather and anyone else back home. He needed the competitive edge of anonymity. Within months, Heather tracked him down. She showed up at Kapiolani Park after his workouts or at the finish line of practice races, always begging to talk to him. She said she needed closure, which in his mind meant keeping the door open, something he wasn't willing to entertain until after he stood on the podium wearing a gold medal.

Heather, who was usually a composed anchorwoman even when she wasn't on screen, became unglued, sobbing and begging for another chance. Brad ignored her, wondering what about Heather had attracted him in the first place. He no longer noticed her thin, sexy body, silky blonde hair and bright blue eyes, which boosted the ratings of Channel 7 news. All he saw was a woman lacking confidence and charisma.

"You're a selfish bastard!" Heather had shouted at him on one of those occasions when she'd flown to Hawaii to watch him compete in a world cup event.

"I've always been like this," Brad said. "When we met, you didn't seem to care."

"I've always cared," Heather sobbed.

"What happened to you?" Brad asked. "When we were in high school, you were so cool. You were only focused on your own goals. Not following me around like a puppy."

"Your indifference has destroyed me," she had said and crumpled to the ground. Brad saw this as a theatrical performance and didn't take the bait. He walked away from her just as he always did when she lost control.

After the accident and throughout his lengthy hospitalization and in-patient rehabilitation, Brad preferred his privacy. His parents wanted to fly him back to Seattle and take care of him, but he refused. If he moved back home, it would be like giving up. Becoming a child again. In his mind, he was still an Olympic champion and even though his legs were shot, he wasn't about to let all his dreams die. He hadn't told his mom and dad about the money Mansfield had promised him. He also didn't want them to know about the pills he collected under his mattress in case the pain he suffered became greater than his dream of being a millionaire.

Brad was used to being the center of attention and seldom listened to the problems he heard his family and friends talk to each other about around him. Although he was surprised when his sister Michelle came to Hawaii to see him without her husband, he didn't think to ask her what was going on. Instead, he complained to her about the hospital food. It wasn't until after she left that his mother interrupted his physical therapy session and asked to speak to him alone. She'd wheeled him to a private room and stood over him.

"I'm used to your shitty attitude, but you will not disrespect your sister," his mother had said. Her hands were shaking and Brad wondered if she was going to slap him.

"I really don't know what you're talking about," he'd said.

"Your sister is going through the worst time in her life."

"What about me?" He had grimaced as if he was in pain, but she ignored him.

"Did you even know she's going through a divorce?" She put her hands on her hips.

"No," Brad's eyes widened. "I thought Derek was on a business trip or something."

She shook her head.

"What?" he asked.

"You're just as selfish now as you were as a triathlete," she said, wagging her finger at him.

Brad's parents stayed as long as they could, but had to get back to Seattle for work and to care for their dogs. After they left, he felt pangs of loneliness he'd never before experienced. The pills under his mattress were tempting. One night, after soaking his pillow with tears, he called

Heather and begged her to come to Hawaii, but to his surprise he found out she was already there. She was at his hospital bedside within the half hour even though it was well after visiting hours. He took her back into his arms and she confessed her recent move to Oahu. She had taken a job at a local station with lower pay in a smaller market, but closer to him. Before he could think things through, she agreed to help him, which quickly evolved into the resumption of their relationship. They soon settled into a routine of her working and caring for him while he waited for the insurance companies to come to their senses and write him some fat checks.

***

After Brad brushed his teeth, shaved, and stretched his legs gingerly in the shower, he took the chain off the door and slunk back in his wheelchair, ready for Heather's arrival and dinner. He took a swig out of the fresh Tri-Grapetini he had made and was mindlessly flipping through the T.V. channels when he heard the jiggling of the door open with her key.

"How are you feeling, sweetie pie?" Heather asked in the baby talk tone she used with him since the accident. She leaned over and kissed him lightly on the lips.

Brad groaned in response.

"Are you hungry?" she asked.

"Yeah. What are we having for dinner?" Brad said in the most pathetic voice he could muster.

"I'm making your favorite—pork chops, mashed potatoes and asparagus," Heather said, pushing Brad in his wheelchair closer to the kitchen. She then began picking up magazines strewn about on the floor and a dirty dish and glass left on the coffee table.

"You know, you could pick things up a little around here, honey," Heather said.

"How would you like to be confined to a chair for the rest of your life?" Brad raised his voice.

"I know you're having a hard time, Brad. Remember the doctor said it would be good for you to do what you can around the house. It's like physical therapy," she said. "You need to move."

"I'll move after the case is settled. You heard what my attorney said. The insurance companies have private investigators who could be videotaping my every move."

"Well, they aren't here in your apartment. I don't think they will film you picking up your dirty dishes or your soiled underwear."

"If all you're going to do is give me shit, why don't you just leave." Brad could feel his face become hotter. He didn't care if Heather left as long as he got his dinner first.

"I'm sorry, honey. I'm just tired. Let me help you get comfortable and I'll pour you some cranberry juice," Heather said, fetching a small pillow from the couch for his back.

Brad tolerated her attempt to make him comfortable and exaggerated his pain with a few moans and groans when she tucked the pillow behind his low back.

"Is that better, sweetie?" Heather smiled.

"Yeah. Thank you," he said softly.

Brad had gotten accustomed to being waited on by Heather years before the accident so he rarely bothered to make any effort, even when he had been fit and capable of working out as much as six hours each day. In addition to Heather's heavy workload, she had always cleaned, cooked and done every household chore. It had always been Brad's role to train to become an Olympian. Now, it was Brad's role to hide the traces of his vodka consumption, make sure to behave in a manner consistent with an invalid, and to follow Mansfield's instructions so he could collect millions. He didn't care anymore what Heather did.

Chapter 6

@Zlaw The only #triathletes who date are injured.

Heather slammed her front door and headed straight for the freezer. It was empty save for a Ziploc bag of frozen organic blueberries, which she began mindlessly popping into her mouth. She wanted to call Megan and complain about Brad like the old days, but she didn't want to hear her say, "I told you so." Even worse, she didn't want to hear herself make excuses for his behavior.

When he was training for triathlons, he was a future Olympian with no time to give her the attention she deserved. Now, he was paralyzed and needed her support. In a weird way, she liked Brad confined to a wheelchair and his apartment. At least now, she was able to see him periodically and the control was finally shifted to her. And even though he would never admit it, he needed her.

Heather's friends and family had been telling her she could do better since the first time he blew off her birthday party to go on a 100 mile bike ride shortly after they first started dating. Of course she *could* do better. Even last week a commercial pilot who struck up a conversation with her at the dry cleaners had asked for her number. She smiled and flashed a cubic zirconia faux engagement ring she wore to fend off potential suitors.

She usually remembered to stash the ring in her wallet before seeing Brad, but last week he noticed it when she served lunch to him on a tray while he watched the game.

"What the fuck is that?" Brad shouted.

"A ring," she said.

"Are you fucking engaged or something?"

"I'm just keeping my finger warm. Waiting for you," Heather had said, feeling her face flush.

"Good idea, since hell will freeze over before we're engaged."

A shouting match ensued, ending with them making out on the couch. Since he had become paralyzed, they couldn't make up in bed as they had in the past, but it wasn't sex she craved. She got what she needed—his tender kisses and touches. No other man had ever captured her heart like he did.

Ever since Heather could remember, she had gotten favorable attention from almost every human being who crossed her path. People had been telling her she was *beautiful, adorable, pretty,* and *gorgeous* since she was a little girl. By the time she was sixteen years old she was being called *sexy* and a *knockout.*

Boys in her class began giving Heather attention when she was in the second grade. In high school, she accompanied the most popular and handsome young men to every school dance or social, but even though they fawned over her, she lost interest before they summoned the courage to kiss her. She had learned to turn her head so they caught a cheek rather than her virgin lips. She thought it strange that her twin dated the same boy for most of high school, but Heather couldn't sustain a crush on a boy if he reciprocated her interest.

A few months after she turned seventeen, she was practicing hitting tennis balls against a wall. She noticed a boy she had seen at school walk past her, rolling a racing bicycle and holding a helmet in his hand. He was wearing a cycling jersey and padded bike shorts, and his shoes clicked on the cement as he walked. He looked right at her but nothing seemed to register. He didn't smile or give her a cheesy pick-up line. His look was total concentration. Heather stopped hitting balls and smiled, but he didn't smile back.

After her first encounter with the boy, she learned his name was Brad Jordan and started noticing him in the school hallways and in her AP math class. She tried to elicit a reaction from him, but even when she smiled and said hello, he wouldn't look her in the eye.

Heather kept trying, because whenever she saw him she felt butterflies in her stomach—a glorious new sensation. According to her friend, Nathalie, whose mother was the vice principal, Brad had transferred to their school because of its superior track and swim teams.

Heather stopped accepting dates from other boys and became obsessed with her goal of going to senior prom with Brad. She sat next to him in math class, making sure to wear the shortest skirts, tightest sweaters and the highest heels allowed by the school dress code. She accidentally brushed him when she walked past and leaned over to pick up a pen so he could get a good look at her cleavage made more prominent by a new push-up bra.

When those tactics failed, she asked him questions about homework to which she already knew the answers. Brad responded politely, but didn't register much emotion, keeping his focus on magazines he hid in his three-ring binder.

Heather's girlfriends ventured that he might be gay and speculated he was reading *Details* and *GQ* for the pictures. "No, he's just shy," Heather told them, not wanting her future boyfriend to earn an undeserved reputation.

Her obsession with Brad had become painful. After Heather got her driver's license, she would ask her mother to borrow her car to go on some unnecessary errand so she could drive past Brad's house.

One day, as she was slowing down to look at his house, she heard a voice say, "May I help you?"

She looked over to the passenger window and was startled to see Brad riding his bike alongside her car. "I'm looking for a friend's house," Heather had stuttered.

He had looked at her strangely, but the incident seemed to break the ice.

They began talking in math class. At first, they only talked about homework and how lame their teacher was. But one day, she caught a glimpse of a magazine he was reading before class.

"What's that?" she asked.

"Nothing," he said, closing his notebook.

"What magazine are you reading?" She craned her neck to see.

"Shhhhh." Brad looked at their teacher who was talking with a student at the front of the room.

"Are you looking at porn?" Heather prodded.

"Of course not. It's a triathlon magazine, see." Brad opened up his notebook and showed her.

"What's a triathlon?" she asked, twisting a strand of her long blonde hair around her finger.

"Are you kidding?" Brad laughed. "You don't know what a triathlon is?"

"Sorry, no."

"It's a swimming, biking and running event." He smiled, not seeming to mind her ignorance.

"I thought that was an Ironman," Heather said.

"An Ironman is the long distance triathlon event. There are shorter triathlons, too."

"Do you do those?"

"Yeah. I'm ranked number one in my age group for the intermediate distance triathlon for the U.S.," Brad said, raising his head higher as if he was demonstrating his superiority.

"That's amazing!" Heather said. "Can I have your autograph?"

For the first time, Brad looked Heather directly into her eyes and held her gaze. He was smiling broadly, showing perfect white teeth. His brown eyes were crinkling on the edges and she could see a few freckles dotting his cheeks.

She smiled back, feeling warmth and a tingling sensation in her body. But he didn't give her his autograph. Instead, he carefully drew the Olympic rings on the cover of her notebook.

From then on, Heather asked Brad about triathlons every day. He described his bike in minute detail, explaining to her about each of the components, from the freewheel to the aerobars. He could recite his split times for every swim, bike, and run of any race. Because she always listened intently, he went on and on, explaining how he hoped to cut off a tenth of a second of his run time, and how he was working on sighting so he could swim in a more direct route.

Heather pretended to understand by nodding and smiling. But all she really wanted was to spend time with him.

One day, he surprised her when he suddenly shifted topics.

"What about you?" Brad asked.

"What do you mean?" Heather said.

"What are you interested in?" Brad locked eyes with her.

"I'm really hoping to go to prom," Heather said, instantly wondering if she had made a huge mistake in relaying too much information.

"You mean you don't have a date already?"

"Not yet," Heather said softly.

"When is it?" he asked, his voice raising a pitch.

"Friday, May 7th."

"My race that Sunday is just a sprint," Brad said. "If you'd like, I could take you."

And he had. Prom was the night of their first kiss, beginning their romance. As they settled into an exclusive relationship while she attended the University of Washington and he became a professional athlete, he continued to dominate their conversations, seldom talking about anything but triathlons. Heather finally had what she wanted and happily fell into a routine revolving her life around his sport. Her friends and family often wondered out loud how such an average-looking, sullen guy ended up with a vivacious, stunning blonde. They asked how she put up with his busy training and racing schedule while she went to many of her college sorority functions dateless.

But Heather didn't mind. She was with the man she loved and was able to focus on her own career aspiration of being a television news anchor someday. Her sorority sisters who dated frat boys were so busy with social obligations they barely kept up with homework. Heather had plenty of time to study, complete internships and network with local television executives so her career became just as promising as Brad's.

Mid-way through her sophomore year, Heather began working as a weather girl for Channel 5, which fueled her ambitions. After college graduation, she landed a coveted news anchor job at Channel 7 over hundreds of applicants, which gave her the same thrill she had when she first met Brad. She thrived on whatever was hard to get.

Throwing herself into her job, Heather began winning awards because of her knack for investigating difficult stories. She wasn't above telling lies or manipulating sources to get whatever information she needed. Her ratings were high and she felt on top of the world so she invited Brad to move into her apartment.

Living with Brad, who was mostly out-of-town or training, wasn't much different for their lifestyle than having separate apartments. Heather was able to focus almost exclusively on work, and when he was home, she listened to him talk about triathlons while he ate the delicious dinners she prepared for him. It seemed as if she had everything she wanted...until Brad announced they were moving to Hawaii so he could train for the Olympic trials.

Heather had been torn between her shiny new job and her boyfriend, who kept his distance enough to make her work for his attention. She hoped to convince him to stay. There were plenty of indoor training opportunities in rainy Seattle, their families lived close by, and he was in driving and short flying distance to many races.

Brad dropped the subject.

They continued with their routines until one day Heather saw the post-it note on the refrigerator door. His clothes, bikes, and stereo equipment were gone. After she discovered his cell phone was disconnected and none of his family members or friends knew where he was, she tore the place up looking for clues. Her obsession to find him and win him back left her with no other option.

Brad had moved to Hawaii, but she couldn't be sure what city he chose. Kona or Honolulu would be the obvious choices, since Kona was home to the world championship Ironman event and Honolulu would be the location for the Olympic trials. Heather sent an email to her sorority sisters, asking them to donate any airline miles they could spare so she could commute to Hawaii on weekends while her boyfriend was training for the Olympic trials. She didn't dare tell them he had left her. Soon, she had enough miles for flights to find and then stalk Brad.

Her twin, Megan, who was now a high school P.E. teacher and had been bitten by the triathlon bug after hearing Brad talk non-stop about the sport, was happy to join Heather for a few weekend trips. She was excited about swimming in the warm Pacific Ocean rather than in the chilly Puget Sound. She confided to Heather that she had been seeing a well-known Honolulu attorney and had decided to quit her job and move to paradise to be closer to him.

Although Megan wasn't ready to introduce her to her new beau, Heather was happy to help her sister get settled into a Waikiki apartment as she secretly thought she'd be moving to Hawaii soon after Brad came to his senses. They were unloading boxes of kitchen supplies when Heather heard her cell phone ringing from her purse in the bedroom.

"I'm busy, can you get it?" Heather called.

After a few minutes, Megan came into the kitchen. "Why don't you sit down," Megan said.

"There's a lot to do." Heather didn't look up from the box of mismatched coffee cups.

Megan put her hand on her twin's arm and pulled her gently away from the task. "There's been an accident," Megan said.

"Mom and Dad?" Heather slumped in the only kitchen chair.

"Brad," Megan said. "His sister said he was hit by a car this morning."

"Is he alive?"

"Yes," Megan said. "The doctors said he's paralyzed."

"Oh, my God!" Heather shrieked.

Megan went to give her sister a hug.

"What else did Michelle say?"

"It was so weird. I gave her the name of an excellent attorney, but she said he's already there."

"The same guy?" Heather looked at her, curious.

"Yeah," Megan said, her brows furrowed.

"Can I see Brad?" Heather asked.

"No, Michelle said only family can visit right now." Megan held Heather in her arms.

"And, attorneys, apparently."

Megan grimaced.

Even though Heather wasn't able to visit Brad for the first month, she was determined to stay nearby, so she used her obsessive-compulsive skills to drop off resumes, CD's of her work, and badger every local television executive until she was offered a job as an anchor with the NBC affiliate in Honolulu. She kept her visits with Brad short and infrequent and didn't tell him of her recent move. He'd find out soon enough when he saw her on T.V. Her position wasn't starting for weeks, and so she spent her free time strategizing every move until he finally begged her to take him back. Heather always got what she wanted. Their relationship resumed largely where it had left off.

***

Heather munched on a few more frozen blueberries and then put them back in the freezer. She was often exhausted by her work at the station so by the time she got to Brad's place, she didn't have much energy to cook and clean. She was up at 2:30 a.m. in order to start work at 4:00 a.m., and by the time she finished, did Pilates or Zumba at the gym, it was 4:00 p.m. Since she had to be in bed by 8:00, she didn't have much time to help Brad.

On weekends, Heather often had functions to attend, so she was secretly relieved when Megan broke up with her mysterious boyfriend and had some time to help her. Heather leaned back on her couch remembering her call to Megan a few months ago.

"Are you busy with your boyfriend this weekend?"

"It's over. I caught him with another woman," Megan said, her voice shaking.

"That's horrible," Heather said, feeling the sympathetic pain she sometimes felt when her twin was suffering. "Are you okay?"

"Not really. I can't believe I gave up my job to move here for him. I should have known this would happen," Megan said, quietly. It sounded to Heather like she was crying.

"How would you have known he would cheat on you?" Heather asked.

"Yeah, the perfect gentleman. I should have stayed put."

"Hey, Meg, you were just following your heart."

"He didn't ask me to move here, but he didn't object," Megan said. "I never told you, but he gave me money and helped me get my job here."

"I wondered how you could afford the move," Heather said. She swallowed hard. She hadn't realized her twin kept so many secrets from her.

"I wish I hadn't come with you when you were stalking Brad."

Heather sighed. "Don't blame me."

"I can't believe I fell for his bullshit. He only had time for me about once or twice a week and never introduced me to his family or friends. He rarely took me out in public. If we did go out, it was usually to restaurants in Waikiki where only tourists go," Megan said.

"That sucks. There's something wrong if a guy won't go out in public with a woman," Heather said.

"Yeah, what really hurt was on Sunday when I went to Starbucks with a few friends after a run—you know the one in Kahala. It was pretty early in the morning and he strolled in with this chick who looked like she was wearing her clothes from the night before."

"You must have been freaking out."

"Yeah, and it pissed me off that he never took me to Starbucks in the morning. We stayed at his house and he always had some excuse to leave before dawn," Megan said. "It was jarring to see him there...with that woman."

"Did he see you?" Heather asked.

Megan grinned. "Actually, no."

"Don't tell me you hid?"

"Yup. I ducked behind my friends."

"I'm so sorry, Meg. Are you sure it's over?" Heather asked, trying to be as gentle as possible.

"Oh, it's over all right. I never want to see that bastard again," Megan said. "I will get even with him."

"If you're not too busy plotting revenge, could you help Brad out this weekend? It might keep your mind off things," Heather said, remembering how she had felt when he dumped her.

"Why? What are you doing?" Megan asked.

"I'm emceeing a charity function on Maui. Please, will you help me?" Heather pleaded.

"Sure. Just give me Brad's key. He probably won't even know I'm not you."

"Thanks, Meg. I owe you," Heather said. "Now that you and your secret lover are history, will you tell me who he is?"

"Sorry, no. There is no way I'm going to tell you. He's too well-known. I can't have you getting your little reporter nose into his business," Megan said. "I'll deal with this myself."

She's definitely my twin, Heather thought.

Chapter 7

@Zlaw Living in my #office prison cell.

Frank Gravelle grabbed his phone the instant he saw Caron Rossi's name on the caller I.D. He'd never been a fan of this technology, but it came in handy when important clients called and expected personal service from one of the firm's partners.

But Caron wasn't just any client. Frank and her went back years to a time when the ink on his law school diploma was barely dry and his buddies still called her "a looker." She had been thin, her skin creamy white and her hair as jet black as his. Now, they both carried twenty or so extra pounds, wore the lines of age on their faces, and had abandoned attempts to turn back time with hair color, both accepting their natural gray.

He smiled into the phone. Frank was one of the few people who could see right through Caron's gruffness so incongruous with the 1950s style dresses and suits she wore. He had born witness to Caron's struggles up the corporate ladder, starting from the mailroom until she was finally promoted to claims manager after she tactfully mentioned grounds for a gender discrimination suit to her boss, despite Frank's urging to accept her lot as a supervisor. She wanted more from life than Frank thought she was entitled to as a woman and so their romantic relationship didn't last, but their friendship did. He still lost himself in conversations with her, like he had when they were an item long ago. Today, she brought back those old memories when she gave him the news of one of their contemporaries—Boyd Campbell and his death from a heart attack.

After Frank recovered from his initial shock, he said, "Remember when Boyd had a crush on you?"

"No, he didn't. Boyd only had eyes for Edith," Caron said.

"Not true. He only went after her when you turned him down." Distracted by his memories, Frank gazed out his office window at a cruise ship pulling into the pier at Aloha Tower.

"I doubt that very much. I'll see you at the funeral then?"

He frowned. "I wouldn't miss it."

"Uh, Frank. I actually called you to discuss the Jordan case."

"Isn't Alexia the adjuster?"

"Yes, but I'll be watching this one closely."

"Well, the policy limits are high enough," Frank said. "My team is working very hard on this case."

"Your office is a revolving door. I hope you assigned an associate you plan on keeping around for a while," Caron said.

"Zana West," Frank said. "She's a hard worker and a triathlete. She even knows our client."

"Good choice."

"She reminds me of you, Carrie. So far, she's been tough—she doesn't take shit from anyone."

"I've heard *that* before. I don't think you've ever kept a female associate more than a few months," Caron said.

Frank chuckled. "Maybe I'll prove you wrong."

"I doubt it. Just make sure I'm copied on anything important. Okay then, see you at the funeral." Caron hung up before he could ask her about their son.

Frank yearned to tell Lucas that he was his father. He had been thinking more about this, but then dismissed such soap opera thoughts, despising drama outside of a courtroom or deposition. Pushing his emotions aside, he began dictating letters and emails.

Frank was old school. He hadn't owned a computer, cell phone, or any other technology introduced to the rest of the world post-1985 until a few months ago. He hadn't learned how to use email until Caron threatened to pull his cases if she couldn't communicate with him instantly. He finally relented, but directed his secretary, Libby, to print his emails so he could dictate his responses. He'd never learned how to type and lacked the patience for hunting and pecking, unless doing so was unavoidable. He had not embraced e-readers, iPhones, iPads or iPods; he had no idea how to Google, tweet, or text and was no one's friend on Facebook. He even refused his wife, Arlene, a microwave until last year. Associates who annoyed Frank by peeking at their smartphones under the conference table during firm meetings now had to drop them into a basket placed by the door. He was trying to bring back the legal pad and pen, but when even his partners began pushing for laptops, tablets and electronic calendars, he began wondering if Arlene would complain if he retired a few years early.

As Frank dictated the memos for Libby to convert to emails, Joseph Parsons walked into his office without a knock and plopped on one of the chairs facing Frank's imposing desk. Frank kept dictating for a few more minutes while Joe gazed at the expansive ocean and Diamond Head view, made dramatic from the corner office with its floor to ceiling windows and their vantage point on the 27th floor.

When Frank sensed Joe's impatience, he put the Dictaphone down and turned his full attention to his partner.

"What can I do for you, Joe?" Frank always started their conversations this way.

"I've got a new Oahu Insurance Company case. The plaintiff, a thirty-five-year-old woman, was walking in a wooded area next to a grocery store and was allegedly raped by two men. She's claiming the grocery store and our client, the security company, were negligent. Didn't you handle a similar case about twenty-five years ago?" Joe stuck a wad of chewing tobacco under his lip and every so often made use of the spittoon, which Frank had bought specifically for Joe's disgusting habit.

"If I recall correctly, we appealed after the jury awarded six figures and we ultimately won," Frank said.

"You have a good memory."

Frank nodded at him. "Only because it was one of our firm's few victories against Mansfield."

Frank and Joe talked for at least an hour every afternoon. They were two of the "boys" who made up the "old boys" network in Honolulu. After practicing law together for forty years, they regularly entertained the associates and junior partners with war stories, which consisted mostly of gossip about their peers and trial victories. They were less concerned about their own billable hours as they once had been, having already made their fortunes. Now, much of their time was spent supervising the firm's junior partners and associate attorneys, attempting to inspire them to bill as many hours as humanly possible. But they didn't impose a limit of twenty-four billable hours in a day.

Joe was five years older than Frank and still dyed his full head of hair jet black. He embraced new technology and had supervised the creation of a law firm website, which he claimed was the first of its kind for the Honolulu legal community. When Joe wasn't in front of his computer screen in his posh corner office, he could usually be found at home with his pure bred whippets that were frequent winners in local dog shows. He sometimes brought one of his precious dogs to the office, violating the building lease, which only permitted service animals.

Frank turned his attention away from Joe when he heard a quiet knock on the door.

"Come in," Joe bellowed.

"Excuse me," Zana said, entering the office.

"What can we do for you?" Frank asked. It wasn't uncommon for senior associates or junior partners to stop by during their meetings and discuss cases, but it was rare when a new associate ventured from the Ewa-facing substandard offices. The new ones usually were too timid to walk past Libby's cubicle, and so directed their questions to her or their peers.

"Ed Fairbanks, the president of Aloha Athletics, called about Mansfield's demand of five million dollars. He's concerned that with the severity of the Plaintiff's injuries, his company will be on the hook for much more if the insurance company doesn't pay policy limits. I told him we need to do more discovery before evaluating the case, and he hit the roof. He was yelling and screaming at me on the phone. He's wondering what his premiums paid for if the carrier won't pay." Zana took a seat on the couch and waited for their response.

"Premiums pay for the insurance company's parties in Vegas, of course!" Joe piped in with his usual sarcasm as he spat a wad of tobacco.

"He'll calm down," Frank said. "The carrier is not going to pay five million on this claim before discovery *and* an MSJ. Did you explain that we have a reasonable chance of having this case dismissed by the court through a motion for summary judgment? Did you tell him that if we win, the insurance company would not *have* to pay a dime?" Frank knew he had to communicate simply to associates on these matters, because in his experience, even the Ivy League law school grads sometimes didn't have a clue about the fundamentals of litigation.

"Unfortunately, Ed wouldn't let me get a word in edgewise. He was ranting and raving about the demand letter, and then hung up on me," Zana said in a shaky voice, rubbing her knee.

Frank wasn't surprised by this young attorney's apparent stress. It took years of practice to learn how to handle irate clients, and Frank had gotten very good at it. He had a way of reassuring them so they never lost a minute of sleep, even if faced with judgments of millions of dollars in excess of insurance policy limits.

"Why did Ed talk to you, Zana, and not one of the partners?" Joe turned to her. "The reason we have litigation teams for high value lawsuits and Mansfield cases is to avoid this very situation."

"Good question. Zana, is there a reason why the call was not directed to me, Tom or even Lori?" Frank asked.

"Maybe because Ed asked for me," Zana said. "I'm not really sure what happened."

"I'll have Libby set up a meeting with our client. Once I straighten him out, he can meet with the team." Frank picked up the phone and gave Libby instructions.

Since it was Libby who had directed the call to Zana, Frank couldn't really blame the new associate for their angry client. He wondered why his secretary let an attorney fresh out of law school talk to Ed at all. Associates were sequestered in their offices and kept away from clients for several years, or at least until they had proven they had social skills, experience and brains capable of conversing without major incident. It was common to start the associates with small matters of little consequence and gradually promote them to handling bigger cases as they demonstrated their capabilities. Frank had felt that Zana was capable of doing much of the grunt work on this case, but now was wondering if he had been wrong.

Joe and Frank were skilled at shifting a conversation so any associate in the room would get the hint it was time to exit. Zana apparently didn't need any coaxing and left abruptly. After Joe and Frank exhausted their daily banter and Joe left, Frank asked Libby to step into his office.

"Why did our client talk to a brand new associate, Lib?" Frank got to the point.

"Ed insisted I put her on the phone," Libby responded calmly.

"This is a big case, with a lot at stake. Why would this client want to talk to someone who doesn't even know what she's doing?"

"Apparently, Ed knows and trusts Zana. As much as I tried to connect him to you, Tom, or Lori, he wouldn't hear of it," Libby said.

"Hmmm…" Frank peered over his reading glasses at Libby. "Set up an appointment with Ed. Since he wants to work with Zana, tell her to join us. I'm sure I can straighten things out. Schedule Tom and Lori for the meeting as well."

"Anything else?" Libby asked before she stepped out the door.

Frank shook his head and picked up his Dictaphone, finishing his emails. He checked to see if Libby had closed the door before he opened the top drawer to his desk. Then, he pulled out a photograph from a large envelope Caron had sent labeled "Personal and Confidential". He stared at the image of a twenty-seven-year-old man wearing an elaborate robe, mortarboard, and tassel at his graduation from Stanford Law School a few weeks ago. The resemblance between Lucas and Frank was unmistakable. Frank recalled that his own law school graduation picture taken more than forty years ago looked almost identical, except it was in black and white. Also in the large envelope was a smaller sealed envelope addressed to Frank Gravelle, Esq. with Lucas's San Francisco address in the upper left hand corner. He opened a formal cover letter addressed to Mr. Gravelle from Lucas F. Rossi along with a resume. Lucas had written to Frank, whom he considered to be an old friend of his mother, asking for a job.

Frank leaned back in his chair and rubbed his chin. There were no associate offices available, but he could always fire one of the female associates to make room for his son.

Chapter 8

@Zlaw Would you recognize your #swimming buddies in clothes?

Zana stared at her computer screen. She was frozen, paralyzed by fear, unable to strike the keyboard with her fingertips. She breathed in deeply, trying to remember lessons from a yoga class she hadn't attended since before beginning her studies for the Hawaii Bar exam. She focused her gaze on the tropical flowers she had picked from her yard and arranged in the vase she kept on her desk amid the clutter of files. It gave her a small taste of the tropical paradise she thought she moved to before she started working at the firm. Her office door was closed and for the time being, no partners were bombarding her with more work and she hadn't been hassled by any of the attorney-boys for at least an hour.

Zana texted Shelby: I think I fucked up. This time adding a frowny face emoticon.

R U sure?

Her cell phone rang with Shelby's picture on the screen.

"What's going on?" Shelby asked.

"I didn't mean to interrupt you," Zana said, but was relieved to hear her friend's voice.

"It's okay. My boss is in a meeting. What did you do this time?"

"Nothing. Jeez." Zana sighed and leaned back in her chair. She was surprised Shelby called rather than carrying on the conversation by text, which sometimes went on throughout the day if one of them had a problem.

"How did you fuck up?" Shelby asked.

"I'm not really supposed to talk about this. It's about a client."

"Don't use a name," Shelby said. "Just call the person client."

"Okay," Zana said, she paused to plug in the head set to her iPhone so her hands were free to rearrange her flowers, something she did when she was anxious. "A client who I know personally called me directly about a case."

"So. What did you do, hang up on him?"

"Just the opposite. The client hung up on me." Zana pulled a wilting stem out of the vase and tossed it into the small trashcan under her desk.

"That doesn't sound good."

"Yeah, tell me about it. Frank has scheduled a meeting with the client to smooth things over."

"Makes sense."

"He's going to fire me," Zana said, her voice catching.

"If he does, you'll just find another job. No biggie, right?"

"Right. Except no law firms are hiring."

"Restaurants are always hiring."

"Yeah, I guess. Thanks. I've got to go," Zana said and hung up. There was no way she was going to talk out loud about her fear of being a waitress with a law degree.

Zana wished she could have told Shelby the client was Ed, but she didn't want to violate the attorney/client privilege. It was Shelby who had introduced them when they were out for dinner with a group of athletes one evening. Ed often worked out with her group, but while they swam, biked and ran, talking was never easy. Over dinner, they all chattered incessantly about triathlons and training, to the exclusion of anything personal. Few people in their extended group even knew each other's day jobs, marital status, or kid's names. What mattered most were upcoming races, gear, nutrition, hydration, and the weather. And she had heard far too much from men about shaving their legs. They did it in order to avoid the added pain and discomfort when they suffered road rash from falls off their bikes. Such endless talk amused but sometimes annoyed Zana, who at least tried to put triathlons in perspective.

As she contemplated her relationship with Ed, she realized that before his phone call they had never had a single conversation about anything other than triathlons. She wondered how he even knew she was an attorney or that she worked at this firm.

Libby walked in without knocking. "You'll be meeting with Frank and Mr. Fairbanks tomorrow afternoon in Conference Room 1." She placed some papers on Zana's desk. "Pretty flowers."

"Mahalo. Is there anything I should do to prepare?" Zana asked, having heard about Libby's reputation for being among the most knowledgeable and powerful people in the office. She had been working for the firm since its inception and could answer any question about maneuvering around state or federal court. She was also known to discretely assist associates so they could better meet Frank's expectations in fulfilling assignments.

"I suggest you know the file inside and out. Also, wear a suit," Libby said, eyeing Zana's short-sleeved pink jersey top and black pants.

"Anything else?" Zana asked, embarrassed she had forgotten to bring a suit jacket today in her rush out the door.

"Let Frank take the lead even though you already know the client," Libby advised, giving Zana a wink before returning to her cubicle.

Why did she wink at me? Zana thought. *Does she think I have some sort of elicit relationship with Ed, because he wanted to talk with me?*

***

The next afternoon, Zana, wearing a proper black suit, freshly shined sensible black pumps, and pantyhose sans runs, made her way to Conference Room 1 at 2:45 p.m., with a fresh legal pad, an outline of the facts of the case, and a file with the key documents. As she read over her outline, Frank came in, dressed in the navy blue suit he, like all the other male attorneys, probably kept on the back of his door for court appearances.

Frank nodded in Zana's direction, and then sat at the head of the long conference table precisely at 3:00 p.m.

Before she could respond, the door opened with Libby escorting their client.

"Good afternoon, Mr. Fairbanks. I'm your attorney, Frank Gravelle," he said as he jumped out of his seat, extending his right hand to firmly shake hands with their client, whose gray hair didn't quite match his suntanned face and fit body. Ed wore a triathlon race T-shirt, khaki shorts and running shoes.

"Hi Frank. You can call me Ed," he said, shaking the senior partner's hand firmly.

"And, you know my associate," Frank gestured to Zana.

"Hey, Zana, you look great. I almost didn't recognize you with clothes on." Ed laughed and gave Zana a warm hug as she blushed in response to his comment. Zana knew what he meant. She was always wearing a bathing suit or skimpy shorts and running bras when training. The comment was meant to be a joke, but she worried Frank might not understand Ed's humor and think they might be sleeping together.

"I pay huge insurance premiums every year. So, why isn't F.I.M. settling this case?" Ed asked after they sat down at the conference table.

"I understand your concern, Ed," Frank said. "Insurance companies need to investigate cases before they settle claims."

"Brad Jordan is paralyzed, for God's sake. He lost his pro triathlete career and he'll never walk again. I would think that's worth millions," Ed said, emphasizing his words with his hands.

"Well," Frank said, "we've made the request to get his medical records— make sure he doesn't have any pre-existing conditions."

"How could he have any pre-existing conditions? The guy is, I mean— was—a world-class athlete," Ed said, raising his voice.

"We just need to make sure we check everything out, Mr. Fairbanks. Sorry—Ed. Just like you don't do a running race without training, we don't settle or go to trial without completing discovery," Frank said.

Tom and Lori walked in, both wearing suits and carrying legal pads. Frank made the introductions, explaining how the litigation team worked and that Zana would be offering support by providing valuable help behind the scenes with discovery.

"Since Zana is the only one here who knows anything about triathlons, she should handle this case," Ed said, taking a sip from the plastic water bottle he brought with him.

"Mr. Fairbanks, I must caution you that your request is not in the best interest of your company. Rip Mansfield is a tough opponent and Zana will not be able to effectively represent you without the involvement of our litigation team," Frank explained calmly.

Zana hoped her face wasn't turning red. She busily took notes on her legal pad, hoping Ed would somehow get the hint that her skills were more suited as a scribe than a litigator at this early stage of her career. She knew her place.

"Okay." Ed was silent for what seemed like a full minute as the team stared at him in disbelief. "I understand what you're saying. But since Zana is the only one here with a clue about triathlons, that is, I assume none of you are triathletes, she should play a major role in our defense. She should be taking depositions and going to court. I hope *you* understand my position."

"Sure, Ed, I do understand," Frank said. "I'll see to it personally that Zana takes depositions and is involved every step of the way—with partner supervision, of course."

Lori gave Zana a dirty look—"stink eye"—as it's called in the islands.

Zana continued to focus her attention on her boss, feeling a little dizzy and so she sipped water from her Hydro Flask.

Lori had been slaving away for four years in the bowels of the firm with few opportunities to take depositions or argue motions in court. Zana felt bad for her co-worker, but what could she do? It wasn't as if she had asked Ed to come here.

When she looked up from her notes, she met Lori's stare again, shrugged her shoulders and cast her a sympathetic glance. According to Andrew, Lori's days at the firm were numbered if she wasn't given a chance to prove herself soon.

Frank stood up, signaling an end to the meeting, and then shook hands with his client.

When Ed gave Zana a goodbye hug, his body was more relaxed, despite the scary possibility of a runaway verdict if the case should proceed to trial.

Zana hoped her embarrassment hadn't been evident to her colleagues. She pretended to take some post meeting notes in order to avoid eye contact. Even though she was a lowly associate, she knew she was being put in a position above her rank and if she blew it, her career could end abruptly.

Her stomach churned. She hadn't expected to be given any responsibility at all for at least a year. Now the firm's client was counting on her to take on tasks no one would imagine her doing so soon after being sworn into the Hawaii State Bar. It was common knowledge that partners weeded out associates by making them unhappy with their continued lack of responsibility, forcing them to seek employment elsewhere. Associates who were perceived to be up-and-coming junior partners were given nicer offices, deposition assignments, and independence in handling some of their own small cases. The most gifted associates found themselves taking deposition trips to the mainland as a reward for their potential, like Tom, who had traveled to Los Angeles, Phoenix and Washington, D.C. on a two-week deposition trip last year. Zana wondered whether the good old boy partners would ever let a woman move up the ladder like Tom had. Or, was she being set up to fail?

After the meeting, Frank did something unprecedented. He asked Zana to come to his office for a private chat behind closed doors, an honor often granted to junior partners or senior associates, but never to newbies. Her boss only talked to new associates on their own turf in their crummy offices for the purpose of giving them instruction on assignments, but most often to chastise or fire them.

She saw the surprised look on Libby's face when they walked past her cubicle and into Frank's office. Zana knew she was hardly worthy of his $400 per hour billing rate, but for the first time, she wasn't fearful of being fired. At least not today.

Frank motioned for her to sit in one of the chairs across from his desk usually reserved for partners. She breathed in the faint scent of chewing tobacco from the spittoon positioned against the chair leg and got a rare glimpse of the ocean and Diamond Head view.

"Zana, even though you'll be given a visibility in this case that will be witnessed by the client, Tom and I will be monitoring everything you do. All conversations between you and Ed about anything related to this case must be reported to me. Do you understand?" Frank asked, leaning back in his oversized Italian leather chair.

"No problem," Zana said, listening intently. She made a mental note to talk to Andrew about this new development, hoping for some pointers.

"Is there anything about your relationship with Ed that I should know about?" Frank looked down at the papers on his desk while waiting for her answer.

"I'm not sure what you mean," Zana said, blushing again. She wished Ed hadn't hugged her.

"Well…," Frank paused, apparently trying to formulate the most politically correct words. His chin rubbing was almost frantic.

"Oh, you mean… God, no!" Zana said.

Frank nodded, dropping his hand to his lap.

"Just so you know, I believe Ed is dating a triathlete in my training group. I don't know him well, but we do have mutual friends." Zana hoped this would put Frank's mind at ease, or at least wipe away any sexual images he had conjured up. The thought of her and Ed together grossed Zana out, but she had to be realistic. At least Frank hadn't linked Zana with the guy she *did* have her eye on.

Chapter 9

@Zlaw How to kick your #dreamguy out of your office in 3 easy steps.

Jerry Hirano sunk into the buttery softness of his new red leather chair, his latest acquisition from Japan. When he walked into his law office early that morning, bleary-eyed from jet lag, he was surprised to see the chair already behind his desk. There, too, was the equally modern painting hung on his office wall just as he had envisioned when he purchased it from the trendy shop in Tokyo. Red was his signature color. He chose it for his Ferrari, many of his shirts, and was helpless against the charms of a woman with cherry red lips and matching nail polish.

His office re-decorating project was far more interesting than the new case file in his inbox. Jerry sighed, then sipped from a bottle of water and stretched his legs under his desk before opening the file. The case was unusual only because the accident causing injury happened at the Honolulu Olympic trials for the men's triathlon. Otherwise, it was much the same old stuff he worked on all the time—an injured plaintiff seeking money from his client, South Shore, Inc. Since they were self-insured, Jerry had been hired by their third party administrator claims adjuster, rather than an insurance company. He suppressed a yawn.

After reviewing the pile of documents and studying the complaint filed by Rip Mansfield on behalf of his client, Jerry penciled notes on the document for his paralegal to use when she drafted the answer.

Without knocking, Gina, his assistant walked in and dropped off a pile of documents on his desk.

"Nice outfit," Jerry said, appraising her long legs, short lace skirt and low cut top. Gina winked as she did every day in response to her boss's frequent flirtations.

Ever since he was a small child, he had watched his Japanese father flirt with every woman in his path, and so Jerry did the same. His mother, a locally well-known Caucasian singer, always reacted with a smile when her husband used his charm without discrimination to any woman, whether she was a size 24 or size 2; seventy-four years old or a college student. Jerry's brand of flirting was just as innocent as his father's. His law school buddies had used the "catch and release" method of dating, but Jerry couldn't quite master the "catch" part, unless a young lady asked him out. If a woman invited him out for a drink or to dinner, he would always say "yes" and they would invariably end up in a 3 to 5 month relationship usually ending when someone more interesting made the first move. His friends called him a serial monogamist, but he hoped to one day meet a special woman and have a loving relationship like his parents who had been married for forty-five years.

Jerry made some additional notes to the Brad Jordan complaint before tackling the pile of accumulated mail. On top was an envelope with the return address of Bamboo Entertainment, the production company for his cable T.V. show, "Fighting In Paradise", in which he played Jerry Ho, the loveable Waikiki resort security manager who had reason to use mixed martial arts to thwart bad guys on every episode. After two seasons, the show had become a local hit and was gradually acquiring a wider audience. Recently, his fan emails and Twitter followers from the U.S. mainland, Japan, Korea, and South America had increased. He didn't bother to slice open the envelope containing his paltry paycheck. For now, Jerry spent most evenings acting in front of a camera and his days billing hours at his law office in order to make a living and fund his hobbies.

At forty-two, he had been practicing law far too long and was simply biding his time before he could pursue his real passions. Along with his dream of being a full-time actor, he hoped to retire from his law practice so he could use his "all-you-can-fly" pass to travel the world. Early in his career, when he was handling a plaintiff's personal injury case, he had taken a large settlement and paid for a pass that allowed him to hop on any World Airlines flight free of charge for life. He'd become the envy of anyone who heard about the deal he negotiated with the airline, but he didn't yet have the money to utilize the pass as much as he'd like.

Jerry had blown most of his cash on his Ferrari and the string of girlfriends he took for rides. Still living with his parents—or, more accurately, in a cottage 100 feet away from their house, he felt a need to go overboard with gifts of flowers, jewelry and shoes. Every Tax Day, his accountant advised him to invest his money. Aside from purchasing a condo for rental income years ago, Jerry didn't listen. He was waiting for the right girl, and until she came along, he had no plans to economize.

Jerry had what he called LADD—Law Attention Deficit Disorder. He could not concentrate on any legal document for more than five minutes. Despite this challenge, he was a formidable opponent, even against heavy hitters like Rip Mansfield. Jerry could charm a jury made up of any demographic, and if he didn't become distracted by his quest for fame and the drama of frequent all-encompassing new romances and messy breakups, his colleagues thought he'd be one of the islands' great attorneys.

Wendy, the adjuster who assigned him the Jordan case, even joked that "he could charm the pants off of any juror—female or male." She and Jerry had enjoyed a 5-week fling until a lengthy deposition trip led to his next relationship with a flight attendant. It took a few years for Wendy to move on, but after she found herself a proper boyfriend, she continued her earlier practice of giving him litigation cases.

Jerry cringed when he saw Mansfield listed as the Plaintiff's attorney, but was pleased to see Frank Gravelle's law firm representing one of the defendants. He enjoyed working with the firm that had given him his start in the practice of law. The alumni of G, P & D were spread all over Honolulu's legal community and even had a Facebook page where they often posted funny anecdotes and criticisms. Just like so many other young attorneys at the time, he had worked a stint at the firm. He remembered when Frank hurled a file at him from across the room when a document Jerry had written hadn't met his boss's high standards. Jerry's experience at G, P & D's boot camp-like atmosphere had honed his legal thinking and taught him about being an insurance defense attorney enough so he could open his own practice, taking several of the firm's client's with him.

Initially, after parting ways, there had been hard feelings between him and Frank. The two of them didn't speak for a few years. Jerry wasn't sure if Frank was pissed off because he didn't get to fire him or if he was unhappy for losing the clients. Eventually, they had a case together, became friendly again and now on occasion got together for lunch or drinks.

Jerry's office was in a tall building adjacent to the high rise where G, P & D had been located for 20 years. After he enjoyed some take-out sushi, Jerry decided to pop up to Frank's firm and chat with him about the case—an excuse to avoid addressing the hundreds of emails still awaiting his attention.

"Is Frank in?" Jerry asked, leaning against Libby's desk in his usual seductive manner.

"He's in a deposition," Libby said curtly without taking her fingers off her keyboard. "What case are you here to see him about?"

"You look beautiful today, Libby," Jerry winked at her.

"What case was that?" Libby asked again, still striking her keyboard.

"Blue really compliments your skin," Jerry said.

"Thank you. I've got a rush, Jerry. Which case, please?"

"Sorry to interrupt. The Brad Jordan case; I represent South Shore, Inc."

"Lori and Tom are on the team. Both of them are out," Libby said, not looking up.

"I'm sure there's a lowly associate slaving away in the bowels of the firm I can talk to," Jerry said.

"That would be Zana West."

"Don't tell me the old man actually hired a woman."

"She's in Ned Harris's old office." Libby looked up at Jerry briefly and he winked at her again. He remembered the days when she would return his flirtatious banter. Over the years, her enthusiasm had waned after he politely declined an invitation for dinner one night. It was hard for him to say no to a beautiful woman, but he hadn't wanted to mix work with pleasure, especially since she was Frank's secretary and at least fifteen years his senior. Since then, she had been icy towards him. But he wasn't here to think of *what ifs*.

"Hi there," Jerry greeted Zana as he walked into her office. He made himself comfortable in one of the old brown leather chairs facing her desk, which he recognized from his days at the firm. He guessed the desk and chairs were mismatched rejects from partners' offices after they redecorated. Most of her framed diplomas and certificates were lined up on the windowsill and leaning against an empty box. Above them, he could see the large Dole Cannery pineapple atop the old factory-turned office building in the distance. The walls were empty except for one lone diploma, and her desk was a messy heap of papers that would multiply with her tenure at the firm, assuming she could please Frank enough to hold onto her job. Jerry thought this was unlikely.

"Hello," Zana said, staring at him. Jerry suspected Zana recognized him from T.V. as most people in Hawaii did. "May I help you?"

"I'm Jerry Hirano. I represent South Shore, Inc. in the Jordan case." Jerry extended his hand. She rose from her chair and stepped around the large wooden desk. He noticed her wipe her hand on her skirt before shaking his. She stood a few inches taller than him. After she withdrew her hand, he saw her red nail polish, which was a shade darker than her lipstick. She had a unique look with her shoulder-length straight black hair and bangs—Egyptian-style. But her green eyes made her look Irish. Whatever her ancestry, Jerry was mesmerized.

"Oh, yes. You haven't filed an answer yet," Zana said as they both sat down.

"I'm working on it," Jerry said. "I was an associate at this firm years ago. My office was next to yours. It was my first attorney job."

"Really?"

"It took me awhile to hang up my certificates as well. I had hoped the partners would see what a brilliant lawyer I was and promptly move me to an office with a better view—and better furniture," Jerry said, smiling. They locked eyes briefly and then she quickly looked away.

"I can relate," Zana said. "Did you want to talk about the case?"

"Who do you think was responsible for the accident?" Jerry asked, tilting his head, trying to get her to make eye contact again.

"What do you mean?" Zana said, turning to her computer.

"Don't you think it's strange?" What he really thought was strange was the way Zana avoided looking him in the eye. He wondered if she was shy or stuck-up, but there was something intriguing about her. Apart from her lack of eye contact, she appeared to be professional, but much too young and innocent to be an attorney.

"What?" Zana asked, abruptly turning and leaning back in her chair, now staring at him directly.

"Who would drive through a triathlon course, hit a cyclist and drive away without stopping?" Jerry said, surprised by Zana's sudden surge of confidence.

"Maybe someone who wasn't paying attention. It happens all the time in car accidents," Zana said. "You know that."

"But, the driver didn't even stop to render aid."

"Well, the driver probably got scared and didn't want to be caught," Zana said, playing with her hair.

"Hawaii Revised Statutes, section 291 requires the driver of any vehicle involved in an accident resulting in injury or death to render reasonable assistance. If we can identify the driver of the vehicle and bring that person into this action, the jury will be so disgusted they will most likely let our clients off the hook," Jerry said, hoping to impress her with his legal knowledge.

"How can we find the driver?" Zana asked.

"I just got this assignment and haven't had a chance to look at the investigation," Jerry said. "Don't you think it makes sense to work together and not point fingers at each other?"

"You know I'm not lead counsel. You'll have to talk with Frank."

"I'm not sure I want to risk being smacked on the head with a brief."

Zana giggled and flashed a smile, which lit up her face. He smiled back, his face hot.

"How long have you worked at G, P & D?" Jerry asked.

"Not long." Zana looked away again.

"When I was here, we used to wait until all of the partners left for the day and the associates would have parties in the lunch room. One time, Ernie Hayashida got so drunk he threw up in Frank's wastebasket after the cleaning crew left. Frank was so pissed off when he came into work the next morning. His office stunk. I was off-island that day, but I heard he went on a tirade and Ernie got the boot." Jerry chuckled.

Zana seemed to ignore his anecdote and stood up, giving him the universal office executive's signal to leave, but he remained planted in his chair, leaning back. He stared at her. She was nothing like most women who delighted in his monologues and every move. Her apathy was intriguing. And, she was beautiful, yet seemed not to realize it. Jerry was usually the one to end an encounter, so her attempts to shoo him away made him yearn to stay.

"I've got a meeting," Zana said.

Jerry could tell she was lying.

"So, I'll wait until you get back." He sat for what seemed like a full minute, watching her ruby red lips open in surprise.

"I'm just kidding. I've got to get back to my office," he said, enjoying her startled expression. He had noticed she was wearing red kitten heels, making her long legs look shapely. Her skirt was higher than knee length, probably because she was so tall.

"Think about what I said. If we can figure out who the driver of the vehicle was, we should be able to get our clients out of this case."

"Okay, I'll think about it," Zana said.

Before leaving, Jerry picked a red hibiscus from the tropical arrangement on her desk and handed it to her. "For your hair," he said, watching her place it carefully in front of her ear on the right side, signaling she was unmarried.

Jerry walked out of her office feeling confused. *Who was this girl who would dare fake a meeting in order to kick him out of her office?* Since the show had taken off in the last year, he was much more accustomed to women seeking his autograph, tossing their panties at him or even professing their desire to have his baby. He had even had to learn to say "no" and for the first time since passing the Bar, he found himself between girlfriends.

As soon as he got back to his office, he did something he had never done in the ten years since he had his own law practice. He opened the liquor cabinet used for occasional client parties, pouring a shot of tequila and downing it without need for salt or a lime wedge. He then sat back in his new red leather chair thinking of Zana and her electric green eyes.

Chapter 10

@Zlaw The fighter in paradise is #out-of-my-league.

Zana aimed the remote control at Andrew's 60-inch screen, one of the perks of sharing the house with him and his girlfriend, Kelly. Another perk was their shared taste for white wines. Although Zana preferred Chardonnay, she didn't complain about the pinot grigio she found in the fridge that her housemates had opened the night before. She grabbed her wine glass in one hand and clicked on "Fighting in Paradise" with the other. The cable channel played five episodes in a row every evening, most of them re-runs. If Andrew was watching sports, she had to watch T.V. in her room, but Kelly usually didn't mind watching Zana's favorite show with her as they both thought Jerry Ho, the lead character played by Jerry Hirano, was fierce.

After a few commercials, Jerry Ho appeared on screen wearing tight fitting black slacks and an Aloha shirt with a gold nametag. He walked through the lush grounds of the Waikiki hotel where he worked until he encountered a man hassling a young woman and warned him to stop. A verbal altercation ensued, and when the man pulled out a gun, Jerry knocked it out of his hand with a lightning fast roundhouse kick followed by a series of mixed martial arts moves until the man was lying on the ground.

Zana stared intently at the screen, trying to reconcile the character in the show with the man who had sat across from her earlier in the day. There was something about being in his presence—maybe his scent or energy—quite distinct from Jerry Ho, the simple guy who spoke Pidgin English and fought bad guys for a living. Jerry Hirano's voice was buttery smooth, his diction perfect after many years of Punahou schooling like President Obama. That was it. Jerry seemed to have Obama-swagger—a sort of relaxed confidence she knew she would never possess. She was anxious about almost everything and put all efforts into at least appearing calm. Jerry's serenity came naturally. Perhaps that was why she felt so intensely drawn to him.

Zana heard a key in the front door, but didn't want to turn away from the T.V. to see which of her roommates had gotten home first.

"Hey Zana, howzit?" Kelly asked, throwing her Michael Kors bag onto the counter.

"Just kickin' back after a long day. As usual," Zana sighed. "What's up with you?"

"Not much. Why are you home so early?" Kelly said. "Did you get fired?"

"Not today."

"Sorry, I didn't mean to…"

"It's okay. With Frank as a boss, you never know. Where's Andrew?"

"He texted. He's on his way home," Kelly said, leaning against the Lazy Boy and looking down at her roommate who was sitting on the couch. "You look weird."

"How so?"

"You're smiling."

"I smile." Zana smiled to prove her point.

"No you don't. If you ever smiled, you'd have crows' feet or laugh lines on your face. It's perfectly smooth."

Zana grinned even more.

"You have a flower in your hair," Kelly said. "Did you suddenly become a kama'aina?"

Zana laughed.

"Why are you so damn happy today?" Kelly asked, plopping onto the Lazy Boy next to the couch. She was still wearing her nametag from the hotel where she worked as an assistant front desk manager.

"I met *him* today," Zana said, nodding her head toward the T.V.

"You met him…you mean Jerry Hirano!" Kelly said, leaning forward.

"Yes. I met Jerry Ho." Zana clapped her hands together. "He came into my office."

"OMG! You rock, girl! Is he as good-looking in person as he is on T.V.?"

"Better. He's hot!" she said, sitting forward.

"Why was he in your office?"

"You're not going to believe it," Zana giggled.

"You're being cast for the show?"

"No—silly." Zana touched the flower in her hair. "We've got a case together."

"Well, that would have happened eventually. You knew he's an attorney." Kelly rose from her chair and poured herself a glass of wine.

"Yeah, but I never thought he'd show up at my office out of the blue."

"What did he say to you?" Kelly said, taking a sip of wine.

"Not much. We talked about the case and then I kicked him out."

"No!" Kelly sprayed her wine onto Zana's bare shoulder. "Sorry."

"I freaked out," Zana wiped herself with a napkin. "I didn't want him to think I have a crush on him."

"Actually, you're *obsessed* with the guy," Kelly said, laughing. "Let's be truthful, Zana."

"I am not. I just…really like his show," Zana said, embarrassed Kelly had noticed.

"Did he give you the flower?"

Zana nodded, smiling. "He pulled it out of the vase on my desk."

"Tell me what happened," Kelly said.

"I was so nervous, I lied and said I had a meeting," Zana said.

"Who did you lie to this time?" Andrew asked, walking into the apartment and giving his girlfriend a quick kiss.

"Well, I didn't really lie." Zana exchanged a look with Kelly.

"Come on, you can tell me," Andrew said, opening another bottle of wine.

"It's nothing. Another attorney came by to see me today," Zana said. "That's all."

"Was it Jerry-T.V. Star-Hirano?" Andrew asked, with a smirk.

At first Zana hesitated, but then she figured, what the hell. "Yeah," Zana said. "How did you know?"

"Facebook, Twitter, Instagram. All of the secretaries posted pictures of him the minute he walked into the office," Andrew said.

Zana picked up her phone to check Facebook.

"Sorry, but you don't have a chance with him," Andrew said, his tone serious.

"I'm sure she does," Kelly put in before she sipped her wine.

"That mother fucker has so many women," Andrew said, sitting down next to Zana. "He's got his own fan club. No offense, Zana, but he's not going to date an attorney when he can date models and actresses. I'm just sayin'."

"Can we change the subject?" Zana picked up the remote, no longer in the mood to watch Jerry Ho.

"You should date someone more appropriate. How 'bout Kim?" Andrew said.

"Kim McCall?" Zana snapped her head to look at him. "Are you kidding me?"

"Is that the guy in your office with a comb over?" Kelly asked.

"Not anymore. He shaved his head," Andrew said. "I think he likes you, Zana."

"I'm not dating anyone, especially not someone from the office. I need to focus on work and training. I've got the Bronzeman coming up next weekend," Zana said, horrified at the thought Andrew would even think she should date Kim.

"What about Brian Ching? He's like a puppy dog. He follows you everywhere," he said.

Zana rolled her eyes and then looked at her phone showing all the pictures of Jerry posted on Facebook by the receptionist and secretaries that day.

"I think she should hold out for Jerry. Don't you think they'd make a cute couple, honey?" Kelly asked.

"Maybe for a few months," Andrew said. "He's not exactly a long-term relationship guy. Just look at the tabloids."

"Can we *please* change the subject?" Zana pleaded.

"Sure. What's for dinner? I expect dinner to be on the table when I get home, women," Andrew said, pounding his fist on the coffee table.

"Yeah, where's my dinner? I expect you to bring take-out for us when you get home, man!" Kelly said, sitting down between Andrew and Zana and putting her arm around her boyfriend's shoulder.

"We can order take-out—again," Andrew said, kissing his girlfriend.

"I've already eaten. It's time for me to go to bed." Zana got up and moved toward the hallway.

"But it's only eight-thirty," Kelly said.

"Yeah, I think I'll do some reading and hit the hay," Zana said, taking her wine glass with her. "Good night!"

"Now, see what you did…" Zana heard Kelly say, and giggled to herself.

In her room, she plopped on her bed and grabbed a few magazines from the pile on her nightstand. The latest *Honolulu Magazine* had a small article about Jerry with a picture of him and a young model, recently arrested for a DUI. Another magazine showed a close-up of Jerry wearing board shorts, accentuating his 6-pack abs, surfing in Waikiki. HI-Luxury Magazine published shortly after Jerry won a Hawaii People's Choice award said he was "looking to meet that special someone."

Sounds promising, Zana thought, but knew deep down inside Andrew was right. Jerry could have any woman he wanted. There was no way he would be interested in an associate attorney too scared to even look him in the eye.

Chapter 11

@Zlaw No time to grocery shop. #Wine for dinner...again.

Heather placed a bag of pre-washed baby spinach in her cart and crossed "salad" off her list. Grocery shopping took twice as long because strangers recognized her as a morning news anchor. She didn't mind, but they also wanted to chat as if she was an intimate friend.

"Hi Heather," said a large woman wearing a faded purple mu'u mu'u. She was also wearing ancient rubber slippers called flip flops by U.S. mainlanders.

"Hello," Heather said, smiling at the unfamiliar face.

"I enjoyed your story about the schools yesterday," the woman said, grabbing a couple of cans of Spam from a stacked display.

"Thanks. I hope the Board of Education watched it."

"I'll bet they did. It's about time teachers got the supplies and support they need." The woman kept pace with Heather as she walked down the cereal aisle.

Heather nodded, adding a box of Special K to her cart.

"Would you mind signing an autograph for me? My name is Bernice." She pulled out a crumpled piece of paper from her purse and rummaged for a pen.

"Oh, sure. I'm happy to. I have a pen," Heather offered. She grabbed a box of Wheaties for Brad, dropping it into her cart alongside the baby spinach, a bunch of bananas, a bag of dried mangoes, and a half dozen Fuji apples. She placed the crumpled paper on a box of her favorite cereal, Captain Crunch, and signed her name and then returned the sugary treat to the shelf.

Bernice scowled at the paper where Heather had written: "Aloha Bernice! Heather Alexander" in her squiggly handwriting.

Heather heard her stomach growl and felt the beginning of a headache forming. She wasn't in the mood to write mushy sentiments her older fans seemed to prefer. The younger fans were easier—they only wanted selfies.

"Are you Heather Alexander?" a bearded man asked, parking his cart behind Bernice's. A little boy with chocolate smeared on his face darted from the man's side and raced down the aisle.

"Yes, that's me," Heather said.

Bernice sighed loudly and pushed her cart to the peanut butter section.

"My wife and daughters love you. We watch you every morning," the man said. "You remind me of my oldest daughter who is in engineering school at the University of Washington."

"Ahh, well that makes sense. I'm from Seattle," Heather said.

"Yeah, I know. My daughter watched you on the news there before you moved to Hawaii."

"Thank you. It's nice to know that a few people watch me here," Heather said. "You must be proud of your daughter."

"I'm proud of all my kids. My son just graduated from dental school," the man said, turning toward the little boy who had grabbed a box of Lucky Charms from the shelf. "This is my grandson, Trevor."

"Cute boy," Heather said, not even looking at him. She wasn't a fan of children and felt her headache worsen. "Excuse me, it's been nice talking with you, but my boyfriend's waiting."

Heather returned to her shopping list, hearing her doctor's voice in her head warning her to stay focused while grocery shopping and not to enter the store hungry. She looked at the bananas in her cart longingly. She knew that following her well-planned list was of grave importance—"a matter of life and death"—Dr. Weiss had said. But, fame had its price and Heather enjoyed it. She pushed her cart to the bakery section near the whole grain bread where the shelves were blocked by a table displaying samples of baked goods.

"Would you like to try some brownies, Ms. Alexander?" the plump woman behind the table asked.

"Oh, no thank you," Heather said, trying to squeeze through the narrow space between the table and the only 8-grain loaves on sale.

"They're delicious. Right out of the oven," the woman said.

Heather wedged between the woman's chair and the Wonder Bread.

"Try this double chocolate fudge—here, have a small piece." The woman thrust a chunk of brownie on the end of a toothpick into Heather's face.

"I'm trying to reach that bread." Heather pointed to the highest shelf.

"Eat this first." The woman was now holding brownie samples in both hands within an inch of Heather's mouth, which was now watering from the scent. Without regard for her diet, Heather grabbed both brownies and stuffed them into her mouth, closing her eyes as she chewed, tasting the rich chocolate.

"Try this toffee crunch. It's my favorite," the woman said and handed another sample to Heather, who was still trapped between the table and bread shelves.

Heather stuffed the third chunk into her already full mouth. Chocolate crumbs spilled onto her silk blouse.

"Here, this one is raspberry chocolate swirl." The woman pressed another brownie into Heather's hand.

Heather leaned against the Wonder Bread, spewing stray bits of chocolate onto the packages as she chewed.

"Try this chocolate decadence; it's the most popular."

Heather grabbed the fifth brownie and stuffed it into her already full mouth.

"Each package is four dollars and fifty cents," the woman said. "I'm sure your family would love them."

"Yes, they would," Heather said around a mouthful of brownie. "I'll take a package of each."

After the woman added five packages of brownies to her cart, Heather unwedged herself out from behind the table, abandoning the bread and her shopping list. She paid for her groceries and hurried to her BMW, parked on the far end of the lot on purpose so she could walk extra steps in order to burn calories. She sat in the car and wolfed down most of the brownies. When Heather was stuffed, she brushed the chocolate crumbs off her face, hands, and blouse before slipping back into the store to use the bathroom. Once she was in the privacy of a locked stall and had waited for the last patron to leave, she fastened her hair with a large clip, leaned over the toilet, and stuck her fingers in her mouth to make herself vomit.

After Brad left her last year, Heather's eating disorder had gotten so serious her weight plummeted to 86 pounds resulting in a two-month hospital stay. If it were up to her, she would have continued on her destructive path, but Megan threatened to tell their parents about her anorexia and bulimia. The station manager had been ready to fire her if she didn't undergo an intensive program of counseling and instruction from a dietician and medical staff.

She agreed, but because of her notoriety as a T.V. news anchor, Heather had entered the hospital under a pseudonym. She was so gaunt and pallid few people recognized her. Eventually she gained 19 pounds, returning to work with a new eating regime and tools to combat her anxiety.

Heather and Megan had experienced a "Leave It To Beaver"-like childhood with doting parents, Shawn and Sherry, who married young as high school sweethearts. The little blonde twins were unlike their friends whose parents were divorced. Heather and Megan never experienced shuffling from one parent's house to the other; they never heard their parents call each other names or fight about child support; and they never received double presents on their birthday and Christmas. They lived in the suburbs, with their stay-at-home mom and their father who was an early employee of Microsoft. Their friends would congregate at the Alexander house, which was clean and smelled of freshly baked chocolate chip cookies and homemade bread.

As a twin, Heather had tried to be perfect to match their surroundings.

She and her sister watched their mother eat small green salads with dressing on-the-side for dinner and take step aerobics at their local gym, always bikini ready for their annual vacation to Hawaii. Sherry cooked delicious meals for her family, which the girls and her husband eagerly consumed. Heather alternated between binging and purging and starving herself in secret. Megan exercised compulsively, as they both emulated their mother's self-discipline.

Heather hid her strange relationship with food from Brad, and on the occasions he caught her vomiting, she feigned illness. Since her hospital stay, she had managed to follow her doctor's orders and maintain her 105 pound weight with frequent scale checks and alternating between five small meals a day and juice fasts.

As she leaned against the toilet in the grocery store bathroom, she felt hot from shame. Tight control over her life was slipping away. It was only a few weeks ago when Megan had pointed out that her twin replaced control over food with control over Brad—calling her his jailer.

Heather denied it, but felt less anxiety knowing Brad was confined to a wheelchair and his small apartment, relying on her for food and everything else he needed.

She had planned to go directly to Brad's apartment from the grocery store, but decided to head home and wash up first.

Before she stepped into the shower, she purged herself again. Her reflection in the mirror told her she looked fat, but the scale read 107 pounds, which according to her doctor was still underweight for her 5'7" height. If she were to keep her news job, she'd have to channel her self-discipline into staying healthy. So, she pulled the untrustworthy cheap, long mirror off its nail on the wall and stowed it in a closet.

Relapse! Heather texted Megan.

Megan called Heather immediately, asking, "Are you okay?"

"I think so."

"You threw up?"

"Yup."

"Can you get back on track?"

Heather nodded, realizing Megan couldn't see her. Then added, "Yeah, I'll be okay. My weight's a few pounds over."

"Do you want me to take you to your therapist?" Megan said. "I can take care of Brad."

"No need. I've got an appointment in a few days."

"Should I come over and throw out any food?"

"I ate it already."

"What was it this time?"

"Brownies. Free samples and a few packages."

"Oh, shit!"

"Got to go." Heather dropped the phone onto her bed without disconnecting and wretched again into the toilet. This time, it was involuntary.

She finally reached Brad's apartment two hours later. As she opened the door, she immediately sensed something was wrong. She placed the bag of groceries she was carrying on the small table in the entryway. Brad's wheelchair was sitting in the middle of the room—unattended. She looked around and saw him sprawled out on the floor with his head propped against the sofa.

"You bitch!" he yelled.

"Brad, I'm sorry. I had an emergen…," she started to explain.

"You fucking bitch," he continued. "I'm sitting here and you're taking your goddamned time."

"I'm sorry," she pleaded. "Are you okay? Let me help you."

"Where the fuck have you been?" Brad screamed as she approached him. Heather smelled alcohol on his breath. As she leaned down to help him, he hit her hard across the mouth with his open hand.

Heather reacted by slapping him in the eye.

"I'm sorry, Brad," Heather gasped as she saw Brad's look of hurt and anger.

"Get out! You slut! Leave!" Brad bellowed.

As Heather started to walk out, he hurled an empty vodka bottle at her. It hit the doorframe, smashing onto the tile. Heather turned to look, and saw the broken bottle with jagged edges lying on the floor. It had become a dangerous weapon she didn't want to leave in Brad's hands. She grabbed it before bolting out the door. She tossed the bottle in the large trash bin, thankful Brad couldn't use it to hurt himself. Who knows what he'd do in the state he was in. She then ran to her car, hoping she wouldn't be recognized. She wondered how he was going to get himself back into his chair and into bed without help.

As she drove away, she looked up at the window of Brad's apartment and saw a silhouette walking behind the curtained window. She assumed a neighbor had heard the commotion and had come to his aid. Who else could it be?

On the way home, Heather drove through the McDonald's drive thru and ordered a Big Mac, large fries, a chocolate shake, and a cup of ice for her swollen face. As she waited for her order, she put her hand on her sore jaw. Her eyes welled with tears. She wished she could have a do-over so she could shop quickly and get to his place on time, cook his dinner, help him get ready for bed and tidy up. It was her fault. She should have resisted the woman with the brownies.

Heather never gave a thought to leaving Brad—even after his occasional physical assaults. Giving up on her dreams of their lives together was not an option. For years, she had imagined her future with an Olympic gold medalist. Secretly, she had replaced that dream with the fantasy of living with a multi-millionaire, and although she could barely admit it to herself, she felt empowered that he would never leave her now that he was a paraplegic.

Chapter 12

@Zlaw Should I clean my phone after talking with someone who had #diarrhea-of-the-mouth?

Her energy fueled by her morning latte, Zana arrived at the office shortly after 5 a.m. There were a handful of associates and partners gathered around the coffee pot, but no one had started work at such an early hour. Most of them would spend the next forty-five minutes reading the newspaper at their desks before getting a start on billable time, but they would score points with Frank for arriving before the sun came up. The attorneys who read the paper at home and rolled in past 7 a.m. lacked law firm intelligence and would soon be searching Monster.com for their next gig.

By 10 a.m., Zana was nodding off. She hoped Frank didn't notice her head bob forward when he popped into her office unexpectedly.

"Good morning," Frank said, planting himself in a chair.

"Hi Frank," Zana said, startled out of her momentary nap, surprised he had dropped by her office rather than sending a junior partner, or even a secretary, to give her the pile of papers he was carrying. "Are those for me?"

"Yes, they're Plaintiff Brad Jordan's first request for answers to interrogatories." Frank thumbed through the thick stack, licking his finger in order to separate the pages. "As usual, Mansfield has outdone himself. There are 50 questions, but with subparts—a grand total of about 200. Ridiculous!"

"Do you suggest I object to all of them and provide as vague and non-responsive answers as possible?" Zana asked, lifting an arched eyebrow and smiling.

"I suppose you should answer a reasonable number of questions so we don't find ourselves on the wrong end of a motion to compel," Frank said, rubbing his chin, a habit that invited imitation and mocking amongst the firm's associates. "Don't give away the store."

"I'll do my best," Zana said. Frank didn't crack a smile, so she wondered if he knew she had been sarcastic.

"We have thirty days. Get the draft on my desk in two weeks," Frank ordered, marching out.

Zana plopped the stack of papers on a pile in her inbox before she finished a letter summarizing a deposition transcript for an insurance adjuster. After her mid-morning nap, she felt energized now and her fingers flew across the keyboard as she made her way through the stack of depositions delegated by the partners and senior associates too lazy to summarize them. She didn't mind. It was far better to have mountains of work convertible to billable hours than to have an empty desk. Whenever she was given an assignment, she felt like she had received an unwrapped Christmas gift. Assignments implied that her superiors had confidence in her abilities, which could translate into longevity with the firm.

She had been summarizing depositions for several hours, earning her a Twitter break. After she re-tweeted some triathlon training tips, on a whim she searched "Brad Jordan". Thousands of tweets appeared. She scrolled through and noticed that Heather Alexander, using @NewsBlonde, tweeted about the plaintiff almost every day. The tweets promoted his career or cheered him on at races, with #GoBrad! or #FutureOlympicGold, the amazing #BradJordan. The tweets were consistent with a few breaks of time, but then stopped a few days before the Olympic trials. She then looked at all of Heather's tweets and saw she shifted from Brad Jordan to tweeting about movie and T.V. stars, which made sense because of the accident. There were even a few tweets with #JerryHirano. Zana smiled when she saw his name.

By 3:00, Zana was getting loopy from constant typing and staring at her computer screen. She was hungry and wondered if any restaurants remained open to grab a bite of lunch. She calculated three hours, at least, before she could leave for an evening training run and the few energy bars in her desk didn't sound appetizing.

She looked out the floor-to-ceiling window for the first time all day and noticed the sun's reflection sparkling on the ocean beyond the industrial area. She imagined catching up with Ed in the park and asking him the questions on the request for answers to interrogatories and dictating the answers while running, billing for her time. She chuckled at the absurdity of the scenario. It was time to grab a salad from downstairs and another latte to keep her awake—and sane.

After Zana returned from her lunch break, her landline rang for the second time that day. Young associates weren't the most popular employees at the firm, so the ring surprised her.

"Good afternoon. This is Zana West. May I help you?" Zana said, even though she saw the name on the caller I.D.

"Hi Zana. This is Alexia Moore."

"What can I do for you?"

"I'm wondering, what's the status of the Jordan case? It's on my diary today."

"I was just going over the Plaintiff's long request for answers to interrogatories."

"Oh, that's Mansfield for you," Alexia said. "Did you read *The Honolulu Daily* today?"

"Not yet. Why?" Zana wasn't like the other attorneys in the firm. She got her news from what was trending on Twitter and began work as soon as she finished applying makeup and flat ironing her hair in front of the mirror on the back of her door.

"There was a front page article on the positive economic impact of sports in Hawaii. Towards the end of the story, there were a few paragraphs about the Olympic trials and how a tragic accident will likely mean the end of triathlons in the Kahala area of Honolulu."

"Oh, I'm sorry to hear that," Zana said, at first thinking about how it would impact the races she wanted to enter, but she also wondered what the story had to do with the Jordan case.

"There was an interesting quote—just a minute, I'll find it," Alexia said, and Zana could hear her rustling some papers on the other end of the line. "Oh, here it is. It says, and I quote, 'a witness believed the person driving the car intentionally drove through cones blocking off traffic and caused the accident. The matter is still under investigation.' I wonder who the witness was."

"Who wrote the article?" Zana asked, sitting up in her chair and grabbing a pen.

"Sam Belmont. Do you want me to send you a copy?"

She set her pen down and put her fingers to the keyboard. "No need," Zana said as she clicked away on her computer. "I'm Googling it. I'll call the paper and see if Mr. Belmont will reveal the witness."

"Let me know what you find out. If we can locate him or her, we might be able to get out of this. Could you please call or text me what you find out?" Alexia said, giving Zana her cell number.

"Sure, I'll let you know," Zana said, entering Alexia's number into her iPhone.

After they hung up, Zana called *The Honolulu Daily*. She was disappointed to hear a recording saying Sam Belmont had left the office for the day. She left a message.

As Zana was gathering up her workout gear to leave for the day, Lori and Tom stepped into her office, both wearing suits and carrying briefcases.

"Frank told us you need help," Tom said, setting his briefcase on the floor and sitting down in a chair facing Zana. Lori sat next to him.

"Why are you so dressed up? Were you in court?" Zana said.

"We just finished a two-day arbitration. I'd rather get a drink and deal with this tomorrow," Lori said. "What's going on?"

"Oh, we just got two inches of interrogatories from Mansfield," Zana said, sitting back in her chair and stashing her workout gear under her desk. She hoped she wouldn't have to stay late and forgo her workout again.

"Nothing unusual. We've got thirty days, right?" Tom said.

"Yeah, no rush," Zana said.

"I just heard the Supreme Court rendered a decision in a case in which Mansfield got his ass kicked at trial," Lori said.

"Oh, yeah." Tom's face lit up. "There was a defense verdict on a wrongful death case. Mansfield represented the estate of a kid who died from an allergy to jellyfish. He sued South Shore, Inc., alleging negligence for failure to warn. Mansfield spent a shitload of money to try the case. It took about a month. He appealed, but the Supreme Court ruled in favor of South Shore."

"It's always good to hear about that motherfucker losing a case," Lori said. "He must be a fucking idiot to think South Shore had any negligence for a jellyfish sting. What a stupid asshole!"

"You have quite a mouth on you, Lori," Tom said, feigning surprise. "Zana, you'll be talking like a sailor soon enough after having a few cases against Mansfucker."

"You should talk," Lori sneered. "Guess who represented South Shore in the jellyfish case?"

"Who?" Zana checked her Twitter feed on her phone.

"Jerry Hirano. You know, the attorney who stars in the cable T.V. sitcom?" Lori said.

"He represents the South Shore on the Jordan case, too," Zana said, looking up from her phone. "He stopped by the other day."

"He's one sexy dude. All the support staff have the hots for him," Lori said, grinning.

"You should have heard the stories about Jerry while he worked here," Tom said.

"Is that so?" Zana said, wanting to probe for the gossip, but not wanting to raise their suspicion of her interest. Lori stood up and motioned for Tom to follow.

"Let's get a drink," Tom said, standing up. "It's been a long day. Wanna come, Zana?"

"I'm tempted, but I'm going for a run," she said, as she bent down to grab her gear and the new ASICS running shoes she looked forward to trying out. Zana had no interest in spending an evening with Lori and Tom, and she certainly didn't want to get drunk or spill the beans about her crush on Jerry Hirano. It was challenging enough to work with them. They were in their forties, but always seemed less mature than her twenty-something friends. As they turned their back to her, she couldn't help but roll her eyes.

***

The next morning, Zana was immersed in computer research for Brian Ching when her office phone rang for the fourth time that week.

"May I speak to Zana West, please," a woman said in a southern accent.

"This is Zana."

"My name is Sam; I'm returning your call."

Zana sat up straighter in her chair. "Are you calling from the newspaper?"

"Yes. You left a message."

"Oh, sorry. I thought you were a man," Zana said.

"Everyone thinks that." Sam laughed.

"I was calling about the article about the economic impact of sports in yesterday's paper," Zana said, hoping she could get the witness's name quickly, without a lot of small talk. She had piles of work to do.

"I hope you liked my article. It was the first feature I've ever written. I just started at the paper. I moved here from Nebraska last year. My husband thought I should get a job at the newspaper. I have a degree in journalism, and since my younger boy was born, I just—" Sam rambled.

"I'm sorry to interrupt. I'm so glad you got the feature story. Actually, it was really good," Zana said. She decided she'd better be nice or she wouldn't get what she wanted. "I was wondering, can you please tell me the name of the witness who you quoted at the end of the story?"

"Oh, I can't do that. It's a confidential source. Is there anything else I can help you with? I know you're busy. I am, too. I've got an assignment to write about a wedding. You see the groom is a helicopter pilot and wanted—"

"Sorry to interrupt again, but is there anything you *can* tell me about the witness? Where does the person work? How did you find the witness?" Zana said, trying to be tactful.

"I suppose I can tell you how I found the witness," Sam said, lowering her voice as if she was going to tell a juicy secret.

"Please," Zana said, trying not to sound as impatient as she felt.

"My mother-in-law makes this delicious apple pie. Well, I really love apple pie...actually all kinds of pie. I went to a bakery on Kapiolani Boulevard. You might know the bakery; it's really popular. I went there one morning, and while I stood in line, I was talking on my cell to a source for the feature. A man standing next to me overheard me and told me he'd been at the Olympic triathlon trials. He told me what I quoted in the paper. He insisted I not use his name. The line for the bakery was long, but I did get a few of their apple pies for a potluck. It was delicious and I ate several pieces."

Zana resisted the urge to interrupt a third time.

When Sam was done talking, Zana asked, "Can you tell me anything else about him? Where does he work? What did he look like?"

"You have been so nice. His name is John. I can't remember his last name off the top of my head. It was one of those short Asian names like Fong, Wu, Chang...you know, something like that," Sam said. "I hope I don't get into trouble for this. I love my job. It's so hard to get a good job in journalism. I've always worked as a waitress. I'm really hoping my husband doesn't get orders to leave so I can keep this job…"

"Sam, what day and time did you go to the bakery?" Zana asked.

"Hmm… It was early in the morning, because I bought some coffee there. And the only time I buy coffee is before 9 a.m. It was delicious— French roast, I think," she said.

"What day was it?"

"I can't remember. Maybe Saturday. Let's see. I was buying pie for a potluck. It must have been a Saturday, because on Sunday I would have been in church."

"Okay. That helps a lot. Can you remember anything else?" Zana said as she typed notes from their conversation.

"No, nothing, except that the guy was wearing scrubs. You know, like what you see in hospitals," Sam added. "Or, on the show ER."

"If you think of anything else, please call me," Zana said. "Thank you. You've been a big help." She hung up the phone before Sam could reply and texted Alexia her notes.

She immediately received a smiley face emoticon in reply.

***

It was after 5 p.m., and Alexia was the only adjuster still at her cubicle. She rarely stayed late, but had attended a settlement conference earlier in the day and needed to catch up on her diary before she went home. She heard vacuum cleaner noise coming from across the expansive room with its fifty cubicles surrounded by private offices for managers and supervisors. She assumed everyone, including her superiors, had cleared out for the three-day weekend until she heard the voices of Caron and a man—probably another adjuster—as they walked past her cubicle on their way to her boss's office.

Alexia added the latest investigation notes to her report about the Brad Jordan case. She hoped Caron would be pleased with the possibility of finding an eyewitness to the tragic accident. It might not mean much to the outcome, but at least there was a possibility of getting out of the case relatively cheaply—maybe for $250,000 or so. She wanted to give Caron some good news for once.

Alexia had talked to Caron earlier in the day, requesting more authority for the Henderson wrongful death case at settlement conference. To her surprise, Caron had refused to authorize $200,000 for a case she evaluated at close to $500,000. Judge Lee called Alexia into his chambers and berated her for not being reasonable. She listened politely. What could she do without Caron's cooperation?

Alexia made the finishing touches to her report, printed it and decided to present it to Caron in person. Maybe, they could discuss the Henderson case and figure out how to resolve it. She grabbed the file along with the report and smoothed her long hair down before dropping into her boss's office unannounced. When she approached the partly open door, she heard voices and stopped in her tracks.

"It's a major blow," Caron said.

"There's nothing else we can do," a man's voice said.

"If we can avoid paying out on any claims for the next six months, would that change anything?" Caron asked in a shaky voice.

"I'm sure that would be impossible, but it would help," he said.

"What about costs?" Caron asked.

"They're budgeted for. This is serious, Caron," the man said.

Caron sighed. "We have hundreds of employees who will be out of work."

Alexia turned and walked back to her cubicle as quickly as she could. At least the vacuum noises drowned out the sound of her footsteps. She slumped into her chair and clicked off her computer. Her heart was racing. No wonder Caron wouldn't authorize settling the case today. It might be possible to delay payments on her pending cases—nothing was scheduled for trial for months, but there were arbitrations and mediations on the calendar. If she were to keep her job, she'd have to do everything in her power to reschedule upcoming matters and make sure Mansfield didn't squeeze a dime from them in the Brad Jordan case.

Chapter 13

@Zlaw If I got the best spot in the transition area for my #bike in a #triathlon, do I win?

Zana's iPhone alarm jolted her out of a half-night's sleep. It was 3:30 a.m. Her body was used to rousing before dawn to be the first one in the office, or to bike or run before the heat of the day. This early morning was the culmination of months of training for the Bronzeman Triathlon—an intermediate distance, which meant an 800 meter swim, a 25 mile bike ride and a 10k run.

Her checklist was taped on her bedroom door so she could cross off each item of equipment before leaving the house. Shelby always teased Zana for being so anal, but preparation helped her relax. She was wearing her one-piece form-fitting triathlon suit and rubber slippers. She put her swim cap and goggles, a pan for water to wash sand off her feet, and a towel for wiping her feet after the swim into her backpack. Her running shoes, socks and hat were already in it and checked off the list. Her bike was in the car along with her helmet, bike shoes, and sunglasses. Zana pulled three bottles of water and two energy drinks out of the fridge as quietly as possible, trying not to wake Andrew and Kelly. She also grabbed a plain bagel and banana for her breakfast to eat in the car as she drove to Ala Moana Beach Park. She'd listen to the theme from Rocky cranked at high volume for motivation once she pulled out of her driveway.

She had trained with Pete Sander's triathlon club for four months in preparation for the race. Pete wasn't a professional coach, but liked to train with a group of like-minded athletes, so he organized three training sessions each week for the club members. If Zana found time, she swam, biked or ran the other four days of the week with her friends or by herself. She had no expectation of winning or even placing in her age group, but wanted to get a P.R.—personal record. She took her mental game as seriously as her equipment preparation, planning some visualization time after setting up her transition area and stretching.

After ten minutes on the road, Zana pulled into the parking lot of the boat harbor adjacent to the race venue. She had scoped out this spot weeks ago and thought it would be the perfect place to park so she would only have to ride her bike a block to the transition area. Her SUV, when placed into 4-wheel drive, could jump the curb and park where passenger cars couldn't drive without breaking their oil pans. She noticed one other vehicle beyond the high curb with the personalized license plate TRIBAD, which caught her eye because the word seemed to be a play on the phrase, "my bad". Zana chuckled as she thought of obnoxious teenagers using the sarcastic phrase instead of a proper apology.

She grabbed her backpack, replaced her rubber slippers with bike shoes, strapped on her helmet, snapped her feet into her clipless pedals and rode to the transition area. She was so early only a handful of athletes were waiting in line for the volunteers to open up, allowing her to choose an ideal spot for her bike and gear.

After a few minutes, a volunteer wearing a Bronzeman Triathlon T-shirt moved some cones, inviting the group of waiting triathletes to rack their bikes. It made strategic sense to pick a space closest to the swim exit so she would not have to run far to her bike in her bare feet after running out of the water. She would then trot alongside her bike through the transition area surrounded by fencing with sponsor logos to the mount line, and then ride out the exit, hopefully getting a head start.

"Good morning, athletes! Welcome to the 8th Annual Bronzeman Triathlon!" the announcer boomed over the loudspeaker. "It's going to be a hot day. Slather on that sunscreen."

Zana appreciated the reminder. After she stood in line to have her body marked with her race number 436, she carefully applied a thin layer of waterproof sunscreen to all of her exposed skin, making sure not to smear the race numbers a volunteer had written with a black Sharpie.

"The water temperature is 80 degrees this morning, so balmy you will not be allowed to wear wetsuits," the announcer said. "Competitive rules apply today and so no drafting behind other bikes is allowed. You'll have to stay 3 bike lengths behind the bike ahead of you. Remember to ride as far to the right as safely possible."

Zana was almost done with her pre-race checklist. Her bike was racked. Her helmet was placed carefully on top of her aero bars with her sunglasses inside. She had laid out a towel and a small tub of water to wash and dry the sand from her feet after the swim. Her running shoes, hat and socks were placed neatly next to the towel and her bike shoes were ready to jump into after the swim. She swigged water from her bottle and walked toward the beach to look at the ocean conditions.

"Race numbers 521, 82, and 436 report to the announcer. Let me repeat, numbers 521, 82, and 436. Your bikes need bar end plugs before you begin the race. If you don't solidly plug your handlebars, you will be disqualified. Numbers 521, 82, and 436 report to the announcer," the voice said.

Zana heard her number, but not much else. She wasn't sure where the announcer was located and so asked a volunteer who was handing out T-shirts. She was directed to a tent in a far corner of the large transition area in the parking lot. As she made her way to the tent, she ran into Shelby.

"Are you ready?" Shelby asked, falling into step with Zana.

"As ready as I'll ever be. My number was called by the announcer," Zana said. "Where are you going?"

"I found someone's cell phone. The announcer can probably find the owner," Shelby said as they approached the tent. A pile of boxes of extra T-shirts and tables stacked with an assortment of orange cones, signage, tools, marking pens, duct tape and other items were all inside the tent area. On a table next to the side of the tent was a tray piled high with Costco muffins and an empty pizza box. Sitting in a wheelchair with a microphone in his hand was a young, athletic-looking man. Zana thought he looked familiar and assumed he was a wheelchair athlete.

"Hi. I'm race number 436. You called my number?" she said.

"The official said you're missing a bar end plug," the announcer said without looking away from a small notepad. He pointed to a jar of plugs on the table. Shelby was waiting to interrupt him to ask about the cell phone when the race director walked into the tent.

"Brad, I need you to announce that the athletes should start moving towards the water. It's a half hour until the race starts. In a few minutes, I want to get you out there. Carl will come by with his golf cart," the race director said.

"Sounds good," Brad said and then swigged from a plastic bottle.

Oh my God, Zana thought. *That's Plaintiff Brad Jordan!* Zana snuck another peek at him while she grabbed a few plugs from the jar. He looked tan and healthy and not nearly as miserable as Mansfield had described in his demand letter. She noticed the muscle tone in his arms. His legs were a little skinny, but not too bad. Zana caught Brad's eye. Embarrassed, she quickly turned her head and walked out of the tent.

"Wait up, Zana," Shelby said, rushing to catch up with her. "Do you know the announcer?"

"No. Do you?"

"No, but I saw you checking him out. I just wondered if you knew him. He looks kind of familiar."

"Why do you ask?" Zana said, not wanting to get into a discussion about the case.

"He reeks of alcohol. I think he's drinking and it's only 5:30 in the morning," Shelby said.

"He looks like a para-triathlete. I'm sure what you smelled wasn't alcohol," Zana said. She couldn't imagine anyone living the multi-sport lifestyle drinking in the wee hours of the morning.

"Good luck, Shelby," Zana said before rushing to her bike to replace the missing bar end plugs. She took her iPhone out of her bike bag. She had to act fast since the transition area was closing soon and she would barely have time to make it to the start, let alone pee. The phone rang quite a few times before Alexia Moore picked up.

"Hi Alexia. This is Zana West from G, P & D. I'm so sorry to wake you up so early on a Saturday morning, but this is important."

"That's okay. What's up?" Alexia said, sounding groggy.

"I'm competing in the Bronzeman Triathlon at Ala Moana Beach Park," Zana lowered her voice to a whisper. "Brad Jordan is the announcer. He looks pretty good, but he reeks of alcohol. Can you get an investigator out here to film ASAP?"

"I'll see what I can do," Alexia said, now sounding wide awake. "Focus on doing well in the race. I'll take care of Jordan. Good luck!"

"Thanks, I'll need it!" Zana said and hung up. She put the phone into her backpack.

"The transition area is closing in two minutes," Brad announced.

Zana grabbed her swim cap, goggles, and water bottle. Most of the participants had already walked the 800 meters to the swim start. The athletes were broken up into groups, called "waves" starting with the pros, followed by each age group, starting five minutes apart in order to spread the competitors safely across the course. Each athlete wore a timing chip on a Velcro strap around his or her ankle, recording their split times for each segment of the triathlon and a total time for placement by age group and overall standings.

Zana was relieved that her wave was the fourth group to start the race, giving her an extra 15 minutes to warm-up. She jogged slowly, but conserved her energy as much as possible. It was time to get her mind focused on the race, rather than on Brad Jordan's surprise appearance.

By the time Zana reached the start line, the gun had fired and the pro athletes were swimming towards the bike transition. She tugged on her cap and adjusted her goggles before easing into the water for a relaxed 50-yard freestyle swim.

Brad called Zana's group, 25 to 29 year old females, to line up between two guys on surfboards, forming an imaginary line between them to serve as the starting line for the triathlon. Zana knew she was one of the faster swimmers and so positioned herself in the front row so she wouldn't run over her competitors.

"Boom!" the gun sounded.

She launched into a sprint to find clear water, but another swimmer clung to her side, apparently trying to run her over. Zana slowed down slightly so with each stroke her elbow and fist deterred her competitor from infringing on her space. She finally wrestled away and found open water.

Her pace slowed as she fell into a rhythm that would allow her to conserve energy for the bike and run legs of the race. She had practiced spotting this course many times, intermittently lifting her head up so she could see the water exit until she was about 200 yards from the shore. She then turned about 15 degrees so she would swim the most efficient and straight line in.

At the 600-yard buoy, Zana was ahead of most of the other swimmers in her group and had caught up with the slowest competitors in the wave before. As she approached the large orange buoy situated about 50 yards from the swim finish, she put her head down and swam at about 75% of her fastest speed. Once Zana's hand touched the sand in shallow water, she pulled herself onto her feet and ran the rest of the way through the water and up the beach. She wasn't certain of it, but she thought she had finished the swim in the top three of her age group.

She ran up the path through the sand and towards the paved area leading to the transition spot where her bike was racked as close to the ocean as possible, which she quickly located. Other competitors had to run across the hot asphalt in bare feet, searching for their bikes amongst approximately 1500 others.

Zana stepped in and out of her water pan, washing the sand off her feet and then quickly dried them on her towel as she yanked off her swim cap and goggles. Sunglasses on; helmet on and buckled, and on with her bike shoes in less than 30 seconds. Zana ran with her bike, taking the shortest route amongst dozens of racks to a blue line at the transition entrance. Then, with no wasted motion, mounted it and clipped into her pedals. She rode cautiously over some speed bumps to the entrance of the park and took a long drink from one of her water bottles. It was time to get serious. She placed her forearms on her bike's aero bars so her upper body was flat in an aerodynamic position and pedaled fast so she could begin passing other cyclists ahead of her.

She felt energized riding through Waikiki, passing slower cyclists, one after another. The cheers of tourists lining Kalakaua Avenue encouraged her to go faster. At one point she heard a few voices cheer her on. "Go, Zana, go! You can do it, Zana! You're doing great!"

She picked up her pace to impress her friends; their voices seemed to give her superhuman strength. It wasn't until she reached the top of Diamond Head Road, near the lookout, that her progress slowed.

At first she passed a few bikes going up the precipitous grade. But as she reached the steepest part of the hill and had to stand up out of her saddle, about a half dozen strong cyclists passed her—as if she were standing still. Once on the straightaway on level ground, Zana's cadence evened out and she got into a rhythm she kept for the next 15 miles.

As she came close to the next transition area, T-2, she marveled at how well the race was going so far. She was surprised few other cyclists were passing her and wondered if she might still be in contention as a top three finisher in her age group. She made a mental note to make sure not to unbuckle her helmet before she racked her bike so as not to risk a two-minute penalty. She replaced her bike helmet with a running hat and her bike shoes with running shoes.

The first two blocks after dismounting her bike felt like running in quicksand. Her quads and hamstrings ached from the long ride and so it took every bit of effort Zana had to move forward. She made sure to drink water at the first aid station and quickly downed an energy gel for a calorie boost to get through the 10K run.

After about five blocks, her legs loosened up and she increased her pace. Normally, when she trained, she listened to hip hop music on her iPod. Since headphones were banned from races, she hummed the theme to Hawaii 5-0 in her head.

Zana focused her eyes forward and her mind on the imaginary music, moving her feet in sync with the beat. Soon, her legs moved quickly and easily. She zoned in on one athlete in front of her at a time. She imagined lassoing each of them and pulling them towards her as she passed. This worked for several miles aiding her in passing about 25 runners, mostly older men who had probably burned out on the bike and had nothing left for the run. It took experience to pace a triathlon just right.

As she passed some of the athletes, it was clear from their slumped shoulders and hands on bellies that they were experiencing stomach upset or cramping. Zana had been there before. Fortunately, today, she was feeling strong. Running up the backside of Diamond Head, within a mile of the finish line, she increased her pace.

Cresting the hill, Zana came upon a young woman who had a "25" written in black marking pen on the back of her calf to signify she was in the 25-29 age group. As Zana passed her, she saw it was Leslie Hamakua, who often earned a spot on the podium at local races. Leslie must have quickly identified Zana as a competitor, because she started running just a half-step behind her, almost on her shoulder. If they kept this up, there would be an all-out sprint to the finish line. Zana increased her pace to stay ahead of Leslie, leading down the hill.

As they reached the bottom, still inches apart, Zana could hear her own labored breathing and her thigh muscles started to cramp. She finally gave in to her body's painful cries and let Leslie pass her. Once Leslie was about 10 feet ahead, Zana fell into a rhythm behind her. A guy Zana had seen training in her neighborhood began running next to her, which made it easier to pace.

It wasn't long before the finish line was in sight. She focused on Leslie and began to reel her in. Zana picked up her knees, increased her cadence and sprinted, zipping past Leslie just in time to cross over the finish line first.

Relieved, Zana bumped fists with Leslie as the volunteers pulled the black straps with timing chips off their ankles. Another volunteer gave Zana a shell lei and a kiss on the cheek. She would have to wait for the results to find out where she had placed in her age group.

"Zana!" A voice yelled from the crowd of people gathered around the finish line.

She looked around to see who was calling her. A tanned blonde with a curvy, but muscular body, wearing a low cut white T-shirt and pink shorts, walked towards her. "I know we haven't met in person. I'm Alexia. They announced your name as you crossed the finish line."

"Hi Alexia," Zana said. She had expected the adjuster to be frumpy looking, but instead she was stunning.

"Congratulations! Great job!" Alexia opened her arms to give her a hug.

"I'm sweaty," Zana said. Alexia hugged her anyway. "Thanks. I felt good today. I'm surprised you came down."

"I didn't want to miss the chance to see Brad Jordan for myself," Alexia said softly.

"So, what have you observed?" Zana asked, stretching her right calf.

"He seems like he's plastered. He's been slurring his words. I think the race director figured it out, because I saw him replace his plastic bottle with a water bottle."

"That's so bizarre," Zana said, switching to her other calf.

"Yeah. Tell me about it."

"Did you get someone to film him?"

"My buddy, Rick, a private investigator, lives close by. Luckily, I had his cell number and he was able to get here right away. He said he normally doesn't bring his equipment home, but was on a job last night and so had everything he needed."

"Lucky us. You'll have to excuse me, Alexia. I should get something to drink and I'm desperate to use the restroom," Zana said, grabbing a Gatorade from a trash bin converted to drink cooler filled with ice, and then popping into a vacant port-o-potty.

When she exited the bathroom, Alexia was talking with three sweaty male triathletes. *That figures,* thought Zana.

Rather than join them, Zana looked for the race results near the timer's tent. A crowd surrounded the postings on a large board. After a bit of elbowing and patience, Zana saw that she came in second place in her age group, a distant 3.5 minutes behind first-place winner "M. Alexander." Zana grinned. This was the best she had ever done and since she was so far behind the first-place finisher, there was no reason to be disappointed. Usually, she took off as soon as she saw the race results, but this time she would stay and accept her prize at the awards ceremony.

Giddy with excitement, Zana sought out Alexia, who had made her way over to the bandstand where Brad Jordan was making announcements. Alexia was aiming a camera with a zoom lens at Brad.

"Anything interesting?" Zana asked.

"He seems to have sobered up a bit," Alexia said, snapping a few more pictures. "A blonde chick was hovering over him—I think she's his girlfriend."

"Is that her over there?" Zana pointed to a thin blonde with Jackie O. sunglasses and a floppy straw hat.

Alexia nodded.

Later, at the awards ceremony, Miss Hawaii and the Mayor of Honolulu handed out medals to the first, second and third place competitors who stood on the tiered stand. A costumed Bronzeman posed for photographs with each group of winners.

When it was Zana's turn, she stepped onto the second tier with M. Alexander positioned on the first. The woman wore a skintight dark gray triathlon suit, running hat and sunglasses. *She looks so familiar*, Zana thought, but couldn't pinpoint why.

Brad introduced the winner and announced that she was Megan Alexander from Seattle. She bent down to give Brad a hug and kiss before she left the stand.

"Congratulations!" Shelby and Moana squealed, now changed out of their race clothes. Zana was the first of their training group to place in the top three of her age group. Her friends usually placed in the middle of the pack where, before today, Zana had consistently finished. They examined the second-place medal she was wearing around her neck and the packet of gift certificates and goodies she had received as part of her prize.

"Who's that guy?" Shelby whispered, gesturing to a tall, athletic-looking man wearing a baseball cap, Ray-ban sunglasses and a black T-shirt, standing several feet away and staring at Zana.

She shrugged.

"May I help you?" Moana boldly asked the guy.

"No," the guy looked embarrassed and quickly walked away.

Zana wondered if the guy might have been Rick, the investigator whom Alexia had hired. He probably wanted to talk with her in private.

"Excuse me—I'll call you later," Zana said to Shelby and Moana, and rushed off to look for the man.

When she spotted him again, he was standing next to Brad Jordan whispering in his ear. Zana's heart jumped in her throat. What if Brad was aware that she was opposing counsel in his lawsuit? He must have seen her name on the court documents. Maybe that guy was one of his attorneys or an investigator for the Plaintiff?

Zana started to feel sick to her stomach as she quickly walked to her car. The SUV with the license plate TRIBAD was still there. Zana smiled but decided she would enjoy the rest of her weekend. She'd deal with work again on Monday.

Chapter 14

@Zlaw Have you read the tabloids this week? Oh, good. While you were reading, I was #swimming, #biking and #running. #Winning!

Brad lay in the filth of his sweaty, crumb-encrusted sheets as the sun's heat woke him up from another fitful sleep. A handful of Ritz crackers and empty packets of string cheese were scattered on his pillow. A small cockroach scurried across his nose, making it itch, and then darted under the crumpled bed sheet when he reached up to scratch. He gradually opened his eyes.

He groaned as he squinted, reaching for the sunglasses on his bedside table to shield his eyes. Through his Oakleys, he was able to adjust his gaze and rest it on the bike helmet on his desk. He wished he could strap it on and take out one of his bikes for a spin to enjoy the beautiful sunny day. He was tired of being cooped up in his apartment, wondering if this was what being in prison felt like. If it weren't for Heather and Mansfield's monitoring of his every movement, he would be able to get out for a run or ride more often.

As it was, he only dared exercise outside when Heather was out of town and when he could come up with a good excuse for not being home when Mansfield's staff called or stopped by to see him.

Brad wiped away a tear, only to have it replaced by a stream of others. Triathlon had defined who he was ever since he could remember. Now, he could only be defined by this scam. He longed to resolve the lawsuit and enjoy the freedom the settlement would buy him. Resolution of the case would also release him from the chains of litigation—he would be able to go anywhere without fear of witnesses. The more his negative thoughts flowed through his brain without alcohol to dull them, the more he felt hopeless—destroyed. He had no doubt that he was the one who deserved to die in the crash and not Vic. He couldn't help but feel guilty about Vic's death. His initial physical suffering had felt like sufficient punishment for his survival, but as he had recovered the feeling in his legs and then the ability to stand and walk, his helplessness was replaced with anger and self-loathing. He heard himself whimper, groan, and sob, but somehow it soothed him.

***

Heather knocked a half dozen times before letting herself in. She wanted to respect Brad's privacy, but was alarmed when she heard him moaning. For a split second, she had a panicked feeling that he was in his room with another woman. She then remembered Brad was impotent, because of his paralysis. Her feelings of relief were suddenly replaced by fear. Had Brad tried to kill himself?

She raced into his bedroom, finding him lying in bed with his hands on his tear-soaked face, rocking back and forth on the bed. He was hysterical.

"Brad, it's okay. I'm here now," Heather said softly, placing her hands gently on his shoulder and head. "Is there anything I can get you to make you feel better?"

His eyes closed, Brad shook his head.

"Chocolate always makes me feel good. Can I bring you some of that delicious Belgium chocolate Megan brought over?" Heather propped up his pillows on the bed and brushed the food crumbs away. Then she sat on the bed and gently stroked his hair.

"I could use a drink," Brad said with his eyes still closed.

"Coffee? I brought some orange juice for you," Heather said. "I'm pretty sure we have some herbal tea left, too."

"O.J.," Brad perked up. "Can you make it a screwdriver?"

"Orange juice's coming up," Heather laughed. She went into the kitchen and poured it in a glass. She then texted Megan: Need U @ B's ASAP!!

Heather's mouth was still sore from him hitting her a few days ago. She had hoped they could talk about the incident, but one look at him and she could see he was still incredibly upset about it. She hadn't called him or come by the day before. From the looks of things, he must have been miserable and utterly helpless without her.

Back in the bedroom, she rummaged through prescription bottles on the dresser until she found the bottle of Ambien.

"Take one of these so you can sleep," Heather handed him the pill. "You'll feel better."

Brad nodded and swallowed the Ambien with the juice.

She then straightened his bedding, brushing off any stray crumbs she missed before and threw the cracker and cheese packets into a plastic trash bag. "This place is a pit," she said.

"You need to clean it more often," he said, raising his voice.

"You must be feeling better," Heather said. "Can we talk about our fight?"

Brad shut his eyes and almost instantly began snoring.

Heather sighed and continued straightening his bedroom. She placed his bike helmet in a drawer, thinking, *this will only remind him of what he can no longer do.* She then heard her cell phone from the living room and hurried to answer it.

"Hi Robert," Heather said as she answered her phone, noticing the call was from Robert Hightower of Epic Press. She spoke softly as she shut the bedroom door, hoping the call wouldn't disturb Brad.

"How are you doing?" Robert said.

"Fine, did you get my email?" Heather asked.

"Yes, I have a few questions."

"Just a second. Someone just knocked at the door." Heather let Megan in, motioning she was on the phone. "Okay, I'm back. What are your questions?"

"How did you know Petra Deutsche is cheating on her husband? And where did you get the pictures anyway?" Richard said.

"I have my sources. How much will you pay? I can email better pictures once we decide on a price."

"For the story and pictures: eight hundred fifty," Robert said.

"I can't do less than twelve fifty. Another tabloid has already offered twelve hundred. You've been helpful in the past, Robert. I'd like to do business with you." Heather mouthed the words, "just a minute" to her sister and motioned for her to sit on the couch.

"Sorry, Heather. My budget is only a thousand. I wish I had more. If you have to sell them to someone else, I understand," Robert said.

"Okay. I'll take it. I want to help you out and I like working with you. I'll email you the full story and photographs tomorrow." She ended the call.

"What's that all about? Are you selling to a tabloid?" Megan asked, thumbing through a triathlon magazine.

"Yeah," Heather nodded. "I know this guy who will pay me good money for stories I can't use for the nightly news—celebrity gossip and such."

"That's quite a gig," Megan's eyes widened. "How much money are you raking in doing that?"

"A few grand every month." Heather straightened up some newspapers and magazines strewn across the floor.

"Let me know if I can do anything. I could use some cash," Megan said, leaning over to help her twin.

"I could pay you for Brad-sitting."

"I don't mind helping out. I'm teaching half-days so I'm only making a little money," Megan said raising her voice.

Heather poked her nose into Brad's room and then closed the door. "Shhhhhh," she whispered. "He's asleep."

"Sorry," Megan whispered. "Did you puke again?"

"No. I'm back on track." Heather picked up a pile of dirty T-shirts and shorts from the floor.

"So, what's the problem this time?"

"When I texted you, he was hysterical. I was worried he might be suicidal," Heather said, keeping her voice low. "I wasn't sure what to do. I guess I needed your support."

"Do you think he's okay?"

"Yeah. I gave him a sleeping pill." She dropped the soiled clothes in a pile next to the washing machine, grabbed her purse, found her checkbook and began writing out a check.

"It must have worked. I can hear him snoring."

"Hey, how did you get here so fast? Were you lurking outside the door?"

"I was at the Starbuck's down the street," Megan said, standing up and putting a hand supportively on Heather's shoulder. "I can understand why you'd be upset."

"I'm worried about him. I think I should be here with him around the clock," Heather said, handing Megan a check. "I'd be horrified if something happened while I was gone."

"Wow! I mean, thank you," Megan said, looking at the amount on the check. "Isn't this your day off?"

"It's supposed to be. Chuck called this morning and wants me to fill in for the weekend anchor. She's sick and there's no one else available."

"Go ahead. I don't mind staying with Brad," Megan said, folding the check in half and tucking it safely in her purse.

"I was sort of hoping you'd offer. They're really in a bind with all the cutbacks. I'm worried that if I don't help out whenever I'm asked, they'll replace me. Are you sure you can do this?"

"No problem, Sis. It's not like I have a date or anything. I can watch T.V., read the paper and keep Brad company after he wakes up."

"I should go home and get ready," Heather said, putting her hands on her twin's hands as she often did.

"No worries. I'll take good care of your man," Megan smiled.

After grabbing her bag, she peeked in on Brad one last time. Seeing he was sleeping soundly, Heather closed his bedroom door as softly as she could and left the apartment.

***

When she had heard Heather's car drive away, Megan slipped off her clothes and climbed into bed next to Brad, spooning him under the filthy covers. His skin felt hot against her body. She breathed in his musky scent and kissed him on the neck. She watched his chest rise and fall steadily, even after she placed her hand on his erection, not disturbing his Ambien sleep.

Chapter 15

@Zlaw Shopping for cute outfit for sort of #date. Does that mean I get a sort of #kiss?

*L*itigation attorney meeting in Conference Room B at 2:30 p.m. today, the instant message popped up on Zana's computer screen at precisely 2:05 p.m. She wondered how many attorneys were actually sitting at their computers and would do as commanded on such short notice. Her first thought was to pretend she didn't see the message. But, curiosity got the better of her and soon Zana followed a handful of attorneys down the hallway.

She saw Frank dressed in a suit and tie talking to a twenty-something man who Zana assumed was his son. They both had broad shoulders, stood over six feet tall, had the same strong chins, slightly bulbous noses and bushy eyebrows. Frank's wavy hair was mostly gray, but bits of black still peppered it, making Zana wonder why he didn't color it. Most older attorneys did. The younger version of Frank had black straight hair and flashed a gorgeous smile at her.

Attorneys, mostly focused on their smart phones, began filling into the conference room. Rather than talking with each other, they scrolled and tapped while Zana stood watching. She regretted leaving her phone on her desk. After a few minutes, while she shifted her weight and examined a chipped fingernail, Frank cleared his throat. The phone tapping abruptly stopped.

"Good afternoon gentlemen and lady," Frank said, nodding in Zana's direction. "I want to introduce you to our newest associate, Lucas Rossi. Mr. Rossi just graduated from Stanford Law School and will be working in the litigation department."

"Hi everyone," Lucas said, giving a jerky wave and smiling with straight white teeth.

"Lucas is Caron Rossi's son," Frank said.

Zana noticed the surprised looks on Kim and Tom's faces and wondered if they had thought the same thing. At least she hadn't put her foot in her mouth. It was unusual for Frank to make a fuss about a new associate. Usually, new hires went unnoticed until they toted their belongings out the door a few months later when Frank tired of them.

"Lucas will be a valuable asset to our litigation team. Make sure you introduce yourself to him," Frank said. "You can all get back to work, now."

The attorneys hurried out the door, most of them picking up where they left off on their phones. Before Zana could leave, Frank motioned for her.

"Lucas, I'd like you to meet Zana West. She's in an office near yours," Frank said.

"Welcome, Lucas," Zana said, surprised his handshake was so moist and flaccid. She wondered if Lucas just shook women's hands like that.

"Nice to meet you," the younger man grinned.

"Lucas will be working closely with you, since you are the other newest kid on the block," Frank said.

"Wonderful," Zana said, trying to look enthused. If this "kid" was as lifeless as his handshake and as idiotic as his grin, she hoped he would be assigned to help someone else soon.

"I'm looking forward to it," Lucas said, continuing to smile.

"Nice meeting you," she said. "Excuse me, I've got work to do."

Behind her, Zana heard someone call her name.

"Zana, duck into my office," Andrew said, catching up to her.

She nudged Andrew on the shoulder. "Sure. I've got a minute."

"OMG," Andrew said as soon as he closed the door behind her.

"Are you thinking what I'm thinking?" Zana said.

"Lucas is Frank's 'Mini-Me'," Andrew said.

"Yeah. It's so weird. I thought Lucas was Frank's son when I first saw them standing next to each other," Zana said, plopping into a chair facing Andrew who sat down behind his desk.

"Frank's entire family was at last summer's firm picnic. He doesn't have any sons. He has two grown daughters who are younger than Lucas."

"Hmm…" Zana mused. "Isn't it strange that Lucas is Caron Rossi's son?"

"I know. I think Lucas looks a whole lot more like Frank than Caron."

"Could Lucas be Frank and Caron's secret love child?" Zana said, snickering.

"It's probably a weird coincidence they look so much alike. Caron's an old battleax, but Frank's wife, Arlene, is still gorgeous," Andrew said. "There's no way Frank would have done the nasty with Caron."

"Well, it would have had to have been a long time ago. Lucas must be pushing 30," Zana said. "Just in case Lucas *is* Frank's pride and joy, it's probably a good idea to err on the side of caution and treat him well."

"I'm not the one who has to worry," Andrew laughed. "It sounds like you'll be working with the dude."

"Yeah. I hope he's intelligent. He'll probably run to his mommy or

Frank if he hears me complain."

"Good luck!"

"Gee, thanks." Zana rolled her eyes and left Andrew's office to go back to her own to tackle the Jordan interrogatories. Not two minutes after she returned, she heard a feeble knock at her door.

"Come in," she said loudly.

"Excuse me," Lucas said. "I just wanted to let you know that I'm next door if you need any help."

"Thanks. I'll keep that in mind," Zana said. "Are you sure you're next door? Rex is on one side and Lori is on the other."

"I'm in Lori's old office," Lucas said, rubbing his chin. His Cheshire Cat smile was gone, replaced by a serious look—similar to Frank's when he was about to berate an underling.

"Where did she move?" Zana said. Although Lori had a corner office, it was small and was on the wrong side of the tracks, so to speak.

"Oh, um. Lori was fired," Lucas said. "Didn't you know?"

"No, I hadn't heard. Do you know why?" Zana asked, her eyes widening.

"I'm probably not supposed to say this, but I heard there were no job openings so I'm pretty sure she was fired to make room for me," Lucas said. "I heard she was on her way out anyway."

"Hmmm. Okay," she said, frowning.

"I'll let you get back to work," Lucas said and then stepped out, closing the door behind him.

Zana put her face in her hands, wondering if she would be next. Did Caron have any more sons? Although Lori was foul-mouthed around other associates, she billed *beaucoup* hours and clients adored her. Now, there were only four women attorneys left in the entire firm, including the real estate, transaction and sports sections upstairs. Even though Lucas seemed charming, she got a glimpse of his tough edge—similar to his mother. She'd have to keep a close eye on her new next door neighbor.

Zana texted Andrew. Did you know Lori was fired?

Andrew texted back. You mean, you didn't?

Mini-Me is now in her office.

Lucky you.

He's a chip off the ole block.

I'm thinkin' sperm donor.

Zana texted a smiley face emoticon and then put her phone back into her purse. She had work to do on the Jordan case, but before she lost her courage, there was one phone call she needed to make.

***

Jerry leaned back in his red leather chair and laced his fingers behind his head. He had just spent the morning reviewing Brad Jordan's medical records, including several treating neurological and orthopedic surgeons' reports stating their opinions that his surgeries were successful and their prognosis was good. He *would* regain his ability to ambulate. *So, if his own doctors were correct, why did Brad continue to use a wheelchair?* Jerry scratched his head.

He thumbed through the records, locating discharge summaries from the rehabilitation hospital. On all of the final documents, the conclusion was the same. Brad had not met his goal of walking. He had complied with the prescribed exercises and had been released to do home exercises, but still could not ambulate. The measurements of atrophy were insignificant and the patient's ranges of motions in his lower extremities measured only slightly below normal. He had sensation in his legs according to the discharge summary, but other physician reports noted that Brad reported no sensation. Jerry wondered about the discrepancy and made a note on a post-it to ask questions about it when he took the Plaintiff's health care providers' depositions.

Jerry pressed a speed dial button on his desk phone and then clicked the speaker button to connect with Tony at Lanikai Investigations.

"Hey, my friend. You guys are the best in the business," Jerry said after Tony picked up. "I need your help."

"Thanks, Jer. You are too kind. What's up?"

"I need you to do some surveillance on a plaintiff—Brad Jordan. He claims he's paralyzed, but doctors' reports suggest otherwise. I'll give you a $50,000 budget. See if you can catch him walking," Jerry said. "I'll email you the address, photos and other details. Can you have your boys get on this right away?"

"Sure. But that's an unusually high budget for this type of surveillance, Jerry. Is there anything else I need to know?" Tony asked.

"It's a Mansfield case."

"Oh, that explains it—The Ripper—there's probably something up," Tony said. "I smell fraud in the air."

"You might have seen a triathlon accident on the news about a year ago. Brad Jordan was one of the competitors hit by a car. His medical records look fishy. My suspicion is that the day after the case is settled, the guy will jump out of his wheelchair and miraculously be cured. I've seen it before."

"Wouldn't be anything new. I'll bet the guy is still competing in triathlons in Russia or something," Tony said.

"Probably. Do you have any suggestions?"

"Let's start with three days of surveillance and we'll report back. You'll hear from us earlier if we get something good. Hopefully, we'll catch the guy on film dancing or running."

"Walking would be enough," Jerry said. "Thanks. Your staff always does a terrific job."

After hanging up, Jerry drummed his fingers on his desk, trying to figure out what else was bothering him about the Jordan case. According to articles Jerry had read on the Internet, Brad was extremely competitive and had his heart set on being an Olympian for years. Why didn't he get right back out there and race as a disabled athlete? There were so many stories about servicemen who had body parts blown off who were racing as para-athletes in triathlons, playing wheelchair basketball or completing in marathons. *With such an athletic background, why would this guy sit around and do nothing?*

Jerry's thoughts were disrupted when his new paralegal, Debbie, walked into his office, carrying a pile of documents. She was wearing a short black skirt and a sheer teal blouse, revealing a black tank top and abundant cleavage underneath. Usually, he didn't mind his female employees dressing more like streetwalkers than legal professionals, but it bothered him today. He barely knew her and felt like he should be buying her a drink, rather than discussing cases.

"New assignments?" Jerry said, trying to look at her face and not her bust-line.

"How did you know?" Debbie said, leaning over to lay the document on his desk.

"A lucky guess." He maintained eye contact.

"I hope you're busy enough," Debbie said, holding his gaze.

"Absolutely. Is there anything else?" Jerry said, turning to his computer.

"Oh, I almost forgot—an attorney called for you," Debbie said, fumbling with a pink message slip. "Her name is written here. Zana West. She wants you to call her."

"I think this is important," Jerry said, grabbing the paper. "Could you please close the door behind you?"

"Will do." She set the rest of the files down on his desk and left the room.

Jerry felt an unfamiliar flutter in his stomach when he saw "Zana West" written on the pink slip. He immediately picked up his phone to call back, but he got her voicemail.

"Hmmmm, hi, Zana. It's me. I mean it's Jerry…Hirano? Uh, can you call me? Uhm, it's about the Jorgan— Oh, uh, the Brad Jordan case. Okay. Just call me." Jerry dropped the phone into the receiver cradle and sighed, shaking his head. He then picked up his phone again.

"Debbie," Jerry said into his phone, clicking the intercom button. "Could you please bring me some chicken Pho from the Vietnamese restaurant on the corner? I need to eat lunch in my office so I can stay by the phone."

"I can give her your cell phone number if she calls back," Debbie said.

"That's okay, lunch please?" Jerry said, feeling his face flush. This was the first time he could remember waiting by the phone for a woman to call.

After eating his Pho at his desk, he didn't feel like working anymore. *My LADD must be kicking in,* he thought. For the next hour, he read martial arts magazines and a few articles about himself in *Honolulu Magazine* and *People*.

Then the phone rang, startling him out of his concentration. "Hello," Jerry picked up the phone after the first ring when he saw it was Zana's office on the caller I.D.

"Hi Jerry, this is Zana West. Thanks for returning my call," she said.

"Hi Zana," Jerry said with a smile.

"You said you'd like to work together on the Jordan case," Zana said. "Well, I was wondering if we could share our investigation findings."

"What a great idea," Jerry said, excited at the thought of seeing her again. "Do you have anything interesting yet?"

"I'm sorry, I'm having trouble hearing you. I think someone is playing a computer game in the next office or something."

"I asked about your investigation."

"Yes. I've got some news. When can we meet to discuss it?" Zana said. "It's a tad noisy here."

"Dinner tonight?" Jerry said. He was expected on the set to re-shoot a scene, but he was almost certain the director would give him the night off if he promised to come in first thing in the morning.

"I could do that. Where would you like to meet?"

"Where do you live?" Jerry asked, excited to see this exquisite woman's home base.

"Kahala."

"I'll pick you up. Would seven o'clock work for you?" Jerry said, his hands shaking. He was so used to accepting invitations from women for dinner, it felt weird to be the initiator.

Zana said yes.

Jerry beamed as he passed Debbie on his way out, heading home early to shower and shave.

"Looks like you've got a date," Debbie said.

"Just a meeting," Jerry said, trying to suppress his smile. But hopefully, it would lead to something more.

Chapter 16

@Zlaw A #Ferrari driver is by definition sexy.

Zana watched the clock tick slowly waiting for her evening with Jerry. It felt like a date because he was picking her up at home, but mostly, because of her own wishful thinking. Jerry could have invited her to his office to discuss the case, but instead he suggested dinner. True, they both had to eat, but if this wasn't a date, what was it?

She had rushed to the mall after work and bought some cute strappy black wedge sandals, resisting the temptation to buy stilettos. The thought of falling off of them steered her to the more sensible purchase. She didn't mind towering over Jerry, having seen photos of him arm in arm with skyscraper-tall models.

Zana knew she was dressed a little over the top for a "work" meeting, but decided to make the most of this opportunity. There might not be another. She was wearing her hair loose and had taken the trouble to curl the ends, even though she knew it would be stick straight by the time their appetizers arrived. She had attempted to create a smoky eye look using gray eyeliner and eye shadow with instruction from a Youtube.com tutorial. But that had made her look like a domestic abuse victim and so she reverted to her day look of mascara and a hint of gray shadow. Her skirt was short and her V-neck lace T-shirt plunged low enough that if she had cleavage, it would have shown.

Jerry's movie star looks took Zana's breath away the moment she answered the door. She wanted to run her hands through his thick, black hair. His almond-shaped eyes made him look exotic, inviting questions of ethnicity. He had changed out of his business attire too, and was wearing a black T-shirt and tight gray jeans that accentuated his physique.

"Hey, Jerry," she said, trying to sound casual. She hoped he couldn't see the sweat pooling under her arms or hear the catch in her throat from her heart racing so fast.

"Howzit Zana?" Jerry asked, giving her a Hawaiian style kiss on the cheek, causing her to blush.

"Can I get you a drink before we leave?"

"Sure, Counselor," Jerry said.

She felt tingly all over hearing him call her "counselor." She was still getting used to being an attorney and hearing the word in reference to her career. She had learned Jerry was fourteen years older than she was by reading about him online, but she found him so much more attractive than guys her age. He stood tall with his shoulders back, maintained eye contact when most people would look away, and he always found something to compliment in everyone. He even smelled like a grown-up, wearing what she thought was Polo Cologne.

While they sipped their wine, she showed Jerry around the house Kelly had tastefully decorated. Zana was relieved Andrew and Kelly were still at work so she could spend time with him alone. If Andrew were there, he would surely blurt out something embarrassing about her. He'd tell Jerry he had never seen her go out to dinner with a man before or had only seen her wear athletic clothes outside of the office. He would be telling the truth, but Zana would much rather give Jerry the impression she was more sophisticated—more like the women she saw him pose next to on magazine covers.

And when Zana saw Jerry's red Ferrari, she was even more convinced he was out of her league. If this was the only time she ever had dinner with Jerry Hirano, at least she could say she had ridden in his Ferrari, too.

She was surprised when he opened the car door for her and continued this chivalrous practice with every door they encountered that evening.

The short ride to a new restaurant on Waialae Avenue didn't give Zana much time to experience the joy of her first Ferrari ride with their highest speed reaching 25 mph. But that was okay with her. The restaurant was almost empty, so they made themselves comfortable at a square corner table. Instead of sitting across from her, Jerry sat next to her, as if he was her boyfriend.

"Have you been here before?" Zana asked.

"It just opened. I know the owner, Steve. He was an extra on my T.V. show," Jerry said. "I have a little cable show—'Fighting in Paradise'— have you heard of it?"

"Oh, yes. I've watched it a few times," Zana lied. "It's very entertaining." She was still having trouble looking him in the eye. She fiddled with her napkin and wondered if Jerry could see her hands shake.

"I'm glad you enjoyed it. It's a lot of fun," he said.

"What looks good?" Zana grabbed the menu a little too quickly. She wondered if she should offer to split the check. Isn't that what colleagues did at business dinners?

"So, what do you think about going out with me tonight?" Jerry asked as if he was reading her mind.

"I think it's a good idea. I have some interesting things to tell you about my investigation," Zana stammered, still not knowing how to act around him.

"You seem a little uncomfortable."

"Oh, no, I'm fine," Zana said, ripping a paper napkin apart in her hands under the table.

"We're just having dinner. Relax."

Zana felt her face flush. She studied the menu intently, feeling Jerry's eyes on her.

"Are you okay with Steve making recommendations for our dinner?" Jerry said.

"That's fine," she said, putting the menu down. "Let me tell you about what we discovered in our investigation." She started to relax when she decided to think of him as just another attorney instead of a T.V. star.

"Shhhhhh," Jerry motioned for her to look at the couple who had just arrived and sat down at a table across the room.

"That's Pierce Brosnan," Zana whispered.

"No, that's Rip Mansfield," Jerry corrected her.

"Oh, shit!" Zana said, slapping her hand over her mouth. "Excuse my French."

"That's not French, but you're excused. My sentiments exactly," Jerry whispered.

"I guess we won't be talking about the case."

"At least not here. So, let's enjoy our dinner and get to know each other."

"Sounds good," Zana said, finally meeting Jerry's eyes and smiling.

"Would you like some wine?" Jerry produced a bottle from a paper bag he had brought with him.

"Sure," Zana said, laughing. "Do you always carry a bottle in a bag like a wino?"

"Yes, I do." Jerry laughed with her, pouring wine into the empty wine glasses on the table. "The restaurant doesn't have a liquor license yet and so the State of Hawaii allows me to be my own sommelier."

"You're a man of many talents." Zana raised her glass to him.

"You seem like you have a few," Jerry said.

"Good evening," a tall man wearing an Aloha shirt and navy slacks said as he approached the table. "I see you have drinks already."

"Hey, Steve," Jerry said. "This is Zana—she's an attorney working on a case with me."

"Hi," Zana said, disappointed about his introduction, though she realized she shouldn't be.

"If all lady lawyers are this hot, I want your job, Jerry," Steve said.

Jerry winked at Zana. "What's good tonight?"

"We have fresh Opakapaka and a delightful seared ahi appetizer," Steve said.

"I hope you like fresh fish," Jerry said.

"Absolutely," Zana said. "It's one of the best things about living in Hawaii."

"Surprise us," Jerry said, gathering their menus and handing them to Steve.

"He seems like a nice guy," Zana said after Steve left the table.

Jerry nodded. "He is. What were we talking about?"

"Your many talents."

"Not nearly enough," Jerry said. "Aren't you a cyclist? I saw a racing bike in your office."

"I'm a triathlete."

"Ah. That explains your fit body. How did you get involved in that?"

Zana shrugged. "When I was a kid, my parents were endurance athletes. My dad competed in the Kona Ironman World Championship," Zana said. "They got me involved with swimming, biking and running at a young age."

"Do your parents live in the islands?"

"No. My mom had a heart attack during a marathon when I was young. My dad pretty much fell apart after she died. He got into drugs. I haven't seen him since I was a teenager," Zana said, surprised at herself for telling him this. She hadn't told anyone else in Hawaii about her past. Why now? And why Jerry?

"Wow, you've had it rough," Jerry said. He reached over and put his hand on her shoulder.

"It was, but I made it out okay. I won an emancipation lawsuit when I was sixteen. I've lived on my own ever since then."

"It's remarkable you were able to become an attorney."

"I was lucky. I couldn't have done it without some great mentors," Zana said, hoping they could shift to a different subject. "So, how 'bout you— are your parents living here?"

"Yes. You might have heard of my mom, Malia Michaels. She sings contemporary Hawaiian music," Jerry said. "She's also super popular in Japan and the Philippines."

"Yeah, I've heard her on the radio. I love her song 'Rainbows'," Zana said. "And your father?"

"Dad's my mom's biggest fan. He's her manager," Jerry said. "We live in an old house in Manoa, near the University."

"You live with your parents?" Zana said, trying not to laugh. The hot T.V. star she was so nervous about meeting still lives with his parents! She could hardly believe it.

"Yeah. That's between you and I. It's not something I advertise," Jerry said, fidgeting with his wine glass.

"I don't get it. How do you still live with your parents? Didn't you go away to law school and college?" Zana asked.

Jerry shrugged. "I went to UH for both. It's walking distance from the house," he said. "I live in a cottage on my parent's property, near the main house. It has two bedrooms, 2 baths, a kitchen and living room. So in a lot of ways, it's like having my own house, but I'm still nearby if they need help with something. When they're traveling, I take care of their dog."

"Well, that's convenient," Zana said, seeing him less as a superstar and more as a devoted son. Maybe he wasn't out of her league after all.

She was much more relaxed during dinner, partly because of the wine and partly because he didn't seem quite so intimidating when she thought of him living in a cottage within voice range of his mom and dad. She wondered if he was more down-to-earth than he appeared. She wished she was still part of a family, but hoped to someday start her own.

As they enjoyed their fish dinner, they talked about their childhoods. He told her stories about life in Hawaii and learning hula and karate with his younger sister, Jennifer. And Zana told Jerry stories about bouncing between foster homes while trying to keep her grades up and compete in the occasional triathlon. Even though she graduated from high school in 2002 and he in 1988, they laughed as they shared some favorite songs and movies—oldies to her, introduced to her by her mother when she was a child.

After dinner, as they were sipping coffee, Rip Mansfield approached their table, standing over them. "You're an asshole, Hirano," Rip sneered.

"The Supreme Court apparently didn't think so," Jerry said, flashing a genuine smile.

"Next time you won't be so lucky," Rip said, walking away.

Zana was relieved he hadn't looked her way. She didn't want Mansfield to remember he saw her and Jerry together.

"He's a sore loser," Jerry said. "You probably heard about the Supreme Court opinion. I kicked his ass at trial—oh, excuse *my* French," Jerry put his hand over his mouth dramatically.

Zana laughed out loud. "Apparently, he deserved it."

Jerry's eyes lit up. "Let's destroy him in our case."

"Yes. Let's."

The waiter put the check down next to Jerry, who quickly placed his Platinum American Express on it. Zana was impressed with the ease at which he took control of Mansfield and the check. Maybe living with his parents wasn't what she thought. It certainly took guts. Maybe, Jerry *was* husband material.

Chapter 17

@Zlaw Mean #attorneys suck.

When Zana emerged from the parking garage, she squinted, then rummaged around in her knock-off Coach bag for her sunglasses. Her iPhone said 7:26 a.m. but it felt much later to her. The elevator was usually empty when she arrived before dawn, but now she endured 27 floors of stopping as workers stepped off a few at a time, eventually giving her some elbow room. Ordinarily, there would be no eyebrows raised about such a respectable work arrival time, but Frank, sitting in her guest chair, tapped his wristwatch when Zana strolled through her office door.

"Don't get comfortable. I need you to cover for me at a status conference with Judge Huang. Libby will prep you on your way to court," Frank said, getting out of the chair.

"Okay," Zana nodded, stunned that the only day she arrived after seven was the first time she was entrusted to go to court by herself.

"Now, hurry along. I have a deposition to get to," Frank said.

Zana grabbed the suit jacket hanging on the back of her door before joining Libby for the twenty-minute walk to court.

"This construction case has 16 parties, many of them are represented by different attorneys," Libby said as they walked out the door to the building. "Frank's printed calendar is in the file."

"Do I need to say anything?" Zana asked.

"Just tell the judge you're filling in for Frank. Speak up if there's a conflict in his calendar," Libby said, keeping up with Zana. "Any more questions?"

"No. Thanks, Libby."

After Libby left to walk back to the office, Zana quickened her pace. *Why had she shown up late for work on the one day Frank needed her?* Zana's mind was swirling with the events of the last 24 hours. If she hadn't been out with Jerry and unable to sleep with sexy thoughts of him running through her mind all night, she would have been in her office working when Frank appeared this morning. Nothing good could come of her irrational dreams of romance with Jerry. He wasn't a one-woman guy and she had no interest in having her heart broken. It was time to focus on work.

Leaving early yesterday and arriving late today might not lead to a pink slip just yet, but keeping up such slothful habits would surely get her fired. Frank had dumped Lori to make room for Lucas. There was no reason why he wouldn't give her the boot for a minor infraction.

When Zana arrived at the courtroom, the other lawyers were already present—all men, most of them wearing Aloha shirts and slacks, because it was an informal status conference rather than a hearing.

Zana saw one attorney she recognized—Rip Mansfield.

Mansfield was seated at the counsel table, talking to a tall man standing over him. The men turned to look at Zana the instant she walked in.

She smiled and walked past those sitting on the benches open to the public and through the low swinging doors beyond the bar where only attorneys were allowed. She squeezed in next to a few men sitting on a bench and consulted her file, while the others turned back to their conversations with one another.

"May I have your name please?" the clerk asked as he approached Zana with a clipboard.

"Zana West, here for Frank Gravelle. We represent Nakashima & Sons Welding," Zana said as the clerk wrote down her name.

Zana noticed Mansfield had immediately turned to look at her after she said her name.

"Did you just start working for Frank?" a man with a dark weathered face asked her.

"A few months ago, yes," Zana said, looking up from her file.

"I'm Wayne Kahanamoku. Frank and I have known each other for years," he said.

"It's nice meeting you. What firm are you with?" Zana asked, just as Judge Huang walked into the room, wearing a shirt and tie rather than his black robe.

"Good morning, counsel," the judge said.

As the attention turned to Judge Huang, Zana saw from the corner of her eye that Mansfield was staring at her. His gaze moved from her short-heeled navy pumps up her long legs to her navy skirt and to her beige suit jacket. Zana tried to concentrate on what the Judge was saying about using a discovery master and mediation, but felt uncomfortable under Mansfield's stare.

She turned her head and stared back. She moved her eyes from his Italian leather shoes, up his black creased pants to his muted black Aloha shirt to his chiseled face framed with thick, dark hair flecked with gray. She looked straight into his blue eyes, widened with surprise.

Mansfield winked and mouthed a word.

Zana wasn't sure what he had said, but thought it might have been "whore". Disgusted and offended, she turned away and re-focused, remembering to take notes for her report to Frank.

When the conference was over, Zana walked out of the courtroom at race-walker pace in order to avoid Mansfield. She ducked into the ladies room well ahead of the men she heard talking behind her. She took her time washing her hands and drying them thoroughly, hoping to walk back to the office alone. The hall had cleared out while she was in the bathroom, and was empty now as she waited for the elevator doors to open.

"You must be tired after your romp with Jerry Hirano last night," Mansfield said, appearing next to her.

"It's none of your concern, but Mr. Hirano and I had a business meeting last night," Zana said, keeping her eyes on the closed elevator doors.

"Do you always wear slutty dresses and cum-fuck-me shoes for business meetings?" Rip said, standing only inches from her.

Zana kept her cool. "What were you doing looking at my outfit?"

"It's hard not to notice a whore. How much did Hirano pay for you?" Mansfield asked in a low voice, stepping into the empty elevator.

"You go ahead. I'll wait for the next one," Zana said.

"Suit yourself, you sexy thing. I wouldn't mind getting you alone—I'm hungry," Mansfield said, holding the elevator door open. He then licked his lips as the elevator door closed.

Zana swallowed hard and turned away. She stepped back into the ladies room, scrubbing her hands again with soap and water. *Had she done something to elicit Mansfield's vulgarity? Should she tell someone?* She knew that if she told any of the other male attorneys, they would tell her to shrug it off. "That's Mansfield. If you can't stand the heat, get out of the kitchen," they would say. Frank would fire her if she couldn't handle "a little ribbing" from opposing counsel. And Zana couldn't tell Andrew about this incident. He was upset enough about Mansfield and there was nothing he could do to help anyway. She'd just have to suck it up.

When she heard someone coming into the restroom, Zana stepped into a stall not wanting anyone to see the tears welling in her eyes or her flushed cheeks. She sat down on the toilet seat lid, slumping down, pulling her legs up and hugging her shaking body with her arms. Zana recognized her feelings, which she thought had finally healed after years of counseling.

She thought of her past, still lurking in her mind. Her father had been arrested for selling heroin a few years after her mother died. Her first foster family appeared from the outside to be respectable and middle class. She had her own room and was starting to feel comfortable attending a new high school and getting to know the family. But one night, their son, Ted, who was home from college, walked into her room naked and used the same tone and some of the same words Mansfield had said to her before he had raped her. Reliving that awful night all over, the tears spilled down her face.

She had run away after her attacker's parents didn't believe her and her social worker refused to reassign her to a new home. She was painted by authorities as a liar until she met Felicity Holmes, a legal aid attorney, who helped her become an emancipated minor and directed her to social programs and counseling. Felicity had been Zana's role model and mentor, urging her to graduate from high school, college and then ultimately law school.

Hearing the person leave, she got up and left the stall. Then, Zana washed her face, composing herself before walking back to the office. She bit her lip, knowing that as a new attorney, she held no power. She had no recourse against wealthy Mansfield who would deny any allegations of impropriety. Plus, there were no witnesses.

As she stood before the elevator, she again felt tears form in her eyes and then remembered her vow that Mansfield would never make her cry like he had to so many other women and probably men before her. She closed her eyes for a few seconds. He was trying to intimidate her with words. As she tried to convince herself everything would be okay, she saw a group of men walking towards her and pressed the elevator button.

"Hey Zana," Kim McCall said, following her into the elevator.

"What are you up to?" Zana asked, startled by his friendly voice.

"I had a hearing on a motion. Are you heading back to the office?" Kim asked.

"Yeah, are you?"

"After I file an answer that's due today. I don't trust having it done by a messenger at the last minute," Kim said. "Do you have a moment to wait for me and we can walk together?"

"Sure, sounds good," Zana said. She was relieved she wouldn't have to walk back alone.

"Why don't you have a seat here," Kim said, motioning to a row of chairs outside the document filing area. "I'll be right back."

After Zana sat down, she saw three male attorneys walking purposefully towards the elevator. One of them was Jerry Hirano. They were wearing suits and ties and carrying briefcases, obviously headed upstairs for court. Zana admired the way Jerry moved, his body fit from martial arts training and his movements fluid like a cat's. She could imagine that if a fight broke out, Jerry would quickly destroy his opponents as she had seen him do so many times on "Fighting in Paradise". She wished she could tell him about how Mansfield had treated her this morning. She pictured how the fight between them would go down, with Jerry knocking Mansfield out with a powerful punch or roundhouse kick.

Before Jerry stepped into the open elevator, he turned and grinned. This caught Zana by surprise. She smiled back and wished he had been alone and not hurrying up to court. She would've liked to hear his soothing voice.

"Okay, all done," Kim said beside her. "Sorry to keep you waiting."

"No problem," Zana said in a shaky voice. She stood up on wobbly legs.

"Are you okay?" he asked.

"I'm fine," Zana said, hoping Kim hadn't noticed how upset she was.

"I think the reason they call it the *practice* of law is because the learning curve is so steep even seasoned attorneys never get the hang of it," Kim said as they walked down the courthouse steps.

"Makes sense," Zana said, putting on her sunglasses to shield her eyes from the morning sun. She stopped to take off her jacket.

"I've been practicing law for three years now and it's still stressful."

"What do you find stressful?"

"Mistakes. We all make them, and trying to resolve them without getting into trouble with partners and clients keeps me awake at night," Kim said as they walked across a busy intersection.

"What about dealing with other attorneys? Do you find it stressful?" Zana asked, hoping Kim wouldn't ask her directly about who was giving her stress.

"Generally, the attorneys here are civil, but I always dread getting cases against the few jerk attorneys," Kim said.

"What do you do when you encounter a 'jerk'?"

"I try to be nice to him, which sometimes turns him around. I've been surprised by guys who were in fighting mode when we first met and became cooperative in response to my being friendly," Kim explained.

"What about someone who is legendarily horrible?"

"Like Rip Mansfield?"

"Yeah, I've heard he's an ass."

Kim laughed, lightening the mood. "Well, he's unredeemable. No one can penetrate that guy."

"So how do *you* handle him?"

"Just survive," Kim said. "The only way to handle Mansfucker is to not let him get under your skin. Survive. Don't try to conquer. Why all the questions?"

"No reason." Zana gulped. She could feel her eyes welling with tears under her sunglasses.

"Zana, you'll get through this first year of law practice. It's not easy for any of us, but we all make it," Kim said, looking at her as they walked.

"I'm not so sure," Zana said softly.

Chapter 18

@Zlaw I want to be a #private-eye when I grow up, if that should ever happen.

Under the spray of the tiny showerhead, Zana washed the chlorine out of her hair with special protective shampoo. After her stressful morning with Mansfield, she had popped over to the YMCA for a quick one-mile swim. Moving in the weightless water felt therapeutic, and combined with Kim's wisdom, allowed her to relax. Rather than focus on Mansfield, Zana thought about Jerry's smile and imagined having a real dinner date with him.

"My ohana, my love," a woman was belting out a song from an adjacent shower stall.

Zana rolled her eyes.

"My keiki, my love."

Shut Up! Zana thought to herself. *Can't that woman ever stop singing?*

"Washing over me so tenderly… Hmmmm."

Oh My God! Zana hurriedly finished her shower. She had hoped to shift her focus from Jerry to the triathlon case and work out some issues in her mind while showering. Not today apparently.

"So tender is your love."

"I can't hear myself think," Zana said out loud. She wrapped a towel around her body and passed the woman who was also leaving her shower stall. She gave her stink eye, but the woman kept singing to herself.

Zana dried off and dressed quickly, disappointed she couldn't do some serious shower-thinking before heading back to work. She didn't bother drying her hair, but rather, put it in a ponytail. The goggle marks around her eyes wouldn't be noticed, since she planned to spend the afternoon at her desk. She could always use the mirror behind her office door to apply more makeup or flat iron her hair if an unexpected meeting arose, which was highly unlikely.

After she escaped the annoying woman and slid into her car, she cranked up the air conditioner and unwrapped a Kind Bar. She leaned back in her leather seat and pondered the documents Mansfield produced the day before in response to their request for production. There were a few years of tax records, the police and incident reports, photographs of the plaintiff and recorded statements, and some medical records.

What bothered Zana the most was a photograph of a scar on Brad Jordan's hip. She noticed the area of skin around the scar was tan and the hip and leg looked more like a triathlete's than a paraplegic's.

The winter before her mother died, Zana broke her leg skiing. After only a few weeks in a cast, her leg was atrophied and took months of rehab before it started to return to its usual muscular shape. Something just felt wrong about Brad.

Back at her desk, Zana googled "Brad Jordan." The results were the same as her last search. He was a professional triathlete with pages of references of race results, the Olympic trials, and the accident. Zana clicked on each reference, noting that all of the races were before the accident.

On a whim, she googled "Bradley Jordan." There was an attorney, a vice president of a company, a deceased person and quite a number of others with the name "Bradley Jordan." She then typed in "Bradley Jordan triathlon."

This time, the Plaintiff's race results from the late 1990s and early 2000s came up. When she compared the data with what she saw when she googled "Brad Jordan," she discovered the plaintiff used the name "Bradley" when he first started competing, but raced under the name "Brad" when he became a pro.

Zana went back to her googled results for "Bradley Jordan" and began adding the data to an Excel chart she had prepared several weeks ago. She finished the 1990s and then added six races he had competed in during the early 2000s. She then x'd out of the Excel spreadsheet, assuming she was finished.

She pressed "next" three or four more times on her Google search, not seeing anything pertaining to the plaintiff, but then spotted an entry about a Bradley Jordan who had competed in the Antler Lake Triathlon in Minnesota about fourteen months after the accident. He came in 4th place in his age group, with a total of seven competitors. Using the plaintiff's birthday, she calculated that the Bradley Jordan who had raced at Antler Lake was in the same age group as the plaintiff. She wondered if the athlete happened to coincidentally have the same name, which was possible.

She clicked onto the race website to the photographs. The final results listed about 200 competitors and Bradley Jordan's bib number was 57. She studied the pictures, but didn't see any athletes with that number.

Zana phoned investigator Rick, who picked up after the first ring. She explained what she was working on and directed him to the website.

"I wonder if anyone who competed in the race would be able to I.D. him," Rick said.

"I doubt it. It's been almost a year," Zana said.

"What's this on the results?"

"What are you looking at?" Zana asked, studying her computer screen.

"There's a notation of 2 minutes after his finishing time."

"A penalty, I think."

"You mean a penalty was imposed on him for doing something wrong?"

"Yeah. This athlete must have violated the rules." Zana squinted at the data.

"What rule?"

"It's impossible to determine from these results." She scrolled down to see if there was any explanation, but she didn't see any.

"How do we get that information?" Rick asked.

"We could subpoena the timing company or the race director," Zana said. "Maybe there was a report about penalties."

"Maybe the official who issued the penalty remembers this guy."

"Very doubtful," Zana said. "I'm sure the officials wouldn't remember a random penalty from a year ago."

"It looks like this guy would have placed second in his age group if he hadn't gotten the penalty," Rick said.

"That's interesting. I'll bet Bradley Jordan was pissed." Zana leaned back in her chair.

"Do you really think if the Bradley Jordan in the race was the plaintiff he would have gotten mad? He's won so many races. Why would he care about some little race in Nowheresville, Minnesota?"

"He probably has a big ego," Zana said. "I have an idea. I'll put you on hold and conference you in. Don't say anything. Just a second." Zana clicked the hold button. She found the race director's name and phone number on the website, then tapped a few numbers to disable caller I.D. before inputting the digits.

"Hello, is this Pete Hirsch?" Zana pressed the conference button, bringing Rick on the line to listen in.

"Yes."

"Hi, my name is Brenda Layton. My boss is thinking about sponsoring a triathlon and wanted me to ask you some questions about your race," Zana said in a fake Minnesota accent.

"Oh, that would be terrific," Pete said. "What would you like to know?"

"Is your race an American Triathlon Association certified race?"

"Yes, it is," the man responded.

"Do you use officials?" Zana asked.

"Yes."

"My boss only wants to sponsor certified and officiated races so they're fair and safe," Zana said.

"Oh, well that makes sense," Pete said.

"My boss wants me to talk to a few athletes and officials who participated in the race last year to ask their opinions about whether it was a well-organized race. If it is, he'll probably be interested in talking to you further. Can you give me their contact information?"

"Unfortunately, I don't feel comfortable giving you phone numbers," Pete said.

"Sure, I understand. Could you tell me the officials' names? We really want to give you sponsorship money if they liked the race."

"Last year, we only had one official," Pete said. "No, we actually had two, come to think of it. The second official was brand new. It was his first race."

"So, do you remember who they were?" Zana crossed her fingers.

"Grady Jones—he's been our head official since the race started. I'm sure he'll have great things to say about it. That new official, he had an unusual name, but I can't think of it right now."

"Can you text me if you remember it? I can give you my number."

"Hmmm. I remember now—Devere was his first name. He had to spell it for me so I could put him on our volunteer list."

"Do you remember his last name?" Zana asked, already feeling like she hit the jackpot.

"Levinson. His name is Devere Levinson. I think he's still working in Hibbing as a personal trainer. I could ask around," Pete said. "How much money is your boss thinking about?"

"We'll be getting back with you." Forgetting her Minnesota accent, she said, "Mahalo."

"Excuse me?"

"Uh. Thank you. I said, thank you," she covered.

"No—thank you. Tell your boss we really appreciate this," Pete said.

"We will. I mean, I will. Good afternoon." Zana clicked the line to hang up with Pete and then giggled.

"With just a little practice, you could be an investigator, but I wouldn't quit your day job," Rick said.

"Yeah, I almost blew it with the mahalo. Jeez. I guess I'm assimilating into Hawaii culture faster than I thought I would," Zana said.

"No problem. You recovered well. Way to think on your feet, counselor."

"Poor guy, he thinks he's got a sponsor on the hook," Zana said, her voice cracking. She wiped beads of sweat from her forehead with the back of her hand.

"He'll survive. Okay, my turn now," Rick said.

Zana heard the computer keys clicking through the line.

"I've found Devere Levinson's phone number. Hold on, Zana."

"Hello," said a male voice.

"Hi, is this Devere Levinson?" Rick asked.

"Yeah."

"I want to ask you about a triathlon you may have officiated last year," Rick said.

"You must want to talk with my son. Dev! Dev! There's someone on the phone for you," the man yelled. "Just a minute."

"Hello," another male voice said after a long pause.

"Are you Devere Levinson?" Rick asked.

"I am. Who is this?"

"My name is Ron. I've been asked to follow up on penalties in a triathlon. I understand you officiated a race last year. The Antler Lake Triathlon?"

"Call me Dev. My dad is Devere. Yeah, I remember that one," Dev said. "What do you want to know?"

"How many penalties did you give out to the athletes?"

"How would I remember that?" Dev said. Zana could hear indignation in his voice.

"Do you remember giving a penalty to an athlete named Bradley Jordan?"

"No."

"Do you keep records of your penalties?"

"I turn my penalties over to the head ref after the race is over."

"Do you remember anything about that particular triathlon?" Rick said.

"Oh, yeah. It was the first triathlon I officiated," he said.

"Is there anything you remember about the race or penalties you issued?"

"Yeah, this guy. He got pissed off because I gave him a penalty. He was yelling at me. He said he would have won if I hadn't given him a penalty," Dev said.

"Do you remember what age group or how old the guy was?" Rick said.

"Yeah, in his twenties…maybe twenty-five or so. He was a jerk."

"Do you remember what his name is?"

"No," Dev said.

"Do you remember his race number?"

"No."

"What did he say to you, Dev?"

"That I remember. He said, 'You fucking asshole! Do you know who I am?' Something like that."

"Do you have any idea why he asked you if you knew who he was?" Rick said.

"I think he might have been some kind of big shot, but I don't really know. It was my first officiating gig. I really don't know much about the sport. I was asked to go through the certification program, because they needed another official for the race," Dev said. "I'm a personal trainer."

"Dev, if I email you a picture of a triathlete, would you be able to tell me if he's the guy you gave the penalty to?" Rick asked.

"Probably. The guy was in my face. I thought he was going to take a swing at me," Dev said.

"Will you give me your email address?"

"Sure, it's devlev@gmail.com."

"I'll email the picture in a few minutes. If it's the same guy who was at the race, email me back and say, yes. If it's not the same guy, email back and say, no. Do you understand?" Rick confirmed as Zana listened on the other line.

"Yes, I understand. I'll fire up my laptop right now, but it's getting pretty late here. I've got work in the morning," Dev said.

"Yes, right away. Thanks so much for your help, Dev," Rick said. "I appreciate it."

After they hung up, Zana received a blind copy of Rick's email attaching a photograph of Brad Jordan wearing triathlon bike gear. She stared at her computer, waiting for an email from Rick. She then started working on another project until she heard a "click".

The email was from Rick. Dev's answer was "Yes."

Chapter 19

@Zlaw I'm convinced #evil people all have an evil laugh so they can be easily identified.

Heather scowled and massaged her temples. She had finished her black coffee, read the morning paper, and checked her phone a dozen times for a text or email from Megan. Starbucks was so crowded the line of people waiting to order snaked alongside her table. A young man with Polynesian tattoos covering his arms, with pants riding so low on his hips she could see most of his floral print boxer shorts, stood so close they were almost touching.

She moved her chair against the wall to avoid being part of a candid cell phone picture, if his pants fell down as she predicted.

She scanned the que for celebrities who frequented the coffee shop, being the closest to the finest Waikiki resorts. On occasion, she'd spot an A-list actor in a ball cap and dark glasses, though the disguises never fooled her.

Ordinarily, she didn't mind waiting for her twin if she had something to fill her time, but this morning the only entertainment was the guy whose pants had inched to his knees. Time to start her video.

While filming, Heather stuck her foot out to touch the guy's calf, startling him. She got the footage she had hoped for. His pants fell to the floor.

As she posted the video on her Youtube channel, she felt a tap on her shoulder. It was Megan.

"You're late," Heather said.

"Sorry, we rode 50 miles this morning. One of the guys had a flat tire and slowed us up," Megan said. "Just a second, I'm going to order coffee. I'll get you a refill."

"The line's too long," Heather said. "I'll order your drink on my app."

"I've got it." Megan punched in her order on her phone.

Heather watched her twin walk to the counter to pick up the coffees. Megan was her carbon copy with the same golden blonde, shoulder length hair parted slightly on the side, blue eyes and heart-shaped face. The best way to distinguish them from each other was by their clothes and body types. Megan had more defined muscles from her constant training and wore athletic gear almost exclusively. Heather usually dressed in suits and looked thin even with the 20 pounds added by television cameras.

"This place is hopping today," Megan said, placing their coffees on the table along with a croissant and a packet of dried mangoes.

"I can't believe you're eating that fatty thing," Heather said, frowning.

"I've already burned it off." Megan sat and took a bite.

"I guess 50 miles earned you some carbs. I wish I had time to do a long workout."

"Speaking of workouts, guess who I ran into at the gym yesterday?" Megan asked.

"Who?"

"Jessica Pang."

"That bitch. I wanted to kill her." Heather leaned towards Megan. She felt her stomach tightening in knots, hearing the woman's name for the first time in over a year. After walking out on Heather, Brad had a brief affair with Jessica after he moved to Hawaii, even though he now claimed it didn't mean anything.

"She's pregnant," Megan confirmed. "She only knew the guy for two weeks and he totally blew her off."

"She told you that?"

"Yeah. We were on spinning bikes next to each other and we both forgot to bring headphones," Megan said. "Do you know what happened to her and Brad?"

"No." Heather fiddled with her paper coffee cup.

"Come on—I know when you're covering something up."

"Okay. It's hard to hide anything from you," Heather said. "I emailed her."

"You emailed Jessica? Are you serious?" Megan's eyes widened. "What did you say?"

"Something about Brad and I still being together. It was public knowledge that her ex-husband was having an affair during their marriage, and so I called Brad a cheater. It worked, because the bitch dumped him," Heather said in a low voice.

"Are you kidding? How did you know they were dating?" Megan put her coffee cup down hard on the table, almost spilling it.

"I have my sources." Heather leaned back and took a sip of coffee.

"Did you hire an investigator or something?"

"Well, sort of. Brad and I belong together. He was using her."

"You don't know that. Sometimes, I can't believe we're related." Megan grimaced.

"You should talk," Heather said. "I'm not the one who swore revenge on the guy who was two-timing you. *You're* the evil twin."

"No—you're far more evil than me, Heather," Megan said. "I don't know what you're up to, but I have serious questions about your side business."

Heather shrugged. "I'm just doing it to make a little extra money."

"Remember what you did when we were kids to make extra cash?"

"You mean, my babysitting jobs?" Heather rummaged in her purse for a piece of gum. She could usually trust Megan with her secrets—they had always been partners in crime, but now she wondered.

"You know what I'm talking about. Taking the neighbor's pets and collecting the reward money," Megan whispered.

"You remember that?" Heather continued to rummage through her purse, not allowing her twin to see she was surprised. She had hoped everyone in her family had forgotten her childhood shenanigans.

"Yeah. I can't believe you got away with it."

"Mom and Dad still think I'm a perfect angel," Heather said in the sweet tone she reserved for their parents. She put down her purse and looked back at her sister.

"If they only knew. You're definitely the more evil twin." Megan laughed.

"I'll take that as a compliment," Heather said. They had always kept each other's secrets. Usually, they were both behaving badly. Now, she was asking her twin to keep her eating disorder and her tabloid business a secret, and for once, Megan wasn't trying to cover anything up. "You're not going to tell them, are you?"

"Of course not." Megan sighed, and touched her twin's hand. "Be careful."

"Is Jessica keeping the baby?" Heather asked, bringing the conversation back to Brad's ex.

"She didn't say anything about *not* keeping it."

"If you were her, would you?" Heather leaned forward.

"I'm not sure," Megan said, looking down at her phone. "I wouldn't want to raise a kid without a father."

"No, you wouldn't want to give up triathlons." Heather smirked.

"What about you? What if you get pregnant?" Megan put her phone down and took a last bite of croissant.

Heather shook her head. "There's no chance of that. Brad's paralyzed."

"But are you sure he can't have sex?" Megan whispered.

"He's paralyzed, Megan," Heather spat.

Megan shrugged and wiped her mouth with a napkin.

"Right. Did you really think we were having sex?"

"I hadn't thought about it." Megan looked down at her phone again.

"Do you think he's been jumping out of his wheelchair and into bed with me?" Heather reached over and pulled Megan's phone out of her hand and placed it on the table.

"Keep your voice down," Megan whispered, picking her phone up again. "The thought didn't cross my mind."

"Well, you're just a P.E. teacher, not a doctor." Heather grabbed Megan's phone again.

"Okay, stop right there. Just because you're pissed off doesn't mean you have to attack me."

"Sorry," Heather said. "You know I want to have kids with Brad. I've always dreamed of having a boy and a girl."

"I know. Your perfect life plan." Megan rolled her eyes.

"What's that about?" Heather said loudly.

"Come on. I'm joking," Megan said and stood up to hug her sister. "I've got an appointment with a hot bath."

"Yeah, I've got to go, too. Time for me to check on Brad," Heather said, handing Megan her phone.

Heather was anxious to get to Brad's place. He had been even more depressed lately so she didn't like leaving him alone very long.

When she pulled up to his apartment building, she spotted his SUV with the TRIBAD plates. She remembered being with him when he picked up the car after it had been converted so he could operate it with his hands.

The mechanic had asked, "Hey Brad, you want new plates or what?"

"My legs are shot, what am I going to do with those plates?"

"You'll be racing as a wheelchair athlete soon. You might as well keep them," Heather had said.

Brad exploded with a tirade of expletives at her suggestion. But he kept the plates. When they got home, he drank a half bottle of vodka and passed out in his chair. When he woke up, she had yelled at him about drinking so much and he had responded with a hard slap to her face, then the silent treatment for a week. Since then, he had made an effort to hide his drinking and she pretended not to notice.

She hoped, once the case was settled, he would become one of those inspirational guys racing as a paraplegic triathlete. Then, they would marry and have sperm donor children—a boy and a girl. Everyone would think she was an angel marrying the Olympic hopeful paralyzed in a tragic accident. Heather imagined Brad writing a best-selling motivational book and appearing on talk shows. Their lives would be perfect.

When she opened the door with her key, Brad was watching football. He didn't even look up at her when she kissed him. "Hey, sweetie," Heather said.

"Hi Meg."

"It's Heather," she said, standing between Brad and the T.V. "Your girlfriend. Remember."

"Oh sorry, babe. You said you were doing errands today. I assumed your sister was coming over."

"Does *she* kiss you on the lips?"

"No. Did you kiss me on the lips? I was focusing on the game," Brad said. "Sorry, sweetheart."

"Well, okay, you just seemed disappointed it was me and not Megan,"

Heather sat on the couch next to Brad.

Brad stared at her. "Don't be like that—of course I'm happy you're here. Now, do you mind if I watch the game?"

Heather walked over to the sliding glass door. She flung it open so the cool island breeze would air out the stuffy room. Breathing in the scent of Plumeria flowers growing in the trees below relaxed her. She then retreated to the kitchen, wiping a tear from her cheek with the back of her hand. Was Brad's mistake her fault? She had been so busy with work and her side tabloid job she had been pawning off his care to her twin a lot lately. Even their parents sometimes confused them. She needed to do something creative to shift her focus, otherwise she'd ruminate on Brad's misspeak all day.

Heather logged onto her laptop she'd set on the kitchen table and checked her email. She googled "Jessica Pang images" and thirty-eight pictures of the well-known Hawaii pop artist appeared. She selected the most unflattering picture and copied it, pasting it into an email addressed to Benny Carvalho, a reporter with Hawaiistyle.com. And she wrote:

Hi Benny,

I have some good dirt for you. Jessica Pang is pregnant. She doesn't know who the father is. No need to pay me for this one. It's a freebie. Let me know if you have any questions.

Aloha,
Heather

She closed her laptop and joined Brad on the couch. She snuggled close, put her arms around him and kissed him on the neck. He still didn't seem to notice.

Chapter 20

@Zlaw What would be cuter—my #JimmyChoos or #ManoloBlaniks with a black ski mask?

"Mr. Ho, can I please have your autograph?"

Jerry looked up from his newspaper at a familiar face and laughed.

"Sorry, Jerry, I couldn't resist. What are you doing here this morning?" Celia Ching said. "I thought you only hung out at Starbucks."

Jerry and Celia had been law school classmates. Now, she was an attorney with the State Prosecutor's Office.

"I'm hoping to run into a witness to an accident. We only have a first name and a description, but I understand he might be a regular here," Jerry said, tucking his newspaper into his briefcase.

It had been years since he had stepped into Patty's Bakery. There were few office buildings or stores nearby, so patrons tended to be locals with time on their hands or tourists who read about Patty's famous pies and malasadas in Oahu guidebooks. Jerry had seen a local news story reporting on customers' complaints about the parking. If anyone was caught parking illegally in the tiny lot, a man lurking nearby clamped a boot on a back rear tire and demanded $160.00 bail money.

"Do you mind if I have a seat while I wait for my order?" Celia asked.

"Sure, be my guest. You must be really hungry if you have to wait."

"Very funny. I ordered a few dozen malasadas for the office. What does this guy look like, anyway?" Celia brushed crumbs off the chair and sat down next to Jerry.

"He's an older Chinese man named John," Jerry said.

"That describes about one third of the men in my extended family. Do you have anything else to go on?"

"Not much. He was here on a Saturday at about 9 a.m. wearing scrubs."

"A lot of people wear scrubs. They're comfortable," Celia said. "What did the guy witness?"

"An accident on Kilauea Avenue during the triathlon Olympic trials,"

Jerry said.

"Oh yeah, that case. My cousin, Brian, mentioned it—the Mansfield case," Celia said. "This bakery isn't much of a hang-out. The parking sucks, there are so few tables and the coffee isn't very good. My bet is the guy isn't a regular."

"Good point, but I have nothing else to go on," Jerry said.

"From what Brian told me, the accident occurred on the top of Kilauea Avenue, where few people were lined up to watch it—it's so steep."

"What does that have to do with this witness?"

"At the prosecutor's office, we always have to think like criminals and witnesses," Celia said. "I'll tell you how I would analyze this situation."

"I guess I ran into the right person, then," Jerry said, smiling.

"Maybe… The guy was wearing scrubs and not athletic wear on a weekend so that tells me he probably isn't an athlete," Celia said, and then paused, looking deep in thought. "I'll bet he didn't plan to be at the triathlon the morning of the accident. He may have just been on his way home from somewhere and happened upon it."

"The accident occurred shortly after dawn. Where could he have been so early in Waikiki, or even around that area?"

"I can think of a handful of places. He was probably having breakfast at a restaurant on Maunakea or at Waikiki Denny's. Or, he could have been at Starbuck's near the Honolulu Zoo."

"That doesn't narrow it down much. There are a lot of other places in Waikiki. There's also Kahala Mall nearby."

"No, the mall doesn't open until later." Celia shook her head. "And, if he were coming from the mall, he would have walked on the back roads rather than up steep Kilauea Avenue. It makes a lot more sense if he came from Waikiki," Celia said.

"Sure, that makes sense," Jerry said.

"That's me. They just called my number. Good luck, Jerry. You're going to need it," Celia said, and kissed his cheek.

Jerry looked around the bakery and saw no one remotely matching the witness's description and decided to head back to his office.

While walking out to his Ferrari, he saw a guy affixing a boot to another car's rear tire.

"Good morning, sir," Jerry said to the man.

"Hey, you look familiar," the guy said. "You're Jerry Ho."

"Naw, I just look like him," Jerry said. "I get that a lot."

"Well, you talk like him, too," the guy said.

Jerry shrugged. "Do you ever see an older Chinese man named John who wears scrubs around here?" he said.

"Yeah, I saw a guy like that a few times. What do you wanna know?"

"I'm trying to find him, but I don't know his last name or contact information. Is there anything about him you remember?"

"I've seen him about four or five times in the last few months. He rides

The Bus. I saw him get off at The Bus stop across the street. He carries a black backpack with an old L.A. Raiders logo. I'm still a fan so I asked him about it one time. He said he's from L.A. but he isn't very talkative." The man crouched down next to the boot he had just attached.

"Did he say anything else to you?" Jerry asked.

"He mentioned he's retired."

"Can you think of anything else—clothing, jewelry, tattoo—anything else he carries?" Jerry said.

"He's an old guy, about five-nine, about my height. He's pretty thin," the boot guy said.

"You're pretty observant. Anything else you can think of that might help?"

"I only saw him wear scrubs a few times, usually he wears shorts and a T-shirt," the boot guy said. "Oh, and he sometimes carries a Starbuck's coffee cup. I remember, because he asked me if there was a garbage can so he could throw it away."

"Why do you remember so much about this guy?"

"I've got a good memory, I guess. I sit here all day watching cars go in and out of the parking lot—I remember the SUVs, the Toyotas, and the Mercedes. There aren't many people who take The Bus here. Those are the people I remember."

"Fair enough. Thank you very much," Jerry said, handing the guy a $20 tip after he had signed "Jerry Hirano" on it.

Shortly after Jerry pulled out of the parking lot, he pressed the Siri button on his iPhone.

"Call Zana West, office."

"Calling Zana West—Office," Siri said.

"Good morning, this is Zana."

"Good morning, this is Jerry," he said.

"Jerry who?" Zana said. "Just kidding. Hi Jerry."

He laughed. "I would have said Jerry Seinfeld."

"And I would have believed you…except my caller I.D. had your name on it."

"I got a lead on that guy, John, at the bakery."

"Terrific. Who is he?"

"I don't know yet. I think he hangs out at the Waikiki Starbucks in the mornings. Can I interest you in an early morning stakeout?" Jerry asked.

"Hmm, maybe… How early?"

"I'll pick you up at six at your house."

"Do I have to wear a ski mask and all black?"

Jerry laughed again. "Leave your ski mask at home. That would attract the wrong kind of attention. A short skirt and high heels would be nice," Jerry said, feeling comfortable enough to engage in a bit of flirting, something he hadn't felt comfortable doing with Zana up to this point.

"Would that be for your benefit?" Zana said.

"Definitely. You should also bring your laptop. We're going to be there for a while. We should at least *act* like we're working."

"Is there a reason why you're not having an investigator do this? We're sort of clueless."

"Speak for yourself. It's more fun if we do it. And, as an added bonus, I get to see you," Jerry said, smiling.

"Yes, that is a bonus," Zana said. "I'll see you in the morning."

Ending the call and turning on the radio, Jerry listened while he made his way to the parking garage. He carefully maneuvered his Ferrari between the cement pillars in the parking structure of the high rise where his office was located. His reserved stall cost him a whopping $350.00 per month, but it was worth it. He always had a space and the Porsche and Lexus on either side had conscientious owners who were vigilant when opening their car doors.

Jerry bounced out of his car, humming the last song he had heard on the radio. He jogged to the elevator to open it for an elderly man, and then gave him a wide grin. Once he was in his office, he looked at his watch and calculated the number of hours before he would see Zana. Twenty-one.

"Jerry, sorry to interrupt, but the pre-arbitration statement for Higgins is due by five," Debbie said, dropping a file onto his desk. "I've done as much as I can."

"No problem, Debbie. I'll work on it."

"Emily Anderson called to confirm your dinner tonight," Debbie said. "Also, Kenny called and said he needs you on the set after work."

"Can you call Emily and tell her I can't make it?" Jerry asked.

"Sure. Anything else?"

Jerry shook his head and signaled for her to close the door behind her. His late night dinner companion was a flame-haired flight attendant on her weekly layover, something he usually looked forward to doing. They had been seeing each other casually for about six months, but he sensed her impatience during her frequent phone calls. Last week she had suggested they see other people. He had thought that's what they were doing anyway and didn't argue. He doubted he'd ever hear from her again after Debbie called to cancel.

Jerry opened the file, hoping he could quickly draft the document, but was having such a hard time concentrating, he emailed opposing counsel instead. "Do you have any objection to filing our pre-arbitration statements in two days?"

Jerry stared out the window for a few minutes until he heard the click of a new email. He had his extension.

He picked up the Hawaii Bar Directory and thumbed through it to find Zana's picture. Her piercing green eyes stared back at him. There was something different about her when he compared her with the women he usually dated. She wasn't so available. He couldn't imagine her becoming as obsessed with him as many of them did. He had a hard time trusting woman who seemed to think he was the character he played on T.V. He wondered if they were only interested in him for his local fame.

On the other hand, Zana didn't seem at all interested in his T.V. show, the character he played, or his notoriety. She seemed sort of mysterious, but the smile she flashed when he saw her at court yesterday had made her look vulnerable. He had this overwhelming feeling of wanting to protect her for some reason, but he didn't know from what...

Chapter 21

@Zlaw Attorney work doesn't leave me much time for Facebook #stalking. Did you really search #stalking???

Zana couldn't resist a couple minutes of Facebook stalking after getting off the phone with Jerry. First, she checked to see if he had posted anything since the last time she looked two hours ago. Then she viewed her own Facebook page to make sure the posts showed her surrounded by good friends and having fun, just in case he *stalked* her. She didn't care too much about her image, but as a T.V. star, he might. Or, at the very least his publicist cared for him.

Since Jerry had accepted her friend request, his posts were mostly pictures of food, videos of his two Siamese cats playing, and some shares of funny memes. She liked to post selfies taken with her triathlete friends, pictures of sunsets and complaints about the long hours she worked.

Zana's phone dinged, signaling for her to get back to work. In order to avoid wasting all her time on social media, she had started setting an alarm to go off 5 minutes after she began tweeting, checking Instagram, Pinterest, or Facebook. So far, it was working.

She put her phone back in her purse and directed her attention to the interrogatories in the Jordan case. She had already copied and pasted canned objections after each question and so now had to insert substantive responses. She wished Lori hadn't been fired, because it would have been so much easier to do this as a team. She messaged Tom for help, but received no response.

Zana sighed, brushed the hair out of her face, and then went to Lucas's office, opening the door quietly.

"Am I interrupting?" Zana said, seeing he was playing solitaire on his computer. Every time she stopped by she caught him goofing off.

"Sort of," Lucas x'd out of his game and spun his chair around to face her.

"We've got a ton of discovery to do for the triathlon case," Zana said, still standing.

"We?" Lucas said, lifting an eyebrow.

"I thought you were helping me?"

"Sorry, I'm working with Frank to prep for a trial starting in three weeks. I've got depositions to summarize and witnesses to prep," Lucas said. "Frank asked me to be second chair."

"Are you kidding? I heard he didn't assign anyone to be second chair unless they've been practicing for at least four years," Zana said, hands on her hips.

"He recognizes talent when he sees it. Tom is also counsel for the case. All three of us are going to handle the trial," Lucas said, putting his feet on his desk.

"It must be a big case."

"Trial is expected to last at least a month," Lucas said.

"I guess I'm on my own then," Zana said softly.

"Sorry, Zana. I'd help you out if I could." Lucas shrugged.

"I'll let you get back to your important work," Zana said, pausing a moment to watch Lucas resume his solitaire game. "I hope you win."

"Thanks," Lucas said without looking up.

Zana marched down to Andrew's office, ducked in and closed the door.

"You will not believe this!" she said, plopping into one of Andrew's guest chairs.

"What? Do tell," Andrew said, putting down a deposition transcript he was reading and getting into full gossip mode.

"Mini-Frank has been elevated to second chair for Frank's trial after working here for less than a month."

"That's ridiculous."

"I know," Zana said, rolling her eyes. "The dude is playing solitaire while I'm working my ass off. I can't believe he gets rewarded by going to trial."

Andrew put his hands in a steeple position, leaned back and said, "Actually, that's good."

"How could this possibly be good?"

"Frank can now see firsthand Lucas is a lazy loser."

"Good point," Zana nodded.

"He can fool Frank when he has an office to hole up in during the day with the door closed. There's no way he can fool him during a lengthy trial."

"You're brilliant. This is an amusing turn of events, except for one thing," Zana said, furrowing her brow.

"What's that?" Andrew asked.

"Now, I'm stuck doing most of the discovery for the triathlon case. Frank, Tom and Lucas, the rest of my team will be tied up completely for a few months."

"You can handle it, Zana. It's just discovery. It'll be okay."

"You're forgetting one thing."

"What's that?"

"Mansfield."

"Oh. Well, then you're fucked."

"You got that," Zana said, looking down and biting her lip.

***

After she returned to her office, Zana resisted the urge to check Facebook for the fifth time since breakfast. There were no new texts or personal emails. She wished she could get away with playing games all day like Lucas, but she wasn't the golden associate so she had to return to responding to Mansfield's voluminous discovery requests. There was no chance she would get out of the office in time to swim and run with Shelby and Moana as planned today, and the way things were going, she'd be stuck behind her desk until she was old and fat from no exercise. She looked at her running shoes longingly.

At least her inbox was full. Associates about to get axed first experienced a dearth of assignments, and just as they wandered around looking for more work, Frank broke the news. On the bright side, she would have more than enough to keep her occupied while her boss was immersed in trial for sixteen hours a day. She could probably chance coming into the office as late as 6 a.m. and cutting out early to work out. And, Lucas would be out of her hair.

Zana drafted one answer at a time and then moved onto her next task, drafting questions for Brad Jordan to answer. Since she had started her first attorney job, each new assignment felt like climbing a mountain with false peaks. When she thought she had reached the top, there was more climbing. In law school, the professors taught students how to think like lawyers by assigning them dusty appellate court decisions to read, subjecting them to in-class questioning, and testing them on legal principles, but they were never taught how to draft interrogatories.

Once Zana completed the preliminary questions for Jordan, she crafted interrogatories she hoped would put them in a position to win the case. She asked: "Have you participated in any triathlons since the subject accident? If so, state the name of the triathlon(s) and the date of such event(s)." If Jordan answered "no," he was lying. If he answered "yes," he would be admitting he had concealed his physical capabilities. She suspected Brad would attempt to hide his post-injury triathlons. Otherwise, he would have raced in Hawaii rather than in Minnesota.

Zana looked up from her computer to see Frank standing over her desk, rubbing his chin. She jumped slightly in her chair.

"How are you coming with those interrogatories?" he said, sitting down across from her.

"I'm part-way through," Zana said.

"We've got to get cracking on this discovery. I'm sure the adjuster is anxious to move it along."

"I'll get it done," Zana said, fingering her necklace.

"I'm not sure you're aware that Rip Mansfield is…" Frank paused, "… less than trustworthy."

"I got it," Zana nodded, her desk shaking as her foot bounced. "I've heard about him."

"We need to be very careful. I want to see your draft when you're finished," Frank said. "By the way, I'll be in trial with Tom and Lucas next month. I've asked Brian Ching to supervise you, but he's going to be out of the office for depositions a good part of the time, so you'll have to do a lot of discovery on your own. All of our experienced attorneys are tied up."

"Sure," Zana said, trying to sound confident. *If he hadn't fired so many, he wouldn't have such problems.*

"I've told Ed Fairbanks to communicate directly with you for the next few months. Copy me on your weekly reports to the adjuster," Frank said. "Libby will let me know if there's anything amiss."

"Yes, Frank," Zana said, scribbling notes on a legal pad.

"Any questions?" Frank said and then rose swiftly and left the room before she could open her mouth.

Zana felt her heart pounding. For the first time since she started work at the firm, she would be free to work without her superiors breathing down her neck. It felt scary and exhilarating at the same time. She powered through the rest of the interrogatories at a pace fueled by her newly acquired freedom and was able to finish by 7 p.m.

It was too late to run at the park, but she could pop by the mall and pick up something cute to wear tomorrow on her surveillance "date" with Jerry. Before packing up to go, she wrote a quick email to her secretary.

Hi Sylvia,

I won't be in the office until late tomorrow morning. I have a meeting with Jerry Hirano on the Jordan v. Aloha Athletic case.

Email or text if you need me.

Zana

With the thought she would be seeing him in less than 11 hours, she felt a rush of excitement typing Jerry's name.

Chapter 22

@Zlaw #JamesBond and the #Tri-Geek. A blockbuster movie? Or, a weird dream?

Zana's iPhone alarm went off at 5:00 a.m. She was already awake, lying in bed imagining how she'd spend the morning with Jerry, thinking about what she would wear, and feeling anxious about whether she was reading too much into the attention he had been giving her. With no time to spare if she was going to look her best, Zana leapt from her bed to shower. She'd spend extra time on her makeup, hair and ironing her short black skirt and emerald colored blouse, both purchased the night before at Macy's.

Now dressed, she examined her reflection in the mirror. The neck-line of her new top was low enough to attract interest, but still professional, and the short skirt made her legs appear longer and even accentuated her toned thighs and calves. Just as Zana was fastening her necklace, she heard the beep of a text.

I'm here. Should I knock? Don't want to wake peeps. J.

Zana grabbed her laptop bag and purse and quietly let herself out the front door. Jerry was standing next to his shiny red Ferrari, wearing black slacks and a snug black T-shirt revealing the outline of his muscular physique.

"Good morning," Jerry said, kissing her cheek.

"Good morning," Zana whispered, not wanting to wake Andrew and Kelly, who she hadn't told about her early morning excursion.

Jerry walked around the car and opened the door for her. She made a ladylike attempt to slide in, trying to keep her short skirt from rising up.

"You look beautiful," Jerry said after they were both in the car.

"Mahalo. You look terrific yourself. In a James Bondish way," Zana said, smiling at him.

"I think you look a little like Agent 99 from 'Get Smart'."

"That's before my time, but I'll take it as a compliment."

"It's before my time as well, but I'm a sucker for vintage T.V. shows,"

Jerry said. "John might already be there."

"We'll see."

"We're way overdressed for Waikiki Starbucks—we're going to stand out."

"You'd stand out even wearing boxer shorts," Zana said.

"Is that right?" he glanced her way.

"I meant to say, *board* shorts." Zana felt her face flush.

"Sure you did," Jerry said, looking straight ahead as he drove on the dark road. "If John's already there, just follow my lead. I'll talk to him."

"I don't see how this stake out is going to work. You're going to attract a lot of attention, Jerry Ho."

"I've spent a fair amount of time at that Starbucks. People are used to seeing me. But, I usually don't get there at six o'clock," Jerry said. "I'm not much of an early bird."

"I've been there at four-thirty—when they open."

"Are you kidding? You must have had a late night."

"No, I probably go to bed when you're just getting started. I often go running in the early morning, before it gets hot. Especially, if it's a long run," Zana said.

"Oh, that's right, you're a tri-geek," Jerry said, turning into the parking lot at the Honolulu Zoo, across the street from Starbucks. "About ten years ago, I competed in a few triathlons."

"How come you don't do them anymore?"

"I'm too busy with the show and martial arts. I practice law in my spare time."

"I wish I could say the same. Work is seriously interfering with my training," Zana said.

Jerry helped her out of his car and carried both of their laptop cases through the dark parking lot on their way to the café.

"I should get you into martial arts training. Have you ever seen any MMA fights?" Jerry asked.

"Only what I see on your show," she said. "It's pretty cool."

"So you're a fan!" Jerry said, giving Zana a big smile.

"Okay, I admit it. I'm a fan," Zana said. "Don't hold that against me."

"I won't," Jerry said, opening the door for her. "Have a seat, Agent 99. I'll get us breakfast. What's your drink?"

"A latte please, Mr. Bond." Zana placed her laptop bag on a chair near an electrical outlet.

After Jerry came back with a latte for Zana and a chai tea for himself and a few bags of assorted breakfast breads and pastries, they set up their laptops.

"Don't forget our mission, Mr. Bond," Zana said. "I don't want to distract you with my short skirt."

"What mission?" Jerry asked, winking at her.

He answered a call on his cell phone while Zana read emails. They both intermittently scanned the store and watched the door for an older Chinese man with an old L.A. Raiders backpack. When Asian men entered the café, they took turns asking the men if they were John. Mostly, the answers were no, except one man, who upon further questioning had been in Japan at the time of the accident.

By 8:15, Zana had cleared her inbox and finished all the work she could possibly do remotely. She sipped another latte when a thin Asian man with flecks of gray in his hair wearing khaki shorts and a peach colored T-shirt came in. Jerry nodded to Zana when the man's faded L.A. Raider's backpack came into view.

"Let's wait until after he orders and sits down," Jerry said. "He looks familiar."

Zana nodded in agreement.

Jerry picked up a newspaper to peer over, and she looked at her phone while intermittently glancing up at the man, who ordered a coffee, added sugar and cream, and then sat at an empty table near the door. Jerry waited about 30 seconds before approaching him.

"Excuse me, is your name John?" he said, loudly enough for Zana to overhear.

"Maybe, who wants to know?" the man said.

"You look familiar. Have we met?"

"I haven't met you, but I know who you are. You're the guy on that T.V. show," the man said.

"And you're John Chu. I recognize you from the news," Jerry said. "I'm sorry to bother you, but I understand you may have witnessed an accident that happened in the triathlon Olympic trials."

"Could you please leave me out of this?" John reached into his backpack for a newspaper.

"I'm familiar with your situation. Do you mind if I sit down?" Jerry sat across from the man without waiting for an answer.

"I guess I don't have any choice, do I?" John said, opening his newspaper and looking down at an article.

"You know what it's like to be wrongly accused of something, Mr. Chu. I represent someone who was wrongly accused of causing that accident," Jerry said. "My client needs your help to set the record straight."

"I'm not interested. If you know my situation so well, you'll respect my privacy. Good luck," John said. He stuffed his newspaper into his backpack, got up and walked to the door, carrying his coffee with him.

"Mr. Chu, we really need your help. All I need is an affidavit," Jerry said, following John to the door.

"Mr. Hirano, I've had enough dealings with attorneys for a lifetime. I can't stomach the sight of anymore. Now, please leave me alone," John walked out the door.

"Follow him," Jerry said to Zana.

She quickly left the café, spotting John as he crossed the street and walked towards the aquarium. She had her phone with the Bluetooth in her ear, so she called Jerry to report where the witness was going, following him as swiftly as her high-heeled wedge shoes would allow.

"I'll pack up our stuff and grab my car," Jerry said.

"You'll be conspicuous in your Ferrari. Can't you catch a taxi?"

"Not a bad idea. You're smarter than you look."

"Thanks a lot," Zana said, picking up her pace to keep John in sight.

"There's a taxi. He's stopping for me."

"John's walking on Kalakaua Avenue—towards the aquarium. It looks like he's headed to a bus stop. I'll keep following him and let you know if I see him get on a bus," Zana said, picking up her pace.

"Okay, I'm in the taxi," Jerry said.

"Good."

"Okay, I see him. We're pulling over to pick you up. Do you see me?" Jerry said from the taxi that pulled over about 50 feet in front of her.

Zana ran towards the taxi in her high heels and climbed into the backseat next to Jerry.

"You run like a girl. Are you sure you're a triathlete?" Jerry said.

"You try to run in heels," Zana said. "He's getting on that bus."

"Follow that bus," Jerry said to the taxi driver.

"Are you spies or somethin'?" the taxi driver asked.

"Yeah, could you please follow that bus? It's important," Jerry said.

"Okay, Mr. Ho," the taxi driver said. "Are we being filmed?"

"Yeah, so you better not lose him," Jerry said.

"Gotcha. I'm right behind him." The taxi driver sped up, positioning his yellow car right behind The Bus, following it up Diamond Head Road.

The Bus turned left by Triangle Park and then drove towards Kilauea Avenue, the site of the accident. The taxi driver sped up faster and then whipped around the corner, causing Zana to land in Jerry's lap. He momentarily held her and then he released her to return to the other side of the backseat. Zana felt her face flush from a mixture of excitement and embarrassment. She kept her eyes on The Bus ahead of them and watched John as he exited at the stop one street over from where the accident occurred.

"Keep your distance from that man who just got off The Bus. Drive slowly, but keep him in sight," Jerry said, leaning between the front seats.

"I've got it," the taxi driver said.

"We need to get his address, so let's see what house he walks up to. We can pull over and wait until he's inside, and then Zana can walk past the house to write it down," Jerry said.

John turned and walked up a few stairs to the porch of a small house with a tidy yard, landscaped with red ginger plants. The taxi driver pulled over.

Before Zana climbed out, Jerry put his hand on her arm and said, "Be careful. Don't let him see you."

"Why? He's already seen you."

"John Chu was the agent of the famous actor, Lester Braun. He was all over the news about five years ago when he was charged as an accomplice in the murder of his client's wife. He could be dangerous," Jerry said. "Maybe I should do it."

Zana ignored Jerry's warning and jumped out of the cab. The house number was partially obscured by some tropical foliage, but when she saw it, she tapped the digits into her phone. Before she turned away, she saw John staring at her out of the front picture window, which sent a chill up her spine.

"Operation John successful," Zana stammered when she climbed back into the taxi.

"You should have let me get out." Jerry put his hand on her upper back.

"It's okay," she said, feeling more comfortable under Jerry's protection.

"We can now subpoena him to testify," Jerry said.

"When is this show going to be on the air?" the taxi driver asked.

"Oh, probably in a few months, sir. Thanks for your help," Jerry said.

"You did a great job," Zana said to the driver.

"Could you please take us back to the Honolulu Zoo parking lot?" Jerry asked.

"Sure, I'll give you my name and number in case you need me to be a regular," the taxi driver said.

"Great, we'll let you know," Jerry said and flashed his T.V. star smile.

Chapter 23

@Zlaw Washboard #abs are mesmerizing.

It was almost 11 a.m. when Jerry dropped Zana off at her building. After stepping out of his Ferrari, she resisted skipping back to her office. She smiled as she opened the glass door for an elderly man and continued to hold it for a handful of smokers who had been on break. While at Starbucks with Jerry, Zana hadn't received any urgent emails or phone calls so she was sure she hadn't been missed.

"Good morning," Zana said, grinning at Libby as she walked by her cubicle.

"Hi Zana," Libby said, looking up from her computer.

"Where the hell have you been?" Lucas said, standing in front of Libby's cubicle with his hands on his hips.

"I had an early morning meeting," Zana said, wondering why her whereabouts was any of Lucas's concern.

"I dropped by your office two hours ago. Now, you're finally strolling in at lunchtime?" Lucas said, wagging his finger in her face.

"If you had asked Sylvia, she would have told you where I was," Zana said.

"Sylvia is out sick. Your behavior is unacceptable," Lucas said, raising his voice. "I'm sure Frank will agree."

"I'm sure Frank will agree that my 6 a.m. meeting on a high profile case was more important than my being at your beck and call," Zana said, raising her voice. "Excuse me, I need to get to my office."

Zana heard Lucas sigh as she headed there. Her phone was ringing when she walked through the door.

"Zana West speaking."

"It's Libby," the woman whispered.

"Hi," Zana said as she sunk into her chair.

"I wanted to let you know not to worry about Lucas."

"Thanks, but I wasn't really concerned about his temper tantrum." She clicked on her computer.

"He was out of line," Libby said.

"Yeah, he was. Is he in Frank's office tattling on me?"

"I'm not sure. But, yes, he did walk into his office. I'll make sure Frank knows you were meeting with Jerry Hirano this morning on the triathlon case," Libby said.

"How did you know?" Zana asked, frowning.

"It's my business to know everything in this office."

"Okay, well thanks, Libby."

Zana was more disturbed that Libby knew her business than she was about Lucas's tirade. She wondered if Libby monitored everyone's emails and phone calls. It made sense. Lots of businesses policed employee communication. At least if Libby was monitoring her actions, she would know Zana worked hard. And if Libby was checking Lucas's every computer move, she would know he spent most of his time on Facebook and playing computer games. He wasn't much of a threat, except she couldn't compete with him being Frank's Mini-Me.

Zana had gotten through her daily emails while at Starbucks, so the email from hirano@fightinginparadise.com stood out among the few new ones. She hadn't seen that email address before. She assumed it was Jerry's personal address. The subject line was "Tonight".

Hi Zana,

I have a late depo this afternoon so it will be challenging to get to the set on time. I wish I had my own helicopter. Would you mind coming to the Diamond Head sound stage with me? I can pick you up on Alakea Street at 5:15. I don't have time to drop you off at home first (Ferrari is not as speedy as helicopter). You can watch the filming, if you can spare the time and have the patience. Hey, you might get discovered! If you're up for it, join me for dinner afterwards?

Aloha,
Jerry

Zana smiled to herself at the thought of seeing Jerry Ho in action on the set of "Fighting in Paradise". This was her dream come true. Since Jerry had to get to a pre-hearing conference this morning, there wasn't enough time to drive her back to Kahala to pick up her car. Ordinarily, she would have ridden home with Andrew, but he was working on Maui for the day. She wrote back.

Hi Jerry,

No problem. It will be fun to see you in action. Will I get to watch you with your shirt off? I'll see you at 5:15 at the same place you dropped me off this morning.

Aloha,
=Z=

P.S. Your Ferrari will do.

Jerry's email took Zana's mind off Lucas's irrational behavior. After clicking send, she remembered that Libby would likely read her email. She regretted the bit about watching him shirtless. What would Libby think?

Zana leaned back in her chair and swiveled to face the view of the large Dole Pineapple in the distance. She wondered if she should share with Libby that she liked to joke around and assure her there was nothing going on between her and Jerry. They were just colleagues talking business, and only Jerry would have his shirt off. Zana laughed aloud at the thought. No need to act defensive with Frank's secretary. From now on, she'd censor her emails.

All afternoon, she kept busy summarizing medical records. Shortly before 5, she made use of the kit she kept in her desk, complete with toothpaste, toothbrush, cologne, and touch up makeup. She turned her daytime look into an evening one, re-applying mascara and eyeliner and changing into a low cut red top she had hanging on the back of her door, along with the rest of her dry cleaning she hadn't taken home yet.

When Zana stepped onto the elevator, Lucas rushed in behind her.

"Are you going home early?" he asked.

She glanced his way. "Why are you so interested in what I'm doing?"

"It's not fair to the other associates if you're only working part-time and we have to pull your weight," Lucas said, the elevator door closing behind him.

"You might want to focus on your own work. Not on me."

"Lori was fired. There are only four other women left. I wouldn't want there to be only three." Lucas held up his fingers for emphasis.

"What does my being a woman have to do with anything, Lucas?"

"I'm just sayin'." Lucas shifted his stance, staring at the floor numbers above the elevator door, which opened when they reached the lobby level.

"Sounds like sexual harassment to me. You might want to knock it off, especially since there are security cameras in the elevator," Zana said and then walked quickly away.

She was happy to see Jerry's Ferrari already parked on the side of busy Alakea Street, attracting stares from passers-by. She sped up her pace and hopped into the passenger seat.

"I hope I didn't keep you waiting too long," Zana said, pulling her long legs into the cramped cockpit.

"I was reading a text. Sorry Zana, I would have gotten out and opened the door for you," Jerry said, leaning awkwardly across the stick shift to kiss her on the cheek.

"That's okay. I think seeing Jerry Ho getting out of his Ferrari at rush hour on a busy street would create too much of a ruckus. No worries."

"Mahalo. You look beautiful, by the way," Jerry said, raising his eyebrows at her long legs.

They discussed the case while driving to the studio in bumper-to-bumper rush hour traffic. When they finally arrived, Jerry waved at the security guard at the entrance of the Diamond Head Sound Stage parking lot.

"I hope you won't be too bored for the next few hours. I need to go to makeup, then you can watch me kick some ass with my shirt off," Jerry said, winking. He jumped out of the car and raced around to open Zana's door for her.

"I'm sure I'll be well entertained," Zana said. She was still wearing high-heeled wedges and found it challenging to keep up with Jerry's quick pace as they walked towards the set.

A young woman with an "Intern" badge met them at the front door.

"Kaimi, could you please take Zana to the set so she can watch, and get her some coffee?" Jerry said. "I'm late for makeup."

"Sure, Mr. Hirano. You can follow me, Miss Zana," Kaimi said.

Zana followed the young woman. She looked Polynesian with her long, thick braided black hair, dark complexion and big brown eyes. She led her to a handful of folding chairs where a few other people were sitting, engrossed in reading scripts. There were some black directors chairs set up, including a chair that had "Jerry Hirano" in bold, white print. Several cameramen and grips were setting up their shots in front of a green screen.

She saw a man who she thought must be the director hurry into the room with a script in hand, barking out directions to the cameramen. Another man who was Jerry's size stood in to assist with lighting.

After a few minutes, Kaimi offered her steaming coffee in a black ceramic cup with the "Fighting in Paradise" logo on it. Zana took the coffee and with her other hand pulled out her phone.

"Please put it away," Kaimi whispered. "Phones aren't allowed."

"Sorry," Zana said softly. She turned it off and stashed it in her handbag, wishing she had been able to snap a few pictures and text Kelly where she was.

Zana sat up straight, sipped her coffee and smiled at anyone who looked her way. She wondered how many women Jerry had brought to the set before her and hoped she wasn't his *flavor of the week*.

She watched the director, cameramen, stand-in, assistants and countless others talk amongst themselves using unfamiliar terms. With her phone in her bag, Zana had no idea what time it was, but she estimated it had been well over an hour. She didn't dare move. Her coffee cup, she had placed on the floor, was empty. She shifted in the chair now uncomfortable. She wasn't used to being unproductive and longed to check emails, tweet, or scroll through Instagram or Facebook.

Finally, Jerry wearing black slacks and a black Aloha shirt with a gold hotel nametag, which read "Jerry Ho", walked onto the set. Zana suppressed a giggle when she saw his face caked with makeup. A woman wearing an earpiece and carrying a clipboard positioned Jerry in front of the green screen. The director approached him and discussed something in a low voice.

"Quiet on the set."

"'Fighting in Paradise', Episode 27, scene 5, take 1," the guy with a clapboard said.

"Action," the director called.

Jerry ripped off his shirt and executed a roundhouse kick, a series of sharp blocks and punches, making fighting noises as he did.

"Cut!" the director yelled. "Jerry, your angle is off. You need to face left a little bit more. Let's have Annabelle work with you. I think there are too many outside blocks. It's not making sense."

A lithe Asian woman, who Zana assumed was the choreographer, worked with Jerry on a series of blocks, punches, and kicks until his movements were more fluid. The director seemed satisfied and filmed more takes, this time with other actors dressed as thugs.

Zana had seen Jerry fight plenty of bad guys sans shirt on T.V., but she had never seen him this close in the flesh. He was focused on his work, giving her the freedom to stare openly at his muscular chest and six pack abs.

"Cut! That's a wrap," the director said after forty-five minutes of filming. The actors quickly dispersed.

"Did you see anything you liked?" Jerry said to Zana, toweling the sweat off his face.

"All of it," Zana said. "Can I take you home?"

"I need a cold shower after that comment. I'll be right back," Jerry said, raising both eyebrows.

The director left and the cameramen and grips began packing up. After watching them for a while, Zana pulled out her phone. She texted Kelly. At sound stage watching Ho's six pack. Heaven!

Kelly texted back: Yummy!

"Anything you want to share with me?" Jerry said behind her as Zana was reading Kelly's text.

"No, that's okay. Just work stuff," Zana stammered. She closed the screen on her phone.

"Are you hungry?" He had changed into jeans and a red polo shirt.

"Sure, I could eat," Zana said, slipping her phone back into her purse.

"There's a café a few blocks away. It has delicious food. Shall we go there?" Jerry said. "I have something interesting to show you about the investigation."

"Sounds great," Zana said, trying to hide her disappointment. Jerry had shifted the topic quickly to work. She had been imagining again that she and Jerry were actually dating, but knew such thoughts were ridiculous. They were just colleagues, working on a case together. She had to remember to keep her cool.

The café was so packed people were spilling out the front door. Zana was hungry and hoped Jerry would suggest another option so they wouldn't have to wait. Instead, he led her through the front door past the waiting customers.

"Good evening, Mr. Hirano," the hostess said, beaming.

"Hi, Jill. Good to see you."

"Come this way," Jill said, leading them through the busy dining room to the sole empty table in the back. "Enjoy your dinner."

"I'm assuming you made a reservation," Zana said after they sat down.

"It's sort of a standing reservation," Jerry said. "Take a look at the walls."

Zana glanced at the photographs covering the walls. Most of them were of "Fighting in Paradise" actors, with Jerry in various fighting stances or posing with fans. She then noticed the menu cover. The name of the restaurant was Fighting Café.

"Are you the main attraction here?" Zana asked.

"Sort of. Most of the actors in the show come here after work. It's convenient. This café used to be dead until fans got word that we hang out here. It didn't take long with Twitter."

"Why are these people leaving you alone? I've noticed them stare at you, but no one has approached."

Jerry shrugged. "We've been coming here for a few years. We're not much of a novelty anymore. Plus, the café mostly attracts locals. Tourists eat in Waikiki."

"I see," Zana said. "I hope it's Mansfield-free."

"Absolutely, I've never seen that snake here." Jerry laughed.

"That's good. You wanted to tell me about the investigation," Zana said. "What is it?" As much as she wanted to pretend they were on a date, she accepted reality. They had work to do.

After ordering dinner, Jerry pulled photographs and reports out of the manila envelope he had carried in with him and laid everything across the table.

The first picture caught Zana's eye. It showed an SUV parked on the side of a street with a personalized license plate, TRIBAD.

"That's so weird," Zana said. "I've seen that car before."

"You have?"

"Yeah, I'm trying to remember where. The license plate looks familiar."

"Maybe you saw it at a race or something," Jerry said.

"You're right. That's it. I did see it at a race," Zana continued staring at the picture, while the waiter tried to fit glasses of wine and place a breadbasket on the small table.

Jerry shifted the papers on the table to make room. "Recently?"

"Yeah, it was at the Bronzeman Triathlon. The car was the only one parked up on the curb when I got there at zero dark thirty," Zana said, studying the photo.

"Do you realize this is Brad Jordan's SUV?"

"He *was* at the race."

"He was racing?"

"No. He was the emcee. He reeked of alcohol, even though it was very early in the morning. We had surveillance take pictures of him making announcements." Zana picked up another photo.

"Why do you remember his car? I would bet there are other personalized plates at races with triathlon-related words."

Zana studied a photo. "The curb was high and it took a lot of effort to get my car over it. I noticed the only other car that had done the same thing, I guess," Zana said, straining to remember the morning of the triathlon.

"How did Jordan get his wheelchair down the curb?" Jerry said. "Was he with someone else?"

"I'm not sure. But even if he was, it would be hard to move a wheelchair with a grown man down from a high curb."

"I would imagine someone in a wheelchair would park somewhere more accessible," Jerry said, studying the photograph before putting it on the pile.

"Megan Alexander, won my age group," Zana said. She paused while the waiter placed their entrees on the table.

"Who's she?" Jerry asked, looking up from the photo.

"From my Internet research, Brad is dating Megan's twin, Heather. You know the anchorwoman?" Zana picked up her fork.

"I've seen her."

"Megan might have been there helping him at the race."

"That's a possibility, but look at this," Jerry said, pulling another picture out of the envelope.

Zana studied the picture of the silhouette of a man standing behind the curtain in a second story window of an apartment building.

"Is that Jordan?" she asked, taking a bite of fish.

"The investigator thinks so," Jerry said. "He staked out Jordan's apartment the entire day and the only person besides Jordan who entered and exited was Heather Alexander. At about 7:00 p.m., he saw what he thought looked like Jordan walking by the window."

"This is unbelievable," Zana said. "Are you saying Jordan can walk?"

"We don't have enough proof, but we've got inferences. We'll get there," Jerry said, cutting into his steak.

After dinner, Jerry and Zana headed back to his car parked two blocks away. Walking next to him out of the restaurant, she felt Jerry's hand on her lower back and then, as if he remembered she was co-counsel, his hand retreated.

They were silent during the short ride to Zana's house, deep in their own thoughts. Jerry walked her to the door. She noticed his eyes looked serious, almost intense. For a moment she thought he might kiss her lips, but he caught her cheek instead.

When she got inside and shut the door behind her, she did her version of a happy-dance. She had finally gotten a close look at Jerry Ho in action.

Chapter 24

@Zlaw If I were meant to #golf, I'd have been born wearing plaid diapers. The #19thhole? Now we're talking.

Brad was positioned in his wheelchair in front of the T.V. tuned to a reality show Heather liked. He pretended to be interested, but felt restless. He wished Megan was there to relieve his boredom and horniness. All he got from Heather was some G-rated cuddling and like now, she was holding his hand, making it itch and sweat. He knew it wasn't her fault they didn't have sex. She had no idea what he was capable of, but he didn't want to test her. Or tell her the truth.

While Brad considered his predicament, he watched her smile at the silliness on the screen. She didn't get much time off, so he endured the show for her benefit.

From what he knew of Heather, after years of dating, she was hung up on following the rules and being perfect. He assumed she wouldn't tolerate his deception. She was always selling gossip to tabloids and so if she knew he was able to walk, he was afraid she might leak the story or report his current physical status to Mansfield, ruining his chances for a multi-million dollar payday.

Brad had always been laser-focused on his goals ever since he won his first blue ribbon at a swim meet at age seven. Even then, he had envisioned being on the medal stand at the Olympics.

Now, he was completely focused on making someone pay for his losses and he didn't care whom. He was determined to milk as much money out of the lawsuit as possible, equating a huge settlement or judgment to an Olympic medal, because as far as he was concerned, that's all he had left.

He was used to sitting in his wheelchair whenever he was in the company of others. It was more comfortable than the couch. Sometimes, he sat in it even when he was alone. It had occurred to Brad that the wheelchair was sort of a symbol of all that had been taken away from him: his lifestyle, his dreams, and his life's work. His deception would quickly be discovered if he miraculously walked again the minute he cashed his settlement check and he knew he'd have to lay low.

His plan was to leave the country and reappear miraculously healed, perhaps in time for the Olympic trials for Rio in 2016. Between his drinking binges, he had managed to do some Internet research of international triathlon communities where he could race again under an assumed name for a few years. Although Germany seemed the most promising, he was also considering Canada, Mexico, France and Italy.

Brad's thoughts were interrupted when the doorbell rang. Because Heather thought he was an invalid, she hurried to answer it. He wiped his sweaty hand on his shorts and clicked off the T.V.

"I'm here from Rip Mansfield's office," the frumpy woman at the door said, barging in with a packet of legal papers in hand. "I'm Dorothy Kawakami."

"Please come in, Dorothy. I'm Brad's girlfriend, Heather."

"Hello, you must be Brad," Dorothy said, stepping towards him cautiously as if she was approaching a rabid, stray dog.

"Yeah, hi," Brad said, but stayed put, believing that the appearance of disability excused his rudeness. His wheelchair, he believed, allowed him to continue his lifelong entitlement attitude, so he didn't feel any need to be polite.

"Mr. Mansfield sent me here to have you sign your answers to interrogatories," she said, taking a seat on the couch next to Brad.

"That's strange. I don't remember answering any interrogatories. Why should I be signing anything?" Brad said. He remembered Rip telling him he would have to answer quite a few written questions, but was surprised he was now being asked to sign them sight unseen.

"Mr. Mansfield answered them for you. He thinks it's best for your case. Please sign where the post-it flags are," she said, thrusting the document in front of him with a black ballpoint pen.

"Shouldn't he at least read the document first?" Heather said.

"If you'd like, but I've got a bus to catch. I'll notarize it when you're done signing," Dorothy said.

"Okay, if you say so," Brad said. He wasn't exactly sober and was willing to do anything to get this woman to leave. He was relieved she'd showed up when Heather was here. If he was with Megan, her interruption would have been much more inconvenient.

"If you don't mind, I'll have a look at this." Heather reached for the document.

"I'm sorry, Miss, but this isn't any of your concern. I have strict instructions from Mr. Mansfield. This document is due tomorrow and I must leave as soon as he signs." Dorothy got up and positioned her pudgy body between Brad's wheelchair and Heather while he signed the tagged page.

"Very well. Mahalo," Dorothy said and tucked the signed documents into her floral patterned shopping bag.

"Aren't you going to notarize it?" Heather said.

"I'll take care of that later," Dorothy said. "You are Brad Jordan, aren't you?"

He nodded.

"I can get his driver's license for you," Heather said, taking a step towards the bedroom.

"No need. I've really got to catch my bus. Mahalo!" Dorothy said, hurrying out the door.

"I can't believe she didn't check your I.D. or notarize the document in front of you," Heather said after Dorothy left.

"It's not like there are other invalids answering to the name Brad Jordan."

"She was supposed to look at your I.D. and notarize the document in front of you, though," Heather said, taking a seat on the couch. "That's how notarizing works."

"For Pete's sake, it's not like there's a notary jail. Don't worry about it," Brad said, raising his voice. He reached for the remote and turned the T.V. back on, switching the channel to rugby. If Heather was all hung up on the notary following the rules, she surely would never understand or forgive his deception.

***

Rip Mansfield was playing golf with his associates, Chris, Doug, and Randal, the only guys at the office whose company he tolerated for the time it took to play 18 holes. They showed him respect by agreeing with his opinions and even though two of the young men had been on their college golf teams, they seemed to always mess up some shots so their boss won. Rip never minded people sucking up to him. It was a sign of honor.

The foursome had just finished putting the 17th hole. Rip took a moment to lean against the golf cart, breathe in the warm air and watch a red-crested cardinal peck at the grass and then fly away, beyond the palm trees lining the green. His orange shirt and plaid shorts were damp from sweat after hours of playing in the hot sun. His associates studied their scorecards and swigged water bottles allowing Rip time to catch his breath. Doug wore similar plaid shorts and a bright yellow shirt. Chris and Randal, the newer associates, had not yet copied Rip's fashion choice of plaid. They wore khakis and polo shirts with Mansfield's law firm logo.

Rip paid his associates twice as much as their peers. Fely, who had been his secretary for several decades, was not afraid to offer her two cents on the type of personality she believed worked well in the firm. She reminded him to hire attorneys with high levels of "emotional intelligence". She didn't explain her assessment, but he knew what she meant. A psychiatrist friend had once called him a narcissist and he couldn't disagree with such diagnosis and so, he hired "yes" men who he handpicked for their flexible morals. Rip's hiring practices meant background checks revealing checkered pasts. He felt that if an associate had something to hide, he could use the information for "training purposes".

Doug's past history of heroin abuse and rehab allowed Rip to gently "remind" him to do what he was told, because no other firm would hire someone so risky. Doug agreed and eagerly followed Rip's directives, however shady.

And even though Rip worked with his associate attorneys daily, he had a hard time remembering their names. They were young, fresh out of law school, and despite Rip's threats, usually didn't stay with him for more than a few years. The office was a revolving door for new recruits learning the skills it took to become plaintiffs' attorneys. Once they mastered the art of sucking money out of insurance companies with the least amount of effort, they jumped ship, putting their own cheesy advertisements on the Internet and T.V., competing against Rip and their former colleagues for accident victims. Rip got the big cases—he always did—and they would take the scraps, cases usually valued at $20,000 or less, reaping their meager contingency fees.

But Rip didn't mind losing an attorney after a few years. That way, he avoided emotional involvement, and their replacements took orders far better than the more seasoned and confident associates.

He was anxious to escape the banter of the young men now, so as soon as he was declared the victor, he left them at the 19th hole, heading home to his mansion. He was in a foul mood, feeling lonely and miserable. He had settled a case that morning for $1.3 million, and surprisingly, didn't feel any rush of excitement even though the case was at most worth only about $500,000. He was disturbed by his reaction. Usually, a significant win would mean celebrating with an expensive bottle of champagne on the links. He didn't bother this time and didn't even mention the settlement to his underlings. *Had he lost his edge?* He was still pondering it when his cell phone rang as he braked his car at a red light.

"Rip Mansfield, please," the female voice said.

"Speaking."

"This is Alicia Hoshino. I was wondering if you would be agreeable to rescheduling my client's deposition. It's tomorrow afternoon," the woman said in a shaky voice.

"Remind me, what case?" he said.

"Silva versus Aloha Roofing."

"Why do you need to reschedule?"

"My client's in the hospital," the woman said.

"Okay. Call my office and talk to Fely about rescheduling," Rip said, uncharacteristically pleasant to the young attorney.

"I will. Thank you."

Rip disconnected the call and shifted his Porsche into fifth gear on the H-1 Freeway, driving towards Kahala. He hadn't even asked Alicia whether she was horny or about the color of her wet panties. It wasn't like him to pass up an opportunity for wordplay with a powerless female. He put his hand on his forehead to determine whether he might be running a fever. He pulled his monogrammed platinum flask out of his briefcase open on the seat beside him and took a swig of whiskey.

When he rolled into his driveway, he took another long swig as he waited for the iron gate to open, which did nothing to calm his nerves. He wasn't even in the mood for sex so he canceled his girl for the evening with a short text.

He parked his Porsche next to his Bentley, then entered his house through the eight-car garage, tapping in the security code to cut the alarm. He took off his shoes before setting foot inside as was the custom in Hawaii homes. He waved his hand to electronically turn on the lights, walking slowly through the kitchen, the dining room, and the upstairs sitting room and library before going to one of his five wet bars.

Rip pressed a code to open a locked cabinet and pulled out the Nun's Island 25 Year Old Pot Still Whiskey he had purchased from a connection at the Galway Distillery in Ireland last year after he had earned a particularly generous contingency fee.

He gently dusted the unopened bottle that had set him back $195,000, before he carefully opened it. He pulled out a crystal tulip whiskey tasting glass and polished it with a clean cloth before pouring 2-3 seconds' worth of the precious liquid.

Rip took his prize drink into the library, sitting in a well-worn Italian leather chair he reserved for tasting the finest liquor. Tilting and swirling so that the liquid covered the glass equally, his nose and senses fully experienced the powerful aroma. He brought the glass to his face, sticking his nose in, taking a slow, deep whiff. He detected a hint of nutmeg.

He sniffed deeper and got a sense of tree bark, and then he took a small amount of the expensive whiskey into his mouth, swirling it so it covered his tongue and teeth. He breathed through his nose and focused on the sensation of it. Rip then opened his mouth slowly and breathed in through his mouth and nostrils. He took a swig, tasting the spectrum of flavors of the spirit, closing his eyes in full enjoyment. He took another drink, closing his mouth to hold the liquid on his tongue for a long moment and then finally swallowed, tasting the finish of the whisky, detecting flavors he found hard to describe.

After he had enjoyed every last drop from his glass, he locked the Nun's Island back in the cabinet. As much as he savored its flavors and aroma, he still felt uneasy and restless. It was as if he had a hole in his heart that needed filling, but he had no idea how.

He walked into his expansive kitchen that despite its lack of use, sported the most expensive appliances Rip's decorator could find. He opened one of the doors of the La Cambusa, an 8.2 foot-wide refrigerator custom-made to blend with the stainless steel and black décor. At $41,000, the fridge had to be shipped from the Italian company, Meneghini, who had installed all the bells-and-whistles, including a Miele coffee system and a flat screen T.V.

He stared at the glass shelves one of his housekeepers had filled with Greek yoghurt in all different flavors, Odwalla juices, a variety of jarred pickles and olives, brie cheese, and a few cartons of Thai food purchased at a local restaurant. Nothing looked particularly good. He didn't bother to crack open the freezer.

Rip closed the La Cambusa door and walked over to one of the knife blocks on the center island. He selected a sharp paring knife and inspected it. He ran the knife under a stream of hot water from the Miele coffee system and wiped it clean with a fresh dishtowel. He opened the pocket glass door separating his dining area and lanai, not really noticing the full moon shining brightly in the sky. To him, it looked more like a large round lamp.

Restless, he sat down on a giraffe print lanai chair, studying the knife in his hand. Putting his tanned arm on the glass table, he made a slit on his scarred forearm. He pressed the sharp knife into his skin until he felt pain and watched as the blood seeped out of the cut. He blotted it with the dishtowel, sat back, and noticed how glorious the moon was tonight.

Chapter 25

@Zlaw The lengths husbands go to avoid the #honey-do-list. Just hire a handy guy with #six-pack-abs.

Zana felt the tension in her neck and shoulders when she entered the conference room early Saturday morning. She dropped her iPhone into a basket with the other electronics Frank forbid during their meetings. *Didn't these people have lives outside of the office?* She scowled as the others laughed at one of Tom's jokes when she sat next to him at the long table. Lucas sat directly across from her with a silly grin on his face, Andrew on one side and Kim McCall on the other.

Zana didn't mind working long hours all week, but resented the mandatory Saturday meeting. It was held at the same time her friends biked 50 to 75 miles. When she had complained to Andrew about it and asked if there was any way for the group to meet on Friday afternoons, he had laughed. "How do you think the married partners escape doing weekend chores?"

Andrew was right; the guys showed up at the meeting wearing their golf clothes. As soon as the meeting was over, they rushed to the links for pre-arranged tee times. Some of the guys instructed the weekend receptionist to tell their wives they were still in a meeting if they should call. Zana had considered wearing her biking gear, but by the time she'd get to the park, her friends would be returning from their ride.

Her colleagues sipped from the firm's logo coffee cups. Zana wished she would have grabbed a cup before sitting down, but the meeting was about to start.

"Smile, Zana. We're not your executioners," Tom said, eliciting a roar of laughter.

Zana glared at him, but managed a smile.

"That's more like it," Tom said. He was wearing navy blue shorts and a white IZOD shirt, not the new stylish kind with the big polo horse. Without staff or clients present, the attorneys who weren't dressed for golf wore white tennis clothes, surf shorts and to Zana's disgust, Lucas had on ratty jeans and a Stanford hooded sweatshirt. He looked too bundled up for the tropical weather, but just right for the air-conditioned office. Zana wore a conservative blouse with an Aloha print and black pants, but had left her suit jacket on the back of her office door. She hadn't bothered with makeup today and had pulled her hair back in a ponytail.

Frank sat stiffly at the head of the table, flanked by senior partner George Tao and Michael Lee. Zana noticed Rex, Cole and the other newer associates had strategically filled the seats as far away from Frank as possible, probably to avoid being singled out during the briefing of future assignments. The only other woman was senior associate, Suzanne Tong, with her bowl-shaped black hair and stylish glasses. She had glanced at her watch at least three times since Zana sat down. Suzanne normally worked upstairs in the real estate transaction section of the firm, but was filling in for a few months in litigation while they were short-handed.

"Okay, we're all here. Can we move it along? I've got an appointment in an hour," Suzanne said, looking again at her watch. Zana knew her appointment was probably at a salon, while the men likely assumed it was with a client.

"Good morning, ladies and gentlemen," Frank said. He was the only man here who looked more comfortable wearing a suit and tie than the golf shirt and khakis he wore now.

"Good morning, everyone," George said, peering over his reading glasses. Zana rarely saw George, who was usually on the golf course schmoozing clients. He was the firm's rainmaker and she had heard, was considered the most valuable partner even though his monthly billable hours seldom exceeded double digits. Where Frank was intimidating and cold, George was friendly and warm. His eyes were kind, especially to associates, whom he made every effort to mentor. Zana had talked to him a handful of times during Saturday meetings or in the lunchroom, but had never had the opportunity to work with him.

Andrew had been George's right hand man for the past year, which gave him opportunities to take neighbor island depositions and appear in court, but didn't protect him from Frank's critical eye. According to Andrew, Frank had fired the three guys who had preceded him in helping out George. Andrew felt it was just a matter of time before he was next.

After George announced some new clients from Japan and Korea, Frank, Tom and Lucas recapped their trial preparations and discussed the motions they were working on in an attempt to exclude evidence at trial. Lucas boasted about a legal theory he planned to argue in court, while Zana stared at him with her mouth agape, trying not to roll her eyes. She hoped Frank and Tom weren't relying on anything Lucas claimed to be doing.

The group methodically discussed depositions, court hearings, pre-hearing conferences, discovery deadlines and arbitrations scheduled for the upcoming week. Eventually, the topic of the triathlon case came up when Rip Mansfield's name was mentioned.

"He settled a case for over a million dollars last week," Michael said.

"Speaking of Mansfield, Plaintiff Brad Jordan's deposition is scheduled for next Friday," Tom said, clicking his pen while he talked. "We noticed it weeks ago, but now we've got a conflict."

"Tom and I have to be in court for a pre-trial conference, the hearing on the motions in limine, and the final settlement conference for our trial. It's going to take most of the day," Frank said, looking at Zana.

"Of course, we have to reschedule it," Zana said, surprised she had become a participant in the meeting.

"I've asked Mansfield and he refused," Frank said.

"That doesn't surprise me," Brian Ching said, taking a sip of coffee.

"Zana will have to take the plaintiff's deposition," Frank said.

"Are you kidding me?" Lucas said, slamming his coffee cup on the table, causing its contents to splash and soak his legal pad.

Zana had the same reaction as Lucas, but was afraid to say anything. She had no business taking a plaintiff's deposition and certainly not one with Mansfield present. She would be eaten alive. Apparently, all the other attorneys in the room thought that, too, staring at Frank in wonderment.

"That's not going to work, Frank. You know Mansfield," George said. "I've gone to trial against him dozens of times. I'll take the depo with Zana's assistance."

Zana held her breath, hoping Frank would take George up on his offer. Plus, it would give her a chance to see him in action.

"Thanks, but aren't you leaving for Japan?" Frank said.

"We aren't leaving until Sunday," George said, peering over his reading glasses.

"Okay. Thanks, George," Frank said, nodding at his partner.

Zana breathed an audible sigh of relief and felt some of the tension ease in her shoulders.

"George, after you leave," Frank said, rubbing his chin. "Zana will be on her own with discovery while I'm tied up in trial."

"Aren't there any other partners who can step in to help her? She's pretty green," Lucas said.

Zana stared at Lucas, willing herself to keep her mouth shut. Andrew shot her a look of warning.

"I'm afraid not. Joseph will be at a dog show on Kauai and the other litigation partners are in trial, or otherwise tied up. I was planning on having Brian supervise her, but he's heading to California for depositions. Our client wants Zana on the case and so he'll get his wish," Frank said.

Zana bit her lip and rubbed her pant leg under the table. Her hands were sweaty.

"You're working with co-counsel, Jerry Hirano, on this case, right Zana?" Tom glanced at her.

"Yes," Zana nodded. "We've been working on some investigation together." Feeling her face flush, she hoped no one noticed.

"Does Jerry actually work? I thought he was just Kung Fu fighting these days?" Michael said, eliciting laughter from the guys. Lucas snorted.

"Watch out, Zana," Kim said. "Jerry will put the moves on you."

"That's enough, guys. Can't we wrap this up? Suzanne has an appointment," Andrew said.

Zana was relieved when her housemate came to her rescue. She wasn't sure how much Andrew knew about her dinners with Jerry, but was fairly certain Kelly had passed on some of the details.

"What has your investigation revealed?" Frank gestured for her to continue.

"There's some evidence the plaintiff is faking his paralysis," Zana said.

Everyone who was fidgeting with a pen, paper clip, or legal pad stopped and gave her their full attention.

"We have a witness in Minnesota who saw Jordan racing in a triathlon. We also have pictures we believe show him standing in a window," Zana said.

"I suggest you fly to Minnesota and depose that witness," Frank said.

"Jerry's planning to subpoena the witness for deposition in a few weeks." Zana made sure to keep clear eye contact with Frank.

"You better pack your parka, because you're going, too." Frank jotted a note on his legal pad.

"You're sending Zana to a mainland deposition?" Lucas said in a whiny voice.

"Jerry has had successful trials against Mansfield. She'll be in good hands," Frank said.

A few of the attorney-boys exchanged looks between each other.

"There's another development," Zana continued. "We found a witness to the accident. You know that guy, John Chu, who was in the news for his client allegedly poisoning his wife?"

Some of the men nodded.

"He saw the accident, but he's not talking."

"You'll have to take his deposition, too," Frank said. "Where does he live?"

"Jerry's on it. We tracked the guy down to a house near Kilauea Avenue, the accident location, but he just moved to Maui according to our investigator," Zana said. "We think he relocated to avoid involvement in this case."

"Make sure you fly to Maui for Chu's deposition," Frank said, jotting another note on his legal pad.

Zana nodded.

Lucas sighed loudly and shrugged his shoulders.

"Is there anything else we need to discuss?" Suzanne said, looking at her watch again.

"I think that's it. Anyone else?" Frank met each attorney's eyes around the table. Some of the attorney-boys shook their heads. "Enjoy your weekend, everyone. Make sure you get your timesheets into accounting."

Zana grabbed her phone and rushed out of the room, but sensed Lucas following her. She stepped into an open elevator and pressed the "close" button, surprised the door snapped shut before he could step in. It was still early enough to go for a long bike ride by herself. But first, she'd stop by Starbucks for some coffee.

Chapter 26

@Zlaw Sometimes work gets in the way of my #daydreaming. Joking. It always does.

Brad stared at the T.V. screen, not registering what team was playing or even what sport was on. Rip forbade him from drinking any alcohol in preparation for tomorrow's deposition. Brad had been sipping coffee and eating Doritos all afternoon, hoping his craving for vodka would subside. After finishing the last chip, he licked his fingers, crumpled the bag and tossed it across the floor. It hit the rim of the garbage can, bouncing off onto the carpet, scattering a trail of crumbs.

"Fuck it!" Brad leapt out of his chair, scooped the bag into the trash and located a half empty bottle of scotch hidden behind a row of cereal in the cabinet above the fridge. He poured the scotch over a few ice cubes in a glass instead of using his plastic water bottle.

Heather was at work, so no one would be breathing down his neck the entire evening. He could walk around his apartment and if he dared, go for a run. He'd done it a handful of times when he had driven to a carefully selected location wearing a hat with an attached dishwater blonde ponytail so he wouldn't be spotted by an insurance company's surveillance team. Rip had warned him of that possibility.

Brad wondered what Rip actually knew of his physical abilities and drinking. His own attorney might have P.I.s watching him, too, checking up on his investment. Brad wasn't sure what Rip would do if he knew he could walk, but didn't want to test him or make him less motivated to intimidate the insurance adjusters into paying millions. As he swigged his scotch, he did a few squats in front of the T.V.

His thoughts were interrupted by a text from Megan. I'm here, let me in.

Brad sat down and rode to the door in his wheelchair, just in case someone other than Megan was on the other side.

"Hey, Brad," she said, walking in with bags of Burger King take-out.

"You brought dinner. How nice." Brad smiled up at her.

"I know you weren't expecting me, but I figured you needed company before your big day," Megan said, spreading burgers, a chicken sandwich, fries and ketchup packets onto the table.

"They always say not to have sex before the big game, but I've never been one to follow rules," Brad said, standing up and putting his arms around Megan, pulling her body close to his.

"Let's eat first and talk for a change. Are you sure Heather won't be coming over?" Megan ducked out of his embrace and sat at the table.

"No, she worked late and agreed I need my rest before tomorrow. She seemed pleased to have a night off from Brad-sitting." Brad sat next to Megan.

"You aren't that bad. Not too many diapers to change," Megan said, popping a few fries into her mouth.

"I met with Mansfield and his sharkettes this morning."

"Really? What was that like?" Megan looked up from her burger.

"We prepped for over three hours. They asked me question after question about the accident, my injuries, my background, and my personal life."

"Your personal life, eh? Did you tell them that we do it doggie style?" Megan handed the chicken sandwich to Brad.

"No, I just showed them a video. What do you think?" Brad smirked.

"I don't know. Did you tell them you're dating Heather and you can't get it up?"

"Surprisingly, they did ask and that's essentially what I said."

"Good. The only way we're going to make a shitload of money is if you stick to the story," Megan said, her mouth full.

"Man, I'm glad I'm not a lawyer. It would be torture to have to ask tedious questions for a living. They grilled me. I'm exhausted," Brad said, and then took a bite out of the chicken sandwich.

"You better have it together. Hopefully, there won't be any more interrogations until trial."

"I can't wait until tomorrow is over. Will you meet me downtown so I can see you after we're done? It would make me feel better," Brad said, reaching out to stroke Megan's hair.

"Are you sure you don't want Heather there instead?" Megan kept her eyes on her food.

"She'll be working," Brad said. "Besides, she isn't quite as much fun."

"I'll be lurking around the building. Just text me when you're done."

"Thanks, sweetie."

"What was Rip's office like inside?" Megan asked.

"Really cool. He must make big bucks," Brad said. "I wouldn't mind working in a place like that, everything was high tech, black and white granite and fine leather."

"Get a big enough settlement and we'll be living well."

Brad glared at her. "If it weren't for the accident, I would already be living well with a gold medal around my neck."

"Keep that thought in mind tomorrow. They need to see how the accident destroyed your life." Megan wiped her mouth with her hand.

"I'd rather focus on the future. I'm sick of being cooped up in this apartment. I want to ride my bike and run. And…"

"Be patient," she cut him off. "There will be plenty of time for training after we cash the settlement check."

"Would you be willing to move to France or Germany with me?" Brad stuffed the remaining few bites of his sandwich into his mouth.

"Sure. Sounds cool," Megan said.

"When this is all over, I was thinking about getting into pro cycling in Europe. After all, Lance Armstrong started out as a triathlete before his legendary bout with cancer, and look where he ended up," Brad said.

"Yeah, look where he ended up. I think you should skip the doping." Megan sipped her coke.

While they were envisioning the future and him competing in the Tour de France, they heard a few bars from Eminem's "Lose Yourself", Brad's ring tone.

"Hello," Brad said in a weak, sickly voice just in case an investigator was calling.

"Brad, this is Fely, Mr. Mansfield's secretary."

"Yes."

"Mr. Mansfield wants me to remind you that Doug Williams will pick you up at eight tomorrow morning," Fely said. "If you need assistance getting ready, he'll come early."

"No, that's okay. I can manage myself." Brad raised his voice.

"Make sure you wear the clothes you were given this morning."

"Okay," Brad nodded and took another swig of scotch.

"Remember, no drinking alcohol and you can only take the prescription drugs on the list you were given. Do you understand?"

"I think so," Brad said, hoping he wasn't slurring his words.

"Are you having any problem with these instructions?" Fely asked.

"No." Brad took another sip.

"If you are, call me so we can reschedule. Remember, this deposition is like you're in court. You'll not have another opportunity to make a good first impression."

"I understand."

"If your testimony conflicts with any previous statements or your testimony at trial, defendants' counsel will question you about that."

"I know. Rip and the other attorneys told me like five times already." Brad put his phone on speaker so he could talk while stroking Megan's hair.

"Also, I just want to remind you to listen carefully to all questions before responding. If you don't understand a question, make sure you say so."

"Sure." Brad kissed Megan's earlobe.

"Do you remember the code words and sounds you discussed with Mr. Mansfield?"

"Yes, I think so," Brad rolled his eyes and put his hand on Megan's breast, which she swatted away.

"Doug will go over them with you again in the morning. If you cough, that means you need a break to ask for help with a question area. Mr. Mansfield will ask you if you need a glass of water. Do you remember those codes and procedures?"

"Yeah, I've got it. We practiced it all morning," Brad sighed.

"Okay. Do you have any questions for me now?" Fely asked.

"No. Thanks."

"Okay. Good night and good luck," Fely said.

Brad turned his phone on silent. "I'm sick of this. I just want to relax. And, fuck your brains out."

"Let me finish my fries first," Megan said.

***

Zana ran along Ala Moana Beach's curved shoreline, the wind blowing her ponytail. Her bare feet carefully struck the sand with each foot strike, avoiding shells and debris. She inhaled the humid salty air, more relaxed after another stressful day of work. As she ran, Zana thought of her upcoming trips to Maui and Minnesota, butterflies whirling in her stomach. She would travel with Jerry, and hopefully, stay in the same hotel. As she caught herself daydreaming of romance between them, she forced herself to think about the case.

She picked up her pace, feeling the wet sand beneath her feet. She thought about John Chu and after seeing him stare at her out the window, was relieved he had so quickly moved to a neighbor island. He was expected to testify about seeing a mysterious woman plow into the racing bicyclists. But, there were police, volunteers, and barriers everywhere. Why had that woman driven onto the course? Hadn't she seen the road was closed to motor vehicular traffic after sunrise? Anyone who lived in that neighborhood would have seen the signs warning roads would be closed for the race for weeks in advance. The neighborhood was filled with old houses occupied by families. There was no reason to drive through unless someone lived there. On the morning of the accident, the woman must have purposely drove onto the racecourse. *But was her intent to kill or seriously hurt one of the athletes? What was her motivation? Was she exacting revenge?*

So far, their focus had been on Brad Jordan and they had spent little time on Vic Leavitt, the athlete who died. Maybe, someone was trying to kill him and the others were collateral damage? She'd include questions in the notes she prepared for George about this possibility. Jordan could be asked whether he knows of anyone with a motivation to kill Leavitt.

After her run, Zana leaned against her car and stretched her calves. Then, she wiped the sweat from her face and shoulders with a towel. She would love nothing more than to go home and watch recorded episodes of "Fighting in Paradise", but tonight she'd have to review her notes in preparation for Brad Jordan's deposition the next morning. She was looking forward to seeing Jerry, but doubted they'd have much time for a personal conversation.

***

Zana had been working with George and several paralegals all week, prepping for Brad Jordan's deposition. They reviewed investigator reports, medical records, discovery responses, notes, the police report, recorded statement transcripts, scene photos and records summaries. She was charged with preparing an outline of questions and educated George about the details of triathlons and training.

"Zana, you'll need to sit next to me and assist with documents," George told her when she dropped a copy of her outline by his office.

"Sure," she said. "Be happy to."

"This looks very thorough," George said, scanning the document. He then looked at her over his reading glasses.

"I hope so." Zana wished she could spend some time in his office looking at his framed art and shelves filled with mementoes from his travels.

"Have a seat and let's discuss what you can expect tomorrow." George leaned back in his chair. He ran a hand through his thinning gray hair. "I've been practicing law for almost fifty years, but I still remember my first deposition. I was scared shitless."

Zana gave George her full attention. "That's hard to imagine."

"It's true. I was about your age. The firm's partners sent me into the lion's den on my own. I was relieved when it was all over."

"Do you expect there to be problems tomorrow?"

George laughed. "Mansfield always creates some sort of ruckus, especially if he's having difficulty with client control."

"Is there anything we can do in preparation for it?"

"Since plaintiff might not actually be paralyzed, I've hired a surveillance team to install a few extra cameras in the hallways to see what transpires out of view. We probably won't get anything, but it's worth a try. Zana, you won't have any trouble with Mansfield tomorrow with me there," George said, looking at her intently.

"Thank you," she said. "I appreciate that."

"I don't approve of how he treats women. The Attorney's Disciplinary Committee is investigating charges against him."

"Really?" Zana swallowed hard.

"Unfortunately, their investigation has been going on for more than a decade with no move towards sanctioning him or preventing him from behaving inappropriately."

"So, he just gets away with it?"

George gestured with his hands. "He's been getting away with uncivil behavior for more than thirty years. No one has been able to stop him yet," he said. "Frankly, I think the only thing that *will* stop him is retirement or death. Rip Mansfield is a powerful man."

Zana turned away, not wanting George to see the fear in her eyes.

Chapter 27

@Zlaw Sometimes I'm mistaken for a secretary, flight attendant or a pharmaceutical salesperson. I'm really a Land #Shark.

Zana used her key to open the main office door and fumbled around to find the light switch on the wall. The illuminated digital clock behind the receptionist's desk read 5:23. The office was dead silent, except for the low hum of machines. Zana yawned, wishing she had been able to sleep more than two hours. It wasn't as if she was taking the plaintiff's deposition herself, but she felt anxious about sitting across from Mansfield all day.

She had tossed and turned all night, exchanging fears of Mansfield with lustful thoughts of Jerry, who would be sitting on the same side of the conference table—hopefully next to her—for the entire day. She counted seven dinners, lunches, and coffees with him over the past month to "discuss the case". She sensed there was something romantic brewing between them, but wasn't so sure if he wanted to pursue it. So far, Jerry had only pecked her on the cheek, brushed his hand against hers, and draped his arm around her shoulder. Kelly had advised Zana to accept their relationship as platonic, but there was something about the way Jerry looked into her eyes and the softness in his voice when he spoke that gave her hope his feelings matched hers.

For the past few days, she glanced at her iPhone every few minutes to check for an email, text, or phone message from him, but there was nothing. She thought about calling him about the upcoming discovery, but even in this odd business liaison, she had applied *The Rules*, letting him be the one to call her.

Zana settled in front of her computer, making last minute changes to the deposition outline. She reviewed the websites for the Hawaii triathlons held since the accident and found a few photos of Brad Jordan either emceeing or watching from the sidelines in his wheelchair. She printed color copies of the pictures so George could ask the plaintiff about them.

She also made sure there were multiple copies of all exhibits to pass out to each attorney attending.

Zana double-checked everything. Was she missing anything?

***

The pounding in Brad's head grew louder. He feared his head would explode, and pressed a pillow against his right ear. He licked his lips in an effort to sooth his cottonmouth. When he opened his crusty eyes, the light streamed through the window illuminating the medication bottles on the nightstand and Mansfield's clothing pick—an Aloha shirt and slacks—hanging on his closet door.

Brad squinted at the clock. It was only 7:45. *What was that pounding?* He eased out of bed and fished through a pile of clothes on the floor for his bathrobe. He slipped into his wheelchair and wheeled to the door, pulling his robe closed over his boxer shorts.

"Who is it?" he asked in a scratchy voice.

"It's Doug. I know I'm early, but I thought you might need some help getting ready this morning," the man said from the other side of the door.

"Dude, you're going to have to leave. I can get ready by myself," Brad said, cracking open the door.

"Sure. I'll wait in the car and be back in 15 minutes."

"No, give me a half hour. There's a Starbucks down the street."

"That's not going to give us enough time to get there, Brad."

"I don't care." Brad closed the door hard and locked it. He then opened it again after a few seconds and saw Doug still standing there. "Bring me a Venti coffee, will you?"

After he shut the door again, he hid the evidence from the previous evening. Megan had left at midnight after they had emptied a couple bottles of wine and had sex on a makeshift bed made out of pillows on the living room floor. He threw the pillows back on the sofa and tossed the condom wrappers into the kitchen trashcan.

Then, Brad poured a glass of orange juice and took a sip. He had planned on skipping the vodka this morning, but couldn't resist pouring in a generous shot. No one would know. He showered, shaved and put on the blue Aloha shirt and beige slacks Mansfield told him tested well with juries. Since only attorneys would be present during his deposition, Brad didn't understand why it mattered what he wore, but he'd put up with whatever necessary bullshit in order to collect his money. He was settled into his wheelchair when the doorbell rang. He took one last swig of vodka out of the flask he'd stashed in the pouch in the back of his wheelchair, and opened the door to see Doug, who handed him his coffee and a slice of banana bread.

"Eat this on the road," Doug said.

"I'm not hungry," Brad said, pushing it away.

After Brad was settled in Doug's SUV, he sipped his coffee, hoping it would settle his stomach.

"Do you have a trash bag?" Brad said.

"We can throw garbage away when we get there," Doug said.

Brad nodded, hoping he wouldn't hurl on Doug's leather seats. He opened the window a crack and leaned against it. If he could take a short nap on the way to town, he would be okay.

"Let's go over the deposition ground rules," Doug said.

"Let's not."

"Rip's orders," Doug said, flicking on his left hand turn signal as they merged onto the H-1 Freeway on their way downtown. "Listen to each question carefully before you answer."

"Uh uh," Brad nodded.

"Don't let the attorney put words in your mouth. He'll try to trick you."

"I got it." Brad sucked in air from the open window.

"Only answer what you know. Don't speculate or guess," Doug said, focusing on the road.

Brad glared at the man. "You told me all this yesterday."

"Rip insisted I go over it on the way to the depo this morning," Doug said.

"No need. The accident got my legs, not my brain."

"Humor me," Doug said. "Now, some possible questions: How many seconds elapsed from the time you heard the car's engine to when your bike impacted with another bike?"

Brad stared out the window. "I have no idea."

"You'll have to estimate," Doug spat.

"Okay, okay. Fine," Brad said, looking at Doug. "Thirty seconds."

"Do you know how long thirty seconds is?"

"Okay, half a second." Brad sighed and turned back to the window.

Doug clicked on his right hand blinker to take the Vineyard exit off the Freeway. Brad closed his eyes and nodded off. He jolted awake hearing Doug's voice.

"You'll have to answer my question," Doug said loudly.

"What?" Brad opened the small paper bag of banana bread and broke off a piece and popped it into his mouth.

"Did you talk to anyone after the time of the accident and before you were transported to the hospital?"

"I don't know." Brad said with his mouth full.

"You're not even trying, Brad. You talked to ambulance attendants and police." Doug sighed.

"I'll bet opposing counsel will be easier on me than you are. Geez!" Brad said as Doug pulled into the parking garage and pulled into the first empty space.

"I hope so. That's the point. If you can handle what we throw at you, you'll do well today."

"I can't wait until this is over." Brad stuffed the rest of the banana bread into his mouth.

"Do you have any questions or concerns?"

"Yeah, I don't know what I'm supposed to be doing," Brad said, letting Doug help move him into his wheelchair from the car.

"Do I need to go over everything again with you?" Doug asked.

"No, I'm just bullshitting you." Brad laughed. "You attorneys have got to lighten up."

Doug wheeled him through the parking garage toward the elevator. Brad studied the buttons on the panel as they descended in silence. Mansfield was sitting in the lower lobby of the high rise when Doug rolled Brad off the elevator.

"You're late," Rip sneered.

"Good morning, Rip," Brad said.

"Hi Brad. Are you ready?" Rip said, putting his hand on his client's shoulder.

"I was until Doug confused me with a thousand questions on the way over here. I hope I can keep it all straight," Brad said.

"He's doing his job," Rip said. "Doug will take you to the restroom and then we'll go upstairs."

"I don't need to pee," Brad said. "I'm ready for the land sharks."

***

At 8:30, Zana carried the documents and files in her briefcase, along with her laptop, to the large conference room. The court reporter, Dennis, was busy setting up his machine and computer on the far end of the long table. Zana placed a legal pad, pens, and the pile of exhibits in front of the chair next to the court reporter and began setting up her laptop in the spot next to where George would sit.

"Are you a new secretary?" Dennis asked.

"No," Zana blushed. "I'm an associate."

"Sorry. You seem so efficient. I'm not used to seeing attorneys do that," Dennis said, motioning to the neat placement of pad, pens and exhibits on the table in front of the empty chair.

Zana shrugged and plugged her laptop into the outlet under the table, pleased none of the other attorneys were there to hear his comment. The court reporter was in his early sixties. She suspected he had been recording the firm's depositions for well over thirty years. He was probably tight with the partners so it wouldn't surprise her if he told Frank or George that she had behaved more like a secretary than a lawyer.

She opened up a blank word document and typed "Brad Jordan's Deposition" on the top.

"No need to take notes," Dennis said. "I'm using Real Time transcription so you can view the questions and answers during the deposition with only seconds delay."

"Oh, right. My secretary downloaded the software. Thanks for the reminder," Zana said, clicking some keys.

When the door opened, she looked up to see Mansfield's associate entering the room pushing the plaintiff in his wheelchair. Through the glass wall of the conference room, she saw Mansfield talking on his cell phone in the lobby. Her heart skipped a beat when Jerry walked by and shook hands with her nemesis, just ending his phone call. Considering their recent hotly contested trial, their exchange looked cordial.

"Good morning Dennis, Zana. Good morning Doug, Mr. Jordan," Jerry said when he came into the room, smiling and nodding at each person as he said their name.

Mansfield entered the conference room, followed close behind by the other defense attorneys, Ray Sumida and Dean Henderson. Just as everyone got settled, George walked in carrying only a pen and a folder with Zana's outline. He looked younger than his seventy-six years, healthy and fit from frequent golf outings and commanded respect from all the attorneys at the table, including Mansfield. George looked wise in his reading glasses, like a Chinese Mr. Miyagi from "The Karate Kid". He spoke quietly and appeared very calm.

After Brad Jordan raised his right hand and swore to tell the truth, George began his questioning with the court reporter putting the testimony in a question and answer format, which Zana viewed on her laptop.

Q. (George Tao) When did you decide to come to Honolulu for the Olympic trials?

A. (Brad Jordan) I qualified at an early season race and decided to at that time.

Q. Did you know any of the other athletes who were competing?

A. Most of them. We competed against each other for years.

Q. Did you have any expectation of qualifying for the Olympics?

A. Yes.

Q. What was your expectation based on?

A. I was the best athlete of those who were competing.

Q. Why did you consider yourself the best?

Rip Mansfield: Objection. Asked and answered. Argumentative.

Brad Jordan: Do I answer the question?

Rip Mansfield: Go ahead.

A. I was U.S. National Champion at the time. I had raced the top guys in the field in the past and usually won.

Q. Were your relationships with any of the top guys in the field strained in any way?

A. You mean, were any of them my enemies?

Q. Yes.

A. No. We all got along.

Q. What time did you get to the race site on the morning of the accident?

A. I don't remember.

Q. How long before a race did you normally arrive?

A. It depended on the race.

Q. Please describe what you recall about the accident.

A. Jeff, Vic and I swam together. Well, Jeff was in front of us and Vic and I swam mostly side by side. Jeff was out of the water first, then Vic, and I was right behind Vic running into transition. After we got on our bikes, Vic passed Jeff. The pace line was Vic first, then Jeff, then me. I don't think anyone was immediately behind us. We rode up Kilauea in that order. Our wheels were close together. As we approached the top of the hill, we were hit by a car. (long pause) All I remember is that I saw the front of the car hit Vic's bike dead on. Jeff went flying and so did I.

Q. Did any vehicle or bicycle impact with your bicycle?

A. I'm not sure. Maybe Jeff's bike hit mine. It happened so fast.

Q. Was any part of your body impacted with a motor vehicle or bicycle?

A. I don't know.

Q. Where did you land?

A. On the ground.

Q. Where on the ground?

A. I'm not too sure.

Q. In what position did your body land?

A. Hmmm.

Q. [Rip Mansfield] Do you want to take a break?

Brad's eyes welled up with tears. He put his head in his hands and began sobbing.

"We're taking a break," Rip said. He motioned to Doug, who wheeled their client out of the room.

***

Brad was surprised he had broken down when asked about the race. This wasn't part of the plan. He hadn't expected the memory of the accident to evoke such strong emotions. Ever since he was released from the hospital, he had been using alcohol to numb his brain, avoiding any thoughts about the day of the accident as much as possible.

Today, as he answered questions, he vividly remembered Vic dying right there in front of him. He couldn't understand why he lived and Vic didn't. It occurred to Brad that this was the first time he had shown any emotion about the accident. Rip was going to kill him. He had emphatically instructed him to keep it together. Brad's only thought as he was wheeled out of the conference room was his desperate need for a drink.

"It's freezing in there," Brad said.

"Here, wear my jacket," Doug said, taking his suit jacket off and helping Brad into it.

"Thanks," Brad said. "I need to pee."

"Sure, I'll go with you," Rip said, putting his hand on his shoulder.

"No, that's okay. I can go alone," Brad said, using his arms to manually maneuver the wheelchair into the hallway.

He saw Doug head back into the conference room, but Rip ignored his wishes and followed him into the hallway.

"Brad, you need to keep your emotions in check and focus on the questions. You'll have to be in control or you're going to mess up. Do you understand me?" Rip said sternly outside the men's room door.

Brad nodded. "I really need to use the lua."

"Go ahead." Rip started to follow him.

"Alone," Brad said, glaring at him.

Rip backed off.

Brad wheeled himself into the handicap stall. The flask hidden in the pouch on the back of his wheelchair was a calming sight. He took a few gulps and then closed his eyes, steeling himself to go back into the air-conditioned conference room. He slipped the flask into the inside pocket of Doug's jacket so he'd be able to take a swig more easily during the next break.

***

Zana remained in her seat during the entire break. The defense counsel had used the time to strategize. The questioning began again once Brad was wheeled next to the court reporter and the attorneys had put their smart phones down. George started once again and the court reporter carefully recorded every word shown in Real Time on Zana's screen.

Q. Before the break, I had asked you, in what position did your body land?

A. I don't remember.

Q. Did you talk to anyone at the scene of the accident?

A. I don't remember. Probably the—I don't know.

Q. Did you see the person who was driving the vehicle that hit Vic?

A. No.

Q. Did you get a look at the car.

A. Not really. I think it was white.

Q. Do you remember that specific detail?

A. I don't really know. I might have read it in the police report.

Q. Let me give you the police report for your review.

Zana opened a folder and passed copies of the police report around and handed a copy across the table to Brad. As he reached to grab it, the report fell to the floor. She bent down under the table to retrieve it at the same time as Doug and Brad. She noticed the witness bend down farther than she would have expected from someone without use of his legs. But, what caught her attention was the flask she saw when his jacket opened. She could also smell alcohol on his breath. She momentarily locked eyes with Doug and realized they both had seen the same thing.

She noticed Brad quickly close the jacket and sit upright in his wheelchair. She saw Doug put his hand on Rip's elbow. Rip continued to look bored and opened a newspaper, which rustled in the quiet room. Zana wrote on her legal pad, "Witness has been drinking" and pushed the note in front of George. He glanced at it and resumed his questions, which popped up on Zana's computer screen.

Q. Mr. Jordan, please review the portion of the report in front of you under "unit 1". Do you see where the vehicle is described?

A. Yes.

Q. Does that refresh your recollection?

A. I don't have any recollection of the car.

Q. You do agree that a vehicle entered the racecourse and caused the accident, is that correct?

Rip Mansfield: Objection, argumentative, misstates prior evidence.

Zana was surprised Rip had been listening behind the wall of newspaper. It caught her off guard to hear his loud and surly voice, which had been convivial up to that point.

"You can answer the question, Mr. Jordan," George said.

"You will *not* answer the question," Rip stated loudly, standing up, letting the newspaper drop to the floor.

George continued, "Do you have any reason to believe…"

Buzzzzzzzzz… Buzzzzzzzzzzzzzzzzzzzz… Buzzzzzzzzzzzzzzzzzzzz…

A loud alarm sounded. It took a few seconds for Zana to comprehend it was a fire alarm.

"We're leaving," Rip said.

"It's a fire alarm. We need to evacuate the building," Doug said as he bolted out of his chair.

Zana grabbed her purse and followed Jerry and George to the stairwell.

***

Rip yanked Brad's wheelchair away from the table. Doug then wheeled Brad out to the elevator where dozens of employees and attorneys had gathered to walk twenty-seven floors down to the ground. Rip pressed the button on the elevator and the three of them waited for the doors to open.

"Sir, you'll have to be evacuated by the stairs. No one can take the elevators," a man wearing an orange vest and red cap with the words "Fire Marshall" on it advised them.

"Clearly, this gentleman can't take the stairs," Rip said.

"Sir, step away from the elevator. I'll make sure the gentleman gets down safely," the Fire Marshall said loudly, placing his large body between Rip and Brad.

The elevator door opened and Brad rolled in, laughing out loud as the doors snapped shut, leaving Rip and Doug in the hallway.

"Asshole!" Rip bellowed at the Fire Marshall. He had pulled the fire alarm trick a handful of other times and had never had a problem staying with his client.

Rip followed Doug down the stairs. Even though his associate was twenty-five years his junior, Rip's fury gave him a rush of adrenaline, making it easy to keep up with him. He pushed past people who seemed to be taking their time and stopped saying, "excuse me" after they were halfway down. Now he was getting winded and his Aloha shirt was soaked with sweat.

"You jerk!" a woman yelled after Rip when he nudged her out of his way.

He shrugged it off. He didn't care what she thought of him.

The stairwell exited on the Diamond Head side of the building directly across from Cookie Corner. Once Rip and Doug were outside, they pushed through throngs of people to reach the front door blocked by police officers and fire fighters.

"You can't come in here, sir," a police officer said when Rip squeezed past him into the foyer.

"My client's in an elevator alone," Rip said. "He's an invalid."

"Sir, we'll take care of him," the officer said. "Please exit the building."

Rip didn't move an inch, hoping they would relent and let him search for Brad.

"Sir, you must leave now," the police officer said, and then turned to a colleague. "Sergeant, escort this man out."

Another uniformed officer took Rip by the arm and led him to an area about 20 feet away from the building where a crowd of people gathered. Doug followed behind him with his phone up to his ear.

"Has he answered yet?" Rip asked.

"No."

"Try texting," Rip said. "This is a fucking mess!"

"No response yet," Doug said after a few minutes.

"Fucking loser," Rip said. He cracked a smile for a brief moment, thinking about the balls his client had to get drunk during his deposition and then escape. It was something he would do.

After a few minutes, Rip saw a police officer pushing Brad in his wheelchair out of the building towards them.

"Thanks, Officer," Doug said, taking over the handles on Brad's wheelchair and pushing him towards the large planters of tropical foliage.

"All clear. False alarm," an announcer said over a loud speaker. "You may now return to your offices."

Rip led them to the back of the building where there weren't any people congregating.

"You fucking asshole!" Rip towered over Brad in his wheelchair.

"What are you saying?" Brad slurred.

"You're drunk, dude," Doug said.

"So what?" Brad said, reaching into Doug's jacket for his flask.

Rip grabbed Brad's wrist and yanked the flask away, then put it in his own pocket. "No one messes with me, you God-damned prick," Rip bellowed. "Do you know how lucky you are that I agreed to represent you? I don't put up with this crap. You either listen to me and follow my advice, or you end up with nothing—or loser representation."

"Oh, sorry." Brad looked down.

"Sorry, my ass."

"Give me another chance," Brad said. "I'll do what you say."

"Another chance? What the fuck?" Rip said. "Why?"

"Please," Brad begged.

"Didn't we tell you? No drinking or drugs," Rip said.

"Yes."

"Are you stupid?" Rip stared at him.

Brad put his face in his hands.

"My clients get one chance. If they blow it, they get no money."

"I'm sorry. I can do better."

"What pisses me off, Brad, is that I spent all day yesterday telling you how to behave and what to say. You didn't listen to a God-damned thing, did you?" Rip pressed his finger into Brad's chest. "If you had testified as I told you to do, we'd be walking away with millions right now."

"Sorry," Brad slurred.

"Doug, take this cocksucker home. We'll get in touch and let you know if we're going to be filing a motion to withdraw as counsel. I'm the best attorney you'll ever get. Remember that," Rip said.

Rip turned around and walked back to his office. He took a sip from Brad's flask and grimaced. Revolting. Then, he thought about how good his Nun's Island whiskey was going to taste.

***

Megan checked her iPhone to make sure the audio was clear. She played the video over again, watching Rip look down at Brad in his wheelchair, and bellow, "I spent all day yesterday telling you how to behave and what to say." She watched the video again and then snuffed out her cigarette in the ashtray portion of a garbage can outside the building where Brad's deposition had been held.

Even though she was a triathlete, from time to time she enjoyed smoking, a bad habit she picked up when she was a teenager. When the fire alarm sounded, she had been waiting for Brad on the ground floor lobby as promised. She lit the cigarette after evacuating, then ducked behind a large planter when a few people gave her stink eye for smoking too close to the building.

While Megan was kneeling on the ground hidden by the planter, she heard Brad's and Rip's voices. When she peeked out, she saw Rip for the first time since he had two-timed her for that slut at Starbucks. She aimed her smart phone at the three men, clicking on her video camera, not expecting to capture anything helpful or interesting. Heather's antics must be rubbing off on her. Now, reviewing the video and listening to Rip's rant, she wondered how she could use it against him. She smiled, envisioning sweet revenge.

Chapter 28

@Zlaw He couldn't keep his eyes off me!
There are #witnesses.

Zana suspected Rip or one of his minions had set off the fire alarm. According to George, Rip had been pulling similar stunts since he started practicing law years ago, but had never been caught. For that reason, before Brad Jordan's deposition, Caron had authorized payment for extra security cameras. The building management had even allowed them access to the elevator security video recordings and cooperation with their Security Supervisor, Bert Kalakaua. The day after Jordan's failed deposition, Zana and George sat at the conference room table sipping coffee waiting for Bert and their investigator, Rick, to arrive.

"This is the first time our firm has done anything like this," George said.

"I hope there's some useful footage," Zana said, positioning her legal pad and pen on the table.

"We'll see. As I've gotten older, I've become less patient with Mansfield's nonsense. I know Frank is concerned about F.I.M.'s litigation budget, but at some point we have to take a stand."

"Makes sense. Too bad Frank can't be here to see this."

"They're prepping their expert for trial today," George said. "I hope the investigator gets here soon; I've got to pack for my trip. You'll be on your own for a while."

"No problem. I've got it covered. I hope you have fun in Japan," Zana said, her voice shaky.

"You'll be okay," George said, patting her hand in a fatherly fashion. "Have you made your travel arrangements yet?"

"Yes, Sylvia has been out sick so Libby took care of it for me."

Rick and Bert walked in the door. After they shook hands and made introductions, Rick slipped a disc into the DVD player.

"The first video shows Mansfield, Jordan, and another attorney from Mansfield's office," Rick said.

"That's Doug," Zana said, as the video showed the attorney wheeling

Brad into the elevator followed by Mansfield. Doug pressed the close button the moment Brad entered the elevator, blocking a few people who were trying to get on.

"I thought you placed microphones with the cameras," George said. "I'm not hearing any sound."

"We did, and we were able to record their conversations," Rick said, adjusting the volume.

"This is sounding disturbingly illegal," George said. "In my day, we resolved cases through good old-fashioned jury trials."

"Now it's arbitration, mediation and technology. There's no law against having security cameras—they're everywhere," Zana said. "If Brad Jordan is faking his paralysis we need to know."

Rick turned up the volume more using the remote. Zana pushed her chair closer to the flat screen.

"Remember to listen carefully to the questions and tell the truth, Brad," Rip said loudly.

"Okay," Brad said.

"If you don't understand a question, remember to let them know. I'll be right beside you. Everything will be okay as long as you tell the truth," Rip said, and then the elevator opened and the two walked out.

The screen went blue.

"That's weird, it sounded as if he knew he was on camera," Zana said.

"Yeah," Rick said. "Everyone knows there are security cameras in elevators."

"But, there aren't usually microphones," Bert said.

"Do you think Mansfield knew what we're up to?" Zana said.

"I'll bet he's just being careful," George said. "Let's look at the next video."

They watched footage of the three getting off the elevator and as they made their way down the hallway. Doug opened the door of the law office for Brad and Rip, and they walked into the reception area with Doug pushing Brad's wheelchair. Rick switched to the next video, showing the receptionist taking their names and Rip sitting on the black leather sofa, picking up the newspaper from the coffee table. He then answered his phone, standing up while talking. The video showed Brad wheeling his chair up next to the couch and studying his phone. Doug excused himself and walked into the hallway.

"Can we see what Doug is doing?" George asked.

"Sure." Rick pressed some buttons on the remote to show the hallway footage.

They watched an empty hallway for a few minutes. Then Doug walked out the door and waited, studying his phone. After about three minutes, the elevator opened and a teenage boy wearing jeans and a gray T-shirt came out carrying a messenger bag. Doug handed him an envelope.

"I'll text you," he said to the boy. "You know the code?"

The boy nodded, tucked the envelope into his bag and turned to press the button for the elevator. Doug then walked back into the reception area.

Rick switched the video back, which showed Doug walking up to Rip.

"We're all set," Doug said while Rip was still talking into his phone.

"So, he paid the boy to set off the alarm?" Zana said.

"Well, unless there's some evidence the boy set off the alarm, it doesn't look like we can prove it. Why do you think the envelope had money in it?" George asked.

"You've got a point," Zana said.

"You've been watching too many cop shows on T.V.," Rick said.

The surveillance video showed the defense lawyers entering the reception area, making small talk, and ribbing each other. Zana wished they could fast forward the video past the part when Dennis mistook her for a secretary, but to her relief, no one said anything about the incident.

"Things sure have changed," George said when the video showed everyone in the conference room looking at their cell phones.

"I can only imagine," Zana said. She was pleased the footage showed her sitting up straight and reviewing the exhibits rather than staring at her phone like the others.

The video then showed George enter the room, sit down and instruct Dennis to swear in the witness while the attorneys stashed their phones away and opened their laptops for note taking.

George grimaced. "Is that what I look like?"

"Don't worry, the camera adds twenty pounds," Zana said. "You look super fit in person. Walking the golf course every day is paying off."

Zana wasn't focusing on her image. She couldn't keep her eyes off of Jerry, the only attorney at the table who was photogenic. No wonder he was a T.V. star.

"You have an admirer, Zana," George said.

"Who?" Zana said.

"Watch Jerry. He couldn't keep his eyes off you," George said.

"It's just the angle. He's probably watching you ask the questions," she said.

"I've known him a long time, and he does have an eye for beautiful women."

"Look at Brad, don't you think he looks uncomfortable?" Zana said. "He's sweating."

"Good way to change the subject, but you're right," George said. "Rick, can you fast forward to the break?"

They watched the footage of Brad going into the bathroom and drinking from his flask.

"It's weird to have cameras in the men's room," Zana said.

"I hope you erased all other footage," George said. "The last thing the firm needs is a violation of privacy lawsuit."

"We only monitored Rip, Doug and Brad," Bert said. "Brad didn't even take a piss. Looks like he just went in there because he's a lush."

"I saw him drunk when he was emceeing a triathlon," Zana said.

"So, he drank at his deposition. I don't think it's much of a revelation. Rip will argue that the accident impacted his client so badly he started drinking heavily," George said. "I don't think that helps us much."

"Is there any footage of the alarm being pulled?" Zana asked, turning to Rick.

"No, the boy or someone else must have done it on a floor where there were no cameras."

"Is there anything helpful here?" George asked. He studied his watch. "I've got some packing to do."

"Take a look at this," Rick said.

"It's pretty dark. I can't see much," George said.

"That's the elevator Brad went down. For some reason the interior lights were off. I think the only illumination might have been an emergency button light," Bert said.

"Take a look at this." Zana stood up and pointed at the screen. "There's a dark figure in the elevator. It looks like a person is standing next to the wheelchair."

"There must have been a second person," George said.

"I wonder who it was," Rick said. "Do you think it's the boy?"

"No. It looks like a man," Bert said.

They watched the elevator footage over and over and even turned off the light in the room to see if they could make out the identity of the dark figure. Unfortunately, the video cut off before the door opened at the lobby floor.

"I think we need to look at the wheelchair rather than at the man standing," Zana said before they watched it again.

"Good point," George said, before the video ran again.

"The wheelchair is empty. The man standing must have been Brad Jordan," Zana said. "It looks like he was the only one in the elevator."

***

Brad thumbed through *Honolulu Magazine* shifting uncomfortably in his wheelchair as he waited for his meeting with Rip. He thought about heading back to his car where Megan was waiting, but knew she would send him right back up to ask when they were going to get "their" money. If he refused the meeting, she was going to confess their "relationship" to Heather.

He looked at his watch. He had been waiting for more than an hour, longer than he waited for doctor's appointments, because his attorney wasn't interested in talking to him. Brad had to bribe one of Rip's secretaries with a gift card for a spa day in order to finagle a spot on his calendar.

For the tenth time since he'd been there, Brad checked his Twitter and

Facebook feeds on his phone. He found nothing of interest. If he'd been at home, he would have paced, but he had to remember to keep his legs still even though the room, with its modern black chairs and angular chrome and glass tables, was empty. On the walls framed copies of settlement checks with an impressive number of zeros gave the room a focus point, which was far more interesting than the magazine he had tossed onto the shiny black marble floor. Finally, Rip's secretary, wearing a crisp white blouse and black skirt appeared in the doorway.

"Mr. Mansfield is ready to see you. Can I wheel you into his office?" Fely said.

"Sure," Brad said. He could easily wheel himself in, but thought he would look more pitiful if he appeared to need help.

Rip remained seated behind his desk and didn't bother to rise to shake Brad's extended hand as he'd done in the past. Before leaving, Fely positioned Brad behind two black leather guest chairs, which served as a barrier between the two men.

"Hi Rip," Brad said, putting his sweaty hand back on his lap.

"What can I do for you, Brad?" Rip said, spitting out his name, not looking up from a few papers on his otherwise large, empty black desk.

"Well. Uh, I was wondering…"

"I'm busy," Rip frowned, now examining his fingernails.

"I was just wondering when you're going to settle my case," Brad stammered, feeling sweat bead on his forehead. He waited in silence, watching his attorney examine each cuticle.

"Interesting question." Rip looked up and put his well-manicured hands in a steeple position.

"How so?"

"You were stinkin' drunk at your deposition and haven't even finished it. How do you expect any of the insurance companies to write out checks of their hard-earned policy holder's money without even knowing how you're going to testify in court?" Rip said, his voice even.

Brad wanted to shrug but kept his body still. "I'm not really sure."

"You're damned right about that." Rip looked back down at his papers.

"Can we finish my deposition?"

"You mean, start it?"

"Yeah, whatever."

"Listen, *Brad*." This time, Brad could see actual spit eject from Rip's mouth and sprinkle his pristine desk. "You have to get serious. Do you think it's easy to earn your first million?" Rip stood up. He picked up a granite paperweight shaped either like a pineapple or a grenade. Brad couldn't tell.

"No," Brad said, spinning his wheelchair so he could face Rip, who was now standing near the floor to ceiling windows.

"It takes hard work—guts. It takes careful calculation of every move you make 24/7. If you want to be rich, you can't rest for one minute.

You are on stage at all times. You can't lose your concentration or your competitors will destroy you." He looked intently at Brad.

"Okay." Brad squirmed.

"Do you think I got where I am today being a booze head? I can't afford to let alcohol numb my thinking. I would lose my edge."

"I hear you." Brad resisted licking his lips. He could use a drink right now.

"Same thing with you. If you want to win in court or settle this case, you have to focus. No more fucking up. Understood?" Rip moved from the windows and made his way across the room.

"Yes, I'm sorry."

"No more drinking. Not one drop. Do you hear me?" Rip said, now standing over him.

Brad put his head down. Heather had been bitching about his drinking for months, but he'd shrug his shoulders and ignore her. He could do whatever he wanted. He wasn't going to let anyone push him around. He could quit anytime. He had planned to once he got his money and began training again.

He looked up and saw Rip, his hands on his hips and brows furrowed, staring down at him. For the first time since the accident something clicked in Brad's brain. Just like he trained for triathlons—perfect swimming, biking and running, perfect diet, perfect sleep, he would have to train for this litigation. The prize was not sponsorship or a gold medal, but a hefty settlement check. He would train to become the perfect plaintiff, the best witness.

"I'll quit. No problem," Brad said, wheeling back a few feet to gain some distance between them.

"You're going to go to rehab for thirty days," Rip said, sitting back in his chair.

"*What?* No way? I don't need rehab."

"Fely will drive you to an in-house program. She'll stop by your apartment and pick up some clothes and personal items you'll need."

"No way do I need rehab. I'll quit on my own. I swear," Brad said. Beads of sweat dripped from his forehead. There was no way he was going to be stuck in some lame treatment program.

"Okay, have it your way. I'll file the documents to withdraw as your counsel this afternoon," Rip said, looking down at the papers on his desk.

"Wait a minute. Are you giving me an ultimatum?"

"You catch on quick, Jordan. No rehab; no pay day."

"What am I going to tell everyone? Where will I say I am?"

"Who will notice you're gone? It's not like you're working or doing anything worthwhile."

"I need to tell my girlfriend," Brad said.

"Which one?"

Brad stared at Rip. Did he know he'd been seeing both Heather *and*

Megan? Had Rip been spying on him as he suspected?

"My girlfriend...Heather Alexander. I don't know what you're talking about," Brad said, his face getting hot. He hoped Megan had stayed in her car as promised.

"Whatever you say. I've got to get back to work. We'll talk when you're out of rehab. My secretary will arrange everything," Rip said, and then pressed a button on his phone. "Fely, please come in here. I need you and Doug to take Mr. Jordan to Ola Makai."

Chapter 29

@Zlaw Flew through #cloud9 sitting in #firstclass with a first class guy. Still not a member of mile high club.

Zana slipped her laptop back into its case after going through security. She spotted Jerry sitting in a chair, putting his shoes back on. He looked up and smiled warmly before standing, placing his wallet in his back pocket and strapping on his watch.

"You might want to avert your eyes," Jerry said, threading his belt through his pant loops.

"I've seen it all before," Zana said, grinning.

"Have you, now?" Jerry raised his eyebrows.

"I've watched hundreds of men put their belts back on. Unfortunately, it's only been after going through airport security."

Jerry chuckled and picked up his large briefcase.

"We're at Gate 60," he said. "We have time before boarding. Do you want to join me in the Paradise Club Lounge?"

"Sure," Zana said. She'd never been in an airline lounge before and had always wondered what lie behind the doors where she had seen frequent flyers duck into between flights.

"Don't get too excited. The coffee is marginal and there's no food," Jerry said.

"Mediocre coffee is fine with me," Zana said, walking side by side with him to the lounge.

After being buzzed in, Jerry handed his ticket to the agent at the counter.

"Could you possibly change our seats so I can sit next to this lovely woman?" Jerry asked the agent, gesturing to Zana.

"Sure, Mr. Hirano. Would you like me to change your seats for your return flight as well?" the agent asked, batting her false eyelashes.

"If it's no trouble," Jerry said.

"No trouble at all. Miss, may I see your ticket please?" the agent asked Zana and she handed it over.

"I can put you both up front."

"Mahalo," Jerry said, taking the new tickets and then leading Zana to some chairs vacated by two businessmen.

Zana didn't notice the taste of the coffee as she sat across from Jerry at a small table. The large room was crowded, with almost every wicker chair and sofa filled with interisland travelers. The T.V. was tuned to the morning news and sections of the daily Star Advertiser were abandoned on end tables along with empty juice and coffee cups.

"It looks like everyone flying today has access to this lounge," Zana said.

"These early morning flights are filled with commuters. You'll notice the pre-boarding line will be much longer than general boarding. I feel sorry for the tourists who don't have Premium access," Jerry said. "Is this your first outer island trip?"

Zana shook her head. "I went to Kona a few times when I was a kid to watch the Ironman triathlon. But, I've never been to Maui or Kauai."

"You're in for a treat. Maui is beautiful," Jerry said. "When I was a kid, my parents took my sister, Jenny and I there for a few weeks every summer. We drove to Hana, hiked up Haleakala, and went to luaus in Lahaina where my mom would sing and dance hula."

"That sounds wonderful," Zana said, twisting her hair around her finger, wistful of the childhood he described. Her parents' idea of a vacation was driving to an out of state marathon or triathlon when she was a kid. With the exception of their two trips to Kona, they usually stayed in a cheap motel, camped in a tent or slept in their station wagon.

"Now, whenever I go to Maui, it's for a quick court appearance or deposition. I fly in and out, without leaving the air-conditioned rental car or building," Jerry said. "Getting on the plane is similar to taking The Bus to another work location."

"It'll still be exciting to go there even if I only see the sites as I drive by," Zana said.

"Sure—I'll point out the Costco, K-Mart, and Krispy Kreme in Kahului. Let's get to our gate. It's about time to board," Jerry said, standing up.

***

Rip slid his black Salvatore Ferragamo belt off and placed it in a bin along with his iPad in its leather case and his Italian leather loafers. His Rolex usually set off the x-ray buzzers, inviting TSA agents to feel up his pant legs. He'd left it at home for this trip and wore a black sports watch instead. His pockets were empty, save for some lip balm. His driver's license, boarding card, and credit cards were neatly stowed in his iPad case so he was able to avoid the fuss other travelers endured who were loaded down with plastic quart-sized bags filled with small bottles of liquids, laptops, and carryon luggage.

He knew better than to go into the Kokua Airlines Paradise Club Lounge, which was usually packed with attorneys and business people on their way to the outer islands. He wouldn't be able to relax amid opposing counsel, acquaintances, and clients who prattled on about their cases or golf games. Instead, he grabbed a coffee at the Starbucks on the far side of the terminal and found a deserted gate where he could relax and read the morning news on his iPad until his plane boarded.

Rip's paralegal had downloaded the case file for today's deposition on his tablet, his associates had prepped him with memos he'd reviewed the day before, and so there was no need to bother with work at this early hour.

"Hey, Rip. What are you doing over here in the boonies?"

He looked up to see his endodontist, Paul Telford, who he'd seen last year when he had an abscessed tooth several days before a deposition trip to New York. Dr. Telford had done him the favor of getting his tooth taken care of before the trip, and Rip had done him the return favor of handling his messy divorce with claims of domestic abuse by his wife.

"Oh, hey Paul. Just catching up with the news. Where are you off to?"

"Hilo, today. I go there once a month to do some dental work."

"So, how've you been?" Rip asked.

"Life's pretty good. Marilyn and I are engaged."

"Congratulations! It wasn't that long ago when I was helping you with your battle against Vera."

"Yeah," the man grinned. "You know, you and I do the same kind of work. The only difference is that I use anesthetic."

"Root canals are probably less painful," Rip said, giving Paul a lopsided smile. "You're a riot. You'll have to excuse me, but my plane is boarding. Good to see you, pal."

He shook hands with him.

As Rip walked toward his gate, he passed a few familiar faces and nodded to them. He thought they might be clients, but wasn't sure. He seldom had any anonymity in Hawaii and often craved the privacy he had when traveling to the mainland or abroad. On the other hand, he appreciated the notoriety that earned him the best restaurant tables and prime tee times at the private golf clubs. Besides being well known for his T.V. advertisements and news from big cases, he garnered lots of attention because of his close resemblance to Pierce Brosnan. Almost every day, someone asked him if he was the well-known actor. He would say yes or no, depending on his mood.

He arrived at the gate as they were calling for first class patrons to board. He passed the female attorney who worked for Frank Gravelle, but couldn't remember her name so he ignored her. She was standing with the other defense attorneys in the case, probably strategizing, since they had stopped talking when he walked by.

"Good morning, Rip," Jerry Hirano said.

"Hey, Jerry. Howzit going?" Rip said, not waiting for a response as he headed for the plane.

Usually Rip had his people fly outer island for him. He was only given Premium status because of the two first class tickets he purchased for the short 25-minute flight to Maui from Honolulu. He was not a big fan of sitting next to a fatty or chatterbox. It was worth it to pay to sit by himself. Having two first class seats at his disposal also afforded him the luxury of inviting an attractive woman who he might spot in coach to join him. On occasion, he had asked opposing counsel to fill the adjacent seat and sometimes they settled their case before landing.

He relaxed in the front, immediately turning on his iPad. He wasn't interested in watching the line of people try to squeeze their large bodies and stuffed carryon bags through the narrow aisle and he doubted there were any horny single women at this early hour to fill his extra seat. He made sure the flight attendant knew it was purchased and not available for upgrade. Then, he spent the rest of the flight reading the news on his iPad.

***

Zana and Jerry joined Ray and Dean, the two other defense attorneys, in line at the gate. Zana was relieved she'd been rescued from general boarding, so she wouldn't be exposed to Mansfield's taunts when he walked by. He left her alone, saying good morning only to Jerry when he passed them after first class boarding was announced.

"Come on, Zana," Jerry said.

"But they called first class…"

"That's us," Jerry said. Zana could feel the heat from his hand placed on her mid-back to guide her forward.

Zana had never sat in first class before and was surprised the plane only had three rows of wide leather seats separated by a curtain from coach. She followed him to their seats, two rows behind and across from Mansfield, who didn't look up from his iPad when they went by. After sitting next to the window, she leaned back and closed her eyes for a moment.

"You can nap on our way back. Let's go over the questions for John Chu," Jerry said, pulling out a deposition outline from his briefcase.

She nodded, wishing they could enjoy the flight rather than work.

He shifted his body closer to hers and held the outline, placing his forearm so it touched hers on the armrest. Feeling the warmth of his skin, she longed to pull his body closer to her. She could even smell his sweet breath and his musky cologne.

"You've got an eyelash," Jerry leaned close to her, putting his finger on her cheek. His voice was soft in her ear. Their eyes locked for a moment and he moved his face within inches of hers.

"Would you like juice or coffee?" the flight attendant said, interrupting.

"Coffee, please," Jerry said, pulling away suddenly.

"Water for me," Zana said, hoping Jerry would take up where he left off after she stepped away. The flight attendant placed their drinks on their trays along with small bags of macadamia nuts.

"I hope Mr. Chu doesn't mention us following him," Jerry said. The spell was broken and he went back to focusing on the outline for the remainder of the short flight.

When the plane landed, Zana saw Mansfield disembark first.

"Do you think Mansfield paid for first class?" Zana said as she followed Jerry off the plane.

"Absolutely. Did you notice he had two seats to himself?"

Zana nodded.

"He pays for two seats all the time so he doesn't have to sit next to anyone," Jerry said.

"The flight's so short, that doesn't make sense," Zana said. "If someone pays for first class, what do they get?"

"Guava juice and a smile." Jerry grinned.

"Oh, come on. We got that with free upgrades. A paying customer must get more than that?"

"They also get macadamia nuts. It's worth the extra $300 to get a dollar bag of nuts, don't you think?"

"Well, it does show shrewd money management," Zana said.

"Did anyone ever tell you you're sarcastic?" Jerry put his hand on Zana's hair and stroked it, caressing her neck.

"Never," Zana said, surprised by his tenderness.

"Your hair is so soft," Jerry whispered in her ear.

Zana beamed.

They walked side by side onto the sky bridge before she felt Jerry's hand on her elbow leading her into the airport. He held on to her until they got to the escalator. She stepped on in front of him, feeling him place his hand on her shoulder from above.

"What car rental company are you using?" he said.

"Avis."

"Me, too. Do you want to forego your rental car and ride with me?"

Zana realized she watched too many episodes of "The Bachelor" on T.V., because she imagined him asking if she wanted to forego her individual room and join him in the fantasy suite.

"Sure," she said, trying to suppress a giggle. "Are you capable of driving a Ford or Kia? If you don't know how to drive anything other than a Ferrari, I'm not sure it's safe to ride with you."

"I'm out of practice, but I think I can handle it," Jerry said, winking at her.

***

Jerry pulled the rental Kia up to the valet parking area of the ocean front resort in Waialea where the deposition was being held. The attendant helped Zana from the car, asking if she and her "husband" were guests, causing her to blush.

"This is exquisite," Zana said as she and Jerry walked through the foyer, which to her, looked more like a lush garden than a hotel. "Are all outer island depositions held at resorts?"

"No. This is the first one I've been to. We filmed a "Fighting in Paradise" episode here a few weeks ago and the resort's GM overheard me talking on the phone to my secretary about the location for this deposition. He offered his conference room."

The court reporter, Joy, was already set up at the end of the long table. Ray and Dean were helping themselves to coffee, guava juice and muffins set up on a side table and Rip was talking on his cell phone outside the doorway.

"Is Mr. Chu here yet?" Jerry said, setting up his laptop and files next to Joy.

"He went to the bathroom," Joy said as she set up her machine. "He seemed pissed off about having to be here."

"I'm not surprised." Jerry winked at Zana.

Zana opened her laptop next to him, and then grabbed a blueberry muffin while she waited for her computer to connect with the resort's WI-FI.

"Oh, it's you again," John Chu said as he walked into the room.

"Good morning, Mr. Chu," Jerry said, standing up to shake his hand.

"Can we get this over with?" John said, ignoring his hand and sitting down.

"We're going to start," Jerry said, calling to Rip.

"Just start without me," Rip said, but then ended his call and immediately came into the room, taking a seat at the far end of the table.

After Joy swore in the witness, Jerry started his questioning with the court reporter taking down everything they said. Zana followed along by reading the Real Time transcription on her laptop.

Q. [Jerry Hirano] Please state your full name.

A. [Witness] John Fenton Chu.

Q. Where do you live?

A. Kihei, Maui.

Q. How long have you lived here?

A. For about 2 weeks. I just moved here from Oahu.

Q. Why did you move?

A. I was hoping you wouldn't find me. I really don't want to be involved in this. I moved to Hawaii to retire in peace, but got this subpoena.

Q. You understand you're required by law to testify and tell the truth?

A. That's why I'm here. Can we get this over with?

Q. Were you a witness to a car verses bicycle accident that occurred during the Olympic triathlon trials in Honolulu?

A. Yes.

Q. What did you see?

A. I was walking home and I saw a white car driving on the road towards Kilauea Avenue, where the triathlon was going on. I assumed the car would stop at the traffic barriers blocking the road. I was waiting for the bikes to ride past so I could walk across the street. The car slowed down before the barriers and then sped up and ran over the first cyclist. That's all I saw. Can I go now?

Q. How would you describe the car?

A. It was a white compact car. I didn't notice the make. It looked like it hadn't been washed for a while.

Q. Did you see the license plate?

A. I didn't get the number, but I noticed it had a Seattle Seahawks frame.

Q. Did you see the driver of the vehicle?

A. Yes. She had long, black hair. I remember her, because she was strikingly beautiful.

Q. Can you estimate her age?

A. She looked young, probably in her 20s or early 30s.

Q. Did you notice anything else about her?

A. She was wearing a dark colored shirt and she had light eyebrows that didn't match her hair.

Q. How could you see her eyebrows from where you were standing?

A. I saw her face when I was standing on the edge of the corner when she was driving by at a slow pace.

Q. Why did you notice her eyebrows?

A. Okay, you know I lived in Hollywood for years. Women with dark hair have dark eyebrows. This one had light brown eyebrows. It looked weird.

Q. Did you notice anything else?

A. It looked like the driver waited until the first cyclist reached the top before she hit the gas, like she was purposefully mowing him down.

Q. After the car hit the bike, where did it go?

A. It sped up and drove towards the mountains.

Q. Did you see what happened to the athlete or athletes who were hit?

A. No, I didn't want to look.

Q. Why not?

A. I really didn't want to get involved. I saw police officers down the hill running up right after the accident happened. I heard an ambulance siren within a minute. They didn't need me to get in their way.

Q. Were there any other witnesses to the accident near where you were?

A. I didn't see any. The place where I was standing, waiting to cross the road, was the steepest part of the hill. I noticed some spectators, race officials, volunteers, and police officers farther down the hill.

While John Chu was testifying, Zana watched Rip's reaction. He had put down his iPad and was listening to the witness, his jaw set and eyes wide. The testimony would significantly hurt Brad Jordan's case. It would be hard to prove the defendants were negligent with a credible witness who would testify at trial that a woman intentionally drove onto the racecourse and hit the lead cyclist.

"I don't have any further questions," Jerry said. "Rip?"

He moved to the chair next to Zana and leaned forward as he questioned the witness.

Q. (Mansfield): Mr. Chu, isn't it true that your attention was focused on something other than the woman in the car the morning of the accident?

A. (Chu): No. I live a simple life. Immediately before the accident, the only thing I was paying attention to was the woman who plowed into the triathletes.

Q. The triathlon happened a long time ago. Wouldn't you agree that your memory is fuzzy about what happened?

A. Not at all. It was a dramatic event. I remember every detail as clearly as I would have the day it happened.

Q. You know Jerry Hirano is a famous actor, right?

A. I guess so.

Q. Isn't it true that you purposely gave Mr. Hirano answers in order to gain his favor?

A. I don't give a damn that Hirano is an actor. I was subpoenaed here to tell the truth and that's why I'm here. I'd rather be home.

Q. No further questions.

Rip snapped his iPad case shut and stomped out of the room without a word. John left a moment later at Jerry's nod.

"You kicked his ass," Ray said, glancing at Jerry.

"The witness was great for all of us," Dean said. "How did you find him?"

"A little detective work," Jerry said, putting his hand on Zana's knee under the table.

Dean, Ray, and the court reporter quickly packed up their laptops and left, leaving Jerry and Zana in the conference room alone.

"We have hours before our flight boards," Jerry said.

"We do. I didn't expect that to go so fast," Zana said. "Great job!"

"Can I buy you lunch at the Makai Terrace? The view is beautiful this time of year. We might even see whales from the restaurant," Jerry said as they walked out of the conference room. "It's mating season."

Chapter 30

@Zlaw Inspired by #whales mating on #Maui.

As Zana and Jerry stepped out of the air-conditioned building into the mid-day heat, she peeled her suit jacket off and dug her sunglasses out of her purse. They walked side by side down winding paths flanked by red ginger, Bird of Paradise flowers, and swaying palm trees as a gentle breeze blew in from the ocean. A few Zebra Doves pecked at a crust of bread off the path next to a gazebo where a couple was posing for a selfie. Zana breathed in the sea air before the sparkling ocean came into view, feeling the now familiar warmth of Jerry's hand on her back. Before they reached the restaurant, he drew closer, putting his arm around her waist. Her first instinct was to look around to see if any of the other attorneys or the court reporter had witnessed Jerry's display of affection. She only saw tourists.

"Two for lunch," Jerry said to the hostess.

Zana realized she was smiling like a Cheshire cat when one of the hotel staff smiled broadly at her. She didn't want to scare Jerry away, so she made the effort to replace her smile with a more pleasant, neutral expression. She felt butterflies in her stomach when he grabbed her hand and led her to their table.

They were seated on the lanai under the shade of a large umbrella with a magnificent view of the ocean.

"The water is gorgeous today." Zana looked at it in wonderment. She was usually too caught up in her work to notice her surroundings.

"You are, too," Jerry said, looking into her eyes.

Zana blushed and looked away. Changing the subject, she said, "Look how deep blue it is. Oh, look, there's a whale."

Jerry moved his chair within inches of Zana's. She felt his hand on her knee under the table, moving up her thigh.

"I've never seen one so close before," Zana said, trying to keep Jerry's focus on her words.

"Really? You haven't gone whale watching on a boat?" Jerry caressed her thigh.

"Not yet. I've seen pictures of whales breeching, but haven't done any sightseeing since I moved to Hawaii." Zana kept her leg still, not wanting Jerry to stop.

"There's a beach path with a lookout point. We should take a walk after lunch," Jerry said, moving his hand to her waist.

"That would be fun," Zana giggled.

He laughed with her. "Are you ticklish?"

She nodded.

"Let's celebrate with drinks," Jerry said.

"Celebrate Chu's testimony?"

"And, to us."

"During a work day?" Zana asked.

"Sure, you've got to relax sometime. Otherwise, you'll burn yourself out. Have a Mai Tai." Jerry gestured to the table tent with pictures of several tropical drink specials.

"I am relaxed." She purposely dropped her shoulders and slumped forward.

"That's more like it." Jerry laughed.

"Have you decided?" the waitress said, a pen at the ready to take their order.

"Two Mai Tais, please," Jerry said. "What do you recommend for lunch?"

"The fresh mahi mahi fish tacos are excellent," the waitress said.

"That's what I'd like." Zana closed the menu.

"Me, too," he said, handing their menus to the waitress who promptly walked away.

"Did you see Mansfield's expression when Chu testified about telling the truth?" Zana said.

"I did, but do you mind if we don't talk about work?" He reached out to touch Zana's hand resting on the table.

"Sure." She released her grip on her paper napkin and allowed Jerry to take her hand in his. They sat in silence for several minutes and looked out at the ocean.

"See those whales breeching," Jerry said, pointing with his other hand.

Zana nodded, startled briefly by the waitress with their drink orders.

"It's Humpback whale mating season.," he said before sipping the Mai Tai placed before him.

"Is that why they jump out of the water?"

"I'm not sure."

"I'll google it." Zana dropped Jerry's hand and pulled her iPhone out of her purse.

"Stop." Jerry again placed his hand over hers. "Do you always act like an attorney?"

"What do you mean?"

"I'd like to know the *real* Zana." Jerry looked into her eyes.

She put her phone down. "What do you want to know?"

"Do you know how to have fun?"

"Absolutely." Zana raised her glass and took a long sip.

The waitress set their tacos in front of them. "Can I bring you anything else right now?" she asked.

Jerry glanced at Zana. "No, thank you. I think we're fine."

"This is delicious," Zana said after taking a few bites.

"What do you do for fun when you're not working or triathlon training?" Jerry asked before trying his fish taco.

"Not much. That's all I have time for," Zana said.

"What would you do *if* you had the extra time?"

Zana put her taco down and looked at the sparkling ocean. Most of her teenage and early adult years had been consumed with her efforts to survive without parents. There had never been any free time available and no money for hobbies. She earned swimming and academic scholarships for school and often worked full-time jobs to pay for necessities. She didn't know how to answer Jerry's question.

"You look stumped," Jerry said, putting extra guacamole onto his taco.

"What would you *do* if you had extra time?" Zana said.

"Acting, martial arts and travel. But, if I had 48-hour days I'd volunteer at an animal shelter. I love cats and dogs, and so many of them need good homes."

"I've never done that before. Do you have any pets?" Zana pushed her plate away and leaned back in her chair, feeling her body relax.

"I've got two Siamese cats. My sister gave them to me as a gift when they were kittens for my birthday a few years ago. She knew how much I missed having pets. We always had animals when we were growing up. Have you ever had any?" He reached for Zana's hand again.

"Sure. We had a dachshund when I was really young, but he got cancer. I don't remember much, except that he had to be put to sleep. There were some cats at some of the foster homes where I lived, but I never got close to them," Zana said, feeling sad despite her hand being tingly from his touch.

"Did you do anything fun when you were a child that you miss doing?" Jerry asked her, squeezing her hand.

"My mom and I designed and sewed clothes together. Everything I wore was handmade."

"Wow. Would you ever do that again?"

"I loved it. I have such fond memories of my mom from those special days. Yes, if I had endless time, I would definitely make my own clothes again." She grinned, though her eyes were misty at the memory of her mother.

"Have you ever done any modeling? You look like you'd be perfect for the runway."

"Thanks." Zana smiled at the compliment. "I modeled for Macy's when I was about ten, but had to quit because swim meets were on the same days as the fashion shows."

"See, you do have other interests besides triathlon and your law practice," Jerry said, his voice soft. He gently swept a tendril of hair from her face.

Zana nodded. She concentrated on her second Mai Tai, hoping Jerry didn't notice tears welling in her eyes. No one had ever asked her about her passions before or seemed to care about her the way he did. He seemed unapproachable on the T.V. screen, but sitting next to him, holding his hand and sharing their desires, felt intimate.

"I hope you'll be able to sew and model again someday."

Zana laughed. He was so sincere, but she didn't have time to waste. "I'm getting too old for modeling, and it's easier and cheaper to buy clothes in the department stores."

"Be open to living your dreams," Jerry said. "That's what I want to do."

"What are your dreams?" Zana asked.

"I'll tell you someday," he said, sipping the last of his second Mai Tai. "Shall we go take a closer look at those whales?"

"Why not."

Zana was unsteady after drinking so much. Two Mai Tais was more than her usual. Jerry held her hand as they made their way down the steps to the beach walk. The sky was overcast so it wasn't as scorching hot as it normally would be in the afternoon. Zana wished she was wearing shorts and a bathing suit top rather than a blouse and skirt. At least she had decided not to wear pantyhose, so her legs were bare to the cool breeze. She wondered if Jerry was roasting in his long pants and Aloha shirt. They passed a few tourists as they walked, but most of the people they saw were lounging on the beach, in the water, or walking on the grounds of the hotel.

"There's an amazing place up ahead where we should be able to see some whales," Jerry said.

"And, hopefully, not just the white human whales lying on beach towels," Zana said.

"You are cruel, Zana West. But, I'm quite fond of you anyway." As they reached the lookout point, he pulled her close to him.

"Do you treat all opposing counsel so familiarly?" Zana said softly.

"Only you," Jerry whispered in her ear. He kissed her tenderly on the mouth. She returned the deep kiss, tasting his tongue sweetened by the Mai Tais.

As they explored each other's lips and pressed their bodies against each other, Zana felt Jerry's hands move up and down her back and along the contours of her rear end. She wished time would freeze and they would forever be locked together in this beautiful embrace overlooking the deep blue ocean where the whales were mating.

"I'd like to tear your clothes off and make love to you on the beach."

Jerry looked deep into her eyes.

"I'm sure we'd have quite an audience," Zana said. Her body trembled. She, too, wouldn't mind a little exploring.

"I've wanted to kiss you since I first met you in your office," Jerry said.

"Really?"

"Absolutely. But, you didn't seem interested. I guess I've grown on you." Jerry kissed her earlobe.

"Yes, you're an acquired taste," Zana teased.

"So are you." He nibbled on her earlobe and then made his way down to her neck.

"Hmmmm," Zana moaned.

"I hate to say this, but I think it's time we head back to the airport. I suggest we plan on making love on the beach another time." Jerry kissed her again, slower this time.

"I'm looking forward to it," Zana said between breaths, her eyes still closed, enjoying Jerry's gentle kisses, not wanting to pull away from his embrace.

She beamed as they walked with their arms around each other back to the resort, stopping every so often for another kiss. They ducked behind a pillar to make out while waiting for the valet to fetch their rental car.

As they headed back to the airport, Jerry held her hand with his right hand and steered with his left. They listened to 90s music on the radio and compared memories of what they were doing when each song became popular. Jerry had been in college and Zana was in elementary school. But it didn't matter.

"Have you ever dated an older man before?" Jerry asked.

"Are we dating?" Zana said.

"I'd like to."

Zana cocked her head at him. "We're working on a case together. Are you sure that's appropriate?"

"Probably not, but at least our clients have similar interests," Jerry said, eyes on the road.

"Do I need to tell Frank?"

"Why? Do you think he wants to double date?" Jerry grinned.

"You're a nut." Zana pulled her hand away and adjusted the radio to a Hip Hop station.

"You're so young."

"Come on, you date young women all the time—or so I've heard..."

"No comment," Jerry said. "You might want to pull out your boarding pass and I.D."

Zana noticed Jerry's body stiffen when she mentioned him dating other women, which reminded her to guard her heart. From what she'd read in the tabloids, he wasn't the type to settle down or date someone exclusively, but she could have fun. Maybe, she should make an effort to date other men so she wouldn't set herself up for disappointment.

"You look like you're solving the world's problems," Jerry said when they finally pulled up to the rental car agency.

"Sort of," Zana said. She hopped out of the car, grabbing both of their briefcases from the backseat.

Jerry collected the rental car receipt from the agent who checked the car in, and they walked hand in hand to a bench to wait for the transport shuttle.

"I'm looking forward to spending time with you in Minnesota," Jerry said as he helped her aboard the shuttle, which would take them to the terminal.

"And, with Mansfield and the other attorneys?"

"We could stay at a different hotel," Jerry said, winking at her.

"That sounds promising." Her heart fluttered at the thought of being at a hotel with him.

"Think about it."

When they stepped off the shuttle, he pulled her close. "I don't want you to feel uncomfortable."

"I'm fine," Zana said, standing up straighter.

He gently positioned her face so she locked eyes with him. For a split second, she thought she saw a look of vulnerability in Jerry's dark eyes that matched her own. "I just want to make sure."

The security line was short and they got to the gate minutes before boarding.

"Do you think Mansfield or the other attorneys are on our same flight?" Zana asked.

"I doubt it," Jerry said, handing his ticket to the agent. "Those guys probably caught the first plane back and went straight to their offices. You don't have anything to worry about."

"Oh, shit!" Zana said, startled.

"What?"

"That's Michael Lee from my office," Zana said, gesturing to the man on the jet bridge ahead of them.

"So, I guess we won't make out on the plane," Jerry whispered.

"I hope he didn't see anything," she said, her voice shaky.

"Are you embarrassed to be seen with me?"

"No, not at all. I don't want to be fired."

Chapter 31

@Zlaw This is my personality. I'm not #drunk. Okay, I just fell down.

Heather picked up her smart phone again to make sure it wasn't on the "do not disturb" function. She rubbed the back of her neck and sighed. It had been weeks since Brad was admitted to rehab and he hadn't phoned yet. The administrator of the program assured her that Brad would call soon in order to fulfill one of the requirements of his 12-step program.

Remembering the saying about watched pots not boiling, or something like that, she stashed her phone in her purse. She turned on the T.V., hoping to catch the newest episode of "Girls", but settled on a Lifetime movie instead. When she finally heard the music of her Beyonce song ringtone, she dove for her phone.

"Unknown caller" showed on the screen. She answered it anyway and immediately recognized Brad's voice.

"Hey babe," he said.

"Hi honey, are you okay?" Heather said, trying to be sweet, even if she felt more like yelling at him for not calling sooner. She wanted so badly to tell him rehab was a waste of time, but didn't want to risk him hanging up on her.

"I'm okay. I need to tell you I'm sorry for treating you so badly," Brad said stiffly. "I'm an alcoholic and I've lied to you and have yelled at you. I'm sorry, Heather."

"Okay, I forgive you," Heather said quickly without any emotion in her voice. She didn't really believe he was an alcoholic, but it was nice to hear him apologize. Something he had never done before. "When are you coming home?"

"They'll let me out of this hell hole when I finish their program. I'm going as fast as I can. I should be home in a week or two."

"Can't you just tell them you're done?" Heather asked, trying to keep the frustration out of her voice.

"It doesn't work that way."

"I can't wait to see you," she said in the baby talk she reserved only for Brad.

"I have to hang up. I'm only allowed to be on the phone to make amends to people who I've hurt because of my drinking. I'll see you soon."

"Okay. I love you," Heather said, trying not to cry.

"I love you, too," Brad said, his voice cracking.

After Rip Mansfield's secretary called to break the news about taking Brad to rehab, Heather had driven directly to Patty's Bakery and bought a coconut cream pie, eating the whole thing in one sitting. She threw it up, and then didn't eat anything but carrot sticks for two days.

At first she hadn't told anyone about Brad's whereabouts—it was just too embarrassing. He was supposed to be an Olympic gold medalist, not a drunk. Heather confided in Megan during a phone call, who didn't act surprised.

"How can you be so calm?" Heather asked.

"He was drinking quite a bit," Megan said. "I'm sure you noticed."

"I didn't think it was that bad," Heather sobbed.

"He'll be back soon. There's no reason to be upset."

"He's in rehab for God's sake!"

"What's the fucking big deal? Lots of people go to rehab."

"It's embarrassing," Heather said, tears streaming down her face.

"Half the people you report on to the tabloids have either been to rehab or will be going there soon, so who cares," Megan said.

"They're not Olympic athletes."

"Neither is Brad."

What Megan said was the truth, but it stung. Hard. It was so difficult for Heather to see Brad as anything but the athlete she had been in love and obsessed with for so long. She knew he'd started drinking vodka after the accident, but it wasn't a big deal. He could stop anytime he wanted with self-discipline. All she cared about is what people would think if they found out she was dating an alcoholic or even worse, a recovering alcoholic who had done time in rehab. She had kept her eating disorder treatment top secret, but doubted Brad would be able to do the same, especially if he was calling everyone he knew to make amends.

"Why don't you use this time to focus on work," Megan had suggested on the phone.

"I'd rather mope." Heather was still wearing her pajamas.

"No you wouldn't. It's the perfect time to clean his apartment and take care of all the things you complain you don't have time for," Megan said.

"You're right."

"As always."

Heather laughed for the first time in weeks. "Well, at least you don't have to Brad-sit. Rehab has taken over your duties."

"Not all of them."

"Huh?" Heather said, she wondered if they had a bad connection. "Well,

I guess you still have to put up with me."

"No easy task," Megan said and they ended the call.

She didn't see her sister at all during Brad's rehab. Every time she phoned, Megan was either busy with teaching or was swimming, biking, or running, as she prepared for an upcoming triathlon. It was just as well.

While interviewing the mayor for a story on the state of tourism in Waikiki, Heather stumbled upon a chic new off-the-beaten-path restaurant frequented by celebrities visiting the island. The paparazzi were apparently not privy to this latest hangout so Heather began staking it out during her free time. She was able to pay off some credit card bills with the extra cash she earned from selling stories, and to help Brad out, she paid off some of his bills. She stopped by the florist to order an arrangement to be delivered the day he returned home. While she was at it, she ordered a tropical flower assortment for Megan to thank her for Brad-sitting.

***

Brad's legs felt cramped from being confined to his wheelchair for two weeks straight. He didn't dare stand up even when he was alone for fear a counselor or another inmate, as he called them, would walk in on him. Rip's warning was clear. Anything he said or did in rehab would be recorded and discoverable in the litigation. He was counseled to play up his injuries and blame his alcoholism on the accident, which could ultimately lead to a larger settlement. Brad was down with that.

"Hey dude, are you done with the phone?" Chet said, walking into the small office where the patients took turns making calls on the black rotary phone.

"One more call and it's all yours," Brad said. He wished he could use his cell phone, but had to give it up when he was admitted. The number he dialed was from memory and he didn't need to consult the crumpled list Fely had helped him compile. He waited until Chet, who was recovering from an addiction to cocaine, left the room.

"Hey, you," he said softly.

"Hey yourself," she said. "What's going on?"

"Can you help me sneak out of here?"

"Are you kidding me? What if you get caught?"

"It'll be worth it." He laughed.

"It's better if I sneak in," Megan said.

Brad started to get aroused just thinking about Megan's hands on him. "I'll be naked under the covers. Just how you like it, baby."

"I don't think I can sneak in through the window again. I almost got caught."

"Bring me something," Brad said. "You can tell them you're Heather."

"Then what?"

"You can hide, then sneak into my room after lights out."

"That's completely ridiculous," Megan laughed. "You're insane."

"Do you have a better idea?"

"I'll give it some thought," Megan said. "You only have a few more weeks. Can't you wait?"

Chet walked in the room. "Are you almost finished?"

"I've got to go," Brad said into the phone. "Surprise me."

He glared at Chet as he wheeled out of the room. If he weren't trying to play up his injuries, he would have smacked the dude. Who did he think he was treating a guy in a wheelchair like that?

Once back in his room, Brad made sure no one was looking and dove onto his twin bed, kicking off the wheelchair foot rests, causing it to roll and bounce off the wall. He had a few paperback books, some magazines and an old radio on the night stand, but no T.V. to watch, and nothing but water or coffee to drink. He lay on his back and stared at the ceiling. There were still 38 tiles—the same as yesterday.

He'd already been to a group session that morning and didn't have a meeting with his counselor until the next day. The T.V. room was too depressing with all the guys talking about how many days they'd been clean and sober. He didn't have anything in common with them. He said he was an alcoholic to make Rip happy, but he didn't mean it. His rehab experience reminded him of training for triathlons. His coaches told him what to do and how to think, and he followed without question. He was coachable.

The door opened after one knock. It was hard to get used to this place where employees barged in without waiting for his invitation.

"Your physical therapist called and said she's on her way," Rusty said.

"Really?" Brad said.

"I told her we don't allow private sessions with outside providers, but she said your doctor is extremely concerned about your condition deteriorating during your rehabilitation."

"Yeah, I know," Brad said, playing along. "I've been in a lot of pain."

"I insisted I couldn't bend the rules."

Brad grimaced and then groaned loudly.

"She threatened to sue."

"The physical therapy helps a lot with the pain," Brad said, moaning.

"I'll send her in when she gets here, but we'll need to discuss an alternative after today's visit."

Brad's mood changed the moment he saw his physical therapist walk in and close the door behind her. She wedged his wheelchair under the doorknob so no one would interrupt them.

"Are you ready for your physical therapy, Mr. Jordan?"

"Yeah, I'm really stiff. What's this?" Brad said, tugging at her hair.

Megan pulled the long black wig she had worn as a disguise and tossed it to the floor. She then yanked off her lanyard with its fake physical therapist badge and peeled off her clothes so they could begin their therapy session—under the covers.

Chapter 32

@Zlaw #Shoes causing blisters must die.

"You'd better win the motion," Frank said as he passed Zana in the hallway. The tone of his voice was almost threatening to her.

Zana ducked into Andrew's office the minute he arrived— shortly after 7 a.m., hoping for some reassurance. "Is he going to fire me if I lose the motion?" Zana asked. Sweat beaded on her forehead even though the air conditioner was set on freezing temperature.

"I don't know. Frank's the executioner," Andrew said. "We're all on death row."

"This sucks," she said, slumping into a chair. "He told me I better win the motion. He didn't say 'or else', but I'm sure it's implied."

"You talked to him this morning?" Andrew asked.

"Yeah, just a few minutes ago."

"He's probably stressed out. Never talk to Frank the morning of a trial. He has PTS."

"Don't you mean PTSD?"

"Nope. PTS. Pre-Trial Syndrome. It's like male PMS, but before a trial. Don't sweat it too much."

"You're a riot," Zana said with a slight smile.

"Stay out of his way this month if you want to keep your job." He leaned back in his chair with his hands in the steeple position as he always did when doling out advice.

"Good idea. I wish I could get rid of Lucas as easily," Zana said, standing to leave.

"I can't help you there."

***

Before heading to court, Zana read over her motion to compel Plaintiff Brad Jordon's deposition, which was scheduled before Judge Frederick C.K. Lee at 10 a.m.

Mansfield was taking the position that the defense had chosen not to continue after the fire alarm had sounded. In the memorandum in opposition he filed, Mansfield claimed he went back up to the conference room after the all clear was given from fire department officials, and no one was there. It was evident to him and his client that the defense had completed the deposition. According to Mansfield, he didn't receive a call from defense counsel for over a week after the deposition, and to start again and possibly go over the same questions would be prejudicial to his client who had already suffered so much at having become paralyzed because of the gross negligence of the defendants.

Zana had spent hours researching the law regarding depositions and discovery, and had cited cases from Hawaii and other jurisdictions in support of their position. Mansfield had also cited numerous cases, mostly from California.

She left for court at 9:00 even though it was only a twenty-minute walk with comfortable shoes. Before leaving, she had changed out of her sensible flats and into three-inch heels, ordered from late night QVC on a whim and still in their original box. The sky high black pumps would allow her to tower over Mansfield, and at the same time, show off her curvy calves to Jerry.

She hoped he would also be there early so they could chat in person instead of the intermittent texting. After their liaison on Maui a few days ago, they had been open about their feelings for one another. But they were both such busy people. Jerry's texts always said "on set" or "filming" followed by smiling cat emoticons. The studio was five minutes from her home, and while she wasn't expecting a booty call, she thought it'd be nice if he dropped by to pick her up for a late dinner or drink after filming.

Before going through security at the courthouse, Zana removed her black suit jacket, which covered her low cut pink blouse she had also worn for Jerry's benefit. She was quite confident he would suggest lunch after the hearing on the motion—some place where snuggling and kissing wouldn't be noticed.

According to the docket sheet posted in front of the vacant courtroom, they were second on the calendar so she sat towards the front. After a few minutes, she heard the door creak open. She turned her head and there was Mansfield. He gave her a smile and then sat behind her, even though the entire gallery was empty.

"Good morning, Zana," Mansfield said in his slimeball voice. He was so close she caught a whiff of his cologne. It smelled expensive.

"Hello," she said without turning to look at him. She made some notes on her legal pad, hoping he would leave her alone.

"I'm sure you told Frank you're going to lose today," he said.

She could feel his breath on her neck.

"Why do you say that?" she said, trying to appear occupied with her notes.

200

"I own this courtroom. The judges always rule in my favor."

"We'll see about that."

"You poor, sexy thing. You really don't know what you're doing, do you?"

"You're mistaken," Zana said sharply.

"I like your cum-fuck-me heels. They really do it for me."

"Your language is unacceptable," she said, wondering how Mansfield knew about her high heels since she was sitting down. She felt her skin crawl, imagining him following her as she walked to court.

"Well, if you can't handle it, you're in the wrong profession," Mansfield said.

"If *you* can't be civil, you're in the wrong profession."

"I'm civil, you little temptress. You need to wear panties next time," Mansfield said softly, finishing his sentence just before the male law clerk walked in.

Zana noticed the young clerk's crimson face and suspected he had heard what Mansfield said.

"I need to get your appearances," the clerk said curtly without making eye contact.

"Zana West, here for Aloha Athletics," she said.

"I'm here for Plaintiffs in both the first and second matters on the calendar," Mansfield said.

The clerk nodded.

The door to the courtroom opened, letting defense attorneys Ray Sumida, Dean Henderson, and Jerry Hirano in. They were in the middle of a conversation, but Jerry locked eyes with Zana and smiled.

"Appearances please?" the clerk asked the men.

"Jerry Hirano, here for South Shore, Inc.," he said. Zana thought he looked gorgeous in what looked like an Armani suit with a Hermes tie.

"Ray Sumida. I represent American Triathlon Association."

"I'm Dean Henderson, here for Diamond Head Athletics."

The courtroom door opened and another group of attorneys walked into the gallery and pass the bar, taking their seats at the counsel table on the right. Zana inhaled another whiff of Mansfield's cologne as he passed her to take his place at the counsel table on the left. Once Jerry had given his name to the clerk, he motioned for Zana to scoot over and sat next to her. She had to refrain from touching him, although she was tempted to grab his hand. He took out a pen from the leather case he was carrying and wrote on her legal pad. *You look amazing!*

She scribbled a note back to him. *You do, too!*

The law clerk said, "All rise." Judge Lee entered the courtroom from behind the bench, wearing his black robe and a grim look.

"You may be seated," the clerk said. "Calling Civil Number 11-03592, Bangers versus Waipahu Land Group, appearances please."

After the attorneys gave their names and the parties they represented,

Judge Lee told them he was inclined to rule in the plaintiff's favor on the motion. Zana noticed Mansfield's smug look. He nodded expectantly.

"I've read the briefs and all of the exhibits. I don't want to hear any repetitious argument. Does the defense have anything new to add?" Judge Lee asked in a stern tone.

"Your Honor, I must emphasize that in Decker verses City and County, the court ruled…"

"Mr. Hall, I asked for anything new. You cited that case in your brief," Judge Lee said. "Anything else?"

"No, your Honor." The attorney dropped his head and slunk down in his chair.

"Plaintiff's motion is granted. Mr. Mansfield, please prepare the order."

"Yes, thank you, your Honor," Mansfield said, standing up before Judge Lee. As the attorneys were excused and the clerk called Brad Jordan's case, Mansfield turned to look at Zana, flashing an "I told you so" smile.

Mansfield stayed seated at the left-side table while Jerry held the short swinging door open for Zana and joined her at the right-side counsel table. She suddenly felt a rush of fear. Her knees were weak and she regretted wearing heels that made her feel less in control and more wobbly. After sitting down, she closed her eyes and took a few deep breaths, hoping to calm her nerves. The other defense attorneys joined them around the table, but since she had filed the motion, she didn't expect them to add much.

As Zana listened to the other attorneys make their appearances to the court, she hoped her voice wouldn't crack. She desperately needed some water but didn't dare disrupt the proceeding by pouring a cup from the pitchers on the table.

"Zana West, appearing on behalf of Aloha Athletics," she croaked.

"This issue looks pretty cut and dry, anything else, counsel?" Judge Lee asked.

"Ms. West cited Pang verses Kelly, which is distinguishable from this case." Mansfield stood to make his argument, looking relaxed. "In Pang, the deposition was cut short because Plaintiff was having some physical problems and needed medical attention. The case at hand involved a fire alarm that went off."

"Pang is on all fours with the instant case," Zana interrupted. "The facts are very similar to this case and the Hawaii Supreme Court allowed the deposition to continue." She rose to make her argument. As she spoke, she started to feel more comfortable.

"Ms. West is an idiot. It appears she hasn't even read the case, let alone demonstrated any understanding of it," Mansfield said, gesturing with his left hand, flashing his gold Rolex watch.

"I'm no idiot—I think if Mr. Mansfield would bother to read the case, he would perhaps have the mental capacity to understand who the idiot is," Zana said. She then heard some chuckles from the gallery.

"Let's cease with the name calling," Judge Lee said.

"It's important to consider the facts of this case in light of Shell versus Colby. In that case, the defense attorneys wrote to Plaintiff requesting the deposition be continued shortly after it was interrupted. That didn't happen in this case," Mansfield argued, ignoring Zana's attack.

"Mr. Mansfield makes a good point. Ms. West, do you have any response?" Judge Lee said.

"I do, your Honor." Zana thumbed through the file and pulled out a piece of paper with two holes punched at the top. "I have a copy of this email I sent to Mr. Mansfield two days after the deposition. It says, "Please let me know what dates are most convenient for us to continue your client's deposition."

"Ms. West, approach the bench with the document, please," Judge Lee said.

Zana handed it to the clerk who passed it to Judge Lee. After his Honor had the opportunity to review it, he gave it back to the clerk.

"May I see it?" Mansfield said.

The clerk then handed the document over and he reviewed it.

Zana saw Mansfield hide the document under his file.

"The Court hereby grants Defendant Aloha Athletics' Motion to Compel Deposition of Plaintiff. The Plaintiff is to submit to his deposition within a reasonable time at the mutual convenience of all of the parties. Ms. West, you are to prepare the order," Judge Lee said, looking at Zana from behind his reading glasses.

"Thank you, your Honor. May I please ask the court to order Mr. Mansfield to return the document I presented?" Zana asked.

"Mr. Mansfield, return the document to Ms. West," Judge Lee ordered.

"Yes, your Honor," he said. He pulled it out from under his file, tossing it on the counsel table in front of Zana, sneering.

"The Court is in recess. All rise," the clerk said.

Zana grinned at Jerry who was standing next to her. As soon as Judge Lee exited the courtroom, Mansfield grabbed his iPad and turned to leave.

"Your client will pay," Mansfield growled, pointing at Zana.

"Great job, Zana," Jerry said loudly as Mansfield exited the courtroom. The other attorneys congratulated her before they filed out.

"Mansfield said he owns this courtroom," Zana said, gathering her files.

"Some say he does, so kudos to you. It takes courage to fight back against someone like that. I've seldom seen it done," Jerry said.

They walked out of the courtroom together, well behind the other defense attorneys who were already stepping onto the elevator. Mansfield was out of sight.

"Thanks," Zana said and smiled broadly. She stopped to pull off her jacket partly because it was warm, but mostly to reveal her blouse. "Are you ready for our trip to Minnesota?"

"I think so. I've got to check with my secretary about my travel arrangements, but we should be all set," Jerry said, pressing the elevator button.

"Hey, Jerry. Long time no see," a very tall, thin, distinguished-looking man with silver hair, wearing a three-piece suit said as he approached the elevator.

"Doing great, Preston. And you?" Jerry said as he shook the man's hand.

"Can't complain," Preston said. They stepped onto the elevator to go down to the main lobby.

"Preston, this is Zana West—she's with Frank Gravelle's firm. Zana, I'd like to introduce you to Preston Farnsworth," Jerry said, turning to Zana.

"Nice to meet you," Zana said, shaking hands with the rail thin man who was so lean he resembled a skeleton with skin. She had hoped for a few seconds of alone time with Jerry on the elevator. Instead, she listened to Jerry and Preston chat about a case while she watched the floor numbers as the elevator descended at record slow speed.

After they reached the ground floor and Preston had left them, Jerry walked with her to the building's main entrance.

"I've got a meeting. I'm sorry but I really have to run," Jerry said looking at his Tag Heur watch. "I'm already running late. I'll call you."

"Oh, that's okay. It's good to see you, Jerry."

He kissed her on the cheek and walked fast toward the parking garage exit.

She ducked into the restroom before she made her way on foot back to her office. She didn't want to run into Mansfield and so she stalled before leaving through the main entrance, which took her to the intersection of Punchbowl and Halekuwila Streets.

As she stood at the corner, waiting for the walk signal, she saw Jerry drive by in his red Ferrari. At first, Zana smiled at the thought of seeing him, but then her legs went weak and her body stiffened. There was a beautiful blonde woman sitting in the passenger seat next to him. Zana saw Jerry wearing his aviator Prada sunglasses as he drove past. She didn't get a good look at the woman's face since the car drove by so quickly, but immediately she registered why Jerry had been in a rush.

She felt like she had been punched in the gut. She teetered on her too high heels, feeling the backs of the shoes rubbing against her heels, her free hand clenched into a tight fist. Each step was excruciating. When she finally reached the 27th floor, she didn't stop to tell Andrew of her victory against Mansfield, but instead stepped into her office and slammed the door. She tore her shoes off her now bloodied feet and hurled them at the wall, causing the only hung diploma to crash down to the floor.

Chapter 33

@Zlaw #Pack light? No way. I say we bring back the steamer trunk.

Rip leaned back in his chair, feeling the fine Italian leather behind him. He was sitting in his penthouse office with its panoramic view of Diamond Head and the Pacific Ocean. The marble floor reflected cumulous clouds and faint remnants of a rainbow making his black marble desk seem to float in the sky.

Eight computer screens allowed him to scan several email accounts, multiple documents, and social media all at once according to his IT guy, but Rip preferred the appearance of super efficiency over actual function. All he needed was a desk free of messy papers and a set up designed solely to intimidate adversaries and impress clients.

He stared out at a sailboat racing across the water, clearly gaining momentum from a gust of wind, wishing he could open a window to feel the warm breeze rather than the chill of the air-conditioned building.

The sound of several associates discussing a case in the hallway interrupted his meanderings. Rather than rise out of his chair, Rip buzzed one of his assistants to close his door. The office seemed more chaotic lately with so many new attorneys who were stacked three to each small office, and Rip wondered if it might be more productive to have them work in shifts.

The point of having such a large staff was to outperform and outsmart his opponents, but it was of no value this morning. He wasn't used to losing court hearings, especially such a simple matter of protecting Brad Jordan from having his deposition taken more than once. The thought of that bitch's disrespect to him in court made his head throb. He downed a few Aleve with water and drummed his fingers absent mindedly on his desk.

Zana fucking West. His mouth contorted in a scowl he knew made him look like a snarling animal. It was a look he normally reserved for adversaries, but as he sat alone in his office, he couldn't avoid twisting his face as he thought about West and the other young female attorneys who had pissed him off in the past. Rip despised the way they wore their short skirts and high heels to court, taking the Judge's attention away from the logical arguments. The whores would bat their eyelashes and pout in their efforts to prevail, but this chick was the first one who didn't leave the courtroom in tears.

West is more dangerous than most. She looked like a Victoria Secret model wearing too many clothes. She may have won today's battle, but she certainly wouldn't win at trial.

Rip opened up a Word document and made notes to give to his investigators and associates for follow up:

1. Check on Brad's status in rehab. Needs to be sober for trial.

2. Find dirt on witness John Chu. Jury will think he assisted his client in killing his wife and won't believe his testimony about car intentionally hitting cyclists.

3. Investigate Zana West. Check background; weaknesses. Get her fired.

Rip's thoughts were interrupted by a knock on the door.

"Come in," Rip said, giving a more pleasant look to his secretary.

"Can we go over your travel arrangements?" Fely said. She was one of his few employees who didn't seem the least bit intimidated by him, which made her more valuable. She was one of the few people in Rip's life who could openly criticize him without fear of reprisal.

"Just a minute," Rip said, pausing to email his notes to Doug for follow up. "Okay, go ahead."

"I downloaded your boarding pass for your flight to Minnesota tomorrow and emailed it to you. You're flying through Denver. The plane is full, but I have you in a first class aisle seat. You're booked in a suite at the Marquette Hotel in Minneapolis. I scheduled an evening massage for you in your room and have already submitted your room service orders and arranged for a car to pick you up at the airport."

"Where are the other attorneys staying?"

She cocked her head, but otherwise didn't show any emotion. "I've made sure they're not at the Marquette."

"Good girl," Rip said. He preferred his privacy on mainland trips, having no interest in looking over his shoulder in case he sampled some local pussy. "What about the deposition?"

"It's going to be at a court reporter's office in St. Cloud—an hour's drive from Minneapolis. A hotel car and driver will take you," Fely said, consulting her iPad.

"Okay, just email me the details," Rip said. "What time do I need to be at the airport?"

"Eleven-thirty. Do you want one of us to drive you?"

"Yes. Doug can pick me up at eleven. Send him in here, will you?"

"Right away," Fely said and turned with drill team precision to walk out the door, closing it behind her.

Rip downloaded his boarding pass on his iPhone and reviewed his travel itinerary while he waited for Doug.

"Hey, Rip," Doug said, taking a seat in a black leather chair facing his boss.

"I need you to find some dirt on John Chu and Zana West while I'm gone. I've emailed you my notes."

"Got it. Consider it done," Doug said.

"What were you able to find out about the witness being deposed in Minnesota?" Rip asked.

"His name is Devere Levinson. He's a personal trainer at a gym in St. Cloud, Minnesota where he's currently living. He moved there from Hibbing and grew up near Lake Antler. I wasn't able to identify any connection between this witness and Brad."

"That's not good enough." Rip frowned. "What does Brad have to say about him?"

"He's never heard of him. Brad thought Levinson might be a triathlete, but our research didn't find any such evidence."

Placing his elbows on the table and leaning forward in his chair, Rip said, "Did you ask Brad if Levinson was ever his trainer?"

"I did," Doug said. "Brad said it's possible Levinson could have been one of many personal trainers he had in Seattle, but our research didn't find any connection between the witness and Washington State."

"Were there any other possible links?"

"Levinson might have been a trainer at one of the pre-Olympic training camps Brad attended in Colorado Springs or San Diego. We did find Levinson's name on a list of personal trainers who provided clinics at the U.S. Olympic Training Center in Colorado Springs. However, we couldn't determine whether Levinson worked with triathletes."

"Anything else?"

"Nothing. We can't figure out why Defendants are taking this guy's deposition."

"Did you call up Jerry Hirano and straight out ask him?" Rip's patience was finite. He sighed.

"He told me that he's taking the deposition to find out what his relationship is with Plaintiff," Doug said.

"Do you think they're going down a dead end?" Rip fingered his pineapple-shaped paperweight.

"According to Brad, they are."

"Well, I guess I'm going to Minnesota for nothing," Rip said. He put the pineapple down to examine his cuticles.

"I'll go, if you'd rather stay here," Doug offered.

"No." Rip leaned back in his chair and stared out the window at the sailboats in the distance. "I should be there to keep that Zana West in line. Let me know what you find out about this Minnesota witness, or if you get any dirt on Ms. West."

"Sure thing. I'll be at your house at eleven," Doug said, standing up.

***

"Can I help you pack?" Cameron, one of the orderlies at the rehab center, said.

"I'm all set," Brad said. He had crumpled up his clothes in his gym bag, which was sitting on his lap as he waited to be wheeled out into the reception area.

"What about those?" Cameron said, pointing to a stack of paperback books and magazines strewn on the desk and shelf.

"The center can have them." Brad was looking forward to being sprung from rehab. He was excited about seeing Heather, having sex with Megan and had a serious craving for an Absolut vodka martini.

"I hope you're ready for the outside," Cameron said. "There are so many temptations."

"I'll be fine," Brad countered, brushing off the orderly's warning. As an Olympic caliber athlete, he considered himself to be an expert strategist, not just in sport but also in life. He had been careful about what he said in rehab to counselors, psychologists, and other patients, because he knew that every word out of his mouth was evaluated. His words could either extend or shorten his stay. So he added, "It'll be tough, but I'll do my best. Thank God I'm sober. If it weren't for the counselors and all the support here, I'd never have a chance."

Cameron nodded.

"Thanks for all your support, buddy," Brad said, opening his arms to receive Cameron's hug. "Do you mind wheeling me around so I can say goodbye?"

"Not at all," Cameron said, pushing Brad's chair from room to room to say goodbye and proudly tell everyone he was 30 days clean and sober. He expressed his gratitude about starting a new chapter in his life, collected cell phone numbers and promised to stay in touch.

Cameron then wheeled Brad to the reception area where he inquired about the dates and times of AA meetings. He wouldn't miss the room with its rickety chairs, stained carpet and dusty artificial tropical flower arrangements. The fish tank was so cloudy he couldn't see any fish and wondered if it had ever been cleaned.

"Is it okay if I attend more than one meeting in a day?" Brad asked.

"Sure, whatever you need," Dr. Rhodes, his therapist, said. "Call me if you run into any challenges."

"I've got your number," Brad said, smiling. He sat in his wheelchair facing the main doors, knowing Heather would be there any minute to get him.

When she finally walked in, Brad felt a rush of excitement in his body. She was breathtaking. Her blonde hair was sleek, framing her face making it glow.

She flashed a broad smile of perfect white teeth at him and her big blue eyes sparkled when he grabbed her. He pulled her down to his wheelchair and kissed her deeply. He had noticed the staff members turn their heads the moment she had walked in the room. He assumed they either recognized her from the news or were simply enamored by her beauty. Or, maybe they were jealous of the guy in the wheelchair with the hot girlfriend.

"Let's get you out of here," Heather whispered. She picked up his bag and put its handle over her shoulder and pushed him outside.

"I can't wait to get home," Brad said. It felt good to finally be outside in the fresh, tropical air.

When they reached Heather's car in the parking lot, she said, "I'm sure you're looking forward to having some privacy. I had your condo cleaned professionally so you'll be coming home to a spotless place."

"Cool. Thanks, sweetie."

"I asked them to throw out all of your alcohol so you'll be able to make a clean and sober start."

"Are you kidding?" Brad said, staring at her, trying not to sound as angry as he felt. He wondered if he needed to count to ten in order to avoid letting it slip that he had no intention to stop drinking. He had hoped his stash of alcohol at home would hold him over until he could manage to get to a grocery store. He wondered if Megan would buy him some.

"I'm serious, Brad. I tried to make things easier for you," she said, interrupting Brad's thoughts.

"Sure, of course, I appreciate all you've done." But to still his anger from rising, he pressed the side of his face against the passenger window and closed his eyes.

Putting the car into gear, she asked, "Have you talked to Rip Mansfield lately?"

"No—only his associate, Doug."

"What's going on with your case?"

"Rip's going to the mainland for the deposition of some random guy."

"A witness?"

"Apparently," Brad said. "The dude is a personal trainer in Minnesota."

"Odd. How does he have anything to do with you?" Heather said, looking straight ahead at traffic as she drove towards his condo. "Have you ever been to Minnesota?"

"Maybe for a race a long time ago." Suddenly, he recalled his trip to Antler Lake for a triathlon when Heather had gone to Chicago to fill in for an anchor from an affiliate station in order to gain experience in another market.

Brad remembered wearing a long haired scraggly wig, some old jeans and a Green Day T-shirt when he went to the airport in a taxi, which had picked him up a block from his apartment. He had shipped his bike to Minneapolis beforehand and used his full name, Bradley Jordan, when signing up, since he had to show I.D. to buy a one day American Triathlon Association membership for the race. Heather had been away for the entire month, so he was able to train around Antler Lake before race day. He had gained use of his legs only three months earlier so it had been especially painful to run. Swimming required him to arch his back and he had to swallow a few Vicodin before easing into the water. He was able to adjust his bicycle saddle in order to take some of the pressure off his back, but the 25-mile bike segment of the race pushed his limits of pain tolerance.

Since he was racing as an age group athlete rather than an elite or pro athlete as he had done *before* the accident, there was no risk of having to submit to a drug test. On the morning of the race, Brad had taken a handful of pills and had brought extras he could pop at the transitions. He didn't bother to wear a disguise. With less than 500 athletes competing in the race, he didn't expect to run into anyone he knew.

He wondered now if the witness was an athlete who might have recognized him from triathlon magazines or from televised races. Would he regret using his real name? He racked his brain, but couldn't remember if he had seen any professional photographers that day.

"Earth to Brad," Heather said when she opened up his car door.

"That was fast," he said. He had been so deep in his memories he hadn't realized how soon they had gotten to his condo.

Heather helped him out of the car and into his wheelchair. After he was settled comfortably on the couch, she made him a sandwich. She let him have the remote control and sat quietly through an hour of the Golf Channel.

"Honey, would you be terribly upset if I left?" Heather asked. "I really have to get back to the station."

"Of course I'll be upset, but I understand Sugar bear," Brad said. "Do what you need to do. I'll be fine."

"You're so sweet. I promise, I'll call you later and come over tomorrow. Don't you worry about a thing," Heather said, leaning over to kiss him. "Megan might be able to take you to an AA meeting later. I called her and she said she'd be happy to drive you, if you don't feel up to going by yourself."

"Thanks, sweetheart," Brad said.

Heather grabbed her bag and went out the door.

As soon as Brad heard Heather's car leave, he stood up out of his wheelchair and searched his cupboards, fridge and freezer, finding no bottles of vodka, gin, scotch, wine or beer that had been there before his stint in rehab. *Damn.*

He'd call Megan.

"Hey, Megan," Brad said when she answered her cell phone.

"Did you finally get sprung from rehab-prison? " she said.

"Can you come over?"

"Do you need me to take you to an AA meeting? I'm only asking because Heather told me to."

"I just want to see you," Brad said.

"I'll be right over."

"Wait. Can you do me a huge favor?"

"Sure. Anything…"

"Can you bring over some vodka—and maybe, some dry vermouth?"

Chapter 34

@Zlaw No chance of ever getting Mauied. #Spinsters rule.

"You're going to miss your plane," Kelly said, standing in the doorway of Zana's bedroom.

"High-heeled boots or UGGs?" Zana asked. Her feet were still recovering from wearing heels to court.

"I forbid you to wear UGGs." Kelly snatched them out of her hands. She pushed the boots towards Zana. "Put those on and let's go."

Zana groaned. "Can I borrow your pea coat?" She slid her feet into the boots and then zipped the black suitcase she had bought at Costco the previous weekend.

"I put it in the car for you. There are gloves in the pockets and I've also added a pink cashmere scarf and hat so you'll look cute for Jerry."

"Not necessary, but thanks, Kel." Zana wheeled her suitcase to the front door.

"What's going on? Did something happen between you?"

"I saw him with some blonde chick," Zana's voice cracked as they walked toward the driveway to Kelly's car.

"Are you kidding me?" Kelly lifted the suitcase into the trunk.

"They rode past in his Ferrari," Zana said, and then slipped into the passenger seat. "He's moved on."

"I wouldn't be so sure," Kelly said. "I think you should talk to him."

"There's nothing to talk about." She put her sunglasses on so Kelly wouldn't see the hurt in her eyes.

"You're madly in love with him. Even I can see that. You can't give up without a fight."

"I'm not 'madly in love' with him," Zana said, her fingers making quotation marks. "You should take the freeway, it's faster."

"Okay, but I think you should admit your feelings to him. Then see what happens."

"I don't think so. It's a work trip. Besides, Lucas will be there," Zana said, frowning.

"Are you and Lucas on the same flight?"

"Funny you should ask," Zana said. She was relieved to change the subject. "Sylvia is on extended sick leave due to some health issues she's having so Libby made both of our travel arrangements. She did me a huge favor by putting me on the earlier flight through San Francisco. Lucas is leaving a few hours later today with a layover in Denver."

"That'll give you some breathing room," Kelly said. "Aren't you going to have to get a rental car and pick him up at the airport?"

"We're staying at the Marriott by the airport. I'll take the free shuttle and Lucas will pick up the rental car."

"Maybe, you and Lucas can get together for dinner. Work things out."

"No way," Zana said. She would avoid Lucas until their drive to St. Cloud for the deposition.

"You could go to the Mall of America," Kelly suggested.

"Yeah." Zana frowned when she saw the bumper-to-bumper traffic on the H-1 Freeway. "I've never been there before."

"Where's Jerry staying?" Kelly asked, merging into traffic.

"Before I saw him with that chick, we had both decided on the Marriott *and* we were going to ride to St. Cloud together."

"You're going to have to talk to him sometime." Kelly changed lanes. "Is he on your flight?"

"Yeah. He's been texting and emailing that he wants to sit together, but I haven't responded yet," Zana said, adjusting her sunglasses. "I changed my seat online a few hours ago so he has no idea where I'll be."

"Are you kidding? Zana? Come on. Jerry Hirano wants to sit next to you on a five hour flight and you haven't even told him your seat number?"

"I'm not sure I can handle five hours alone with him right now."

"Well, considering how late we are and the traffic, I seriously wonder whether you'll be on that flight," Kelly said. "What time is your flight again?"

"9:15."

"It's 8:05. You're not checking your bag, are you?"

"I was going to, but I won't have time," Zana said, now worrying more about getting to the airport on time than she was about seeing Jerry. Since she had seen him with that woman, she had responded to his emails and texts about the case briefly and impersonally. He had left a few messages on her voice mail, but she hadn't had the courage to listen to them yet.

"You should just sleep with him," Kelly said.

"What?"

"Yeah, just go up to his hotel room wearing only the pea coat. Once he sees what's underneath, he'll forget all about the blonde," Kelly said with a chuckle as she maneuvered through traffic.

"Right. What happens if there's another woman in his room?" Zana said. "Your pea coat is pretty short on me. It wouldn't even cover my vjay-jay. You'll have to come up with a better plan."

"We're almost there. Grab your suitcase and run like hell to security. Since you only have a carry on, no need to go through agriculture inspection," Kelly said. "Do you have your boarding pass and I.D.?"

"Yeah, I've got it. Hopefully, TSA will give me a break this morning. Thanks so much, Kel."

"No problem. Now get your ass to the gate and make sure you have hot sex with Jerry Ho."

Zana jumped out of the car and grabbed her suitcase, purse and briefcase.

"Bye Kelly. I'll text you," Zana said, ignoring her friend's comment. She ran as fast as she could manage in her high-heeled boots.

The security line was fairly short, but Zana was stuck behind a family with a small baby, folding stroller and all of their baby gear so the five minutes it took them to put everything into bins seemed like hours. She tried to be polite and didn't even roll her eyes, not wanting to do anything to attract attention.

"Is this your bag, Miss?" the TSA agent asked Zana.

"Yes."

"I've got to run it again."

"Okay, I'm really running late," she said in a pleading voice.

"Not my problem," the TSA agent said, putting Zana's purse through the x-ray machinery again.

Zana watched as another TSA agent took her purse and motioned for her to follow him while he went through it with his blue latex gloved hands.

"What's this?" the agent pulled a letter opener out of her bag.

"Oh, shit!" Zana said and then covered her mouth. "I'm sorry, sir. That must have fallen off my desk and into my purse at work. I didn't know it was in there. Do you have to confiscate it?"

"No, it's not very sharp. You should put it into your checked bag next time," the TSA agent said, handing the letter opener to Zana who put it back into her purse.

"Can I go now? I'm going to miss my flight," Zana felt a wave of nausea. She would be fired for sure if she didn't show up on time for the Minnesota deposition.

"Next time, give yourself more time," the agent said waving her away.

Zana grabbed her coat, shoes, zip lock bag of 3 oz. liquids, and laptop and quickly put everything back together before she sprinted to her gate. Just as she reached it, the last few people were boarding. She wiped away sweat beading on her forehead and handed her boarding pass to the gate agent.

"Ms. West, I'm sorry, but there isn't any more overhead space left. I'm going to have to gate check your large bag," the agent said. "When you get off the plane in San Francisco, you'll have to wait on the jet bridge for your bag."

"That's fine," Zana said, smiling in relief to have made the flight.

She boarded the plane, trying not to look for Jerry as she walked down the aisle. She kept her gaze straight ahead, focusing on the back of the aircraft. After finding her aisle seat in coach, she was disappointed to find out her seat was next to a woman who she guessed weighed over 350 pounds. The armrest separating their seats was up, allowing her neighbor to fill half of Zana's seat with her expanding girth. She wedged herself in between the woman and the aisle armrest, but could only get one butt cheek on the seat. The left half of her seatbelt had disappeared.

"Miss, you're going to have to fasten your seatbelt before take-off," a red haired flight attendant instructed Zana as she came through the aisle.

"I'm sorry, I can't," Zana said, shrugging her shoulders.

The large woman next to her tried to adjust her body in order to free Zana's seatbelt without success.

"The plane checked in full. We might have to re-book you," the flight attendant said.

"I'll find another seat. I have to be in Minnesota for work," Zana said, barely holding back tears.

"You should have gotten to the airport earlier," the large woman said.

Zana bit her lip. The one butt cheek securely seated was numb.

After what seemed like an eternity, a male flight attendant motioned to Zana to follow him. She grabbed her purse and briefcase and made her way to the front of the plane as directed.

"You may sit in 4B," the flight attendant said, pointing to a first class seat.

"Thank you very much," Zana said, sitting down.

"Hi Zana." Jerry smiled at her from 4A.

"Oh, hi Jerry," Zana said, the color draining from her face.

"I heard there was a problem," he said, leaning over to kiss her lightly on the lips. "I had arranged this seat for you, but you hadn't responded to my messages."

"Oh, I've been busy, but thank you," Zana said flatly, avoiding eye contact.

"What's the matter, Zana?"

"Just stressed about work."

"Tell me," Jerry said. "We'll be in the air for five hours. We have a two-hour layover in San Francisco and then another flight to Minneapolis. I don't want to have to guess what's going on."

Zana blew out a breath. "I saw you drive by after court. There was a woman in your car."

"Oh, now I get it," Jerry said. "I had a meeting with Megan Alexander."

"The triathlete?" Zana said, her eyes widening.

"Yeah, Heather Alexander's twin, the newscaster."

She stared in his eyes. "Why were you meeting with her?"

"She had an interesting video to show me. She's not a fan of Mansfield, to put it lightly."

"So...it wasn't a date?" Zana said, looking at Jerry intently, trying to read his face.

"Are you kidding me? Megan Alexander? No way."

Now she wished she hadn't jumped to conclusions.

"I don't want to have this conversation on the plane, but I will say one thing—I'm not going to justify every woman I talk to or meet with to you," Jerry said quietly. He closed his eyes as the plane safety demonstration was shown on the video screens.

Why am I such an idiot? Zana thought.

She closed her eyes, too, and pretended to nap for the next few hours. But her heart pounded so hard there was no way she could fall asleep. She listened to Jerry snoring next to her. Obviously, he didn't care enough about their relationship.

She pulled out her Kindle and pretended to read. If Jerry woke up, she could feign dozing or duck into the restroom, but he didn't wake up until they landed.

As they gathered their belongings to disembark, the flight attendant announced that anyone who had gate checked a bag should wait for it on the jet way.

"I've got to wait for my bag," Zana said to Jerry as they walked off the plane.

"I've got some work to do; I'll see you on the next flight," Jerry said avoiding eye contact before he walked away from her.

Standing in the cold jet way, Zana felt the tears come. She wished she could run and catch up with Jerry, but as luck would have it her bag was the very last one to be produced from the bowels of the plane. She wandered around the airport for an hour, going into shops and a bookstore, but not really seeing anything that interested her. She ducked into a restroom, parked herself on the toilet in a handicap bathroom stall and finally let the tears roll down her cheeks. She sobbed as quietly as she could with her face in her hands until someone knocked on the stall door, asking to use it.

After Zana washed her face and brushed her teeth, she went to the gate where she saw Jerry working on his laptop.

"I'm sorry," Zana said, sitting down in the empty seat next to him.

"There's nothing to be sorry about," Jerry said without any warmth in his voice.

"It was a misunderstanding, that's all," she said, pleading at Jerry with her eyes. "I was jealous."

He focused on his computer screen, refusing to look up.

"The plane's boarding. I'm going to pop into the bathroom. I'll see you on the plane," Jerry said, putting his computer in its case.

Zana boarded the plane when they called her row in coach. She noticed Jerry had still not returned when they announced first class passengers could board early. At least this time, Zana had a seat she could fit into and fasten the seatbelt. She closed her eyes and drifted off to sleep. The next thing she heard was an announcement to close tray tables and bring seats upright. They were landing in Minneapolis.

By the time Zana disembarked, Jerry was nowhere in sight. Since he had presumably been sitting in the front of the plane, she was hopeful he had disembarked before her. He had probably already picked up his rental car and beat her to the hotel. She called for the free shuttle.

After Zana checked into her room and left a message for Lucas to tell him what time she'd meet him for breakfast in the coffee shop downstairs, she turned on the T.V.

As she lay on her bed, flipping through the channels, she purposely skipped "Fighting in Paradise". She couldn't stop thinking about how she'd blown it with Jerry.

It never would have worked out anyway, she thought, trying to make herself feel better. Andrew had told her over and over again that Jerry was out of her league. Zana hugged a bed pillow and stared at a "King of Queens" rerun.

After watching several hours of sitcoms, she noticed the red light on the hotel phone flashing. Hoping the message was from Jerry, she leapt off the bed and snatched the handset out of its cradle. She pressed the number for voicemail and listened.

"Ms. West, I hope you're wearing those cum-fuck-me shoes at the deposition tomorrow. I'm sure the witness will be as excited as the Judge was." It was Rip Mansfield.

Disgusted, Zana slammed the phone down. Oh, how she hated that creep.

Chapter 35

@Zlaw The pea coat was #lucky and St. Cloud is #Cloud10.

As Zana approached the table, she saw Lucas playing a game on his iPad and eating scrambled eggs. She scanned the restaurant for Jerry. She felt a sudden rush of adrenaline when she saw an Asian man, at first thinking it might be him.

When she realized the man wasn't Jerry, her heart sank even more. She had hoped he would call her about riding to St. Cloud together, but she hadn't heard a word since she apologized at the San Francisco airport.

"You're late," Lucas said without even looking up from his game.

"It's okay, I'm not really hungry," Zana said, sitting down in the booth across from him.

"It could be a long day, you should eat something," Lucas said, uncharacteristically kind. He then looked up from his game and at Zana. "You look terrible. Are you sick or something?"

"I'm okay. Just tired," Zana said.

"Well, if you need me to go without you, I can," Lucas offered.

"No, I'll be fine," Zana said. She would love to take him up on his offer, but feared she'd be fired if she didn't show up.

"If we're going to get there on time, we're going to have to leave in the next fifteen minutes. Waitress!" Lucas said, putting his hand up to signal.

"Coffee, please," Zana said to the waitress when she walked up to the table.

"Anything to eat?" the young woman asked.

Zana shook her head.

"She'll have whole wheat toast," Lucas said. "With jelly."

"Thanks," Zana said, surprised at Lucas's concern.

"If you can't eat all of it, you can take some with you and eat it on the way. I'll drive so you can sleep if you want," Lucas said.

"Why are you acting like this?" Zana said, sipping her coffee.

"What do you mean?"

Zana stared at him. "Nice. You're acting so nice. It's weird."

"You're having a hard time. I know what it's like."

"Sure you do, Mr. Stanford. Everything is easy for you."

"Are you kidding?" Lucas said with a look of surprise. "My life has been shitty."

Zana eyed Lucas. "Hmmm. That's surprising to hear. Frank treats you like a king since you're Caron Rossi's son."

"It hasn't been easy being raised by a single mom. She always worked long hours," Lucas said, slipping his iPad into his briefcase. "She was never around."

"That's rough. But, why are you telling me this?" Zana said, surprised that Lucas would blurt out personal information.

He shrugged. "Because I know you and the other attorneys think I'm a fuck up."

"It's just that you have to prove yourself if you're going to continue working at the firm," Zana said. "It's hard work clawing your way to the top."

The waitress interrupted them, asking if they needed anything else.

"Check please. And, can you bring us a box for the toast so the young lady can eat it in the car?" Lucas asked the waitress in a pleasant tone.

Zana ate a half piece of toast in the restaurant and got her coffee refill to go. Lucas had already punched in the address to the court reporter's office on his phone navigation system, so all she had to do was buckle up and let him do the driving. Even with Kelly's pea coat, pink scarf and gloves, she was shivering by the time they reached the car.

"I'll crank up the heat," Lucas said.

"Thanks," Zana said through chattering teeth.

They waited in silence for the car to warm up and then Lucas followed his phone's verbal directions to the Interstate. Zana munched on the toast and looked out the window, hardly noticing the bare trees buried in snow in the Minnesota landscape even though she had never been here before.

"I've decided I'm going to do a better job," Lucas said, focusing on the freeway ahead of him.

"That's good. I'm sure Frank will appreciate it," Zana said, still surprised Lucas was confiding in her.

"I've had a chip on my shoulder since I started with the firm."

"No kidding. Is that what that was?"

"Yeah, I've resented Frank for years."

"Why is that?" She turned her gaze from the window to stare at him.

"He's my father," Lucas said softly.

"Oh?" Zana said, startled the truth was coming out at last.

"My mom and Frank have no idea I know. Please don't tell them," Lucas said, glancing at Zana, then returning his eyes to the road.

"How do you know he's your father?"

"It's pretty obvious, don't you think?"

"Maybe." Zana smiled for the first time that day. "But when did you find out?"

"When I was in fourth grade. I overheard my mom talking to Frank on the phone about me. She didn't realize it, I'm sure, but I picked up the other line and heard them having a discussion about whether to tell me. They decided to keep it a secret."

"Wow, that's intense," Zana said, suddenly feeling guilty about all the bad things she'd said about her co-worker.

"Tell me about it."

"So, why did you take a job at the firm?"

"I guess I thought if Frank hired me, he'd confess," Lucas said. "I was hoping for the father/son relationship I've always dreamed of."

"I take it he hasn't told you."

"Nope. After a few days, I realized he was going to treat me like any other associate. I was pissed," Lucas said, his eyes narrowed, watching the road. "I guess that's why I've been sabotaging my position at the firm—goofing off and being irresponsible."

"We all make mistakes."

"Yeah, but I've been a real jackass. I want to apologize to you, Zana. I'm really sorry you've taken the brunt of my slacking off. I'm not like this normally," Lucas's voice cracked. "I worked hard at Stanford and graduated in the top fourth of my class. I was even on law review."

"I get it. Thanks, Lucas. I forgive you," Zana said, focusing on someone else other than Jerry. It felt good to get her mind off of her own troubles.

"The plane ride over here gave me a chance to think. I've decided to work hard and make Frank and my mom proud of me. Once I do that, I'm going to tell them I know the truth," Lucas said.

"Sounds like a good plan."

"I'm starting today. Don't worry about taking notes at the deposition or asking questions. I've got it covered. I'll even prepare the summary. Just sit back and listen."

"Wow—really?" Zana said, hoping Lucas was telling the truth. It would be easier to deal with her heartbreak without the added pressure of having to focus on the testimony.

"Yes, really. You're always working long hours. I've heard Frank rave about your hard work," Lucas said. "There aren't very many associates who he has anything good to say about so you should feel proud he thinks you're doing such an amazing job."

"I had no idea. I thought I was totally blowing it," Zana laughed.

"No way. You won the motion to compel against Mansfield," he said. "You're the office hero."

"Thanks, Lucas," Zana said, smiling. "I needed that. Hey, it looks like the exit for St. Cloud is coming up."

It was 9:35 a.m. when Zana and Lucas walked into the court reporter's office. Five minutes late, Zana noted. As they walked in, Rip Mansfield gave them the nastiest look Zana had ever seen on a human face.

"It's about time," Rip said.

"Let's get going," Jerry said, without even looking up at them. He was sitting across from the witness with his laptop open and Mansfield at the end of the table. Dean and Ray sat on the same side as the witness. The court reporter was poised to take down the testimony using Real Time transcription. Zana let Lucas sit in between Jerry and her. They were overdressed, wearing suits. Mansfield, Jerry, and the other defense counsel wore more casual attire—jeans and sweaters.

Zana popped open her laptop so she could follow along by reading the transcript, but this time she'd take Lucas up on his offer and not take any notes.

After the witness had sworn to tell the truth, Jerry started his questioning.

Q. (Jerry Hirano) Please state your full name.

A. Devere Randall Levinson.

Q. Where do you currently reside, Mr. Levinson?

A. St. Cloud, Minnesota.

Q. What is your occupation?

A. I'm a personal trainer.

Q. Have you ever officiated a triathlon?

A. Yes, about five times in the past year and a half.

Q. Did you ever officiate the Antler Lake Triathlon?

A. Yes. That was the first time I ever officiated a race. I remember it well.

Q. I'm going to show you a photograph. It will be Exhibit 1 to the transcript.

Jerry passed copies of the photograph to Mansfield and to Lucas, ignoring Zana. The picture showed Brad Jordan running, wearing bib number 155 with "Antler Lake Triathlon" above the number. There was a mid-2013 date stamp on the photo. Lucas handed the picture to Zana, which she noted was taken the year after the plaintiff was injured at the Olympic trials. She hadn't seen the picture before and guessed that Jerry had gotten it through his investigation in preparation for Levinson's deposition.

A. (Levinson) Okay.

Q. (Hirano) Do you recognize the athlete in the photograph?

Rip Mansfield: Objection. Vague and ambiguous.

A. Do I answer?

Q. Yes, go ahead and answer.

A. What was the question again?

Q. Do you recognize the athlete in this photograph?

Mansfield: Same objection.

A. He looks familiar.

Q. Why does he look familiar?

Mansfield: Objection, argumentative.

A. He's the athlete I gave my first penalty to.

Q. What was the penalty for?

Mansfield: Objection, to form.

Zana noticed Mansfield's face had turned beet red and his forehead was perspiring even though the room was cold. She hadn't taken off her coat, her hands were so icy.

A. I think it was for drafting.

Q. Why do you remember giving a penalty to this athlete?

Mansfield: Objection. Argumentative, vague and ambiguous.

A. The guy got pissed off because I gave him a penalty. He was yelling at me. He said he would have won if I hadn't given him a penalty.

Q. Did you observe the man that you gave the penalty to standing without the aid of a wheelchair or other walking device?

Mansfield: Objection. Argumentative, vague and ambiguous.

A. Yes. He was standing. I also saw him running and cycling.

Q. When you saw him cycling was he using a regular bike or a bike made for a disabled person?

A. It was a normal racing bike.

Q. Do you remember what age group or how old the guy was?

Mansfield: Objection.

A. Yes, in his twenties…maybe twenty-five or so. He was kind of a jerk.

Q. Do you remember his name?

Mansfield: Objection.

By now, Zana noticed Mansfield was standing up and pacing behind the witness. He looked angry.

A. I didn't remember it until I heard about this deposition. I contacted the race director and he checked the records. The guy who I gave the penalty to was Bradley Jordan.

Q. Did Mr. Jordan say anything else to you?

Mansfield: Objection.

Zana was surprised to hear Mansfield shout "objection". Usually, objections at depositions were made in a normal tone of voice with no theatrics. Mansfield now stood over the court reporter.

A. Yes, he said, "You fucking asshole! Do you know who I am?" Something like that.

Q. Do you have any idea why he asked you if you knew who he was?

Mansfield: Objection. Argumentative. Calls for speculation.

Mansfield rushed toward Jerry, knocking the court reporter's machine over. He lunged at Jerry, pushing him against the wall. "You jerk! You are a fucking asshole, Hirano. No one messes with me," Mansfield yelled.

He took a swing at Jerry, which Jerry quickly deflected with an outside block. Before either attorney could make another move towards each other, Lucas rushed in and punched Mansfield hard on his cheek.

Mansfield retreated, shaking his fist at Jerry, yelling, "Hirano, you are a son of a bitch. And, you boy—you fucker!"

As Mansfield grabbed his iPad, he walked towards Zana, wagging his index finger so it almost hit her nose. "You fucking cunt! You're a whore!" As he shouted, Jerry put his body between Mansfield and Zana. Ray and Dean moved forward, both with fists raised towards their opponent.

"Don't you ever talk to this young lady like that, Mansfucker. Ever. Do you hear me?" Jerry shouted.

Mansfield backed away. Maybe realizing he was outnumbered.

After Mansfield left the room with Dean and Ray close behind him, Zana couldn't stop the tears from flowing down her cheeks. She wasn't crying because of the words Mansfield said to her as much as she was feeling emotional about Jerry sticking up for her.

"Are you okay?" Jerry asked, tenderly putting his arm around her. She nodded.

"That bastard," Jerry said.

"Can I go now?" Devere Levinson said, his voice shaking.

"Yes, Mr. Levinson. I'm sorry about all this commotion. You're free to go." Jerry kept his arm around Zana. "Thank you."

"Are you okay?" Lucas asked the court reporter.

"My machine looks like it's still working, so I'm okay," the young woman said. "I'm never going to work on a Hawaii deposition again. You all are crazy."

"Not all of us," Jerry said. "Just him."

She took her machine and walked out of the room, leaving the three lawyers alone.

"Zana, are you sure you're okay?" Jerry asked.

Zana didn't respond. She couldn't. She held her head in her hands, sobbing. She couldn't stop crying.

"I'll take her back to Minneapolis," Lucas said.

"No, why don't you go ahead," Jerry said, kneeling down next to Zana. "I'll make sure she gets back to town."

"Are you okay with that?" Lucas asked Zana. She nodded.

Lucas packed up his computer and put his coat and scarf on. "Okay, Zana. You have my cell phone number. Call me if you need me. See ya, Jerry," Lucas said. "Oh, and Jerry—that was awesome. You really nailed that son of a bitch Mansfield."

"Thanks, man," Jerry said. "Good punch."

"Mahalo," Lucas said, grinning.

After Lucas closed the door, Jerry pulled Zana close to him and kissed her on the lips.

"I'm so sorry," Jerry said softly.

"I'm sorry, too," she said.

"I had no reason to be angry with you."

Zana dried her tears with her hands.

"If I saw you driving with a man in the passenger seat, I'm sure I'd be jealous, too."

"Really?" she asked, meeting his eyes.

"Yeah. When you walked in with Lucas and he pulled the chair out for you, I got it."

"Hmmhmmm…" Zana nodded.

"I really care about you. I haven't been able to stop thinking about you since that day we first met in your office." Jerry leaned forward, his lips meeting hers, and kissed her tenderly. "I only want to be with you."

"Me, too," Zana said, smiling. She put her arms around him. They kissed until the court reporter opened the door and peeked in.

"Oh, sorry to interrupt. I was just checking if we could use this room," she said, looking suspiciously at them.

"We're done in here. Thanks for everything," Jerry said.

On the drive back to Minneapolis, Jerry explained about his meeting with Megan Alexander that led to their disagreement.

"She showed me a videotape of Mansfield and Brad Jordan in an argument. Mansfield admitted he told Jordan what to say in his deposition," Jerry said, grabbing for Zana's gloved hand.

Smiling over his touch, she asked, "Isn't that highly unethical?"

"Absolutely. I've already submitted the video to the Attorney's Disciplinary Committee. Mansfield has some explaining to do."

"Could he be disbarred?"

"That's my hope."

"Mine, too," Zana said, feeling happy about the idea of possibly getting Mansfield out of the way, but mostly because Jerry and she were together again.

As he drove, he continued to hold her hand, and whenever traffic allowed, he glanced at her and smiled.

After they got back to the hotel and made their way through the lobby, he put his arm around Zana and kept pulling her towards him, kissing her.

"What about Lucas?" Zana said, looking in his eyes.

"What about him? Do you think he wants to join us?" Jerry asked somewhat serious and kissed her again.

"No, silly." She laughed.

"Are you hungry? Do you want to eat lunch?"

"Maybe, later. Do you want to show me that video in your room?" Zana said, raising her eyebrows flirtatiously.

"I thought you'd never ask," he said.

When the elevator door closed, he pulled her close and kissed her again, more passionately than they had ever kissed before.

When the elevator doors opened, they went down the hall together, hand in hand. Jerry expertly opened his hotel room door with his key card, and as soon as they were inside, they pulled off each other's clothing as their lips locked together.

"I've wanted to make love to you since the moment you looked at me with your beautiful green eyes," Jerry whispered.

They tumbled onto the bed, enjoying the feel of each other's body for the first time.

Zana sighed. *Paradise.*

Chapter 36

@Zlaw A #smack in the #kisser is always a good idea.

Frank followed the hostess, passing table after table surrounded by rattan chairs filled with state legislators, CEOs, company presidents, lawyers and doctors, nodding greetings to those he recognized. The exclusive Queen's Club, located in a lush tropical garden a few blocks from downtown, was the place where deals were negotiated far away from tourists and underlings. Frank had belonged to the club since he had become a senior partner years ago after he received the necessary sponsorships and was able to afford the steep monthly dues.

Caron was sipping an iced tea, studying her phone at a corner table on the large lanai, which overlooked the tennis courts. She had pushed aside the Anthurium flower centerpiece to make room for a file folder he presumed was a new assignment.

"You're late," Caron said as Frank kissed her cheek.

"You're early as always," Frank said, sitting down. He'd never gotten used to Caron's obsession with arriving 15 minutes early to every appointment, a practice he felt was a waste of precious time. She was wearing her usual 1950s style suit and cat-eye glasses, but he noticed something different about her today. She had dark circles under her eyes and she seemed to slump forward a bit more than usual.

"Your waitress will be with you shortly," the hostess said, handing them menus.

"Mahalo," Frank said.

"Libby told me what happened in Minnesota," Caron said, handing the file to Frank, who took it and tucked it in his briefcase.

"It sounds like Rip provoked him."

"Even if he did, Lucas shouldn't be punching people. He was never like that before he worked at your firm."

"Lucas has been away from home for a long time, Caron." Frank signaled the waitress they were ready to order.

"What's that supposed to mean?" Caron grabbed a menu and gave it a quick glance.

"Would you like to hear the specials?" the waitress asked, interrupting. She placed glasses of water and a plate of taro rolls and butter on the table.

"No, thanks. I'll have the mahi mahi sandwich," Frank said.

"The ahi salad for me," Caron said.

They handed their menus to the waitress.

"Did anyone ever complain to you about Lucas being disruptive or not doing his share of work?" Frank asked. He had made up his mind to fire Lucas and wasn't quite sure how to break the news to Caron.

"His grades were always excellent. He seemed to thrive at his part-time law clerk jobs." Caron picked up a roll and spread butter over it.

"Hmmm." Frank nodded. His sandwich would come with bread, but he busied himself with spreading butter on a roll he didn't intend to eat.

"Perhaps your revolving-door law firm isn't the best fit for a talented boy like Lucas," Caron said, talking with her mouth full.

"It's one of the top firms in the state. I'm not sure there are better opportunities for a young lawyer." Frank could feel his face flush with anger. If she wasn't an important client and the mother of his son, he wouldn't be so tactful. "What do you propose he do?"

"I could talk with one of our other defense firms. I'm sure they'd be happy to have a claims manager's son on board," Caron said in her usual gruff tone.

"I'll have a talk with him about the incident," Frank said, his resolve to fire Lucas wavering. He wasn't about to let F.I.M.'s work slip through his grasp, because he couldn't control his own son. On the other hand, allowing him to stay on put the firm at risk of a malpractice lawsuit should Lucas continue his irresponsible behavior.

"Good idea." She focused on the Anthurium flower in the centerpiece and touched the red waxy part while Frank watched. He wasn't used to her pausing to enjoy anything beautiful.

The waitress placed their food on the table and asked if they would care for anything else. They shook their heads.

After several minutes of silence, Frank said, "How's your salad?"

"I've been thinking," she said, looking into Frank's eyes.

"What about?" he asked.

"Maybe it's time Lucas knew you're his father." She stared down at her food, avoiding his eyes.

"Really?" Frank couldn't think of anything else to say. He'd been so angry with Lucas's bad behavior that he hadn't given any thought to Caron's changing her mind.

"He's old enough, and it might make the transition easier for him," Caron said.

"What transition?"

"Working such long hours." Caron looked up from her salad. "And, being around you all day must make him wonder."

"About what?"

"You and he look so much alike, it's unmistakable." Caron laughed.

"I'm pleased you find something humorous about this," Frank said, serious now. "I'd have to tell Arlene and the girls first. It will be quite a shock."

"Your wife has met Lucas," Caron said. "How could she not suspect you're related?"

"True. She did ask about him once," Frank said, pushing his plate away. "She knows we used to date."

"Believe me, Arlene already knows."

"I don't know about that."

***

After lunch, Frank stopped by another client's office for an impromptu meeting. He wasn't looking forward to facing Lucas, who had flown in the night before and would probably not roll into the office until the afternoon after such a long day of travel. Caron's threat to arrange for Lucas to work for another defense firm was somewhat bothersome, but it might be far better than having an associate play video games while ignoring stacks of work on his desk. Frank had made up his mind to, at the very least, reassign all of Lucas's work that afternoon when he got back to the office. If the boy wanted to play games, so be it. But, he wouldn't be given any attorney work until he proved his commitment to the firm.

As for breaking the news about their relationship, it wasn't the right time. The last thing Frank wanted was for Lucas to have his father fire him from his first attorney job. It would be far better to continue as his old family friend.

Before stepping out of his car to make his way up to his office, Frank pulled out his new smart phone from his briefcase. His youngest daughter, Olivia, had insisted he buy it so they could communicate with texts. She had even set it up so he could read his emails remotely. He entered in his passcode and clumsily clicked on the mail icon. An email from Rip Mansfield caught his attention.

Dear Frank:
Please be advised I'll be filing a lawsuit against Lucas Rossi, your law firm and you, seeking special, general and punitive damages in the amount of $1 million, because of Mr. Rossi's assault and battery to my person, causing serious personal injury at a deposition held in Minneapolis earlier this week. I suggest you put your firm's liability carrier on notice.

Rip Mansfield

Frank sighed. It wasn't the first threat by Mansfield against his firm and probably wouldn't be the last. That was part of the reason their insurance premiums were so high. But, with Mansfield's threat, how could he not fire Lucas? He placed his phone in his shirt pocket, grabbed his briefcase and headed to the office. It was time to face work piled up for the past month while he and Tom were in trial.

"Any calls?" Frank asked as he paused at Libby's cubicle.

"There's an important email from Jerry Hirano. It's with the stack of pink slips on your desk. Here are a few more," Libby said, handing telephone message slips to him. "An email from Mansfield came in you should take a look at."

"I saw it," Frank said.

Libby raised her eyebrows.

"My new phone. Olivia taught me to read emails...and text," Frank said, puffing his chest out with pride.

"Congratulations."

"Did Lucas roll into work today?" Frank asked.

"He's waiting in your office."

Frank was surprised, and he wasn't surprised very often. Lucas sat in a guest chair, wearing a crisp gray suit, white shirt and burgundy tie, and leaned over his laptop, typing. He was freshly shaved and his hair, usually unruly, was combed.

"Lucas?"

"Yes, sir." Lucas put his laptop on the desk, rose and extended his hand, giving Frank a firm handshake.

"What's all this?" Frank asked, referring to stacks of files and documents on his desk.

Lucas returned to his seat. "I know you've been very busy with trial, so instead of going home after my plane arrived last night, I came here. I've caught up with most of the outstanding assignments. I drafted a motion for summary judgment, responded to discovery requests, and summarized several volumes of medical records. There's more to do, but I've got a good start." He sat straight up in his seat, hands resting in his lap.

"Impressive," Frank said. He found himself at a loss for words.

"Frank, I want to apologize for my poor performance and behavior. I appreciate the opportunity you've given me. I promise I won't mess up ever again." His tone was sincere.

"The practice of law isn't anything like cramming for a final exam at school."

"I understand."

"You can't work hard every so often and expect to succeed. You have to be committed to the profession, Lucas." Frank rubbed his chin.

"I know," Lucas said, also rubbing his chin.

Both of the men laughed.

"I know," Lucas said again.

"You know what?"

"You're my father."

Frank's eyes widened. "How long have you known?"

"Since before junior high," Lucas said, looking away, not meeting Frank's eyes.

"I'm sorry." Frank's voice cracked.

"Me, too," Lucas whispered.

They rose out of their seats and hugged in an awkward embrace. After they returned to their seats, a knock on the door sounded before Libby walked in.

"Here's some more message slips," Libby said, handing Frank another pile. "Some are urgent."

After Libby left, Frank asked Lucas, "Do you want to help me return calls?"

"Sure."

Frank handed over a stack of pink slips to Lucas, feeling confident for the first time that his son could handle an important task.

As Lucas headed toward the door, laptop in hand, Frank said, "I hear you gave Mansfield a good smack."

"I might have." Lucas smiled and walked out the door.

Frank sorted through the remaining messages and came across a printed email from Jerry Hirano.

Hi Frank,

Thanks for sending your associate, Lucas Rossi, to the depo in Minn. You may have heard there was an incident afterwards. Mansfield knocked over the court reporter's machine and was threatening Zana West and myself with his fist. He could very well have been armed. We were not hurt due to Lucas's swift and brave action. He punched Mansfield in the face, causing him to quickly retreat. Please let me know if you have any questions about the incident.

Aloha,
Jerry Hirano

Frank grinned, swelling with pride for his son.

Chapter 37

@Zlaw A #dreamy #hero is a thing.

Jerry felt the weight of the humid air as he stepped off the plane in Honolulu. He felt refreshed after a two-hour nap with Zana resting on his shoulder. She followed close behind him as they made their way down the jet way and passed a few airport greeters holding signs and leis. He wished he had thought to change into lighter clothes before getting off the plane. At least he wasn't wearing boots like Zana.

"Do you want to change into rubber slippers?" Jerry asked.

"I didn't bring any, but I'll be okay until I get home," Zana said.

"It's good you packed light, because we're barely going to fit our bags into my trunk," Jerry said as they wheeled their small suitcases toward the airport parking garage.

"I was going to bring my golf clubs to Minnesota, because I do enjoy a few rounds in the snow."

"Always the smart aleck." Jerry laughed and pulled Zana in for a kiss.

Zana giggled. "I feel so much better after my nap."

"You should. You slept almost the entire five hours from San Francisco." There had been an unexpected snowstorm, delaying their flight out of Minneapolis and causing them to miss their connection. Jerry didn't mind. He was able to treat Zana to a night in San Francisco and they caught an early flight back home. She had already posted pictures on Facebook of their selfies taken at Fisherman's Wharf, the Ghiradelli Chocolate Factory, and at a jazz club near Embarcadero.

"Did you get any sleep?" Zana asked as they walked past security.

"A few hours. While you were snoring away, I did some work on my laptop. Thank God for WiFi," Jerry said, grabbing her hand.

"Come on, I don't snore."

He gave her a look but didn't say anything.

Jerry led Zana to his car, parked on the second floor of the parking garage.

"I wish I didn't have to go into the office today, but it's only ten a.m.,"

Zana said as she watched Jerry put their luggage into the trunk. "Are you going to work?"

"After I go home for a shower. While you were dreaming about me on the plane, I emailed our investigator and asked him to do some surveillance on Brad Jordan today." He opened the door for Zana and helped her in.

"Okay, first—why do you assume I was dreaming about you? And, why do you need surveillance when we got Levinson's testimony about Jordan doing the triathlon?" Zana said after Jerry took his seat and started the car.

"You always dream about me, don't you?" Jerry glanced over at her and grinned.

"Okay. Yeah, I admit it," Zana said. "Isn't more surveillance a waste of money?"

"You're probably right, but it's possible Mansfield will stop by Jordan's condo and confront him. If he does, I'd like to get video footage."

Jerry's phone rang after they pulled onto the H-1 Freeway. He saw it was his investigator and put him on speakerphone.

"Hey, Tony. I'm in my car with another defense attorney on the case, Zana West," Jerry said.

"Hi Tony," Zana said.

"Hey, there. It looks like there's some action here at Jordan's condo."

"What do you mean?" Jerry said.

"There's another van here. I'm ninety-nine percent sure it's Rip Mansfield's boys," Tony said.

"What makes you think so?" Zana asked.

"I recognize the driver. He left our company to work for Mansfield, who offered more money," he said. "Where are you?"

"Just passing the Punahou exit."

"Another important thing you should know."

"What's that?" Jerry asked.

"Jordan's girlfriend walked in a few minutes ago."

"Why is that important?" Jerry put his blinker on to take the King Street Exit, heading to Waikiki.

"He's not alone," Tony said. "Not just any…oh, shit! Did you hear that?"

"Hold on, I'll be right there." Jerry pressed his foot on the accelerator.

***

Brad must have nodded off. He felt a woman's small foot on his and moved his foot playfully until his body jolted. At first he thought it was Heather next to him, but as he woke up, he remembered—it was her twin.

"Megan?"

"Hey, sleepy head. Are you sure you want to use my name? What if I were Heather?" Megan gave him a mischievous smile, messing up his hair with her hand.

Brad relaxed his body and lay back against the pillows. He could be himself with her.

"You're pretty hot for being paralyzed, big boy," Megan teased.

She jumped out of bed and Brad watched her naked, tan body walk towards the door. He admired her shapely calves and tight rear end developed from running miles upon miles, and her muscular arms and back acquired from years of swimming. There was not a pucker of cellulite on her smooth skin. Her hair was about a half inch longer than Heather's, and she had a tattoo of two lovebirds in the middle of her lower back. Otherwise, the two women were identical.

But he could tell who was who. Megan's eyes were slightly wider apart and her nose slightly smaller than Heather's, but they were both tall and thin.

Their personalities were so different Brad could instantly distinguish them when they talked. Heather lived by rules and followed lists. She insisted on being in control of everything and despised uncertainty. She was insecure and desperate for his attention. When they had lived together in Seattle, their lovemaking—as she insisted upon calling it—was scheduled for Wednesdays and Saturday nights on a freshly made bed with lights out and two lit candles.

Megan was relaxed, taking life as it came. She enjoyed sex anytime and anywhere. Her confidence was attractive, but she talked of other men so breezily Brad felt he'd never capture her heart. She was playful, always coming up with new ways to have fun.

Every time Brad talked about breaking up with Heather so they could be together, Megan said she didn't want to be tied down and changed the subject. He knew what that meant. Once he had money from the lawsuit, she'd follow him anywhere. She didn't give a damn about her sister's feelings.

But until then, Megan carefully covered their tracks and came over only if Heather had asked for her help to look after him. The whole arrangement was twisted, but he enjoyed having twins at his disposal, especially with so much time on his hands. Heather did his shopping and cleaning. Megan was his "sex twin", which made her laugh when she heard him call her that.

While Megan was out of the room, he turned on his iPod, selecting an old Sade song, hoping her sexy voice would put Megan in the mood for morning sex.

She came back with glasses of orange juice, which were quickly abandoned when Brad pulled her on top of him. She giggled and pretended to ride him like a cowgirl until they came together, sweating in each other's arms.

"You're better when you're not wasted," Megan noted.

"Oh, yeah?" Brad said, reaching for the glass of orange juice on the nightstand. "Did you put vodka in this?"

"No."

"What good are you, woman? I need a screwdriver after my morning screw."

"Have a smoke," Megan said, handing him a Red Vine from a package she had brought with the orange juice. She feigned smoking the Red Vine, moving closer to Brad, lying on top of the crumpled sheets. He grabbed a piece of licorice and put it to his lips, blowing out, and then pulled her close to him.

"Was it good for you, too, baby?" Brad said, laughing. "I'll bet there's a Red Vines vaping flavor."

They lay together on the bed, munching licorice and listening to Sade's music.

"What's that?" Megan sat up in bed.

"What?" Brad said, the licorice hanging from his mouth.

"I thought I heard something."

"I'm sure it's nothing. Come back here." Brad began stroking Megan's breast in time to the music and moved his naked body closer to hers.

"You asshole!" shrieked a female voice.

Brad looked up and saw Heather standing in the bedroom doorway. He instinctively grabbed at the sheets to cover up.

"It's not what you think," Brad said, realizing there was no way it could be anything else. His biggest concern at that moment was Heather finding out he wasn't really paralyzed. "Megan, could you get my wheelchair?"

Megan grabbed a towel hanging from a chair, covered her body and left the room.

"Cheaters," Heather screamed through gritted teeth.

"Heather, honey, stop. She was just comforting me. I was upset and I got drunk. I had a relapse." Brad kept his legs still and continued to lie on the bed as he pleaded to Heather, who was now sobbing and slumped down in the doorway. "I'm sorry. I love you."

"You cheaters," Heather screamed again.

"Heather, no. It's not like that at all. I'm so sorry you misunderstood what happened," Brad said. This wasn't the first time he'd seen her become hysterical. He hoped he could calm her down.

"I know what I saw," Heather said, standing back up, facing Brad, still lying naked in bed.

"I fell asleep. When I woke up, I thought Megan was you."

"Right," Heather said.

"Anyone could make that mistake. I can only tell you apart when I'm awake and paying attention," Brad lied. "You look so damn much alike."

"Hmmmhmmm," Heather said, her face contorted.

"Can you forgive me, sweetheart? I won't ever make that mistake again. You're the one I want to be with," Brad said, pleading.

"You told me you wanted to be alone," Heather said, her body shaking as she sobbed. "Your place is clean."

"I cleaned it," Brad said.

"You're playing sex music. You planned this," Heather shrieked.

"No. Calm down, Heather," Brad said, his voice stern, trying to get through to her. Megan, now dressed in shorts and a tank top, wheeled in his chair.

"I will not calm down!" Heather shouted.

"Last night, I couldn't sleep. I was craving alcohol. I was going to go to an AA meeting, but I stopped at the grocery store and bought a bottle of vodka. I guess I passed out." Brad eased into his wheelchair using one hand to cover his groin area with a T-shirt.

"You're a liar," Heather said.

"I got drunk," Brad said, the excuse felt comfortable on his lips.

"Why is *fucking* Sade playing?" Heather shouted.

"I needed music to help me relax. I always play Sade."

"Right," Heather sneered. "I guess you've forgotten what we used to listen to when we made love, *before* you were paralyzed."

"It's been a long time," Brad said.

Heather walked out of the room and returned holding the half empty bottle of vodka he had left on the kitchen counter.

"Why is Megan here?" Heather stood over Brad.

"I don't really know. I was asleep. I thought she was you."

"Right," Heather said, staring down at him, vodka bottle in hand.

"You can ask Megan. I really don't know."

"I stopped by to see if I could help," Megan said, sitting down on the bed next to Brad.

"Help? Help with what?" Heather shouted and slammed the vodka bottle against the wall, smashing it to pieces. Glass shattered all around them. Megan screamed. Shards of glass flew into the air, penetrating the exposed skin of their arms, legs and Brad's torso.

"What the fuck?" Brad shouted. He dropped the T-shirt he had been holding over his groin and put his hand on his chest and felt the spikes of glass.

Heather held the neck of the bottle in her hand, moving its jagged edges close to Brad's face.

Megan made a move towards her twin.

"Don't come any closer or I'm going to kill him," Heather said.

"Sugar bear," Brad said weakly.

"Sugar bear, my ass! You are both fucking liars. Do you think I believe this shit? You've been sleeping together for months. I had a feeling you were having sex. I could smell it, but I couldn't prove it."

"I'm paralyzed."

"Sure you are," Heather said. "I wish I would have killed you when I had the chance."

"What are you talking about?" Brad said, staying calm. "You're hysterical."

"I've always been here for you. I've done everything for you." Heather's hand was shaking as she held the jagged bottle close to Brad's nose.

"I know, sweetheart," Brad said. He closed his eyes afraid pieces of glass would dislodge. "I know."

"Don't you call me *sweetheart*, you traitor! I cooked and cleaned. I gave you money. You wanted to be an Olympic champion. I did everything to support you."

"Yes, you did," Brad said, keeping his head still.

"You were so worried that you wouldn't make the Olympic team. There were only two slots and Jeff and Vic were faster." Heather moved the bottle away from Brad's face and held it a few inches away from his exposed groin.

"What does that have to do with anything?" Brad said, stunned to hear his dead rival's name. He tried to stay as still as possible so he wouldn't startle her. He didn't want her to cut him down there.

"Don't you see—I helped you. I knocked them out of the competition. *Just for you,*" Heather screamed, moving the glass even closer to Brad's penis. "I pulled a Tanya *fucking* Harding, just for you, Brad."

"Are you saying *you* were the one driving the car? You ran into us?" Brad asked, incredulous, looking down at Heather's wobbly hand.

"Yes!" Heather screamed. "Now that I caught you and Megan together, I'm not sorry one bit. You deserved it."

"You bitch! You almost killed me!" Brad yelled.

"How could you have possibly gotten away with this?" Megan said.

"I wore a dark wig." Heather shrugged. She had moved back a few feet but held the jagged bottle in front of her like a shield.

"You're insane," Brad said.

"Afterwards, I leaked a story to the tabloids that Ryan Peterson was responsible," Heather said. "It was all so easy."

"You killed Vic!" Brad yelled, jumping out of his wheelchair and lunging toward Heather. She slashed his thigh deeply with the jagged bottle, causing blood to spurt out. Brad felt sharp, excruciating pain. He slumped to the floor, putting his hands to his leg in an effort to stop the bleeding. He looked up at Megan, hoping she could help.

"Oh, my God!" Megan grabbed a pillow and bent down to help Brad.

"Don't you dare," Heather held the bottle close to her sister's face. "The fucking liar doesn't deserve to walk anymore."

"He's going to die if he doesn't get help," Megan pleaded.

"And you're going to die, too. I trusted you, Megan. I trusted you with the love of my life and you screwed him!" Heather thrust the jagged bottle toward her twin.

Brad still lay on the floor, blood pooling all around him. The sound of the twins starting to fade. He felt woozy. He thought he heard a loud noise from the hallway and as he looked up, he saw a familiar man kick the bottle out of Heather's hand. Then everything went black.

Chapter 38

@Zlaw #Hibiscus flowers don't have much of a scent, but #love and #victory are sweet.

Zana paid her Uber driver and rolled her suitcase up the driveway, displacing a half dozen Java Sparrows as she headed to the front door. It was only 5:30 p.m. and she could hear the T.V. blaring from the living room. If she weren't so exhausted, she'd wonder if intruders might be watching T.V. No one was ever home at such an early hour.

"You're back!" Kelly called out. She and Andrew were sitting next to each other on the couch, munching on chips and drinking wine.

"Hey," Zana said. "What are you doing home so early?"

"Didn't you hear about the tsunami warning?" Andrew said. "Frank sent everyone home."

"I had no idea." Zana's eyes widened. She'd never been under threat of a tsunami before. "Do we need to evacuate?"

"It was a false alarm. Lots of downtown businesses closed at four o'clock, because of the reports on the Internet," Kelly said. "More importantly, did you see the news? Jerry's on every channel."

Zana tossed Kelly's pea coat on a straight back chair and fell heavily onto the Lazy Boy. She felt the weight of a long day spent mostly at the police station while Jerry was questioned at length about his involvement in Brad Jordan's death. They had planned to get a bite to eat, but journalists from every T.V. channel and news medium were anxious to interview him. Finally, she used her Uber app to get a ride home. As far as she knew, he was still being questioned about the kick he used to save Megan Alexander's life.

"Were you there?" Kelly asked.

"I was outside." Zana sighed.

Zana turned her attention to the flat screen image of Jerry being interviewed by one of the newscasters she recognized from the grassy area outside the police station.

"Was he still alive when you entered the room?" the woman asked, holding the microphone up to Jerry's mouth.

"I'm not sure. My focus was on protecting Megan Alexander. Once I kicked the bottle out of her sister's hand, I noticed Mr. Jordan passed out on the floor in a pool of blood," Jerry said.

"Then, what did you do?" the reporter asked.

"I physically restrained Ms. Heather Alexander until the police came about a minute later."

"What about the ambulance? How long did it take?"

"First responders arrived a couple minutes later. They tried for about ten minutes to stop the bleeding and revive him, but it was too late," Jerry said into the microphone.

"I understand the weapon was a jagged bottle. Were you injured when you kicked it out of Ms. Alexander's hand?"

"No, I'm fine."

"What will happen with the pending lawsuit?"

"I can't comment on that," Jerry said into the camera.

"What's going to happen with the case?" Kelly asked her roommates and turned down the T.V.

"I'm sure Brad Jordan's estate will continue it," Andrew said. "Mansfield won't want to lose out on his share. He's like a tiger shark, he'll feed on the case until there's no meat left on the carcass. Vultures go hungry when he's around."

"Hey, don't be insulting tiger sharks," Zana said, her mouth full of chips.

"From what you've said about Mansfield, he's a true land shark," Kelly said.

"Ain't that the truth?" Andrew put his arm around his girlfriend.

"From your texts, it sounds like my pea coat was lucky after all." Kelly winked at Zana.

Zana beamed. "You could say that."

"I think I'm missing something here," Andrew said.

"It sounds to me like our roomie has herself a shiny new boyfriend," Kelly said.

"I'm not sure I'd go that far," Zana said.

"You were gone long enough for one depo. Were you on vacation with Jerry Ho?" Andrew asked.

"We got snowed in," Zana said, covering her smile with her hands. She wasn't sure if she wanted her co-worker to know any details, but at least he had proven he was trustworthy.

"Say no more," Andrew said.

"Sounds romantic," Kelly squealed.

"You better get used to the paparazzi. I have a feeling you'll soon be posing next to Jerry on magazine covers." Andrew smiled at her.

"We've got to get done with our case, first," Zana said.

"Any chance it'll be over anytime soon?" Kelly asked.

Zana nodded. "Lucas emailed me his draft of a motion for summary judgment. Once the details of Jordan's death are added, it can be filed."

"Really? Lucas did some work?" Andrew said.

Zana nodded. "He's turning into a super associate. More competition for us."

"From what Andrew tells me, you guys did an amazing job on your case," Kelly said. "I suppose you're no longer in fear of being fired."

"I wouldn't go that far," Zana said. "You know Frank. It's one day at a time."

"Yeah. That's why my boyfriend is never here." Kelly patted Andrew's thigh.

***

Two weeks later, Lucas appeared in Zana's doorway, wearing a sharp black suit and a gray tie.

"Wow!" Zana said, when she looked up from her computer. "Are you arguing before the United States Supreme Court?"

"I wish." Lucas laughed. "I'm going to carry your briefcase for your big day."

"I hope we win this motion," Zana said. She filled her briefcase with the file and handed it to Lucas. "I'm holding you to your offer."

When they reached the sidewalk, Zana led her colleague into the sundry store on the corner. "I need a Red Bull if I'm going to survive the day," she said.

Lucas opened the door for her and shadowed her as she paid for her drink.

"Look at this," Lucas said, holding up the latest issue of Hawaii People Magazine.

"OMG! That's Heather Alexander," Zana said. She picked up a magazine and read the front caption: "Alexander Confesses to Murdering Olympic Hopefuls".

"She's lucky Hawaii doesn't have the death penalty," Lucas said as they walked out of the store.

They walked in silence towards the court. This time, Zana wore sensible Ann Klein flats she had picked up at Nordstrom Rack and so Lucas stood a few inches taller than her. As they walked, Zana looked in the windows of the shops and restaurants; she smelled fresh baked manapua and mango bread and she noticed most workers heading into a high rise were each carrying a coffee cup of some sort. She took a long sip of Red Bull, already feeling energized.

Judge Lee had expedited the hearing on their motion for summary judgment at their request. Since coming back from Minnesota, Lucas had kept his promise of helping her and for the first time since she had been with the firm, she was able to leave early to swim, bike, run or spend time with Jerry. She didn't tell Lucas about the latter activity. Frank had been in a good mood since his son had shaped up and they won the trial.

When they arrived at the courtroom, Zana saw Caron Rossi and Alexia Moore already seated. Lucas smiled at his mother as they passed the bar to the counsel tables where the attorneys would argue their motion in front of Judge Lee. If they prevailed, the case would be thrown out of court and Aloha Athletics and their insurance company, F.I.M., wouldn't have to pay even a dollar to Brad Jordan's estate.

"I didn't know my mother was going to be here," Lucas whispered to Zana.

"I called Alexia and told her she might want to bring her boss since this motion is…important," Zana whispered.

"Good idea."

"I want you to argue the motion."

He shook his head, setting her briefcase down. "No, Zana. It's your case. I don't want to take away your chance for glory."

"Lucas, you are totally prepared. You know this case just as well as I do. Make your mother proud," Zana kept her voice low.

"Are you sure?"

"I already won a motion in this case. Now, it's your turn."

"Okay," Lucas said, smiling nervously. "Thanks, Zana."

While they were talking, Jerry Hirano, Dean Henderson and Ray Sumida joined them at the defense counsel table. Rip Mansfield had taken his seat at the opposing counsel table. Zana noticed that he still had remnants of a black eye, thanks to Lucas's well-placed punch. It was obvious he had tried to cover it with makeup, but Zana thought it looked worse.

"Your dad just walked in," Zana whispered in Lucas's ear.

"Is he going to sit at the counsel table with us?" Lucas said.

"No, he sat next to your mom," Zana said.

"Maybe you better argue the motion."

"No, Lucas, you'll do great." Zana patted his hand in reassurance.

"All rise," the court clerk said. Judge Lee entered the courtroom from behind the bench, wearing his black robe.

"You may be seated," the clerk said. "Calling Civil Number 12-05868, Brad Jordan verses Aloha Athletics, et al., Appearances please.

After the attorneys gave their names and the parties they represent, Judge Lee told them they could proceed.

"Your Honor," Lucas said, "the overwhelming evidence supports that a vehicle entered the Olympic trials triathlon race course and intentionally killed a competitor and allegedly injured Plaintiff Brad Jordan. I'm sure the court is aware of Mr. Jordan's recent death and that his estate has chosen to proceed forward with his claims of negligence against our client. As you can see from the transcript of the deposition of John Chu, he was an eyewitness to the intentional actions of the driver of the white car. On this basis alone, the motion should be granted. However, we also have evidence that Mr. Jordan was not paralyzed as he claimed from the accident. Witness Devere Levinson testified that Plaintiff competed in a triathlon and he observed him standing, running and cycling without the use of any wheelchair or any special equipment. The evidence shows that Plaintiff's run split time for the Antler Lake Triathlon was 7:10, which our affidavits establish is consistent with the split time an elite male athlete would have if he were recovering from an injury. We've submitted affidavits and photograph evidence with our motion to prove Plaintiff was standing in an elevator and parked his car on a high curb, which suggest he was capable of walking and was not paralyzed before his recent death."

"Excuse me a moment," Judge Lee said.

His clerk handed him a piece of paper.

Zana noticed that Judge Lee had a strange look on his face when reading the document. She wondered if there was something amiss—maybe another tsunami warning or a bomb threat, and that at any moment he'd order them to evacuate. She wouldn't put it past Mansfield to arrange delivery of such a message. She could hear whispering in the gallery as everyone waited for Judge Lee to speak. He continued to sit motionless, staring at the paper for several minutes.

"I've just received notice from the Attorney's Disciplinary Committee," Judge Lee said. "Mr. Rip Mansfield has been suspended from the practice of law for the State of Hawaii, effective as of 12:01 a.m. today. Bailiff, please escort Mr. Mansfield out of the courtroom."

"Your Honor, this is ridiculous," Mansfield said.

"Mr. Mansfield, we are on the record. Anything you say in court today is in violation of your suspension. You are to leave the courtroom immediately. I will not entertain another word from you," Judge Lee said.

Mansfield grabbed his iPad and briskly walked out, without need for a bailiff escort.

The Judge addressed the courtroom. "As for the motion before us, ordinarily I would have to continue it to allow Plaintiff's estate to obtain new counsel. However, due to the fact that there is overwhelming evidence that there was no accident and that the incident involved a criminal act in which a person entered the race course with the intention to cause death and/or injury, and that there is evidence establishing that the deceased Plaintiff fraudulently claimed to be paralyzed when he was able to walk and competed in a triathlon, the Court rules in favor of Defendant Aloha Athletic Company and the Defendants who joined in their motion, South Shore, Inc., C&C Racing and Pikaki Security. The Court will not address the issue of sanctions. Mr. Rossi, please prepare the order."

"Thank you, your Honor," Lucas said.

"All rise. Court is in recess," the clerk said.

"Good job, Lucas," Zana said, smiling broadly.

"Thanks," Lucas said, beaming. "I owe you one."

"All in a day's work. Isn't that right, counselor?" Jerry said to Zana, winking.

Caron rushed past the bar and hugged her son and Frank, following a few steps behind her, patted him on the back.

"I'm proud of you, son," Frank said.

"Thanks, Dad," Lucas said.

Jerry and Zana, with briefcases in hand, headed to the doorway where Alexia was waiting for her boss.

"Great job, Zana," Alexia said. "You've saved F.I.M. a lot of money."

"Yeah, thank you Zana. We really appreciate your hard work," Caron said, her arm around her son.

"It's nice to have this one resolved," Zana said.

"Oh, you don't know the half of it," Caron said, beaming.

As Alexia, Caron, Lucas and Frank lingered in the courtroom, Jerry and Zana ducked out and walked down the hall towards the elevator.

"I have a surprise for you," Jerry said as they reached the lobby. Once they had left the building, he took her hand and led her to his car.

"Where are we going?" Zana asked. "I've got to get back to work."

"This won't take long." Jerry helped Zana into his Ferrari and they drove down the road where he turned into Ala Moana Beach Park and drove along the road adjacent to the beach to the Magic Island parking lot. After she climbed out of the car, Zana stretched her arms above her head and inhaled the fresh scent of the ocean.

"Are you hungry?" Jerry asked as he reached into his trunk and pulled out a picnic basket.

"I'm starved," Zana said. "You must have known we were going to win."

"I had a hunch." Jerry led Zana by the hand to a grassy area with a view of the marina and spread out a palaka print cloth under a cluster of palm trees. He then laid out plates of croissants, cheese, grapes and strawberries. He poured some cups of guava juice from a thermos. "Sorry, I didn't bring champagne. Frank wouldn't approve of you going back to work drunk at ten in the morning."

"You are so thoughtful." Zana made herself comfortable next to Jerry.

"Here's to us." Jerry raised his cup of guava juice and touched it against Zana's.

They ate breakfast in silence as they looked out at the glistening ocean and outrigger canoes paddling through the rough water.

"This morning has been amazing," she said, looking into his eyes.

Jerry reached into the picnic basket and pulled out the most beautiful red hibiscus flower Zana had ever seen.

"For you," Jerry said, handing it to her.

Zana put it to her nose and breathed in. She then tucked it in her hair in front of her right ear. Jerry then gently took the flower from the right side and moved it to the left ear.

"This means you're taken," Jerry said and kissed her tenderly, allowing the kiss to linger.

Zana's heart beat fast and her mind squealed inside. She looked deeply into his eyes and said, "You are, too."

Dear Reader,

Thank you for purchasing **Land Sharks**. I hope you enjoyed reading the story. Here's a sneak peek at an excerpt of **Freewheel**, Book 2, in the series. For updates on the other books in the series, please visit my website: www.katharinenohr.com. I love to hear from my readers. Please feel free to leave a review on the website where you purchased the book.

Thank you!
Katharine M. Nohr

~~~

After Ryan Peterson reached the transition area, he changed quickly into his running shoes, tossed off his helmet and took a swig of water before beginning the 10k run. He glanced behind, looking to see who might be on his heels, but it wasn't until his coach yelled out to him on mile two that he had a 56-second lead that he started to feel a bit more confident. The thought of prize money gave Ryan the energy to kick into gear. He increased his pace, feeling his legs move fluidly as he pumped his arms and kept his body in an efficient running position.

As he reached the top of Diamond Head, he glanced behind his shoulder again and saw Eric at least 100 yards behind him. Ryan knew Eric was a slightly slower runner so if nothing went wrong, he could hold him off.

He felt the wind pushing him forward and let his body relax as he moved swiftly, each step carrying him towards the finish line. He focused on his breathing and on the rhythm of his feet against the pavement.

As he approached within 150 yards of the finish line, the crowd became wild, yelling his name, encouraging him to finish strong. The shouting and whooping, along with Ryan's thoughts of $20,000 made him forget about the pain he was feeling. As he crossed over the finish line, hearing the announcer affirm he was the first place winner, Ryan's legs became jelly and he almost collapsed to the ground. A bikini-clad blonde placed a purple orchid lei over his head and kissed him on his sweaty cheek. Cameras appeared in his face and someone handed him a towel with sponsorship logos on it.

"How does it feel to win the prize money?" the female television announcer asked Ryan as he was trying to catch his breath.

"Great. What can I say? I'm very happy," Ryan managed to respond.

"Did you realize you had such a big lead over your competitors?"

"Not really. I was just trying to run my own race," Ryan said into the microphone, feeling sweat drip from his forehead.

"How do you feel about Terry Schubert?"

"I don't know. What about him?" Ryan's eyes widened behind his sunglasses.

"Did you know he was taken away by ambulance?"

"Oh, that's terrible. I hope he's okay," Ryan said. In the heat of the race, he had forgotten their handlebars had touched, causing Terry to fall down. "If you'll excuse me, I really need to hydrate and talk to my coach. Thank you."

Hal, one of his coaches, was waiting for him to finish talking with the reporter. As soon as they walked away from the finish line and ducked into the massage tent, Hal whispered into Ryan's ear, "Terry Schubert is dead."

Acknowledgements

Thank you to My Heavenly Father for His constant blessings. Mahalo to my boyfriend, Bill Touth, and my brother, Kim Nohr and my sister-in-law, Hannah Nohr, who have patiently been there for me through this entire journey.

Special thanks to my editor and publisher, Brittiany Koren, who made this project a reality with her skill and enthusiasm. Thank you to my writers group, Brian Malanaphy, Steve Novak, and Karin O'Mahony, who have provided feedback, encouragement and support since the day I penned the first chapter, and to our new member and friend, Nathalie Pettit, for her kind support in the final months before publication. I'm grateful to Mary Alexander, who put much time and effort into an earlier edit, which taught me so much about writing fiction. There were many cheerleaders who believed in me after reading early drafts, who deserve a mahalo: Donna Good, Dianne Johannson; Emily Schmit, Teresa Tico, Ruth Chun, Debra Stevens and Angie Sullivan. Thank you to Arielle Eckstut of The Book Doctors, who deemed me the winner of the Pitchapalooza Contest at the Honolulu Writers Conference in 2009. Arielle has been very helpful and responsive to emails in my quest to publish Land Sharks. I'm so appreciative of agent Susan Crawford who understood my vision and was so generous with her time. A shout out to Kelly "Rae" Monet and Rick Shewey for their patient support and work on my author website.

Thank you to all of my friends who lent me their ears through character and plot development in the books and in life: Cindi John, Kristina Selset, Lisa Ghahremani, Tamara Gerrard, Ramona Emerson, Cheri Moore, Cheri Huber, Angela Hayslett, Prebah Covetz, Ayse Demir, Colleen Graham, Winston Dang, Chay Somvilay, Angela Bushman, Abdusselam Kose, Debra Stevens, Cindy Prud'homme, roz horton, Mitula Patel, Tracy Adams, Kristie Byrum, Emmy Nation, Lesia Schafer, Melissa Deats, Carol Himalaya-Fidele and my many and cherished Facebook friends.

Thank you to my wonderful family for being my rock: Gerrie Nohr, Ed Haney, Jill, Gordy and Drew Gradwohl, Jeff Iversen, Jay Iversen, Sandy Crouse, Wendy Monette, Sharon Beals, Shane and Joyce Sullivan, Jerry and Rose Moore (AZ-parents) and my extended Christensen family—Paul and Lois Wilson, Christian Wilson, Marsha Fu, and my other aunts, uncles, cousins their spouses, and their children.

And, last but not least, purrs to my late kitty, Bucky, and my feline children, Tashi and Ninja.

About the Author

Katharine M. Nohr is the author of *Managing Risk in Sport and Recreation: The Essential Guide for Loss Prevention* and her first fiction novel in the Tri-Angle Series, *Land Sharks.* She speaks internationally on Olympic Games and professional athlete risk management. Ms. Nohr served as Regional Coordinator of Officials, appellate hearings officer and member of the Pacific Northwest Council for USA Triathlon. Ms. Nohr served as a Judge (per diem) of the Honolulu District Court and continues to practice insurance defense litigation in Hawaii. Ms. Nohr is a past Regional Vice President for International Association of Insurance Professionals and was awarded Insurance Professional of the Year in 2012. She is a principal of Nohr Sports Risk Management, LLC and Claim Crazy, Inc. and the owner of the Law Offices of Katharine M. Nohr, LLC. Currently, she is writing the sequel to Land Sharks. Visit her websites at KatharineNohr. com, nohrsports.com; or claimcrazy.com. She's also on social media on: Twitter: @TriathlonNovels, Linkedin: Katharine Nohr, and on Facebook: Katharine M. Nohr.

CPSIA information can be obtained
at www.ICGtesting.com
Printed in the USA
FSOW02n1338070616
21255FS